One

Knights of Virtue

Copyright © 2006, 2012 by Joseph A. Giunta

10-Digit ISBN 1938190041
13-Digit ISBN 978-1-938190-04-9

All rights reserved. No part of this publication may be reproduced, stored in a retrieval system, or transmitted in any form or by any means, electronic, mechanical, recording or otherwise, without the prior written permission of the author.

Printed in the United States of America.

The characters and events in this book are fictitious. Any similarity to real persons, living or dead, is coincidental and not intended by the author.

Cover Illustration by Henning Ludvigsen.
Interior Illustrations by Henning Ludvigsen.

Brick Cave Media
Brickcavebooks.com
2012

For Mel Griffin
A little encouragement goes a long way

By J.A. Giunta

THE ASCENSION
Book One: *The Last Incarnation*
Book Two: *The Mists of Faeron*
Book Three: *Out of the Dark* *

THE GUARDIANS
Book One: *Knights of Virtue*

* Forthcoming

Knights of Virtue

J.A. Giunta

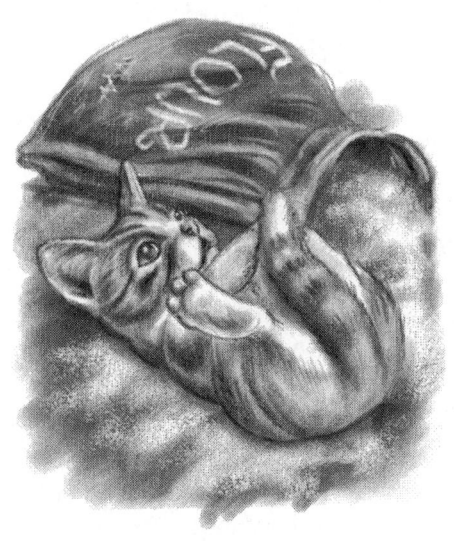

Part One:
Keepers of the Magic

Samuel was a man in his late 40's, sporting the salt and pepper hair that arrives with age, and kept himself in good shape with a rigorous daily routine. An unfortunate side effect to his strenuous activities was his love of sleep. He always managed to pull himself from the warmth of the bed, thanking his alarm clock as he did so, but still enjoyed the days when he allowed himself to sleep in.

Just one such day found Samuel waking not to his alarm clock but to the incessant chittering of two love birds having a spat outside his window. Opening an eye and feeling sympathy for the little fellow, he turned over and let the blue and green female berate its mate in privacy. Rays of sunlight shone through the open window, casting a silhouette of the two lovers against the far wall. From the garden below came scents of blue magnolia, wild roses and yellow jasmine, his wife's pride and joy.

Through the lids of his eyes, he could see the glowing red light from the clock pushing its way into his thoughts. Opening his eyes once more, he could see "9:03" staring back at him. A calendar rested beside the clock with rows of X's leading up to a circled date, and then Samuel remembered why he hadn't been woken by the obnoxious alarm.

It was the anniversary of the Oath of Virtue.

He sat up in bed as memories flooded his mind, his hand unconsciously reaching for the steel amulet hanging from his neck. His thumb played over the surface as a smile crossed his lips, and he shook his head at the youthful adventures he'd taken part in. The amulet, hanging from a steel chain wrapped in leather, depicted the emblem of the Guardians: two men in royal livery, shouldering large cooking spoons as weapons, each standing on either side of an equally large cauldron. Underneath the emblem were inscribed the words "Cookie Brigade," an affectionate name given the knights by the peasants and commoners of an older day.

Samuel stood and stretched, seeing the empty space in bed where Laura had slept, and could smell a breakfast of eggs, bacon and toast being prepared downstairs. He went to the top drawer of his dresser and opened it, revealing five medallions identical to his own. The beginnings of tears reached his eyes when he touched them. A soft glow emanated from each emblem, a white radiance that carried with it the memories of previous owners.

He could feel his brothers there, though they'd been gone for several years now. His fingers traced the worn edges of each necklace, touching once more the brothers he loved so much. It soon became harder to fight back the tears, but Samuel drew his hand back and blinked them away. His was the virtue of Strength, and it was upon his shoulders the responsibility rested.

Samuel was the last Guardian of the Recipe.

He took a deep breath and grasped the medallion around his neck, drawing strength from its reserve like a snake of light coiling about his hand. There would be more time for contemplation later that night, when he could gather all six children together for a discussion. The anniversary of the Oath of Virtue had come and with it the time for a new generation of Guardians. All six virtues needed to be represented, lest the Recipe fall into the hands of those without the knowledge or character to use it wisely. There were far too many stories of people thinking themselves able to control the magic, only to go mad when faced with their true essence.

All would need to be explained to the children, but he would do it later. What Samuel needed most was a warm shower and a hot breakfast. Since Laura was graciously working on one of those, he closed the drawer and said a prayer for his fallen brothers. Turning towards the window once more, he saw the love birds now nestling together, chirping the melody they were meant to sing. He gave the two a smile and headed for the shower.

Samuel was soon whistling a tune of his own.

* * *

After dinner that same day, Samuel was ready to talk with his children. Laura gave him a hug and wished him luck.

"You'll be fine, Sam," she whispered in his ear. He ran his hand through her long, blonde hair, feeling its softness while looking into the comfort of her crystal blue eyes.

"I know," Samuel replied and kissed her. "I just like to hear you say it."

She gave him a playful shove as if to say, "Go on." He then called all six children into the living room, directing each to a seat on the couch or in a chair. It's going to be a long discussion, he thought, so they might as well get comfortable.

Before speaking, though, he was truly taken back by the three boys and three girls. Had it been so long since he'd stopped to look closely at them that he could only now see how much they'd grown? His children had become individuals – there was no doubt in his mind about that – each with diverse needs and interests. He could literally see the essence of each virtue emanating from his sons and daughters.

Trudy was the oldest of the six, being 17 years old, and had the long, flowing blonde hair and deep blue eyes of her mother. Her ready smile and softness of voice put people at ease, often gaining her the confidence of others before it was even asked for. Her love of poetry and music only added to her honest and trustworthy character. Samuel didn't have to look too far into his eldest daughter to see the virtue of Truth staring back at him.

Sitting next to Trudy were the twins, Courtney and John. Both were nearly identical in appearance, were 16 years of age, had short dark hair, slate-gray eyes and a love of the physical endeavors. Courtney and John shared an unusual bond that linked the two together in ways that amplified each other's strengths and lent support to the other when needed. Courtney held an air of authority and undaunted stance, but the young woman of stone would melt when around those she loved. John was a more outgoing person, but he spent as much time with his sister as with any group of friends. Though the two were younger than Trudy, they both stood inches taller than her. Courtney's interest in gymnastics and swimming, as well as John's interest in weight-lifting and wrestling, left the two with a muscular and athletic appearance. Courtney was the walking image of Courage, and her empathic brother that of Honor.

Beside the twins sat Stephany, a petite girl of 15 years. Her long hair of deep chestnut and amber eyes with flecks of gold made the small girl adorable and endearing. Barely reaching her older brother's shoulders, her small frame and fragile appearance only served to hide the enormous strength of spirit within. Her love of horseback riding and medieval fantasy stories often left the girl to daydreaming, but the fire that sparked her soul shone bright, to those with an eye to see, and marked her with the virtue of Strength.

In front of the couch and on the floor sat Alan, a 13 year old boy with hair so black as to seem almost blue. Piercing eyes of azure and a bold, outgoing attitude made the boy a pleasure to be with, but he lacked the forethought and restraint needed to accompany such qualities. He possessed an enthusiasm for all sports and activities but quickly lost interest in them, only to return later again on a whim. The boy's entire being screamed the manners of Valor.

Sitting off by himself in a chair away from the others was the youngest boy, Morgan. At ten years of age, he was just old enough to enjoy doing the things his brothers and sisters did but also young enough to be excluded from them. Left to himself more often than not, the boy with short brown hair and soft amber eyes occupied his time with books and nature. Seeming almost reclusive, he found friends among the trees and foliage, discovering a strange affinity to animals. It would not be uncommon for Morgan to disappear for hours at a time on long walks through the woods, conversing with its denizens or studying herbs and other plant life. It wasn't difficult at all to see the virtue of Humility within the youngest of the six.

Placing a wooden box on the coffee table, Samuel opened the lid to reveal the five medallions resting atop a velvet interior. The amulets began to glow with a hazy luminescence that spread to encompass the room, as if searching the hearts of each present. Taking the necklaces from the box and passing them among the children, Samuel smiled at the looks of wonder on their faces, the shock of first feeling the magic within the warm steel.

"These," he explained, "are your birthright and family heirlooms passed down for over twenty generations now." He removed his own amulet and gave it to Stephany, the rightful holder of Strength. Samuel beamed with pride as each of his children took the medallion intended for them without knowing why or how and passed the remaining ones on.

Each of the six felt the tingling sensation rush through their bodies, felt the storm of emotions and memories from the medallions' predecessors, the unexplainable impression of rightness and could only let themselves be swept away in the flood. Alan, overcome with curiosity and delight, lifted the necklace to his head but was stopped at his father's request.

"No one put on their medallion until I say, alright?" Samuel looked each of his children in the eye, seeing their nods of acknowledgment before continuing.

"I need to explain what all this is about, and it may seem a bit far-fetched at first. Just bare with me, and I'll answer any questions you have once I'm through.

"In each of these medallions is magic. I know," he said, holding off their looks of disbelief and comments with his hands. "Feel the amulets with more than your hands, and you'll know it to be true. What it is you sense, that electric awareness of events and emotions not your own, is magic. The medallions themselves are not magic, but they store a magic put there by my ancestors... your ancestors.

"Our family has undertaken the task of protecting the ingredients to a special kind of magic, a spell if you will, called the Recipe. The magic itself is called essence, but what we protect is the formula to unlocking that essence, that inner core of being that taps into the very nature of things. Think of yourself in terms of emotions and how they sometimes help or hinder you. Essence magic intensifies those emotions to immeasurable limits, creating a great potential for both good and bad.

"It's for that reason that the Guardians, your great-grandfathers twenty times over, first took the Oath of Virtue."

Samuel watched their reactions and was pleased to see he had their full attention. Perhaps it was the medallions that made the story more acceptable, the memories of past Guardians first taking the oath lending strength and plausibility to the tale of their heritage.

"We keep others from obtaining the Recipe because of its danger, to those who would have it and those affected by them. The danger lies in the intensity of the magic, the enhancing of a person's being rather than the manipulation of external energies. It would not be unlikely for someone to be literally burned up, exhausting their life force by overdoing things. Nor would it be unlikely for someone to go mad when made to see the true nature of their souls, the very core of their hearts and minds.

"Each of you has within you one of the six virtues, the moral essence of man," Samuel went on, pointing to them one at a time for emphasis as he spoke aloud their corresponding virtue, "Truth, Courage, Honor, Strength, Valor and Humility. It is this that sets you apart from others and makes you more able to protect and defend the Recipe.

"But before you can do that, you must know and understand yourselves and the story of your ancestors."

Samuel then closed the box that once housed the medallions and touched his hand to the golden band along it side. Reacting to the touch of a Guardian, the band slowly dissipated. In its place, as if hidden beneath the precious metal, were the pages of a book, yellowed by time but preserved by magic. Samuel opened the book to the beginning page, where the faces of six brothers, the original Guardians, stared back through the vellum.

"This is the story of your ancestors..."

* * *

Noria was a small kingdom on the northern edge of Astoria, but its size was not what made it enviable. Thick, lush grasslands stretched across its girth as a sea of emerald, the blades of grass reaching chest-high at times. Its winding valleys of the deep greenery seemed like an ocean when the wind passed through to make waves transverse its length. The rich soil that accounted for the unusual growth led to the most fertile grounds in all the kingdoms, and the most beautiful forest known to man: Lightwood.

Also known as Flamegrove to some, the forest was said to look as if the skies were on fire when the morning sun shone through its tops. Named so for the light bark of the birch that made up the majority of its trees, the woodland held others that lent to its worth. The alder were prized for their bark, as well as their use in building, and were sold to tanners from every kingdom. Providing much of the shade in Lightwood were the heavy elm trees, treasured for their hardness. A good many people, moreover, would go hungry if not for the nuts supplied by the ruddy hazel. And lastly the hornbeam, of which its polished white wood was used to make handles for tools and weapons.

The fact that Noria was a coastal realm furnished it with a bountiful fishing craft, one that afforded lucrative trades among the neighboring kingdoms. Many alliances and favors were gained by the delicacies procured in those fishing beds. Kings may prevail upon their subjects to forgo some of the finer things life has to offer, but few were willing to do without variety in diet.

Immense cliffs of jagged rock, with only ocean to its back, served as a buttress for the kingdom's castle. As if the precipice were not protection enough, the dense forest and deep hollows offered sufficient defense for any attempts made by presumptuous neighbors or brazen brigands. While no kingdom is without highwaymen or gangs of ruffians, Noria was amply guarded. Each of the townships, villages and hamlets that comprised its domain had its own force of soldiers and trained militia according its size and need. The culmination made for a well-managed, highly secured and greatly desired kingdom.

All of which King Marik was exceedingly proud.

Rising the ranks of the mercenary band he was born into, Marik became a master swordsman and tactician by the age of fifteen. Wanted by any who could pay his heavy price, the young man learned the ways of books and men by the greatest of sages – an unusual pastime for a sellsword. With his gained knowledge and abilities, Marik led his own band of hired soldiers until he had accrued a sizable army.

As payment for various excursions and completed tasks, the mercenary leader would accept land in place of gold. Establishing a home for his men and their families was a new beginning for Marik. Governing the property and its people came easy, and his borders increased with each additional hire. Whether by gold or guile, the growing boundaries of his land worried the surrounding kings. It was only a matter of time before he set his sights upon governing a realm of his own.

Using the peasants' discontent and the poor ruling of King Jaril II to his advantage was a simple task. Marik's prosperous and well-maintained home, Mercenvale, sparked envy in the eyes of Jaril's subjects. Implementing his studies in philosophy and government, Marik skillfully interjected the question of inherited rulership by way of his men. It was the duty of his soldiers to pass through each hamlet and village with word of the young successful ruler to the south. The challenge of Jaril's ability to reign only served to enrage him and drive his mind to foolish acts – a behavior adeptly foreseen.

When the King's soldiers tried to take Mercenvale, they were sorely beaten back and taken all the way to the heart of Noria. Marik was determined to oust Jaril from his throne and wasted no time in doing so. During the entire skirmish, not one life was lost, though many suffered injuries. The mercenary leader was strict in his orders that none should be killed, and his men were skilled enough to succeed under the constraint. The last thing Marik wanted to be viewed as was a tyrant. Instead he was considered just in his reaction and supported by the neighboring kings. Jaril and those of his royal blood were generously exiled and his soldiers allowed to remain under the new monarch, once their loyalties were pledged.

The commoners were only too glad to accept Marik as King.

Ten years had passed since that brilliant exercise of skill and tact had gained him a kingdom, and Marik was satisfied to watch Noria prosper under his reign. Having lived through thirty winters, he could feel the weight and burden of rule upon his shoulders. Though still strong in body and mind, his raven hair was graying at the sides. He still possessed a large and powerful body, vigorous for any young man, and he was considered by many an incisive and thoughtful king. Earning his realm by cunning and skill, Marik was the most respected man in all the lands.

Nonetheless, the man who seemed to be without flaw had but one failing. The marketplace within his castle walls housed a bakery that concocted the most unusual of confections, a pastry of which originated in that very bakehouse. Marik's love of the sweetcakes, as well as every common man's in Noria, led to the specialization of their make. Leaving the baking of breads to other merchants, the Esrald family made a point of perfecting their creation. Cookies, named simply for their cooking process, were crispier than the average sweetcakes and came in a wide variety of flavors – one of which included the grounds of cacao beans, an expensive treat more generally known as chocolate.

Gerard Esrald, the elderly baker who carried on his father's craft, was made Royal Baker just six years before his passing away. His weak heart had finally given out after enduring forty-three harsh winters, a reputable and fulfilling number of years. The loss of his wife, in one of the many barbarian raids before Marik's rule, left the diligent man with the task of raising his six sons. Of the six, however, only the oldest was made an apprentice, and it was Tristan who inherited his father's position among the King's staff. Allowed to continue his shop in the marketplace, the hardy baker visited his liege once a week with a new batch of cookies. Though Marik enjoyed all of the different tastes produced by the master baker, it was Tristan's unending goal to find the one flavor Marik could truly be contented with. Entire leather-bound volumes were dedicated to that end, as the Royal Baker made a point to ask his King precise questions about flavor, texture and crispness. Marik's capricious tastes were difficult to chronicle, but Tristan was up to the task.

The other five sons followed their pursuits to fruition and never strayed too far from Noria or the father they dearly loved. When Gerard was upon his deathbed, weary from his many years, he asked his grown sons for one last wish.

"Help your brother whenever you can," he whispered, feeling their youthful hands upon his own more aged ones. "I won't ask you to give up what you have... there was never a man more proud than I at what you boys've become." Moisture tinged his gray eyes and ran into silvery locks. "I only ask you give a hand when needed. Ours is a proud line, fair and strong! Don't let our good King down..."

With one last smile, he closed his eyes forever.

Keeping his promise, Tristan worked hard at his craft. Over fifty entries were made in his journals, each with a different ingredient for the vague taste Marik sought.

There'll be twice that many if need be, the baker thought to himself. *So long as King Marik sees fit to pay for the exotic herbs and spices, I'll continue to try new variations.*

Wagons carrying the strange packages of precious ingredients arrived on a regular basis. As both baker and Court Magician required the imported fare, they often worked together in placing orders with foreign merchants. If the reclusive mage could be said to have a friend, the master baker would be he. Marik was charitably free with his coin, but he rarely placed price with his one fault. Magarius, the King's advisor and magician, was allotted any coin he requested. Marik trusted him utterly and always saw merit in his unusual experiments – with their doubly unique necessities and results.

Neatly stacking his newest parcel of spices, placing them upon sturdy shelves in the dry storage room, Tristan prepared for his trip to the castle. A simple carrying basket, filled with the most recent batch of cookies, rested atop the table of elm. Past experience, through trial and error, showed that Marik should be amenable towards the mixture of crushed walnut, shredded coconut and ground cacao beans. There were other variations in the cooking procedure, but the sable-haired baker felt confident of his choice. If he should meet with disappointment, the usual procedures of recording the results would ensue.

Tristan was a plain man in his tastes of clothes, so the charcoal-purple jerkin and leggings he wore were not overly expensive. The royal colors fit him well though, being as used to an authoritative position as he was. Standing six feet tall, with a fairly heavy build – a trait he and all his brothers shared – the master baker had a formidable and unquestioning air about him. Few could look to the hard gray eyes with resolve.

Taking up the basket of his latest endeavors, he closed shop for the day and headed up towards the castle entrance. Countless vendors lined the cobblestone streets, hawking their wares with the trained voices of peddlers. The morning sun had barely begun to creep over the castle walls, its rays warming the autumn wind, and yet the avenues were bustling with activity. Rising early, the villagers were quick to start their day.

Accepting nods from many passersby, Tristan took the silent salutes with dignified pride. Known all throughout the marketplace, he was respected and well-liked, though few knew him close enough for more than polite conversation. His crisp attitude always bespoke a busy man with little time for chatter, but he was the epitome of discretion and courteousness. It was the public opinion that a woman once broke his heart and fear of it crumpling again kept him distant and circumspect. But neither would he let his customers go hungry, for the man was fair in his price and equable in his portions. The master baker was a trusted merchant and a credit to his royal position – despite his guardedness.

As the shops and carts melted into the background, a handful of houses and other buildings moved to fore. One of the wooden structures in particular caught the baker's attention, and he strode purposefully up the walk. With a quick glance to either side of the weathered edifice, he took from his basket a package, trimly wrapped with white paper.

He bent to lay the packet down on the creaky porch when the wooden door opened to reveal a tiny, golden-haired angel. A polished steel lantern over the door glittered in the sunlight, reflecting off her dazzlingly bright blue eyes. Seeing the bundle caused her face to light up with wonder and joy, and she looked on the verge of calling her orphaned brothers and sisters to the door.

Covering his embarrassment with a cough, Tristan quickly explained, "This was sitting on your porch... I thought it best to call on you before some cutpurse could pilfer it." Having expounded his intent, the master baker quickly handed over the cookies.

Caring little for justifications, the sprite-like child gave a broad smile and mouthed a thank you. She took the treasured treats, and the door closed behind her as she ran to deliver them to her Nana. The Royal Baker beat a hasty retreat back up the walkway and turned towards the castle doors without looking back. After a minute's brisk walk, he began to breathe more easily again as his heart ceased its pounding in his chest. It could then be heard the whistling of a happy tune, though Tristan would deny it if any accused him of it.

The Royal Baker did not whistle.

* * *

"You've outdone yourself this time, master baker," King Marik commented with relish. "This is a very tasty morsel."

Tristan crinkled a brow at the comment, awaiting the minute exception that must soon follow. Whatever the imperfection, no matter how small or imperceptible to the normal human palate, he would mark them in his notes to be later chronicled in the leather tomes. Thoughts of other avenues began to clutter his mind before the King could determine the cookies' deficiency or voice his displeasure. The master baker had another recipe in mind as he began meticulously prodding his liege.

"However...?"

Marik grinned like a rogue.

He knew Tristan could read his face as plain as any scribe read his work. Shifting in his cushioned seat, the King looked about the room as if searching the plain gray stones for an answer. He leaned forward and took up a quill from the polished table, holding the downy black feather to his cheek to help him think.

"It is not so much the texture," Marik began. "You truly have mastered your craft on that account."

"But...?"

"The flavor seems too familiar, as if I have tasted it only a short time ago." Looking much like a connoisseur tasting a fine wine, Marik savored his third cookie slowly. "An exceptional batch of cacao, but something about the... walnut?... poorly complements its counters. Would not our own hazelnut, or perhaps some pecans from Dunsbury, be sufficient to the task? I think we may have been cozened on these shredded coconuts as well."

Taking notes with chalk and slate, Tristan duly nodded with each intimation. "Pecans are closely related to walnuts, Sire, in genus and taste. Would a mixture of cashew or pistachio not work equally well?"

"Perhaps," the King replied, deep in contemplation. The regrettably small amount of time allotted these visits was drawing to an end, but the break from incessant decision-making was a welcome one. If his schedule would allow it, Marik would have the master baker visit him more often.

The sudden appearance of Flicker, a multi-hued faery dragon, reminded the King that his Advisor, Magarius, awaited him in the throne room. Named so for his unique ability to flicker in and out of existence, like the snuffing of a candle flame, the two-foot long dragon was remarkably excitable and often causing mischief. With whirling eyes of a luminous blue, the tiny reptile chirruped his delight and darted towards the baker. Though startling the man at first, as the abrupt emerging from thin air frequently did, the master baker calmed his heart and welcomed his companion. Claws bit into the thick material of Tristan's tunic but caused him no pain as the spiny tail wrapped around his neck. Resilient scales changed from their intermingled cast of rainbow to a deep and mirthful orange, the saurian head looking about for spare treats.

Tristan chuckled when the dragon crooned into his ear, a warbling that shook his whole body with diminutive vibrations. He reached into his pocket and drew forth a cacao bean, the solid exterior of the seed no trouble for Flicker's strong jaws. He held the gift up for his little friend and placed it gently into the waiting mouth. Careful not to let the needle-sharp teeth touch his fingers, the master baker took the opportunity to scratch behind the elfin ears.

King Marik suppressed a smile. "It would seem our conversation has just been concluded. Would you please keep him occupied while I consult with his master? You have my gratitude... I cannot begin to explain the mishaps that haunt that little fellow."

"There is no need to explain," Tristan remarked and bowed. Flicker grew red with indignation but was soon soothed to a placating blush at the baker's ministrations. "There, that's better now, little one. Why don't you and I go for a walk in the royal garden?"

The small dragon sang out a trill in response and disappeared from view. A perplexing look fell over the King, but he was none too put out by the absence.

"In his excitement," Tristan clarified, "he went to the garden without me. He should be back as soon as he realizes I'm not there with him."

"That could take some time, I would imagine." Marik smiled at his own quip and stood from his chair. Though glad he could hold these visitations away from the royal chambers, he didn't want to keep the wizened mage waiting too long. He extended his arm, and the two grasped forearms in farewell.

"Until next week, Sire?"

"Just so. Fare thee well, master baker."

Then King Marik was through the door and down the stony corridor. Listening to the retreating footsteps, Tristan headed for the royal garden. He was nearly past the glass double-doors when Flicker appeared in the air before him. Flapping his leathery wings, the dragon showed his distress with twirling shades of white and green. Once the fear had subsided to a relaxing earthen tinge, the balmy admonition began. A predominantly forgiving creature, Flicker promptly left the deed in the past and was shortly crooning an enchanted descant.

The high-pitched melody soon filled every corner of the garden.

* * *

A lighthearted song escaped through open windows in the Esrald bakeshop, a baritone rich in timbre that possessed a taste no less than bawdy. With practiced humming to fill the missing gaps of words, the lyric attested the joys discerned from one plying his trade. While baking may not have been Cornelius' original craft, the ex-mercenary found more satisfaction in a day's worth of creating cookies than he ever had as a hired sword. He no longer felt the nagging sense of being dispensable, nonessential – no more could he be easily replaced with coin and a sword. There was a perception of contentedness and gratification in performing a task necessary to those around him, to provide happiness in any measurable degree.

Wiping a smatter of flour from his cheek, managing to smear more on than take off, Cornelius resumed the stirring of his cookie batter. The heavy wooden table before him was littered with countless ingredients. Small glass phials with costly herbs and spices were set aside for the King's special charge, but the veteran warrior couldn't help but flavor the batch from time to time with the precious stuff. It was his task to make enough of the crispy sweetcakes to ensure absolute efficiency. No customer should have to go without the freshly baked goods, but neither should there be an abundance left over at the end of the day.

The ex-mercenary with tawny blonde hair did exceedingly well at his task, though he sometimes surpassed his mark. Engrossed in his work as he customarily was, an extra tray of cookies would occasionally find its way into the stonework oven. Tristan was judiciously lenient at such times, virtually condoning, and he invariably dispensed of the excess fare in an unknown, save expedient, manner.

Throwing his one long braid of hair back over his shoulder, the seasoned soldier worked the batter while keeping a close eye on the falling sands of the hourglass. It was nearly time to pull another tray from the oven, though each batch was subject to his skillful eye and not any unbending time interval.

"Cornelius!" a young boy's voice called from the window. "You're scaring all the cats away with that terrible noise!"

The big man's eyes brightened, and a smirk cut across his tanned complexion. Wiping calloused hands onto the front of his apron, he nodded for the disheveled boy to come in.

"Serve's them right," he said and put down his bowl and spoon. "Those bloody cats do naught but mischief in our refuse box. With them hanging about the place all day long, it's no wonder any customers manage to stumble inside here at all!"

The small boy nodded and licked his lips as he came through the front door. His grimy tunic and torn leggings gave him an overall squalid appearance, but his muddy bare feet better implied his lack of coin. This was no dirtied son of a noble in search of grand adventure within the cobbled avenues. He was a street urchin, living day to day by his wit or luck and on the generosity of those like Cornelius. Whether or not he was orphaned mattered little in the alleys and streets, where the only one to be trusted was yourself – and sometimes not even then.

"You just like to complain," Daren accused, his eyes locked upon the cooking spoon. "You would have made a poor Captain of the Guard with an attitude like yours."

Cornelius raised an eyebrow at that and snatched the boy's hand before it could take up the spoon. "Would I have now? I know someone who would've been spending a night in a cold cell if I did take that job." He crinkled his nose and ruffled Daren's ruddy locks. He then hung the large metal spoon from a rung on his belt – one specially designed by his brother the blacksmith – assuming the old position of his sword.

Taking a tray from the oven with sturdy metal clamps, the veteran asked over his shoulder, "What happened to the coin I gave you for shoes? I realize the changing fashions among you scamps, but..."

"I lost them," Daren explained with a shrug. He reached for a cookie but cleared his throat for permission before taking. With Cornelius' assent, he bit into the steaming morsel and closed his eyes to cherish the taste. The luscious chocolate burned the roof of his mouth and lips, but he hardly noticed the distraction.

"You mean someone took them," Cornelius corrected and took out the remaining trays. He slid four new trays into the oven and closed the iron door. "I thought you could defend yourself better than that, Daren. After all the hours I spent training you, I'd think you should be running these streets – not running from them."

Daren feigned a wounded look. "There are some fights even I can't win, master swordsman. I was sorely outnumbered at the time, though I did manage to give a few of them a lasting memory."

A lump welled up in Cornelius' throat, and he blinked away some haunting memory. "My door is always open to you, lad. You can hole up in the library for only so long before you're discovered. It'd be good for you to stay with me for a bit, and I'd enjoy the company."

"I appreciate that, but I think I'm doing rather well on my own. I've lived in that library for a long time now, and no one would think there's a thirteen year old boy living in the rafters. Besides, I may lose an occasional battle, but I won't lose the war!" The little rogue chuckled and took another cookie. "Do you think we could start training again? I spend more time reading books than I do scouting for food."

The master swordsman nodded mutely as the memories of vagabond children invaded his thoughts. The number of campaigns he had fought left his heart broken and his sword arm useless. He was done with fighting, but he could help some of those children to help themselves. No matter the cost, he would make a difference in Daren's life and any other street-bound child that would let him.

"Day after tomorrow," Cornelius answered. "My brothers and I will be done with our weekly undertaking by then. After that I'm all yours." Seeing the appreciative smile exceeded any purse of coin he gained from warring.

A thought struck the ex-mercenary, and he grabbed up some packing paper. "Would you do me a favor, Daren? I need these cookies delivered to the Merchant's Guild."

Eyes widened in surprise, Daren couldn't find the words to answer. He slowly regained his composure and calmly asked, "You would trust me to do that?"

"Of course I trust you," was the response. "Here's five coppers for your trouble. Just be careful that string doesn't come undone, if you catch my meaning? That's a good lad. Oh, hold on a bit." Cornelius reached into the leather purse on his belt and drew out a silver piece. With a wink, he flipped it to the rapscallion youth.

"Get some new shoes, eh?"

The coins disappeared somewhere onto his person, and Daren held the package under his arm. "Thank you, Corn'. I'll see you day after next!"

The master swordsman gave a proud smile and a nod. "Take care, friend! My offer still stands if you should change your mind."

Daren gave a wink of his own and turned, disappearing into the crowds of people with the skill of his trade. Cornelius took the big spoon from off his belt and went back to stirring his batter. The sands in the hourglass continued to fall without relent as the work was resumed – and the memories faded away.

The deep baritone then played out its song once more.

*   *   *

The forest of Lightwood was called by yet another name but one not so commonly known. Deep in the heart of the dense forest lived a mythical race of people, ones who were recognized only in the legends and stories of small children throughout the realm. The foresters were tall and fair, slight of frame but stout in strength. Their almond-shaped eyes were softer once and pointed ears no more than a dissimilarity, but alien belief in gods and life roughly separated them from mankind. Driven into seclusion by persecution and hatred, their physical differences became the marks of an enemy with irrefutable distinctions. The long-lived woodland people retreated deep into the darkened forest, to areas only skilled woodsmen could reach. For centuries they resided there, until the only memories of their existence among man became flights of fancy and fireside tales. Generations came and went with a mutual peace and distance maintained, but humans are scarcely satisfied with their lot. The expanding villages and merchant exploits cut deeper into the woods on a daily basis, and a barbarian clan saw fit to make a permanent dwelling of the trees in Noria. The sylvan elves were being pushed once more, but this time there was no retreat left for them. Their home and lives were slowly being taken away.

The woodland, Luminarron, was their only home.

King Marik was aware of the elves' existence and met with them whenever the need arose. Though the busy King could not take the time to travel through the depths of the forest, he allowed emissaries into his court to speak on their behalf. Having found such needs of late, the sylvans called upon the man for aid. Cloaked to hide their physical differences, they gained entrance to the castle and met with Marik shortly after.

An agreeable relationship had grown over the years, since the foresters first approached the King at the beginning of his reign. With the elves protecting the southern borders from attack through Lightwood, Noria was able to focus its defenses in other areas. This was the basis for Marik's plan to lessen the raids on his people, to drive the barbarians and renegade highwaymen out of his realm. The plan had initially worked without flaw, but the strategy could not have foreseen the incredible growth of the barbarian clans. Possessing some semblance of civility – or at least intelligence – the savage tribes prospered in the woods. Treating them as a separate entity had only provoked their expansion, and their alien ways made them unapproachable for continued talks. The Clan of the Deer had become unmanageable, even for the skilled woodsmanship of the elves.

"I am afraid I have not been kept abroad of the situation," King Marik said in a stern voice.

Sitting atop his polished wooden throne, he had the overbearing appearance of an indomitable man. Magarius stood to his left, the grizzly beard of gray a stark contrast to his salmon colored robes. The sagacious Advisor listened with intent to the sylvan emissary, hoping to find a plausible solution to the problem at hand.

To Marik's left stood Jonathan Esrald, Protectorate of Noria. The third of Gerard's sons stood over six feet tall and weighed nearly fifteen stone. Were it not for the full plate of shining armor he wore, he might have only seemed intimidating. He was, however, a towering mass of steel that brooked no argument. Under a disciplined brow, his crystal blue eyes absorbed all around him.

With his short blonde hair and neatly trimmed mustache, as was the current style among the order in Garand, Jonathan was an emblem for the Code of Knighthood. Since the kingdom possessed no knights of their own, Marik was swift to create the royal appointment when meeting the unique individual. Nothing was so precious to the King as honor.

The Protectorate was the living embodiment of that virtue.

"We thought the situation well under control," the sylvan replied. Straw-colored hair did little to hide those tapered ears, and his piercing eyes of jade were flinty with resolve. An ornate long sword was sheathed within a leather scabbard on his belt, and only deerskin boots showed from under the heavy fabric of his dark robes. With an unapologetic air, the forester continued in his thickly accented common.

"More of the barbarous ones have migrated north, joining with those of the Deer. Their painted masks are new to the trees, but their minds are not. They live as ones accustomed to the woods, and they hunt endlessly. We can no longer keep them at bay with bow and arrow. Their numbers have grown beyond the hundreds, and more are seen entering Luminarron with each sunrise."

Marik sighed deeply as his stony features visibly softened. "What do you think?" he asked his Advisor. "Is there naught we can do to keep these heathens from our land?"

"I do not know, your Majesty." Magarius then asked the elf, "They do not group together very closely?"

"The Clan is divided into smaller tribes that have spread themselves all throughout the forest. Luminarron is large enough to support such numbers, but it will not be long before their eyes turn outward."

"Indeed," the Protectorate said gravely. "There have been reports of raids in Tillsbury, Dunshire and Varengrove. Though easily repelled by their militias and appointed soldiers, the attacks would have had dire results if the watch were at all lax in their duties. I believe the assaults may have been to determine the village defenses, to test their mettle."

"What you say is true," the elf replied. "The Deer is trying its bonds and stretching its legs."

"Before anything can be done," the King uttered decisively, "I will need to be better appraised of the situation. I would like to send my Protectorate along with you to survey the circumstances." The emissary nodded his solemn approval. "When would be convenient for you, Sir Jonathan?"

"The day after next," he answered. "I will come to the forest and look for you at break of day."

"No," the sylvan smiled thinly. "I will look for you."

* * *

A billowing cloud of ivory steam hissed its way upward, the glowing iron of angry red cooling to a lifeless charcoal-gray in the wooden bucket of water. The incessant ringing of hammer on steel echoed all throughout the smithy, the resonant cries of metals being wrought. Numerous blades of various size and shape lined the stone walls, awaiting handles and the finishing process that will ready them for the market. Dull shields of steel-blue lay ready to be embossed with the insignias of their purchasers and burnished to glossy perfection. Mismatched pieces of armor were strewn about the worktables in preparation for the required suits ordered by King Marik. Once the pieces were fully shaped and hardened, the plates would be sent to the leathersmith. There they would be joined together with straps and buckles, forming the plate mail armor that would be given to each squire at the completion of their intense training in the Code.

Standing before the burning embers was one of the largest men in all of Noria, deeply bronzed from the fires of the forge. Though not very tall, the burly man was a mountain of corded muscle and sinew, with a heavy barrel-chest that delivered merciless hammer blows upon the malleable, heated iron. His shoulder-length black hair was tied back in a leather thong, to keep it from his sweaty brow, as sparkling green eyes directed his hand and hammer. A scruffy beard and mustache did little to hide the toothy smile that was ever present upon the blacksmith's face, and a childlike mirth played behind those jasper eyes. Though no one had ever described the hulking smith as jolly, he was an amiable sort and a pleasure to do business with.

And Stephen Esrald did a lot of business.

Only a year younger than Jonathan's twenty-eight, the fourth son of the first Royal Baker was an amazing craftsman and expert with metals. His sword brand was known to all soldiers and mercenaries within Marik's realm, and his skillful reputation was spreading into neighboring kingdoms. Having sworn fealty to King Marik, Stephen would never sell his wares directly to another monarch, but still some managed to fall into the hands of the nobility and upper crust of society. Merchants who could get a hold of the special swords were rewarded a sizable purse, as the blacksmith's stubborn loyalty to Marik drove prices even higher.

Being trained by a fastidious master smith, Stephen continued his inherited task of particularity and the careful choosing of apprentices. With the King's growing needs for armor, the brawny smith was hard pressed to take on more help. Three fledglings labored diligently under his demanding tutelage, acquiring invaluable knowledge and experience – as well as the tanned skin and stout frames that correspond with the plying of that trade.

"Take care with that blade," Stephen warned a young, blonde-haired apprentice. "Keep the folds steady, or you'll have yourself a fine looking play toy. A brittle sword is rarely appreciated," he chuckled and patted the novice on the back. "Good, that's much better, lad. That's going to be a keen edge. Now drop it in the water, and let it cool before putting it back in the coals."

Wheezing steam swelled up from the drum, a surge of vaporous heat that stole the glowing fire from the blade. When the reddened center lost its gleam, the iron was stabbed back into the bed of fiery coals. What may have seemed a tiresome procedure to some, Stephen saw the forging of iron as a steadily creative process with a multitude of opportunity for mistake and greatness. Each sword was unique, exceptional, and designed to the specific needs of its wielder. While such craftsmanship in itself was rare, the results were unequivocally so. With every sword, shield or piece of armor made, knowledge and skill expanded until a definitive character of style broke free, and a master smith was born.

Such was the lesson Stephen tried to instill in his pupils.

As the three apprentices worked tirelessly on producing the heavy plate mail, a customer entered through the great elm double doors. He had the short cropped hair of the soldier's style, but his slicked raven locks and haughty chin bespoke the burdens of nobility. Adorned in black riding pants, with a silken doublet to match, the man looked as if he was torn between his duties and a day on horseback. Fresh straw bent under his dark riding boots as he strode up towards Stephen, his hawk-like nose protruding under calm, gray eyes.

"How do you, good sir." He spoke as if one used to the comfort of command. "Are you master smith Stephen?"

"I am," Stephen replied and offered his arm. "And how may I be of service to you, sir?"

An almost imperceptible frown creased the nobleman's brow but was immediately erased and restored to polite joviality. He took the smith's forearm in perfunctory greeting, his leather glove stretching in protest.

"I wish to commission a fairly large order from you," he said in a smooth voice. "I have a list with all the necessary arms." He removed a small scroll from his belt and handed it to Stephen. While the hefty smith perused the contents, his eyes unrevealing, the nobleman studied his every reaction.

"This is quite a list you have here, my lord. May I ask for what purpose you require so many blades? I don't mean to be intrusive, but I have certain obligations that restrict what tasks I may undertake."

"Perfectly understandable! I wouldn't want to endanger any relations you have with our Majesty. My soldiers number many, as you can see by that list, and I wish to replace their older weaponry. The shields are a gift for exemplary service, and the rapiers are for my sons – and various other relatives who will soon be visiting." The man paused and forced a sigh for effect. "You see, my daughter is to be wed two months hence. Since I am not on very good terms with my neighboring lord, I want to ensure safety for my guests. Your reputation for fine quality is impeccable, so you were the natural choice for this charge."

Stephen took note of the slower, more cautious speech. "Which lands are yours, my lord?"

"I hold the lands of Dirkemshire and Laudley," was the crisp rejoinder. "I am Lord Hubreys, of the Jondra line. You may be familiar with the name. If it will alleviate your mind, I have publicly sworn fealty to King Marik the day he was crowned. My reputation is, likewise, indefectible."

The master smith visibly brightened at that, his doubts allayed for the moment. Something bothered him about Lord Hubreys, but he shrugged it off as a character flaw and not any traitorous intent.

"This will be a costly endeavor," Stephen warned. "Three gold for each blade, two for each shield and five for each rapier." Lord Hubreys' eyes widened in surprise but quickly resumed the noble disregard for expenditures. "Numbers are not my strong suit, but that comes to a great deal of coin."

"Five hundred and fifty gold, if I'm not mistaken. Don't worry yourself, master smith. Your skill is worth every last copper, and I'll spare no expense for the protection of my daughter. My coin is well spent, I assure you."

Nodding assent, Stephen placed the scroll into his own belt. "Everything will be in readiness a week before the wedding. You can pick them up anytime after that, though I dare say you'll need a large wagon to carry it all."

Lord Hubreys gave a wink and a grin. "No need to worry about that! If anything, I'm well prepared."

With that being said, the lord turned on his heel and walked out the doors. As he was untying his horse, Stephen wondered if he should send one of the lads to inquire at the castle about the good Lord Hubreys. Most customers were required to pay half the commission in advance, but in the case of nobility, an exception was always made. The upper echelon of Noria too often took offense at such things. Chiding his suspicious thoughts, the master smith went back to his craft. The workload had just dramatically increased, while time remained ever rigid.

Feeling rather pleased with himself, the so-called Lord Hubreys rode his charcoal mare down the cobbled venue. The gladiatorial arena loomed ahead as a devious smirk crossed his thin lips. Laughing to himself, the dark man began to mutter.

"What does price matter when I intend to steal the blades anyway?"

* * *

The arena was a circular-shaped structure of unimposing gray stone, capable of holding well over a thousand spectators in its alderwood stands. The lack of covering made the games susceptible to weather, but there were rarely any empty seats to be found. What was typically a fatal match in earlier days had evolved into a show of fighting prowess and practiced skill, no longer the barbaric contest it once was. The gladiators were highly trained warriors whose sole duty was to entertain the crowd. Though death was strictly frowned upon, it regrettably did happen at times.

The majority of gladiators were soldiers from the Barbarian Wars or bandless mercenaries trying their resolution and battle skill. Each win drew a percentage of the attendance, a considerable amount of coin, and a certain amount of fame. Matches were scheduled everyday, with a small army of combatants to choose from. The bouts were a great source of gambling and provided a hefty tithe for King Marik as well.

For those gladiators that were slaves or criminals, freedom was the ultimate reward. Once a week, an elimination contest took place to see which man would earn his liberty. Those gaining such a prize usually continued to perform in the arena, accruing an income able to sustain a comfortable life. Those who left defeated could only persevere, for such competitions had only one victor.

The greatest of these gladiators was a hero, a soldier whose bravery stood above the norm. The Barbarian Wars began twenty years before Marik took the throne but lasted only four years after he began his reign. Entering the fray at the age of thirteen, this courageous warrior rose through the ranks at a rapid pace and was appointed the position of General by its end. A fierce and dauntless man, Valoran Esrald earned respect both on the battlefield and in the Arena. His name was legendary to the folk of the realms – and a source of nightmarish stories intended to scare barbarian children into behaving.

Valoran was only four years old when his mother, Larissa, was lost in a raid on their village. King Jaril II's idea of protection for his subjects was less than adequate, and Gerard's wife paid the price for the King's insufficiency. Though young and unable to avenge his mother's death, Valoran swore that one day he would. He trained with dogged persistence, never faltering in his practice with any weapon he could lay his hands on. Seeing no other way for his son to vent his anger, Gerard encouraged the boy when he could. Keeping a tight rein on his son's passion was difficult, and in the end he could not keep the boy from becoming a soldier. No one anticipated the Barbarian Wars lasting such a long time.

Six years had passed since the end of the wars, and the champion of Noria kept his skills sharp by participating in the Arena. Wealthy nobles traveled from distant realms all throughout Astoria to view the renowned weapons master, some hoping to persuade the young man to join their ranks. Although he only fought on occasion, Valoran practiced indefatigably with the others. He trained each man and woman as best he could and offered special attention to those who sought license from their enslavement. He would have nothing to do with the criminal gladiators, but he could not refuse a man whose only crime was his place of birth.

Standing just under six feet tall, the youthful General was sleek and muscular. He had the grace of a feline, a supple range of controlled motion that was liquid in manner and frightening in usage. His body was completely lacking in hair, shaved from head to toe, and the application of oils before a match made him impossible to engage without weapons. He simply slipped out from any attempted grasp, and that made him a dangerous wrestler. His grim, dark eyes gave many cause to rethink their strategies, but no choice of attack could conquer the man.

The weapons master was insurmountable.

While stretching his legs out under the sun, Valoran let his mind wander to the tune of a mandolin being played by the training grounds. The local bards would often show their appreciation for the gladiators by coming out and playing to them. The practiced warriors would, in turn, move to the thrumming cadence. An elaborate production of song and sword would result, and a tempo was set for the matches to follow.

Valoran enjoyed the festive music and was well-nigh tempted to join in the singing when he saw a man in black approach from the corner of his eye. He paid the man no heed but went about his business of loosening muscles cramped from sleeping on the arena bunks – if the stone slabs could be named such. The gladiator granted himself no such luxury as a soft bed with feather pillows, since he was sure his mind and body might be softened by the indulgences. Neither would his conscience allow him to leave the arena while his comrades did not have that liberty.

"You look familiar," the man in black leggings and doublet remarked when he was close enough. He took a seat in the stands a few feet away and watched the General flex his limbs.

"I have that sort of face," Valoran replied emotionlessly. His instincts told him to mistrust the facile voice, though he wasn't sure why. He switched legs and grabbed a hold of his outstretched foot, pulling his bald pate down towards his knee.

"I see you have the mark of a gladiator," the dark-haired man pointed out. The lightning bolt tattoo upon the left shoulder was clearly visible. "Perhaps I've seen you perform from time to time. Yes, I'm sure of it now! You're name is Torren, isn't it?"

Tiring of the man's voice, Valoran stood and fixed his gaze on him. As other tattoos became perceptible, the nobleman blanched and took on a ghastly pallor.

"Oh my," he remarked as apparent recognition dawned on him. His fear was somewhat forced and dramatic, almost theatrical.

The tattoo of crossed swords over the gladiator's left breast was a mark from the Barbarian Wars, depicting the clashing of two mighty armies. The neighing unicorn upon the right breast was the insignia of an elite soldier outfit, a band that Valoran led for two years. The small flame over his sternum was a symbol of unprecedented valor, an honor bestowed by the men serving under him. The joining of all three in a thick, unbroken triangle was a representation of unity in body, mind and spirit.

He was the incarnation of Valor.

"Quickly speak your peace!" the gladiator commanded. As a General, he was inured to giving orders, and his tolerance for the seedy nobleman had grown thin. "I have neither the time nor the patience for idle talk, and you did not approach me by chance."

"You are correct," the wheedling man acceded. "I am seeking those of a talent for the sword... for a task that will prove most rewarding. Your skill with the blade is legendary, and your fellow gladiators are practiced swordsmen as well. I have heard that some will sell their sword arms if the coin is rich enough."

"I do not speak for the others," Valoran said with steel in his voice. "I only speak for myself. My sword is not for hire, nor was it ever. You would do well to stay clear of my path."

The austere gladiator turned on his heel and walked towards the training areas where others awaited his guidance. He could not put his finger on it, but something about the oily man invoked great uncertainty and unreasonable anger. Valoran's intuition had never failed him, and he trusted it implicitly.

Lord Hubreys simply shrugged and looked for other gladiators.

* * *

Humphrey was three years younger than Valoran's twenty-five, but his soft and caring eyes were ageless. A lighter shade of cacao, those eyes lay placid beneath a brow unused to sorrow, and a small but arrant nose sat fixed above the slender lips of a nobleman. Chest-length hair of dusky brown ran free down his leather jerkin and matched in color the playful squirrel atop his shoulder.

Chittering fondly in his ear, its long bushy tail caressed his neck in a loving embrace.

He walked through the green blanket of foliage that was interspersed with groves of birch and alder. A white palfrey walked by his side, its dark eyes attentive and spotted ears raised in curiosity, as thick rays of sunlight broke through the treetops to guide their way. Humphrey stroked its neck and downy mane as they walked through Lightwood, softly playing a reed pipe while listening to his friend's unending stories. In time to the delicate melody, the squirrel gave its exaggerated narration with all the skill of a master teller. The little fellow could drone on for hours about his forays in the forest, his epic adventures and near-fatal encounters. The gentle horse soon lost interest in the musically borne recounting and nudged the master trainer to resume his ministrations.

"I'm sorry, Ivoren," he told the reproving horse. "I lost myself in Harper's tale. His details are so vivid that I nearly saw myself being attacked by a fire-breathing dragon and running for the safety of the elves! And all for the sake of some hazelnuts!" He chuckled and winked to the palfrey, who nickered its amusement in turn.

Harper recognized sarcasm when he heard it.

"Ow!" Humphrey yelled and grabbed for his ear lobe. The bantam squirrel had nipped the fleshy fold, careful not to cause injury, but enough to express his dislike for laughter at his expense. He turned up his glistening nose and twittered something about learning a grave lesson in manners.

"You little devil!" he laughed and rubbed his ear. "I don't know which hurts more, my ear or my pride. Either way, I'm sorry for poking fun at you. You're not still angry with me? Good. Now, what say we return Ivoren to his Mistress Celena and head back to the stables. Maybe we can prevail upon merchantman Lodren for some of those hazelnuts you're so fond of."

The squirrel heartily agreed and fluttered with anticipation. Humphrey only shook his head at the tiny one's excitability, and reached up to scratch its furry head before putting his lips to the pipe again. A following of songbirds saw fit to join in the music, and the ensuing corollary was one of a summons that all who could hear felt obliged to defer. They soon led the forest in a gathering of song, where rabbits and squirrels came out from hiding to meet. Sparrows and starlings swooped from their branches to sing into the cool breeze, as deer stepped cautiously out into the open. A fawn walked tremulously behind its mother, nuzzling the master trainer's leg as the others pranced to the tune.

It was not long, however, before they came to the edge of the wood, where the others did not feel safe to tread. With the song at its end, Humphrey simply waved to his friends and headed for the marketplace. It gave him time to reflect while entertaining his companions with a tender chord.

Humphrey's uncommon affinity for animals made him the perfect master trainer, and King Marik was sharp to note it. He shrewdly put the young man in charge of the royal stables, an onerous task for one body, but he performed splendidly with help from the stablemen and apprentices. Schooling the mares and stallions of merchants and king alike, the eremitic youth found little time to himself. Fortunately, the time spent instructing was pleasant and not at all laborious.

What spare time he did have left was whiled away in the forest. The discomfort he felt around people seemed but a distant memory when among the likewise modest animals. Humphrey knew each one by name, and he went out of his way to make new friends when one was unfamiliar to him. He lived in a simple cabin of his own design – though a number of grateful soldiers showed up to lend him a hand.

Lightwood was his humble home and the animals a second family.

* * *

The Advisor to King Marik, the wise and venerable sage, was known simply as Magarius. A direct descendant to the line of the Great Joren, believed to be the most powerful wizard the world had ever known, the aged counselor had weighty expectations to fulfill. By far surpassing the might and magical strength of his ancestor, Magarius was a modest man with little in regards to fanfare. He was an astute individual, tempered by an unusual number of years, and was rarely moved to passionate displays. His fascination for his work often kept him from the company of others, but his duties as Advisor to the King took precedence.

The work that so consumed the white-haired mage was an untested theory in an area of the Art he discovered called essence. It was nothing like the other known realms of practical magic, for it dealt with the nature of all things, the very core of the item in question. Magarius did not limit his studies to the living but strove to discover the inner being of inanimate objects as well. This one aspect is what set his realm apart from those of druidic, sympathetic and spiritual magic – the more commonly practiced Arts at the time. An essence mage sought to draw from the intense energy of all that was in nature, in the trees and people surrounding him. The true danger involved was in over-extending the pull, which could drain the entirety of life force from the directed subject. Magarius was unable to prove the existence of essence magic up to that point, as none of his experiments could yield conclusive results.

His colleagues in the Wizard's Guild held little belief in the theories of essence, but none would discredit the enormous mastery Magarius held in the Arts. His perceived eminence made him a difficult man to address, which contributed to his already reserved manner. Knowing the feelings of uneasiness among his peers, he decided to abstain from council meetings until more solid evidence of essence magic could be obtained.

That was eighty-seven years ago.

Having no one else to confer with on his findings or failures, Magarius found himself talking with his familiar, Flicker. The faery dragon was notably helpful at times, understanding in his limited capacity, and always a soothing relief in times of distress. Though Magarius had lived well over three-hundred years, he had the strength and wit of a young man. Not even Flicker's illusory pranks could unsettle him – and the dragon was known expressly for his mischievous antics. The impish tricks that time and again would set the castle astir were tiresome and amusing only to their maker, but they were not the cause for the wizard's frosty gray hair.

Sitting at his disorganized worktable, penetrating blue eyes peering down upon pages written in his own hand, Magarius toiled away the night with little more than lighted tallow to aid his burden. The flowing silk robes he wore, colored the orange of a summer sunrise, were appropriate in the Royal Chamber when addressing an emissary from the elven people, but they were not up to the task of keeping out the biting chill of autumn. Flicker crooned softly in his master's ear, sensing the cold that nipped at his tired body. Slipping his tail around the mage's neck, under robe and beard, he quietly warmed the seemingly fragile man – quietly inasmuch as casting spells created a special resonance that only magicians could hear or sense. A faint glow emanated from his florid scales, a rosy luminescence that lulled the sage to sleep.

Magarius woke the next morning to the persistent calls of lively sparrows bent on disturbing his rest. Noting how much time he'd wasted by sleeping, he chided the whims of aging bodies and set about his work. A single leaf lay upon his table, its brown edges dried by time. Resembling the hand of an elderly man, its veins ran like a map over its surface. A chalky-white powder clung to the bottom and rim of a stone mortar to the left. With pestle in his hand, Magarius sprinkled a final ingredient into the rounded bowl and proceeded to mix the two together. The last element had just arrived by wagon, though the shipment originated across the ocean in the far east.

When the exotic spice was indistinguishable from the whole, Magarius dotted the leaf with the resultant compound. An immediate change took place, one both surprising and anticipated at the same time.

The once dried and dead leaf sprang to life, a myriad of coruscating colors that vibrated with magic. Almost blinding in intensity, the light filled the room like a second sun, a radiance of heat the mage could feel as he shielded his sensitive eyes. Flicker hid behind the protection of his master's shoulder until the brightness began to fade.

Then the true essence was revealed.

As if it had never fallen, the leaf was full of life. Its deep emerald hue gently shifted to match Magarius' robes, and then again to a spirited red before blending to a tranquil cast of brown. The cycle of changing earth colors continued without variation, the true nature of the leaf released, and forever would that magic be free. What little force the blade drew from the life encircling it was not enough to cause concern, though an entire tree might cause some distress. Many more experiments would take place before anything of such size would be tried.

Just then it dawned on Magarius what the inner being of a leaf was: the changing of the seasons. By watching the colors shift and blend, he could point out each one to Flicker. The tiny dragon was overjoyed at the sight of the leaf – and his master's happy tone – and jumped down onto the table to stand beside the fickle blade. He sniffed at the displacing shades, hearing the light whisper of magic, and his eyes whirled in a restless sea of blue. Throwing his saurian head back in delight, he trilled out a song to rival the leaf. The warbled descant set the mage to chuckling at his little friend's elaborate show of emotion, but he was thoroughly pleased to see Flicker so lighthearted. Scraping a small amount of the powder into a vellum packet, Magarius touched his finger to the stuff.

"Looks like flour, don't you think?" he asked the faery dragon. Elfin ears perked up at the query, but the song still vibrated down his neck like the purring of a cat. "You be sure to keep out of this now! Yes, I realize the pretty colors are quite entrancing, but I am warning you for your own good. I care a great deal about you, little one" – his eyes softened at the corners as he resumed his cautioning – "so I don't want to see you nosing about in there. You change colors as it is, and they're already very beautiful. Enough said? Good."

He sniffed at the powder on his finger but could discern no odor. He nearly placed it on his tongue to try for a taste, when he felt the dragon's icy stare bore through his inquisitive thought. His bushy eyebrows furrowed in defiance, but he eventually shrugged in surrender. Wiping the powder from his hand with a washcloth, Magarius was careful to make sure he removed every mote. In theory, the powder could only affect a person by ingesting a fairly large quantity. However, he didn't want to take any undue chances before solidifying evidence to present to the guild. The others would be greatly surprised, and deeply chagrined, that his theories were sound from the start.

The magic realm of essence truly did exist.

* * *

The morning of Magarius' success dawned with equal luminosity over the Esrald bakeshop. Tristan busily prepared for the day ahead while the sun was peeking its flaming top over the castle walls. There was still a chill wind wending its way through the marketplace, and the dark mass of clouds overhead forebode a possible storm.

"Morning, brother!" Cornelius said cheerfully as he walked through the open door. "Looks like we're in for some rain this day. Did you sleep well?"

"As well as can be expected," the master baker replied with a sigh. "Those cats outside were calling to the moon all night. I barely got in a wink of rest." Tristan had the worktable arranged in an orderly fashion, with spices to one side and herbs to the other. His leather-bound annal was opened, and he ran his finger along the scrawl as he read.

"You do look a bit tired. Why don't you go and get some rest before the others arrive. I can take care of all this without any problem," he shrugged. "It's not as if I've never done it before."

Tristan waved a hand in refusal. "I'm fine, Cornelius. Do I seem so terribly old to you already?" He raised a brow as he smiled, awaiting his younger brother's response.

Cornelius simply bowed. "Far be it from me to imply such a thing! You wear your many seasons quite well, dear brother. Were that I could be as strong, or the time nearly as gracious, when the years come wearily upon me." His grin was roguish as he poked his spoon at Tristan.

"Ahh, my droll brother. Do you suppose we could get about to working this morn?"

The ex-mercenary winked and set about his task. The burlap sacks of flour stood nearly half his height, but it was their weight that caused him to groan. Ignoring Tristan's remark about just who was aging with all due speed, he carried the coarse bags from the storeroom to the front. Just as he lay them unceremoniously against the far wall, Jonathan appeared at the door.

"I hope I'm not late," the Protectorate said in apology. "I was up most of the night making plans for tomorrow."

"You're never late," Cornelius accused.

Tristan rolled his eyes and settled some bowls onto the table. "I see you're not wearing your armor," he noted approvingly. The homespun tunic and plain leather leggings were far better suited to baking than the iron shell most knights wore.

"I could always fetch my cuirass if you so long for the sight." He smoothed his long blonde mustache to hide a smile.

"Please, Jonathan," the master baker sighed. "We already have one jester among us. Must we have two? Come look at this, and tell me what you think. You may know more of Marik's taste than I do, with all the time you've been spending in his castle of late."

The knight clasped one of the long iron spoons to his belt as he moved behind the table. He scanned the latest entry as the rest of his brothers arrived. Greetings were exchanged and the usual clamor commenced. The bakeshop was one of the larger buildings within the marketplace, which left plenty of room for six grown men to adequately perform their task. But for some obscure reason, the Esrald brothers bumped shoulders and bowls as they moved about their various chores.
    For that one day a week, the six brothers worked in unison to concoct the perfect cookie for King Marik. They put their heads together and thought out each possible course, drawing from Tristan's neatly kept journal for reference. By day's end they had baked hundreds of cookies, all of a different variety and style, texture and taste. The last tray of cookies would be the one mixture chosen to present to Marik the following week. The remaining sweetcakes would be sold at a fair price or given away to those of a need. Since Tristan would bake fresh cookies before visiting the King, the last tray was set aside for the brothers. At the end of those weekly gatherings, the six would sit by a fire at the Talon – a local tavern of sorts – and partake of their labors with a warm mug of cider.
    This day, however, posed a dilemma for the bakers. The empty burlap, where once was an abundant source of flour, lay flaccid in the corner. When Cornelius went to the storeroom for another sack, he cried out in shock and doubled in laughter at what he saw.
    The last two sacks of flour lay strewn about the room, fine white powder clinging to every square inch of the place. The wooden shutters swung back and forth in the wind, and a faint mewing could be heard in the mountain of snowy dust. Trails of tiny paw prints were

scattered in every direction, some leading to the culprits responsible for the careless crime.

A dozen ghost-like kittens meowed in protest.

"Oh gods!" Tristan bellowed. "Look what they've done to my shop! It's going to take a lifetime to get this place clean again." His flinty eyes surveyed the disaster and came to land on the once-black furry felines. A chuckle escaped his lips. "They are cute, though, aren't they?"

"That they are," Cornelius laughed. "Why don't you go and borrow some flour from master baker Ferran, and I'll see if I can't get a cupful from merchantman Gerod."

"Yes," Valoran said and took up one of the kittens. "We'll clean this mess up and find a skin of milk for our little friends."

Humphrey was holding three in the folds of his apron as he whispered to them calmly. "They've been abandoned," he remarked. "This one says she hasn't eaten for days."

Holding two in each hand, Stephen asked, "Is that so? Well, I'm sure we can find something for them to eat!" Placing one up to his scruffy beard for a nuzzle, the burly smith looked as if he would eat it whole. One of the slipperier fellows broke free and jumped for the wall of heavy tunic, its claws taking hold in the material. Stephen simply walked back outside with the mewling kitten still hanging precariously to his front.

"Go on, you two," Jonathan said. "We have this situation under control. Don't we, little ones?" he asked the four he took in hand. Sticking one on each shoulder, the knight carefully joined the others by the worktable for milk.

While Tristan and Cornelius went after the flour, the deserted kittens were cleaned and fed. Once the layer of stubborn powder was removed, a shiny coat of coal-gray fur was unveiled. After the twelve were contentedly full, they drifted to sleep with ease. Jonathan grabbed a pillow from Tristan's bed and stuffed it into a basket. With unexpected delicacy, he placed each one in the basket and used a soft cloth as a gentle blanket for warmth. The Protectorate then headed for the door with the basket of sleeping kittens in tow.

"I know an orphanage not far from here with a number of children who will be happy to see these little fellows." The others nodded their approval to the knight before he added, "I'll be back in no time."

As Jonathan disappeared from the doorway, Flicker appeared with an excited trill of salutation. His eyes shone a twirling blue upon seeing the humble master trainer, and he flew to Humphrey's shoulder to croon in his ear.

"He says his master has gone for a while, and he has no one to play with." Humphrey scratched the tender eye ridges and whistled a trill of his own.

"Doesn't Magarius take from the same shipments as Tristan?" Valoran asked in agitation. "Maybe he has some spare flour." The General was unused to waiting for things to be done.

Stephen pulled at the sticky batter that begrimed his scraggly beard. "Would a magician keep flour about?"

"I could ask," the master trainer offered. "Well, Flicker? Does your master have any flour?" Humphrey projected an image of the fine white powder, since the faery dragon did not think in terms of words. Fluttering his translucent wings in a frenzied delight, he warbled a positive reply.

The gladiator smirked at the antics. "I take that as a yes. Tell him to go and get a cupful of the stuff. I'm tired of sitting about here, waiting to do work that we could be getting on with."

Humphrey conveyed the message to the dragon and watched in amazement as Flicker vanished from sight, only to reappear a few breaths later with a large stone bowl in his claws. Without its pestle, the mortar looked like any other bowl a baker might use. Flicker was extremely proud of himself and elated at the praise he received from the three brothers who quickly set to work. The others returned in time to help mix more batter, but Tristan was a little upset at having to disturb the other master baker when it wasn't entirely necessary.

Flicker was more than happy to console him.

Valoran heard the dragon's mellow humming, and an idea struck him. "Why don't you play us a tune on that flute of yours, Humphrey?"

"Anything in particular?"

"Something... musical."

The others trusted his judgment, so a simple melody of working men soon filled the busy bakeshop. Flicker threw his rhythmic notes to the song, while Valoran – of all people – cleared his throat and began to sing. The General had a surprisingly good voice, a flamboyant tenor versed in the hymns of war. All six brothers joined in, with whistling or singing, and carried the notes with lighthearted speed. When the music had finally stopped and all the work was finished, Humphrey became the victim of warm applause and appreciation.

* * *

A low rumble could be heard as quiet descended on the bakeshop, and the rain that threatened the skies since early morning began to fall. The first droplets were far and few, splashing heavily against the dusty red cobbles with the indifference expected of weather. Brilliant flashes of lightning joined the chorus of distant thunder, lighting the way for those still in the marketplace to swiftly head for shelter. What warmth the fading sun could offer was hastily stolen away by a storm that strained the horizon.

"Let's hurry," Cornelius said through pelting rain. "This chill will be the death of us all!" His breath streamed out in a frosty mist as his words were drowned out in the thunder.

The others waited for Tristan to lock the door before moving at a brisk pace for the Talon, where steaming mugs of warmed cider anxiously awaited. The bakeshop had been cursorily cleaned with a promise to do a more thorough job the next day. With the settling of autumn came also the earlier nights and biting cold that inspired many a speedy trip to the fireplace. The basket full of well-deserved sweetcakes was an added incentive for the brothers, but Cornelius could smell the rains creeping up at a rapid pace and urged the others on. Before consenting, Tristan made each give his word to lend a hand in the morning straightening the place, and in exchange they made an early start for the fireside drinks.

When the six arrived in the poorly lit tavern, their bodies steamed and dripped as the warmth of the room fell over them. They shook off as much of the storm as was possible before moving directly for the fire. A handful of patrons sat at their heavy wooden tables, with foaming mugs to ease the wintry grip. Known for its king-sized hearth, the Talon was a welcome escape from the storm. The blazing fire outlined their bodies as they wound their way towards the great square table reserved for them. The stocky birchwood chairs were already scorched by the fire, but the heat was a pleasant relief for tired bodies.

"This is more like it!" Stephen said cheerfully as he rested his bulk into a creaky chair. He threw his legs up onto the stones of the hearth to let the fire seep into his boots. "Only one thing missing."

"Here ya go!" A plump barmaid dropped six hefty mugs of steaming cider onto the table. "Just call fer more when ye need it."

Cornelius took one of the earthenware cups and downed half the fiery drink in one swallow. "Don't you worry about that, lass! I've never been accused of being bashful!"

"Uncouth, maybe," Jonathan dutifully pointed out. He continued to tick off each detriment, "Unmannerly, crude, surly, impertinent –"

"Ahem!" Cornelius cut off his refined brother before he ran out of fingers to count on. "Is this the sort of thing you learn at court?"

Tristan smiled at that. "Cookie anyone? I'd like to offer an early congratulations to you all on a job well done. These are fine looking sweetcakes!"

The edges were crisp and perfectly baked, the center soft and moist. The combination of melting cacao, diced cashew and roasted almond – along with other various spices – was sure to win the King's heart, if not his choosy taste buds.

"Just a sip!" Humphrey told the faery dragon on his shoulder. Flicker reached his serpentine head down to the steamed cup and drank some of the pale-looking liquid. "That's enough, little one. You don't want to get tipsy, now do you?" The whirling shades of adventurous violet were not the answer he sought.

"These are good," Valoran admitted. He ate a cookie in two bites before reaching for another. "Do you mind if I take some of these back to the arena? I know some hard-working people who haven't had a treat in weeks, and this may be just the thing to lift their spirits."

"By all means," Tristan agreed.

Stephen lazily held out his giant hand for more cookies, his other hand busy raising and lowering a nearly depleted mug. Mist continued to rise from his drying boots, but he was too busy to notice. The carved face of a dwarven warrior upon his cup – hence the name *mug* – held him in thrall, its thickset features proud and defiant with a hint of recalcitrant humor in the eyes.

Humphrey took a second cookie as well and saw the pleading look in Flicker's eyes. "Is it alright for Flicker to have some cookie?" he asked Tristan. "Or do you have some cacao beans for him instead?"

Tristan reached into his pocket and came out with a handful of the maroon-colored beans. Flicker vanished from Humphrey's shoulder and reappeared perched on Tristan's wrist before he could toss the beans across the table. His claws were sharp, but he was careful not to scratch the master baker as he casually chewed his treat.

The others laughed and shook their heads at the little dragon. Cornelius was wondering what it would be like to flit in and out of places in less than the time it took to breathe when a sudden ache in his stomach stopped his drinking half way.

"What's wrong?" Valoran asked the ex-mercenary. His eyes were sharper than most, even by the dancing light of a fire. "You look like something doesn't agree with you."

"I don't know," Cornelius said with a tinge of alarm in his voice. "I feel strange... and it's not from the cider."

Stephen had his hand out for another cookie, when he suddenly dropped his mug. The shattered pieces of earthenware crunched underfoot as he stood with a peculiar look on his face. He opened his mouth as if to say something, then doubled in what appeared to be pain.

"Stephen!" Jonathan cried and reached across the table. His hand never quite made it, for some intense force strained his body. Muscles tensed uncontrollably and left him immobile as his body underwent a metamorphosis that only one man could explain.

The others stood and tried to help their kin, but soon they were in the throes of change as well. Bent over the table with muscles tightened by pressure, each brother clenched his fists and roared aloud his struggle. Every mug and tankard in sight burst into countless shards of baked clay, the flying pieces embedding into the tables and walls. A preternatural light encompassed the brothers, an unearthly cast of iridescence that struck a scene in the faery dragon's mind... the shifting colors of a leaf.

Flicker disappeared in search of his master.

Moments later, when Magarius came crashing through the front door of the Talon, he saw the barkeep hiding behind the bar. Other patrons had joined him there, fearing for their lives and cowering unabashedly until the turmoil could be resolved. In the meantime, the eerie brilliance continued to grow until the hearth was little more than a spark of light. Fingers of electricity played along the edges of the luminous sphere, striking chairs and tables and splintering them with its force. The floor was scarred black with burn marks, and wraith-like smoke clawed its way through the air in wispy tendrils.

"Dear god!" the mage shouted, but his voice was drowned out by the sizzling crackle of power and the hoarse cries of the six men held in its iron grasp. "*Sustraff!*" he commanded, calling his roanwood staff to hand.

The gnarled length of grayish yellow wood materialized in his right hand, and he tapped its stolid end against the floor while speaking in the arcane language of magic. A surge of crackling energy spread from the tip of the staff to the blazing globe of radiance, attacking it in a swirling onslaught of electricity. Like the forked fingers of a skeleton, the globe responded with thunderous alacrity. The two forces waged a battle about the Esrald brothers, but Magarius was indeed the stronger. Walking forward, the stalwart mage disbursed the sphere and absorbed its magical power, a rushing wave of incandescence flooding his staff.

All six men collapsed onto the table in exhaustion.

Flicker rushed to Humphrey's shoulder, nuzzling his cheek and ear. The vibrant thrumming invaded the master trainer's senses and brought him from the dark of unconsciousness. The dragon stretched forward his head and pressed his scales to cheek with a twitter of delight.

Humphrey managed a weak smile. "I'm alright, little one. What happened? I feel as if my head might explode."

"Hmph!" the mage snorted. His eyes were stern with disapproval as he surveyed the brothers. "Explain yourself, young man. What on earth possessed you to take an experiment of mine?" He picked up a piece of broken cookie from the floor. "I see," he said critically. "Thought you might improve upon the taste of your confectioneries, eh?"

The others were groggily waking, and the Advisor's steely voice cut like a knife into their brains. "Could you keep it down, please?" Stephen asked gruffly, pulling himself from the floor. "I think I've cracked my skull somehow."

"Be grateful yours is thick," Cornelius offered in consolation. "Mine feels like there's a dwarven smith inside, pounding without mercy." He held his aching head and groaned.

"There could be one pounding on the outside as well," the grizzly master smith warned. "And mercy never was my strong point."

"If you gentlemen are through," Magarius chided, "I'd like to get to the bottom of this. What could you have been thinking when you took that powder from my chamber? You're all lucky to be alive!" His penetrating gaze fell upon each in turn, wilting their shaken bodies.

"I don't understand," Tristan rasped. "We only borrowed a cup of flour –"

"Did you say flour?" The mage perked his ears at the word, recalling a certain conversation between he and his familiar the night before. "Flicker! Did I not warn you to stay away from that mortar?" The dragon shriveled in fear, his scales fading to a milky green as he buried his eyes in Humphrey's hair. "You could have seriously injured these innocent men, you know. This better not have been one of your mischievous pranks," he warned. "Come look at me."

The dragon reluctantly pulled himself from the solace of Humphrey's shoulder and flew to his master's outstretched arm. He slowly raised his fearful eyes to the intense scrutiny of those crystal orbs, unwavering in severity. With a chirrup in defense, Flicker redeemed himself in the eyes of his master and nestled his body in the folds of his robes.

"I'm sorry, my friend," the mage said softly through his ruffled beard. "Your heart was in the right place, but you must learn to think more clearly in the future."

Flicker heard the remonstration but could only snuggle closer. The others numbly rose at the urging of the mage and followed him out the door. The rain had lessened to a bothersome mist, with the far away rolling of thunder looming to the east. Jonathan was kind enough to leave a few gold coins on the bar, nodding in apology to the barkeep as he followed his brothers outside.

Magarius brought the six men to his chamber in the castle. There was much to discuss and a great deal to explain. The foundation of their beliefs might be threatened by what the mage had to say, but there was no other way to broach the subject of their future. The six had been inexorably changed, magically transformed to epitomize their inner beings. They would need to be taught how to control the intense powers housed within them and channel the energy freed by their essence.

It was time for them to learn about magic.

* * *

"You've been exposed to one of my more recent experiments," the Advisor began to explain. He hadn't said a word the entire way from the tavern, and the others were more than anxious for a rationalization of what just occurred. They sat in chairs by a struggling fire, the stuffy room smelling of burnt spice and incense. With aching heads and weary bodies, the brothers settled in for a long talk.

"Regardless of what you may believe or what you hold as truth," the mage went on in a voice that brooked no interruption, "you all were victims of your own spell this night." Looks of disbelief and question were exchanged, but no one offered to argue with the magician. "Good. Digest that for a bit, while I describe just what sort of magic you worked tonight.

"I call it essence, and it is by far the most powerful of all enchantments I've ever worked. There is more to nature than any man may know, but you six may have added insight to that mystery. You see, the essence of a man, or anything for that matter, is the very core of his soul, his strengths intensified and magnified in a concerted end. Be it good or evil in a man's heart, essence will free the magic that resides there. As we are all a part of nature, we hold a certain amount of power we may call upon to aid us. Some are better at it than others, and those like myself, who devote their entire lives to the perfecting of it, are more practiced than normal men. But that inner strength can only be scratched at the surface, for it is bound to the spirit and not the flesh."

Magarius sighed at the confusing looks he received in answer. "In simpler terms, you have freed the magic of your spirit form and joined it with your physical bodies. You are unity of body and soul, the embodiment of your inner self. I do not know in what way this unleashed magic will manifest itself, but I can guess that it will be very difficult for you to control. You'll need help, I'm afraid."

The mage looked markedly older just then, lines of worry etching the corners of his eyes and creasing his brow. He took up a black-feathered quill and dipped it into an ink bottle, his hand a little less steady than might be expected of one so tenacious. After he scrawled a list of instructions onto a thick sheet of vellum, he handed it to Stephen.

"I have a task for you, master smith." Magarius put the dark quill back in its holder and took his seat by the fire again. "I want you to forge six medallions, measuring the ore to those specifications. They need not be anything extraordinary, for they will serve but one purpose: the metal will store and release excess magic when the need arises. If you feel a surge of energy come over you, and you will, simply channel it into the necklace. I shall instruct you as best I can, but the effort must fall on your shoulders."

Stephen read the list over, and a puzzled look crossed his face at the bizarre directions. The speaking of alien words, the gestures of hand and exposing of metal to the four elements were ridiculous enough, but the mixtures of ore were what held his eye. "Are you sure about this?" the master smith asked incredulously. "If I follow these steps, the iron will be so poorly tempered that I won't be able to shape it. It'll crack at the first blow of my hammer!"

"I assure you," Magarius said with confidence, "what you hold in your hand is a mixture for the strongest iron known to man. You must understand that magic works differently from what you know, and it may sometimes seem contrary to what you deem logical."

Listening with all the attention he could muster, Jonathan found his mind wandering to more comfortable thoughts, ones where his existence was firmly rooted without the vagaries of magic. His hand drifted down towards the spoon at his belt, and he chuckled inwardly as he saw he wasn't the only one who forgot to leave the utensil at the bakeshop. He secretly wished his sword was with him, instead of the long iron spoon. Leaving his armor to help bake was one thing, but not wearing –

The spoon began to grow.

Slow enough to see but fast enough to disbelieve, the metal cooking spoon elongated to a sharp point, its dull edges expanding to a keen sharpness. The muted gray surface smoothed to a silvery sheen. The handle rounded and changed to a leather wrap, while the pommel formed an eagle's head in the midst of a shrill cry. Sir Jonathan, Protectorate of Noria, stood holding the sword of his inner heart, the weapon with which he faced all odds. He held the Sword of Honor.

"What in the world!" Stephen gasped. "How did you do that?"

"I... I have no idea!" The knight held the sword for the others to see, as if it were completely at fault. "I was thinking about my sword, and it just changed!" The look in his eyes spoke of the divine, but Magarius was merely intrigued by the sight.

Valoran stood and took the sword, testing its edge with his thumb. "It's real alright," he said and sucked the wounded digit.

"I didn't think we were imagining it," Cornelius smirked. "Well?" he asked the Advisor. "Is this part of the magic you were talking about?"

"Yes, but not your own. Tell me, did you mix the cookies with these spoons?" Understanding dawned on each of them as the mage resumed his train of thought. "I guessed as much. This proves that inanimate objects are subject to essence as well. If you cleaned out the bowls you mixed the batter in, I doubt they would be altered. I wonder what sort of essence a bowl might have," he began to wonder. His mortar was magically protected, so it couldn't possibly be affected.

Tristan cleared his throat. "Proves? You mean you weren't sure about all of this you just explained to us?" Nervousness is quite an infection, and it spread with the speed of a thought. "What's going to happen to us? I mean, will we begin to change like these spoons?" The master baker held his own spoon up, the thought of shifting swords in his mind, and gaped in awe as the metal enlarged of its own volition. The only difference between his and Jonathan's was the pommel. Tristan's had the spiraling horn of the mystical beast of truth, the unicorn.

"Please," Magarius implored. "All of you be seated, and do calm down. You're not in any immediate danger, not so long as I'm here with you. Master smith Stephen will forge your medallions at his earliest convenience" –

the burly man muttered he'd be on his way if the mage would quit his jabbering – "but the only dangers I can perceive are the ones that will arise when all of this spreads. Whatever changes your bodies have undergone are permanent but finished. What will happen next, however, is that every magician within earshot will flock to this kingdom in search of the magic that was unleashed tonight. Magic makes an unavoidable amount of noise that only wizards can hear, and yours was loud enough to reach the ends of Astoria."

Valoran crossed his arms as a stern look came over him. "Will they pose a threat to Noria? I still rank General, you know."

The Advisor staved off their questions with his hand. "No, no, not in the way that you see danger. No wars will come, but the influx of aspiring practitioners might be unsettling to the populace. The Dark Arts usually are, in any case. I will give you all the instructions on how to perform essence, a recipe if you will. By adding the tiniest portions of the spell to your cookies, you would be lifting the spirits of our people immensely – and be doing the King a great service as well. They will not be changed in any way by the magic, but they will be affected. Being able to touch upon the source of their being, the nature of their soul, will give them insight into themselves they could never have otherwise achieved. And I guarantee our good King will have finally found the one flavor he can be contented with," he added with a wink.

Humphrey, quietly holding a restful Flicker in his arms, posed a question that was similarly on Tristan's mind. "Would that not adversely affect those whose hearts may not be as bright?"

"Indeed," the mage replied fervently. "Perhaps they would see something to their dislike and strive to modify their lives for the better. You cannot force a man to change. You can only show him what he is and hope he changes himself. Think of it as enlightening the populace."

Cornelius snickered at that. "Sort of like an unwanted conscience."

"How long," Valoran cut in, "before we can expect these wizards, and how should we prepare?" The mind of a tactician never rests.

"You need only protect the recipe I give you, and keep it from the nosy spell-casters who will find you. Open attack on your person would be doubtful, but use your heads! You know when someone intends ill will towards you, and surely you all know how to defend yourselves."

"And the cookies?" Tristan asked.

"Bake away, my dear fellows. Make our kingdom a happy one!"

"Alright then," Stephen asserted and stood. "I'll go make the amulets, while you all go bake some cookies."

"Coming?" Cornelius asked the mage. "Or would being seen with us after tonight's display tarnish your illustrious reputation?"

"Don't be droll, Cornelius." Magarius held the door open for them. "I must go wake the King and tell him everything that's happened. Take Flicker with you," he told the master trainer. "If you need me, just send him along to fetch me."

The brothers then filed out of the chamber and headed for their respective tasks. Valoran accompanied Stephen to help forge the strange necklaces, and the others set to baking tray upon tray of cookies. It was just before dawn when the six were ready to head back to the castle, to where Magarius and King Marik awaited their arrival in the Royal Chamber. With the medallions complete and hundreds of cookies baked, the brothers were set for whatever came their way.

The Keepers of the Magic were ready.

* * *

It wasn't until much later that an insignia was embossed on the magical necklaces, an emblem that would forever represent the six brothers and the cause they would champion. The two soldiers in royal livery, proffering the enchanted baking spoons and standing guard over a cauldron with the initials C B engraved into the surface, were models for future Guardians to follow. The passing on of medallions to the next generation of Protectors that would follow was easily foreseen and readily planned.

For the time being, however, the medallions were plain and seemingly ordinary. Each wore his own hanging from a makeshift leather thong, rushed as they were to see the King, and had not been tested for the use they were designed. It would be up to Magarius to decide if the work was adequately accomplished.

"My Advisor has been busy of late," King Marik said to the assembled brothers. "He tells me you have been equally busy, and that these related matters may or may not have an affect on my kingdom. What say you, Protectorate?"

"The night has held many wonders, your Majesty." Sir Jonathan was solemn as always, standing beside his brothers with straightened backs and attentive eyes. Though they should have been tired from their taxing experience, none of them felt the nagging pull of sleep.

"As King, it is my duty to ask what your intentions may be. I am a generous and understanding man, with full knowledge of what passes through one's mind when trying the reigns of new-found power, but I do have a kingdom and subjects who look to me for guidance. You have all, at one time or another, pledged your loyalty to this throne. I feel, however, that a renewal of those vows may be in order."

Without being told, all six men fell to one knee and bowed their heads. Even the quipster, Cornelius, had the sense to restrain his humor before the ruling monarch. Humphrey, unaccustomed to the presence of those unfamiliar to him, knew the King well and was versed in the somewhat precarious etiquette of court. The General and Protectorate had a slight advantage, as well as the master baker with his informal weekly visits, but Stephen performed with laudable acumen.

Marik gladly accepted their fealties in turn, then went on to other business. "About this essence," he began. "The Advisor has thoroughly explained its meaning and implications to me, and I have come to a decision regarding your future in this realm." The King stood from his lustrous throne of elmwood and drew his ornately bejeweled sword. He stepped forward to stand before Tristan, the first of the brothers in line, and spoke in his imperious voice while touching his blade to the master baker's shoulder.

"I dub thee, Tristan Esrald, Knight of Virtue and Guardian of Truth." Tristan kept his head bowed low in the sedate manner befitting a knight.

King Marik went from brother to brother, bestowing the rank of knight and additional titles to each, varying only in what virtue each was made a Guardian. Magarius played a large role in discerning that aspect of the change, but Marik knew long before the suggestion what each brother held most dear in life.

Cornelius was given the title Guardian of Courage, Valoran that of Valor – could his parents have known from birth? – , Stephen that of Strength, Jonathan that of Honor and Humphrey, in all his modesty, that of Humility. The virtues of knighthood were amply represented in the six men kneeling before the King, and Noria could not have asked for a purer Order to defend her.

"Rise, my knights," Marik commanded. "From this day forth it will be your duty to protect this kingdom and its subjects to the best of your ability. I have your allegiance, and you have my blessing. Your acts shall reflect upon this throne –" the King smiled suddenly "– and I will rest easier for the knowing."

"And now," Magarius hesitantly interjected, not wanting to spoil the proud moment, "there is much to be learned. We have little time, so let us make the best of it. I'll see you all shortly in my chamber," he said in stern dismissal. A blow to the head might have been less direct, but the six complied to his wish.

"One last thing, Sir Jonathan," Marik called.

"Yes, your Majesty."

"You have a meeting this morn with a certain emissary. Please keep it. Your duties as Protectorate will remain unchanged."

"Yes, your Majesty."

Waiting until the brothers had gone, the King asked his Advisor, "What are your thoughts? Will their judgment be affected by this sudden change?"

"I think they'll do splendidly, Marik. I seem to recall a younger lad, much like each of these men all rolled up into one, who saw fit to shake the world and seize a kingdom from the pieces. You turned out fine," he accused with a slender finger. "I'll keep a close watch over them, but I'm confident they'll follow their hearts."

"In that case," the King of Noria smiled broadly, "consider the discussion concluded. My kingdom is in good hands."

"That it is, young one. That it is."

* * *

When Magarius entered his chambers, he found the newly appointed knights of Noria in a heated discussion over the taking of another vow. At his bewildered expression, Tristan offered, "We feel that another oath may be needed, one that would more specifically describe our task and sufficiently outline our duties."

"I see," the mage said patiently. "Have you decided what this oath shall be, or is that the source of such fervent talk?"

Stephen settled a chilling gaze upon his brothers. "It is," he said and stood, taking the spoon from his belt. "But we have come to an agreement on the matter, haven't we?" His icy tone indicated that things may not have been settled to the satisfaction of all, but their rising to join him showed the lack of importance on the point.

Each spoon elongated to form the swords of their virtue, the only notable variance being in the accommodating length and silvery pommels. The head of a roaring grizzly bear, with a conspicuous likeness to the master smith, adorned Stephen's two-handed blade. Cornelius, having the heart of a lion, possessed the proud bearing of one on his broadsword. Jonathan's eagle and Tristan's unicorn spiral remained the same, though they found their blades could alter to whatever design they imagined. The master baker opted for a long sword, while Sir Jonathan kept the hefty broadsword of his trade in hand. The gladiator and war hero, Guardian of Valor, was not surprised to see the saurian head of a great dragon bedeck his sword, for the magical beast was often praised for its bold gallantry. Humphrey, master trainer and friend to all animals, was puzzled at the feline crown that embellished his pommel, as he always associated the graceful panther with one of enormous pride. Further reflection granted the understanding that what he saw in the feline was not pride but a confidence gained from the knowing of one's shortcomings. It was the striving for perfection, without the need for admiration, that evoked the presence of modesty.

"And this vow?" Magarius asked. He stood clear of the sword-wielding brothers but was a bit curious nonetheless.

"The Oath of Virtue," Tristan replied and put the tip of his sword against the others'. With the Guardian of Truth leading the pledge, the brothers took their solemn oath in unison.

"That which gives us strength shall give all strength; That which empowers us shall empower all, for this day we pledge our hearts to nature and the preservation of life, to keep others from harm or harming themselves – From this day forth, we are The Guardians, Keepers of the Magic and Protectors of the Recipe."

The Advisor could only smile his approval.

* * *

"And that's how it all began," Samuel said to the gathered children. Their mouths were open, absorbed in the story as they were, and looks of wonder became smiles of pride, an esteem for their heritage.

"But," Stephany started in protest, "you didn't finish the story! I want to know what happens next." Her lashes fluttered in a girlish display, as if blinking away the disbelief that her father would stop so suddenly.

John brushed back a dark lock of hair and sat forward in his seat. "What happened to Sir Jonathan and the elves?" He felt Courtney's frosty stare bore into his side, and he muttered an apology before sitting back out of her view.

"Oh, relax," she whispered to him and sat forward also. "I want to hear some more about Cornelius. He's funny. Is there anything else there about the little boy, Daren?"

"Wait," Alan cut in. "What about the guy in black? Lord Whoo-bies, or whatever ya call 'em." His eyes were strikingly blue in the fading light of evening, and his bold manner spoke volumes for one so young. Calling him outspoken would have been an understatement.

"I liked Flicker," Morgan said to no one in particular.

"Me too," Trudy spoke up. "Just hearing what he looks like, I can picture him in my mind. I wonder what his crooning really sounds like?" She exchanged smiles with the youngest brother and gave him a wink. Hearing about Tristan and the relationship he had with his brothers made her realize just how alienated Morgan must feel at times. Though no one else could see it, Trudy grew up in that instant and assumed the mantle of maturity.

Samuel rolled his eyes and laughed aloud. "And here I thought I'd have to tie you all down just to get you to listen." He closed the book and ran his hand along the edge, leaving the golden band in its wake. "There is a very detailed account of all the stories taking place afterwards. The stories are in chronological order and more or less follow right after the others without breaks in time." His smile grew wan and a serious tone crept into his voice. "Our family has been very busy throughout the years, and its been bleak at times."

"So now it's our turn," Alan said excitedly. "When do we start? I wanna see my sword!"

"Right!" Courtney snickered. "Why would anyone give you a sword? Dad, you wouldn't really, would you? He's just a kid!"

"Courtney," Samuel cautioned, "you're *all* just kids. I want to make it clear that none of you has to go through with this. I'll love you just as much as I do now, no matter what you decide to do. If you're scared, that's alright too. This could be dangerous, and being frightened comes with the territory." He ruffled Alan's hair, messing the shiny black lengths. "You'll be a little different if you go through with it, though. You won't be like anyone else in the world, little kids or not, but you'll have more than each other to rely on. If you have any doubts, don't be afraid to say so."

Morgan looked up to his father with inquiring eyes, but no hint of fear could be seen within those brownish orbs. "Is Flicker still alive, Dad? Have you ever seen him?"

Seeing that all six children intended to go through with the Oath, Samuel visibly relaxed. A grin cut his broad cheeks as he reminisced the times of his past. "I've seen him and heard his song but not in person. It's hard to explain, but those medallions bring about some realistic dreams. The memories stored inside sometimes come out."

Laura stepped quietly into the room with a silver tray in hand. Six ordinary-looking cookies adorned the surface, and she knelt beside her husband after depositing them on the coffee table. "What have you all decided," she asked in a musical voice. "Morgan?" Laura felt Sam's hand on her shoulder, and she covered it with her own. "What have you decided, little one?"

"I'm ready. I'm not afraid, if that's what you mean. I think I've been waiting for something like this for a very long time." His eyes took on a far away cast as his thoughts began to wander. He came back from the daydream suddenly and blushed with a smile of embarrassment.

"It's alright, dear." Laura looked to her other children, and a glisten of admiration touched her eyes.

"Why don't we go ahead then," Samuel said decidedly. "I want you all to put on your medallions now. OK, good. Don't be afraid of the feelings. Just let them come to you. This is much easier than it sounded in the story, because you have a slight advantage over your predecessors." He pointed to the necklaces, and each child held tightly to the emblem with a smile of elation. "Once you feel in control, take a cookie and eat it. The Recipe has improved over the generations, so you'll only need one. Just remember to be confident."

Alan was the first to grab for a cookie, but the others soon followed until only crumbs decorated the ornate platter. Watching Morgan for any signs of trouble, Samuel crossed his fingers for his children. He didn't have any sincere doubts, but the memory of his transition was a difficult one. The power released is so intense that all track of time is lost, and channeling into the medallion no longer seemed the easy task it sounded. He readied himself to help if any should falter.

The light that encompassed the six began as a faint glimmer, almost a reflection of some unseen dancing flame. The luminous shimmering intensified within the medallions, and a single beam of thick iridescence exploded from the metal. The ball of glowing power sent a shock wave of energy out from its center that threw

Samuel back in his seat and pressed Laura against the cushioned chair. A high-pitched keen rose from all four corners of the room as the scorching heat intensified. The tendrils of blue-hot electricity appeared then, threatening to take hold with bony fingers of light. The menacing energy passed over each new Guardian, repelled by the hurtful medallions, but two were not so well-protected. With deliberate slowness, the convalescing tendrils snapped and crackled as a single band of vibrant azure loomed before Samuel and Laura.

"No!" Alan said in an unfamiliar voice. He stood with medallion in hand, a sense of presence unearthly in a child. "No," he repeated with more determination, gritting his teeth with exertion. The energy wavered for an instant and then struck like a bolt of lightning, fully hitting Alan in the chest. Like a writhing snake, the light was absorbed into the necklace, taking with it the fading globe of power.

"Alan!" Laura cried and grabbed her son, hugging him close while still kneeling. She pressed her head to his chest and felt the warmth of the emblem on her cheek.

"It's alright now, Mom." He draped his arms over her shoulders and endured the embrace with stoicism. "I thought that's what I was supposed to do," he said in defense.

"You did just fine," Laura whispered with her eyes closed. She reluctantly let him go, realizing the days of babying her children had come to an abrupt end. She wiped the tears from her eyes and sat back against her husband's leg, her composure somewhat restored.

"Thank you," Samuel told his brazen boy. "That's something new to me, but then again, I've only seen one of these in person." The others still hadn't grasped the fact that something went wrong. "All that's left now is the taking of the Oath. Unless one of you has something to say?"

"Well," Trudy sat forward. "What about the spoons?"

Alan stamped his foot. "I was going to ask that!" He turned to his father with a furrowed brow. "You said I could have one, didn't you?"

Samuel could not have sighed any deeper. "Yes, I did, Alan. Don't make me regret it, though. The spoons are inside the medallions. Some time after the original Guardians took the Oath, it became a hazard to keep them anywhere else. You see, they were stolen at one time, and the power within the spoons is almost as great as that within each of you... Almost!"

"I don't get it," Courtney was saying when a large iron spoon appeared in her hand. "Oh, you have to think about them. Ha! That's a neat trick!"

Alan took his sister's advice and had a silvery short sword in his hand before the others could hold him down. He parried and thrust with some unseen foe, dancing the swordsman's shuffle.

"Be careful," Samuel warned. "That is not a toy, nor is it to be used unless absolutely necessary. I'll be more than happy to show you, but you're going to have to learn respect for a weapon before you can wield it."

All six children had the argent blades to fore, closely examining the different pommels and details of each symbol. It was Trudy who first stood, extending her sword so that the others could touch points like in the story. She had a certain flare for the dramatic.

"That which gives us strength," she began reciting the pledge as she had heard it, each word burned into her mind. Her brothers and sisters followed her example, and the Guardian of Truth took pride in leading the Oath of Virtue for the new generation of Protectors.

Samuel and Laura clasped hands, their love for each other as strong as ever. Their children were taking on an age-old responsibility, one that ran through Samuel's bloodline for centuries. The sight would be forever etched into their hearts and minds, the feeling of unrestricted love a force not even time could hope to conquer. A sigh of relief then passed through Samuel's body, the lifting of a burden that only his children could ever begin to understand.

The family obligation passed on once again.

* * *

Martin looked up from his book, a huge leather-bound volume with tracings of worn gold spreading across its surface in an intricate webwork of archaic design. He felt an unusual buzzing at the nape of his neck, and a chill ran from the top of his blonde head to the tips of his bare toes. He pulled off the wire-rimmed glasses and laid them on the tree stump he used for a table. The fragile young man blew a lock of pale hair from his eyes as he waited expectantly for... something.

BOOM!

The explosion of noise was enough to send him flailing from his three-legged stool. Though nothing around him could have been affected, his keen wizard senses heard the release of raw power as clear as if a building had fallen on him. There was no telling where the source of magic was, but he was sure he could trace it. *After all,* he'd say, *what good was a magician who couldn't trace a spell?* What worried him was the immensity of such a casting.

Sensing the alarm in his master's eyes, a concerned little dragon awoke with a start, with whirling eyes the milky azure of disquieted thought. Spreading leathery wings of transparent blue, he disappeared in the wink of an eye, reappearing on Martin's thin shoulder as he lay sprawled on the earthen floor of his tree home.

A familiar crooning soon filled the hollow bole.

Part Two:
Of Honor and Life

One of the many changes a Guardian undergoes when transformed by essence magic is the lessening need of sleep. Taking advantage of that effect, Samuel wasted no time in preparing his children for what lay ahead of them. The incident of unbridled power snaking out its crackling tendrils to strike Alan square in the chest was enough to cause deep concern, for if the boy was not wearing his medallion, the raw energy would have surely ended his short life. Samuel was convinced his children possessed more power than the Knights of Virtue had known in many generations, and that worried him beyond the feigned passivity. Nature is a mystical force but one that works of necessity. If the new generation of Guardians were noticeably stronger in magic, their need of balance was equally so.

Their enemies would be very powerful.

Along with the inherited magical abilities was the enmity of those who strove to obtain the secret of essence, to unearth the Recipe and use it for whatever purpose suited a mind twisted by evil intent. It was commonly thought among those of the Dark Arts that if essence could release the inner core of a being, then a practitioner of pure evil would be insurmountable. This belief was based on the assumption that the path of shadow was the stronger. There was no doubt it was the swifter, but then nothing gained easily came without risk.

With this in mind, Samuel began the process of training his children in the use of magic, the focusing of their inner abilities to affect desired results. At first, merely controlling the immense flow of energy would require all of their concentration, but mastery would eventually be theirs. Time and perseverance were the means to the end, so the lessons commenced with all due speed. Only when the moon hung well past midnight were the mental exercises finished for the night. Samuel still had a business to run, and his little bakeshop drew a crowd of customers that would be waiting for him at sunrise.

Giving his reluctant retreat, he bade his children good night. The six were far too excited for sleep but also tired from the taxing disciplines of magic. The drawing of inner strength and focusing upon one goal was more difficult than any had first thought, much like forcing a river to pour through a funnel. They were somewhat reassured by the medallions hanging from their necks, the warmed metal holding visions and memories that allowed glimpses into victory. Within the heavy emblems, they could feel success and see the mastery of past Guardians in their mind's eye. Such inspiration pushed the six to try harder, but their father warned of going too far too soon. Patience, after all, was the unclaimed virtue.

They all came back inside, leaving the chill air and soft grass of the yard to the night. Resting in the seats where just hours before their lives were irrevocably changed, Trudy noticed the mischievous look in Alan's laughing eyes. He had an arm behind his back, and a smirk creased his cheeks as he leaned back and affected the posture of whistling.

"I know what we can do," he offered innocently.

Trudy refused to rise to the bait and assumed an air of disinterest. "I think we could all use some sleep about now."

"Or," Alan interjected, "we could read another story." He pulled the worn leather volume from behind his back and suppressed a chuckle at the surprised looks of his brothers and sisters. "Well? Here, Trudy, you read it to us. I hate reading out loud!"

"Umm." Stephany looked worried now that her surprise had drained away. "Should we be touching that? I don't think dad would appreciate us playing with it. I mean, think of how old it is!" Her eyes scanned the careworn cover, the tracings of gold faded away from use. She longed to read the stories inside, to delve into the fantasies of knights, magic and monsters. Only her sense of right and wrong kept her from taking up the book to read for herself. She could feel her father's disappointment bore into her heart from the thought, and the guilt that flushed her face a light crimson was mistaken for fear.

"Actually," Morgan said and leaned his elbows onto the coffee table, "it looks like we were meant to read them when we're ready to." He steeled himself against the raised eyebrows and pursued his line of reasoning. "The book was on the table before we came in. Alan might like to act like he took it from dad, but he didn't." Alan scowled as his mirth was stolen from him. "As the new Guardians, our touch can open the book. Why would dad tell us not to touch it?"

Trudy smiled and knelt beside her youngest brother. She took the book from Alan and laid it on the table before her, closing her eyes as the musky smell wafted to her nostrils. Centuries of heritage lay under her fingertips, the stories and deeds of her relatives long gone. She ran a trimmed nail over the smoothed leather and wondered at the magic that could preserve such a book for so many years. She chided herself as her mind turned towards youth replenishing makeup and the possibility of immortal beauty. Her smile was hidden beneath layers of determination as she ran her hand along the golden band, revealing the vellum pages of the tome beneath. The light of magic faded, and the stories were hers to tell.

"OK," Trudy said with a deep breath. "Here we go..."

* * *

Jonathan Esrald, Protectorate of Noria, strode purposefully through the densely grown trees of Lightwood. The shorter alder, with their wiry limbs, comprised most of the forest's outskirts. On either side of the open path were birch and hazel, while deeper into the forest grew the stolid hornbeam. As birds flew from tree to tree, calling out their song, Jonathan mulled over the events of the previous night. He still hadn't slept, as if he no longer needed the luxury, but spent the remaining hours before dawn preparing himself for the journey into

Lightwood. His sword hung loosely in its scabbard, and his hand clenched the leather-wrapped hilt in anticipation of trouble. The barbarian tribes were said to inhabit the woodland in force, so the Knight of Virtue deemed it wise to be wary.

The heavy elm that sprung up from the rich soil around him grew larger as he approached the center of the elven homeland. He'd only traveled a mile or two before the thickset trees had boles large enough for three men to stand around, clasping hands in a circle. Looking up to the webs of branch and leaf, he was struck by the broken rays of sunlight passing through in early morn.

"Flamegrove," he whispered to himself as he went further in. The sun was climbing well into the morning sky when the brazen call of an eagle stopped Jonathan in his tracks. Not a native to Noria, it would be very rare to see the bird of prey with its downy gray and brown feathers, sharpened talons and powerful wings. But still he heard the ringing cry and saw the shadow circle overhead. With the obstruction of trees and blinding light, it was impossible to tell how large the bird was. Never having much of an interest in avians, Jonathan was hard-pressed to note the unusual wing span and prolonged flight above.

"It looks as if you have a new friend," Umbrah said from the shadows of an elm. The elven emissary was leaning against the massive trunk with a polished long bow of white hornbeam over his shoulder. His eyes were cool and impassive, as always, but Jonathan thought he saw something of mirth in the deep recesses of those jade orbs. Wearing the full leather garb of a sylvan, with the streaked paint of green and black, the knight never even saw the woodsman.

And he stood right under his pointed nose.

"Good day," Jonathan said and offered his arm. Grasping Umbrah's forearm in greeting, he studied the practical outfit preferred by the elves. Only the arms were left unprotected by the soft leather, but the capacity for agile movement coupled with effective camouflage made the woodsmen a formidable enemy. He wondered how such freedom of motion would fare against the protection of plate armor.

"I just noticed it," the Protectorate said and nodded towards the circling eagle. "Rather remarkable, considering its origin. I wonder how it could have come to travel so far from its homeland." He caught Umbrah looking at him with a peculiar expectancy and followed his gaze down towards the eagle's head hilt of his silvery sword. "You don't miss much, do you?"

"Not really. Unusual markings like that tend to stand out on a person. My vision may not be at its best during daylight, but it is keen enough to see the enchantment woven round that blade of yours. Actually," the woodsman began, studying the sword more closely, "it doesn't seem to have the patterns of an enchantment after all. It emanates power from the center, encompassing the whole sword. Tell me, where did you come by such a magical blade?"

"Do you know something of magic?" Jonathan asked evasively.

"I do." Umbrah seemed to take the hint and evaded questions of his own. "Perhaps we should be on our way. I will go slow so as not to lose you. Keep your eyes on my back, and leave the worrying of ambush to me. We will reach the heart of Luminarron by nightfall tomorrow."

The sylvan turned and regarded the man in shining armor. "You would do well to leave your metal plates behind when we go in search of the barbarous ones. Already you are blinding with the sun's reflection."

Jonathan raised his eyebrows at that, never once seeing his armor as any sort of deficiency. Before he could offer an apology for careless thinking, the elf continued speaking while moving through the trees like a wraith in shadow. "You have no horse with you."

"No," Jonathan replied evenly. He wasn't sure if it were a question or statement of fact. "I thought it best to go on foot, since we would be doing a great deal of travel through the trees. Horses are fine for trails," he pointed out as he stepped from rotten limbs to moss-slick rocks, "but I doubted you would take me by way of an open path."

Umbrah nodded as he continued, his ear cocked to keep the knight fixed within his range of hearing. He felt turning to view the man's progress would only insult his honor, intimating him unable to carry himself. The elf was appointed emissary many lifetimes ago, as humans recorded time, and spent enough of those years in his position to know humans angered easily. Living only a breath of a life, compared to the longevity of elvenkind, humans were candles burning at both ends – quick to live, quick to fight, and quick to die. Honor among men was a strange thing.

"You were wise," Umbrah acceded. "We will move swiftly without the burden of a mount. There are far more dangers in Luminarron than the barbarous ones. Those of the Deer are as babes in comparison."

That last did little to encourage Jonathan, if such was the intent. His mind began to ponder what creatures could live within the trees of Lightwood and go unnoticed by man. Noria was an old kingdom, having been established hundreds of years before. The forest was clouded in legend and stories of magic and monsters, but the existence of anything of the like would have been noted long before now.

What about the elves? he asked himself. *If they exist, then why not any of the other legends?*

Thoughts of fairies, orcs and dragons cluttered his mind, causing the trees to blur as they went past. The heavy elm gave way to cedar, fir and juniper. Great hills covered in blankets of lush grassland spread as far as his eyes could see, the trees sprouting up from the emerald sea to form walls and columns of impenetrable vastness. Deep troughs allowed the passing of streams, and the mapwork of deer trails fanned out like a maze of inescapable intricacies. Where a practiced woodsman might see a distinguishable landmark to use as guide, Jonathan saw only trees. Birds, deer, squirrels, a fleeting glimpse of fox, rabbits, raccoon, the unending bed of dew-stained grass: all he saw as one landscape, an unchanging view that scrolled itself like the rereading of a fable.

Umbrah stopped long enough to kneel beside a hand-sized stone and sniff the chilly air of autumn. His hardened gaze moved ever forward. Without explanation, he resumed his silent march with all the stealth of a hunter. Passing the stone, Jonathan saw only slimy moss. The center had a white streak where moss might have been chafed away. The deepness of the scrape is what must have concerned Umbrah, for no hoof could have caused such a mark.

"Do the barbarians wear metal-shod boots?" Jonathan asked.

Lightly stepping from stone to stone, Umbrah crossed a slender stream. The water bubbled relentlessly towards its unseen goal, winding through tree and hill alike. Maintaining his furtive gait, the woodsman called back over his shoulder.

"You have sharp eyes. There are some who do, though the older Deer prefer the softer boot of deerskin.

After slaughtering a band of elven hunters, the barbarous ones took their boots as prize. Now they hunt their namesake for more than meat, regardless of need or number."

Gently, Jonathan asked, "Did you know the elves well? It is never an easy thing to lose a friend." Some unspoken memory insinuated itself into his thoughts, forcing its bitter reflection to the front with rough abruptness. "I understand –"

Umbrah wheeled around, his impassive face contorted by anger and helplessness.

"Do you?" His voice held the ring of cold, unforgiving steel. "Can you know what it is to be persecuted from your home, pushed beyond your lands of birth, to live on foreign soil only to be butchered for the boots on your feet?" The bitterness that rimmed his eyes turned slowly to its former hardened luster. Creases unfamiliar to his fair skin smoothed as anger drained away, replaced by the deep-set calm of a hunter. There was a hint of apology in his voice when he turned away, sitting with eyes closed and his back to the soothing assurance of a tree.

"We will rest here for a few moments before continuing."

* * *

The scratching song of the cricket and human-like call of the night owl were welcome sounds in the falling of night. The silent calm, one born of fear, held more sound of alarm than any cry could hope to muster. Umbrah listened for that silence, the lack of noise that ensued when things were not as they should be. No foreign scents invaded the wood, no rustle of unfamiliar limbs thrashing about through the thick underbrush.

Knights of Virtue

Only faint glimmerings of moonlight struck through the panoply of branch and blade, with leaves made heavy from silver drops of dew.

The two made their camp in a grove of closely grown cedar, finding shelter from the biting chill of autumn's breeze. The woodsman sat against a weathered bole, his gaze intent upon the knight before him. No fire could be lit, for fear of calling attention to themselves. As the elf had warned earlier, there were things in the forest worse than barbarians.

"I am sorry," Jonathan began weakly. No words were passed since last they spoke, and the heated passion in Umbrah's eyes came back to haunt him. An emptiness in the pit of his stomach ached his heart as memories of his own lost friends crowded to the front of his mind. Stalwart knight and able swordsman, the Protectorate of Noria was helpless against the pangs of loss.

"No," Umbrah said softly. "I am far too wise to accuse one man for the wrongs of his race. Of any, I should know of what I speak." A deep sigh broke through his reverie, focusing his thoughts on Jonathan. Those green eyes were less severe now, sad and tormented. "You may understand loss, as I see that you do, but the loss of an elf is much more. Ours is a race closely bound to one another. You asked if I knew them well. I tell you, I know them all well. There is no elf I do not know by name, have not passed wine with or stood beside in time of strife."

Jonathan nodded solemnly, allowing Umbrah to choose his words and stave off the intense emotion welling in his chest.

"Elves are long-lived," the woodsman stated finally. "We see many hundreds of years pass before our time to rest, and only violence may cut short that time. Unfortunately, there are only a handful of us born with each passing generation. An elf maiden may give birth only three times in her life, while some none at all, so you see the immense loss of just one elf. Our race is slowly being destroyed by the violence of these barbarous men. Were it not for our peaceful nature, many of our number would still walk this earth. And so you see what has become of us, a hardened lot of fierce hunters who struggle for survival in the midst of their own home."

"I will do everything I can to help you and your people, Umbrah." Jonathan leaned forward, his deep blue eyes reflecting an inner oath. "I would lay down my life if it but meant the continued existence of your race. You have my word on that."

"Strong words," the woodsman warned levelly. "I have never known your kind, the knights, to take such oaths lightly. Whether it is for pride or honor, I could not say, but do not make promises you cannot keep."

Unwavering and steady as the armor he wore, Jonathan stared unblinking as he spoke. "Without honor, my life would be as nothing. My word is all that I have."

"I have seen this honor you speak of, seen it used as weapon and shield. The trappings of knighthood are flaunted when useful and shunned when not."

"I do not profess to speak for any but myself." Jonathan relaxed his back and leaned heavily against the tree behind him. "Honor to me is not what you see in the Order, the knights that once were. Honor is a manner of living, a goal for which I strive to maintain the purest heart and strongest spirit a knight may have. You have no cause to believe what I say, other than your own judgment of my deeds to date, but I ask one thing of you: Do not disregard my words until I have given reason to do so. When I tell you that my honor is my life, I mean just what I say. If ever I betray that honor, I will forfeit my life in failure."

Umbrah studied the man before him, gazing into the crystal depths of his eyes with the probing of a lifetime's experience. Jonathan felt stripped to the bones, utterly naked beneath that penetrating stare and helpless to move under its weight. With the suddenness of a blink, the moment had passed, and Umbrah looked away to the trees of his home.

"You are different," he mused. "I only wish the elves could afford to give such trust. The night grows darker. Perhaps you should rest –"

The breaking of wood, a brittle limb or twig, instantly silenced the elf and brought him to his feet. A long knife of coal-smeared steel was in his hand, but Jonathan saw no weapons on him a moment before. With a curt nod, Umbrah gave all the instruction he dared. To make undue noise with danger on the wind was to court their demise.

Jonathan slid his own blade from its sheath, masking the grate of steel with his gloved fingers, and slipped behind the cedar. Inwardly cursing the reflection of moon on his armor, he knelt and felt the ground. Wet from a recent drizzle, the soil was rich and muddy – just the thing to hide the glare of polished steel. He began to cover his armor with the muck while listening for sounds of the elf and his prey. While another knight would have scoffed at the idea of dirtying his plate mail, Jonathan had no such compunctions. He saw his armor as protection alone, not as a badge of office to be worn for pride, and he would never allow himself to be the cause of injury to a friend.

Umbrah would have been endangered by such pride.

With the clashing of steel just yards away, the time for stealth had passed. Like a muddied ghost, lumbering for its girth, Jonathan crossed the distance in a heartbeat. Umbrah was already engaged in battle, faced off by some cruel beast in darkened chain mail. Thick skin of a leathery green covered its muscled body, the stocky form of a seasoned warrior. Pink eyes glared from under a protruding forehead, seeing plainly in the dark of night as if born to the shadows about. A wet snout with yellowed tusks snickered over a cruel mouth twisted by rage. Its tapered ears, shorter than those of elvenkind, were laughable if the parody not so sinister.

The woodsman dodged a glancing blow of its short sword, a spiked shield blocking his own attack. While Jonathan longed to aid his new companion, he feared putting the elf in danger by interfering.

"Can I help?" the knight called from the dark, his eyes following every step and movement. He could not recall when his sight was so keen but only stored the fact to be pondered some other time.

Turning abruptly, the monster flared its snout and roared at the knight. Apparently, its acute sense of hearing was not enough to notice the big man approach. Umbrah saw his opening and wasted no time in dispatching the foe. Distracted or not, the beast would have killed them both if given the chance.

Dropping to its knees in pain, clutching the broken links of chain at its chest, the orc fell to its back and breathed its last. The woodsman was over its body without hesitation. His face shone clearly in a ray of silver light, as tears ran freely down his cheeks, and his hand threw away the knife as if it burned his flesh. Almost afraid to touch the fallen creature, Umbrah's hands were close to caressing the waxen face he looked upon.

He wept openly as he asked, "What has he done to you?" Jonathan stood over the elf, his shadow blocking the light that betrayed Umbrah's tears. Though shaken with grief, the woodsman looked up to the trees and starry sky.

"I am sorry," was all he could offer.

* * *

Thoughts of rest were the furthest from Umbrah's mind as he sought to put distance between himself and the fallen orc. Fortunately, Jonathan had neither the desire nor the need of sleep but was content to continue the journey to the center of Lightwood. Allowing the woodsman his space to think, Jonathan went over the task set before him.

The city of Pergolai, heart of Luminarron and home to the sylvan elves, was another day away by foot. Message of his safe arrival would be sent by carrier, but the return missive would entail the steps to be taken from there. Sent only to observe and assess the situation at hand, the possibility of action hung over his thoughts like a threatening shadow. More than just a simple representative of the King, Jonathan was Protectorate of Noria. If it became essential to take immediate action, he would do so. The proper dispatch recounting events and requesting help would be sent, but the knight had no misgivings as to how he would proceed. The Protectorate would effect whatever means necessary to safeguard his land and its people.

Jonathan would not hesitate to move against the Deer.

As much as he tried to concentrate on other things, the orc's death and Umbrah's reaction to it tugged relentlessly at his mind. The vision of a kneeling woodsman, crying over the prone form of an enemy, clouded his thoughts until nothing else held substance.

Questions burned and piled one on top of the other as he tried to sort through the scene. Not wanting to open a sore wound in the elf, Jonathan bided his time. He was confident that Umbrah would explain himself when he felt ready, and to ask it sooner of him would only cause undue pain.

Keeping his eyes to the moving ground beneath him, the knight cleared his mind of all thought, allowing only the rocks and grass and trees to entrance him. Stepping gingerly to fill Umbrah's imagined prints – for the woodsman left no trail of his passing – Jonathan let himself fade into the night of the wood, the chorus of nature and its lilting melodies of discord. And through the dissonance of nightly song rang clear one calling friend, implacable in spirit as mysterious in presence.

An eagle cried out above.

* * *

Time passed slowly in the fleeting dark. Glimpses of light struck through the trees, silvery-white beams of broken luminescence that would have made the going more difficult were it not for sharp vision. Where the constant changes from light to dark would normally keep the eyes unfocused and straining to compensate, the perceptive elves relied upon a unique and secondary sense of sight: infravision. Shifting to this lower level of seeing, the darkness of night became a hazy world of crimson with the body heat of living creatures burning like embers. It was this extraordinary vision that allowed the woodsman to move through the closely-packed boles as if the light of day shone all around.

Jonathan had no such advantage, and yet he maintained the arduous pace set by the elf and kept a step behind. He could only focus on Umbrah's darting form, trusting the woodsman to take the safest path with the least treacherous ground. A protruding limb or leaf-covered hole could easily cause an injured leg or worse. Had Jonathan's eyes been anything less than exceptional, he might have ran headlong into the elf when he came to a sudden stop.

Leaning forward with hands on knees, Umbrah seemed to be gasping for breath. Jonathan knew better. The elf was still shaking with grief and struggling to contain his traitorous emotions. With the patience and respect befitting a knight, Jonathan simply sat beside his guide and waited. The ground was wet, soft and yielding to his weight, but the Protectorate only pulled a blade of grass and rolled between his fingers.

"You need rest," Umbrah said eventually and knelt. "I have been inconsiderate of your needs." The unspoken apology was not lost on the knight. "I will watch while you sleep. Elves need only an hour or two of deep meditation a day."

"I'm not tired just yet," Jonathan said honestly. "I think you might need the time to clear your thoughts more than I." Standing and facing out against the woods as if seeing them for the first time, he turned and gave a nod to the elf. "I will take watch."

If tears were uncharacteristic for the woodsman, laughter was equally so. The chuckle that escaped his thin lips took Jonathan off his guard, and he smiled at the lighthearted display. A brow raised in question was all he would venture.

"Your armor," Umbrah explained with a smiling shake of his head. "You look like a salamander –" he turned the knight about to point at his back – "all muddy on one side from slithering in the muck, all shiny on the other." He squinted his delicate eyes against the glare of moonlight, the brightness ten times as intense in the infra spectrum.

"I see." Jonathan feigned a look of seriousness. "Would you be so kind as to oblige?" His eyes went from the sodden earth to his polished shoulder, asking the woodsman to finish his shabby job.

"I can do even better than that."

The elf scanned the area and found the bush he sought, a squat shrub with black berries speckled brown and yellow. He took a handful of the fleshy fruit and mashed them between his hands, grinding down the skin and juice to a workable substance. He then mixed the remaining pulp with dead leaves, compressing the two into a coal-like smudge of dark. He applied the stuff to Jonathan's armor, spreading it thin to cover every inch. The smell was none too sweet, but the knight recalled a long knife smeared a black that did not glow in the moonlight.

"Now," Umbrah said and stepped back to admire his handiwork. "The brackenberry is far more effective than damp earth, and you will find it less likely to rust your armor than mud."

Thinking of Kalik, his squire, made Jonathan wince. The burly youth would be furious at the scrubbing and polishing waiting for him and all as a direct result of Jonathan's carelessness. He smiled inwardly at that, coming to the conclusion that extra work would build character for the young, would-be knight.

"Thank you," he said and clapped the elf on the shoulder. "Now you take what time you need."

Without waiting for a reply, Jonathan turned and walked away. He wanted to search the immediate surroundings and familiarize himself with it, while also allowing Umbrah some time to himself. He kept within close distance but never so near as to disturb the kneeling elf now deep in his meditative trance. Unconsciously, he scanned the breaks in the treetops for what little sky he could see. His eyes searched the clear black expanse with its pinpoints of light, his ears straining to pick out one noise from the many.

Try as he might, he could find no sign of the circling eagle.

* * *

Umbrah was readying himself to leave when Jonathan appeared from the trees, quick enough to startle him. Relaxing the grip on his long knife, the elf mused that even in full armor the knight moved like a woodsman. The hard set to Jonathan's face broke off all such ruminations and brought Umbrah to alertness.

"What is amiss?" the elf asked.

"I saw movement to the east. Scattered forms, crouched low, moving in stealth." The knight then drew his broad sword, the silver blade already smeared black by the berry mixture. "They're coming this way."

Umbrah was heading for one of the larger trees, a white cedar of sizeable girth, before calling back over his shoulder, "Can you climb?"

Without waiting for a reply, the nimble elf began to pull himself up by the thick limbs. Hand over hand, seemingly without the support of his feet, the slender woodsman clambered up the tree with a strength that belied his slight frame. When he reached a branch strong enough to support his weight, some seventy-five feet above the dew-stained grass, he sat back on his haunches to survey the forest below.

Jonathan knelt on a limb underneath him.

"You surprise me again," Umbrah whispered and suppressed a smile. "Not only can you climb like you were born to these trees, but you see better at night than I." Sunrise was beginning to break over the treetops, a sliver of orange flame that streaked the horizon and made the elf's infravision useless.

"There," Jonathan said and pointed. Shadowed figures progressed across the woodland, darting between bole and brook as if an elven hunting party, short bows over the shoulder, naked blades smudged and dark. Only one other group were so at home in the trees, and they were headed straight for the two.

Umbrah nodded as he switched his level of vision. When his eyes had adjusted to the morning light and evasive dark, his jaw fixed in resolve. His penetrating gaze fell over the barbarians, studying their approach, and turned to fix Jonathan with their intensity.

"They hunt," was the elf's conclusion. "They track deer there and there, taking the hides for boots and clothing, the antlers for trophy. The meat they will more than likely leave to rot, so much of it chokes their stores. They will hunt their namesake until no more roam this land." His knuckles were white with tension as his grip tightened about the branch. "And still they will not leave."

The barbarians possessed incredible speed, and they were moments away from where the two sat when Jonathan leaned over to whisper into Umbrah's tapered ear.

"Don't give in to anger. Keep your mind clear, or your judgment will be clouded. You do no service to your people by dying unnecessarily."

Umbrah turned and gave the knight a hard look, the smooth brows furrowed, but visibly softened as reason won over emotion. He nodded and laid a hand on Jonathan's shoulder.

More of human honor? the elf thought to himself. *Or could it be we are not so different, elves and men?*

A handful of deer skirted the uneven land, bounding over fallen branch and winding stream with ease and grace. The barbarians were moments behind when they began to fire, wickedly barbed arrows cutting through the air with a terrible scream. Most arrows fell short of their targets, but for one, the howling bolt struck true, felling a baby doe in its tracks. Kicking and crying out, the wounded female thrashed its spindly legs with the piercing wooden shaft protruding from its side.

Jonathan moved to cry out, but it was then Umbrah's turn to be the voice of reason. "Do not, Sir Knight. The deer may be avenged another time, but our deaths will serve no purpose."

Swallowing the bile in his throat, Jonathan choked back his tears and calmed his torn and broken heart. Oaths of vengeance were futile. All were made to pay for their deeds at one time or another, and the barbarians were no different. He pried his eyes away as the ferocious men arrived to finish the doe, an innocent animal that could not have seen but weeks of life. Another piercing cry rent the morning air, slicing through the bed of mist that hovered over the trees.

The eagle had returned.

A far more attractive sport, the exotic bird became the new trophy for the day. Sights turned skyward with bows in line, firing steel-tipped arrows at the swooping avian. A blur of gray and brown, the eagle flew through the woods like a specter, diving at impossible speeds through treacherously outstretched tree limbs. Its call of challenge sent the barbarians scurrying into the brush, breaking their questionable formation. Dagger-like talons raked a painted face, tearing hair and feather apart and taking to the wind before another volley was launched.

The tenacious raptor flew straight for the Guardian of Honor, its cry no longer challenging but joyous. The word *friend* echoed in his mind as the stray arrow hit the tree, and Jonathan lost his balance, plummeting from its heights in full plate armor.

His own cry, all too human, was of shock and surprise, but mindless fear was quick to take its hold. Branches shattered beneath his weight as he crashed through, descending like a stone. Again and again he screamed until his throat was worn and ragged. Time seemed to slow and stop, the look of horror on Umbrah's delicate features fading into the distance to be crowded by splintered limb and swallowed by emerald leaves. A preternatural warmth encompassed the knight, battling the whipping chill, entangling armor and flesh in tendrils of groping blue light. Still he screamed, a tormented howl that bent and twisted in pitch until it formed the shriek of a falling eagle. Armor, sword, pack and all shimmered in the magical heat. The bird of prey that emerged, its tufts of snowy white and earthen feathers, swooped past the rising ground and skimmed the moistened grass.

Its remarkable eyes were a pure and crystal blue.

* * *

The magic was like a thunderclap, a resounding of power off trees and rock, coursing through the earth to rumble distant ears. Not since the time of the Illuminati, Pergolai's enlightened magicians, had such a sound been made. The life lines crossing the forest in a spidery webwork were undisturbed, their magic untapped, and yet a force had been used. Echoes of the spell did more than wake the dormant spirit of Luminarron, did more than touch upon the lost lore and forgotten bonds with nature. The buzzing whisper woke a one whose name had not been uttered in many winters, save in the legends and tales of his time.

His magic was ancient, of the elder elves, the first elves, the senquil. The last of his kind, sworn to the life of the forest, Randor was both King and protector, provider and champion. One with the elves, and not, he dedicated his long life to Luminarron, but in better times felt the lessening of his need. Entering into a deep sleep, resting within the bole of a cedar, the elf King thought to pass the years in slumber until such time as he was required again, depending on his kin to call with a magic they both possessed. However, the fading of the lore over many generations turned the peaceful confines of the tree to a prison shared by all. For without the lone King, the elves and each within the realm of trees were left to fend for themselves in a world grown darker with each set of the sun.

No more was the forest crawling with orugai, the pure strain of monster that spawned the orcs in a vile crossing of breeds, but new threats have come to grow in the rich soil. Supplanting themselves in the stead of an earlier threat, the barbarians were a cause for greater concern. Other monsters as well, migrating from far away kingdoms or under the earth itself, found their way into the once peaceful wood, attracted by its purity and scent of raw power. The respite that came from a short span of tranquility had led to lifetimes of ravage and suffering, a stripping away of Luminarron's fragile spirit.

The magic of the elves, paled and weakened from what it once was, could no longer rouse the senquil. The secretive nature of magicians was the source of the wearing away of elven heritage. The passing of lore from mage to apprentice, by word or book, was less and less each generation, one withholding a bit more each time until in the end only pieces of the magic could be conjured. The Illuminati, magicians and spiritual leaders, were divided over the centuries to focus their goals and better serve the sylvan nation. The splintering of power led only to a swifter decay, and the elven clerics had suffered a similar fate. What was considered everyday practice to the ancient priests would be nothing short of miraculous to the present spiritualists and healers.

The elves of Luminarron were not helpless, nor were they a race crippled by pride and mistrust. Fully aware of their ancestor's mistakes, they sought daily to remedy the problems at hand, to recapture the magic that sadly eluded them. Desperately needing a reprieve from the fervor of invaders, the elves were hard-pressed to continue their search, having endlessly to stop and defend their homes. The aid they so terribly needed was finally at hand, called not by the magic of their ancestors but by the working of a man. That their persecutors of so many years, the aggressors they fended off for the freedom of living, should bring about their salvation would be amusing if lives were not at stake. The continued survival of the woodsmen was now in the hands of one, an ancient senquil King whose waking was long overdue.

The Guardian of the Wood had finally returned.

* * *

Jonathan shrieked at the group of barbarians as he swooped past them, his shiny black talons stretched out to claw and rake. There was confusion in his eagle eyes, but he gave way to an instinct not his own. The primal urges were hard to resist, self-justified feelings that propelled him to action, to strike out at the man-things who would threaten him. His years of intensive studies, the rudimentary drills in discipline and control, were as voices in the wind, calling out in futility. Bereft of all but the intrinsic desires of a predator, a bird of prey set on defending itself, the solemn raptor turned its form about and circled back for another dive.

To say the barbarians were a superstitious lot could be equated to calling a great dragon an oversized lizard. Deathly afraid of magic, killing instantly any who possess it among them, the barbarian clans lost all sense of courage and ferocity in the face of it. Though some managed to keep hold of their weapons as they ran, others were not so encumbered. The theory of heightened flight by lessened weight was more from an inherent fear than any subjectivity to reasoned thought. Abandoned arrows and bows littered the forest floor, as well as a smattering of coal-stained swords.

Not one barbarian stood his ground.

A shred of human thought, the sense of honor he so stubbornly clung to, was all that kept the eagle from giving chase. Calmed by the lack of barbed arrows crowding the misty air, Jonathan regained his conscious mind. He no longer felt the restraints of confusion or gave in to the unbridled power of the intuitive mannerisms. He managed to exert his will, if only for the moment, and glided towards the tree that housed a stunned and open-mouthed Umbrah. The wind was cool beneath his feathers, his shadow passing like a phantasm over the rolling brush, and his powerful wings brought him to the woodsman's branch with something a little less than dramatic.

"Illuminate!" the elf said in awe, intoning the singular for Illuminati. "What has happened? You fell... I saw you... Jonathan?"

The eagle screeched softly, but the avian throat was not meant for such whisperings. Trying to explain what transpired, the Protectorate succeeded only in shrieking smaller half-notes, a warbled litany of unintelligible cries. Growing frustrated, he flexed his wings to their full span of fifteen feet, breaking the smaller limbs in the dense treetop. Talons gripped deeply into the branch, flaking bark and wood into splinters in agitation.

"You must relax." the elf said from farther back. Retreating out of harm's way, Umbrah still held his wide-eyed look of fear and concern. "Recall what changed you and reverse it. Think backward to yourself, your image reflected in water or polished steel. Control the magic flowing through you, turn it back toward the life lines."

For another elf, the advice would have been well heeded. But since no other elf had managed to change form since the time of the Illuminati, or the fact that Jonathan drew his power from within and not the life lines, the counsel was of no use. It was only through the relentless discipline of the knighthood, the unfailing sense of honor that drove his life, that he was able to recall so clearly his former self. Holding to that knightly probity, Jonathan could see the image of himself in his mind's eye as if he stared into the finest silver mirror. The reflection was one that bared the soul, personified his life in crystal clear alacrity. It was the moral rectitude that ruled his life that allowed him to reclaim his shape, mold himself back into the man, the knight, that he was.

Jonathan shimmered in the failing shadows.

The snow-white feathers elongated, turned liquid and solidified into flesh while darkening to a sullied tan. His sharpened beak grew soft and straight, the pointed nose resting above bristling whiskers no longer smooth and trim. Steady eyes of cornflower blue retained their presence of mind but shifted beneath a brow intent with concentration. Taloned claws extended, thickened, and lost their steely grip. If not for Umbrah's quickness of mind and hand, Jonathan would have plummeted to the ground once more, crouched atop the branch as he was. He no longer wore his full plate armor but donned a suit of tight leather much like the woodsman's. There was a metal tinge to the hide, a silvery coat that reflected the broken beams of sunlight, and the knight marveled at its hardness and resilience.

"I think I might get better at that with time," Jonathan offered with a nod of thanks. He stretched his body, cracking tightened joints, and set himself down on the limb with more stability.

"What did you do?" Umbrah was poorly hiding his awe.

"I did nothing. I fell. I saw your face as I fell and watched you reach for me. I was a bit disappointed in you, by the way, but I forgive you now." Jonathan winked to show his intended mirth, but the elf was too shaken by the experience to see. "I can only guess that this is one of the ways in which I was transformed, a manifestation of the essence magic. My medallion didn't do me much good in eagle form. Or did it?"

Jonathan was still pondering the thought when Umbrah started down the tree, carefully picking his way from limb to limb to let his mind wander ahead. Shrugging his indifference, the knight headed down as well, finding it immeasurably easier to maneuver in the enchanted leather armor. He looked up to the blue expanse of skies, searching for his feathered friend but saw only rolling clouds, dark and ominous, foretelling of a storm to come.

The rains, he knew, would be very cold.

"We must move with haste," the elf said when he reached the bottom. "Pergolai is only a day's walk from here, but we might be able to reach it sooner if we move quickly."

Jonathan was weary from the exertion of changing, but he was not tired enough for sleep. He could press on another day before taking the time to rest. For some strange reason, he felt as if sleep held only a break from the rigors of daily routine and no longer the restorative state it once had. He followed behind the woodsman, working his legs tirelessly to keep the labored pace, when a question edged to the front of his mind.

Illuminate?

The elf was jogging now, his steps light and measured, and only occasionally did he look back to see if the knight followed. Not allowing himself to sort through the endless possibilities of the day's discovery, Umbrah focused his attention on physical effort. Giving himself up to the task at hand, his mind relinquished its pursuits and allowed total attention to the negotiation of the ground that went underfoot.

"Do you need rest?" the woodsman called over his shoulder, his golden locks shaking with his stride.

"No, I'm fine, thank you. My breath could be a little more steady, but I suppose it's for lack of exercise like this that makes me that way. Just why is it we're hurrying now, because of the barbarians or me?"

"You." Umbrah kept his gaze straight ahead, intent on the terrain. "Seeing barbarians is a common occurrence these days. Seeing an Illuminate, on the other hand, is not. We make haste to tell what has happened to the elders of the Council.

"And to inform the King as well."

* * *

The morning sun blazed over the horizon in a streak of orange flame, throwing purple shadows across the hills and trees. Crystal dew clung to the blades of grass, testimony to the biting chill and persistent breeze that laid siege to the forest from day to day. If not for the heavy fur each barbarian wore cloaked about the shoulders, the coming of a new day would be admittedly discomforting, grudgingly harsh. Such was the need for the small fire that offered warmth to the circle of savages, though none would acknowledge its purpose beyond that of cooking the morning meal – the barbarians were not so wild as to eat their meat raw.

The Chieftain was a coarse man, in looks, manner and mind. Under the dusty hide of shaggy black fur, the mountain of a man, with his ragged beard and unkempt hair, looked for all appearances to be the former bear bereft of its skin. His iron helmet with sharpened antlers did little to attest his devotion to the Deer but was worn as a symbol of leadership. Though he led a small part of the Clan, his opinion of himself was not lessened by that truth. Darnoth's word was law in his tribe, and that law was rarely questioned.

"Talk slower!" the Chief commanded, waving a greasy shank. Gray juices ran down his hand and arm while he ate.

A wide-eyed barbarian, with dirt smearing his painted face, was kneeling across the fire. His leathers were torn across the chest, and he had no weapon on his belt save a small dagger for skinning. The loss of a costly steel weapon was not lost upon the man as he explained the magic he had witnessed just heartbeats before.

"Magic! There is magic here!" He looked for support from his fellow hunters and received their fearful nods. "A pointy-ear with silver skin jumped from a tree and changed into a bird! It attacked and cut us with its claws, sharp as a wolf's, and it screamed like a banshee!"

Darnoth noted the deep cuts along his hunters' faces and necks, glorious battle scars if the cowards had not run from the fray. His distaste was badly guarded as it crept into his gravelly voice.

"A bird? Six moons we live in these trees, and only now you see magic? More like you were outnumbered and made this up to keep me from killing you!" The Chief stood and threw his breakfast into the fire, unaware of its hissing and popping as he wiped his hand on the front of his furs. "Be a true warrior, and tell the truth!"

"I have! We have!" The others were not so sure of their confessions anymore, and his supporters numbered less as they slipped farther back from the fire. "I know what I saw! Carolth?"

The shaman shook his feathered helm. Though he had antlers as well, if not as grand, the multi-colored feathers depicted his station as priest and medicine man. His word, too, held authority but not so much as he'd like. The bone necklace he wore rattled about his neck as he reached a restraining hand to seat Darnoth again. With the help of a gnarled length of hornbeam, Carolth stood and leveled his gaze at the hunter.

Their eyes locked, and the dirtied man lost his breath.

"He speaks the truth," the shaman noted without relenting. "The spirit of the wind shows of what he speaks. The one who fell could not be an elf, though. His hair is too dark. The 'silver skin' is armor, my Chief, and only one group wears such a thing."

"Knights!" Darnoth spat.

Though Carolth possessed a magic of his own, he was not killed. In fact, he was praised and revered as the Holy One, shaman of their tribe. Attributing his powers as gifts of the spirits, Carolth could practice great feats of magic and not be accused of witchery. His magic, however, did not come without a price, and the spirits demanded much of the tribe.

So they hunted and offered deer as sacrifice.

"They join the elves," Carolth surmised. "And they possess magic. I warned this place was cursed! I could smell the magic in the trees, feel it in the air when first we came. The spirits will not look on us favorably if we stay."

"So you say." Darnoth was not a stupid man, for all his vicious acts. He recognized the need for the shaman, but often would he question the need for a replacement.

"Consult the spirits!" the others ventured.

"Yes," Carolth smiled devilishly. "The spirits will show us what to do!"

Kneeling before the fire, the shaman began to intone in a sing-song voice, his words falling past one another so that none were recognizable. The circled barbarians joined in by humming along, a rumbling that emanated from deep within the chest, and swayed from side to side. Carolth waved his weathered hands over the fire, holding his staff to jab at the flames and invoke the spirits of fire and earth, water and air. A battered tin cup materialized in the shaman's hand, and he cast its contents into the rising blaze. Striking with a serpent's hiss, the grayish cloud sprang up as a snake in air, wending its way skyward hypnotically.

The barbarians became so engrossed in the casting that the presence of a stranger eluded them. Even Carolth's heightened senses could not feel the shadow of the foreigner befall them, or if he did, he accounted it to the coming of the spirits. In close-fitting leathers of green and brown, one with wild hair streaked green and black stood in the shadows of a tree to the side. He stood confident, strong, and watched with intent the proceedings below. With skin tinged the color of leaves, the outlander blended easily into the foliage, his sword and bow no more than branches in the treetops.

"Spirits of the elements!" Carolth called with head thrown back. His arms were wide as he prostrated himself before their power and might. "Your children are lost and seek your wisdom! How shall we proceed?"

The fires flared and emerald sparks enfolded the circle. A shadow rose up from the flame, shaped like a man but consisting only of darkness. A foul odor stole over the camp, and the icy chill of death crept about the earthen floor like the running of a wound. Raising its inky image of an arm, the thing pointed south and spoke in baneful tones that chilled the heart into fear and obeisance.

"Leave!" the shade commanded. "This is not your home!"

The painted savages all fell back as the darkness dissipated in an explosion of blistering flame, the orange tendrils licking the pitiful stones that encased it. Carolth's eyes were wide with fright, his confidence no longer the monolith of fortitude he thought. It was that very dread clearly written in the shaman's eyes that caused anxiety to spread like wildfire throughout the tribe. Even Darnoth was slightly dismayed at the portending doom lain before them, for to disregard the spirits' warning was to throw their lives to the winds.

"The spirits have spoken!" Carolth said at last, finding his voice. "No more can we stay in this place, in this cursed land of trees and magic! Our true home lies south, in the forests of our birth!" The shaman looked to Darnoth for approval.

The Chieftain gave a curt nod, his features grim and resolute. "We will leave this place." He looked about him, at his tribe of fifty or so, and a sadness touched his hard brown eyes. "Now."

The senquil turned and fled, his feet a whisper in the trees.

* * *

Night was steadily approaching, the shadows of day growing long over the immovable treetops, as Umbrah and Jonathan slowed their arduous pace to a placating walk. Having traveled without stopping for the entire day, the two were weary and worn. Spoken words were not easily drawn, and both used them sparingly. Chewing dried rations as they moved, the two were left with a dryness in their throats that warm water could not quench. Passing the crystal streams, cooled by autumn's chill, was torturous, but neither lessened their forced haste.

"This is Pergolai," Umbrah said when they came to a stop, his arm spread wide to indicate all they beheld. "I'm sure it's nothing like you expected."

Jonathan studied the trees before him, the intermingling of cedar and birch, elm and fir, all with trunks large enough for six men to circle with arms fully extended, and scratched his head in consternation. Along with the powerful scent of verdure and grass came the heady aroma of wild flowers. Whites, yellows, blues and violets were scattered about the boles as only nature could intend, a crown of soft petals for the majestic land. As far as his heightened eyes could see, Jonathan observed only trees, grass and flowers.

"No, actually, it's not what I expected. Somehow, I thought it would be bigger, with lots of people roaming about doing their various tasks." He gave the elf a wry smile. "Either you're very well hidden or I've been struck blind by recent events."

"Perhaps."

A heavy rope of intertwined leather dropped down a nearby tree, dangling in invitation. Umbrah walked over and grabbed hold of the length, his gloves stretching with the strain. As he pulled himself up the sturdy cord, he called back down to the knight.

"As I recall, you're rather good at climbing."

Jonathan reeled as he looked up to where the knotted leather ended. A canopy of intertwined branch loomed above, limbs woven together so tightly as to comprise the floor of Pergolai. It was no wonder that little if no light reached under the elven city, giving the impression of a swift moving nightfall.

"I could always fly up," Jonathan mused as he put his foot to a bulky knot. "Though I doubt your guards and archers would appreciate the sudden appearance of a knight in their midst."

"No, I think not." Umbrah continued to pull his slight form up as if he were weightless and his two days travel little more than light exercise. "Jonathan, it might be in both of our best interests to not mention what happened today until we are in the presence of the King. This sort of thing is upsetting to most people, and elves are no exception."

The Protectorate only nodded and pulled himself further toward the top. He kept just behind the elf, surprising the woodsman with his strength and endurance. If Jonathan was any example of Marik's new Order of knights, the elves had gained valuable allies indeed. When the two reached the top, climbing through a circle of leaf-strewn limbs that grew as if by the will of the woodsmen, Jonathan looked down to a grassy forest floor that must have been no less than two hundred feet away.

No wonder the barbarians can't get them, the knight thought. *Who in his right mind would scale a two hundred foot tree to do battle in the heavens?*

The two stood in an open area where sunlight filtered through the limbs and leaves. Four elven soldiers stood guard by the circle, their silver long swords still sheathed, while two others worked to coil the leather rope. Four more woodsmen approached from a corridor to the east, a corridor being shaped from limbs woven into an arch, and they were led by a regal elf in light blue robes. They all possessed the straw-colored hair and delicate features of elves, their tapered ears jutting past the green forester caps.

"Umbrah!" the lead elf said and gave him a hearty embrace. The two stood facing each as a mirror image, though one was more weather-worn and hardened by travel. "Your presence has been sorely lacking of late. And who have we here?"

Jonathan knew they spoke common for his benefit only, so he assumed the elf must already know with whom Umbrah arrived. The elven emissary smoothly interjected the knight between them and introduced his new-found friend.

"This is Jonathan Esrald, Protectorate of Noria and royal knight to the King Marik." Umbrah gave a nod to his cousin as they took each other's forearm in greeting. "Jonathan, this is Prince Litan, my friend and cousin. We have much to discuss, Litan, and I think it would be wise if King Arboran and the Council were present."

"Indeed?" the Prince asked. "The King is to hear your report upon your return, but to be truthful, he did not expect you until late this evening. If it is that important, we will see him with all speed."

Prince Litan called his four soldiers to attention, and Jonathan, Umbrah and the Prince followed as two guards led and two trailed behind. Though the corridors branched off from the landing in five different directions, the three were led back down the interlaced hall from which the Prince arrived. Jonathan was stunned at the immensity of the elven city, that something so large could exist above the forest floor. The limbs were grown together so tightly that not even rain found its way through to the city where it was not wanted. The knight suspected a great deal of magic went into the making of such a place, and he thought he could actually feel the minute vibrations and hear the distant whisper of magic that Magarius had told them about. He wondered why a race possessing such power to control the trees and nature would need help to drive out a clan of undisciplined savages.

Walking the winding corridor brought them past circular portals with wooden doors snugly fit within the grown openings. Other passages opened up to either side or forked into another direction as they snaked their way to the Council chamber, where they would speak with the King and elders of the sylvan nation. The Prince and Umbrah were walking side by side as their destination wound closer.

"What has been happening here in the city?" Umbrah asked his cousin.

"The usual sort of thing. We keep watch on the barbarians, engage them and draw back. The whole thing is rather tedious, but it's to be expected when dealing with their like." He grunted. "Debates still continue in Council on whether or not we should call our brethren for aid or if we should even consider moving Pergolai again."

"There's no where left to move her!" Umbrah shot back heatedly, fairly summing up the debate's counter point of view.

"Ah, but there are those who think there is. It has been proposed by Landrun, Westran, Rutai and Serah that the elves belong once more in the land of Faeron, away from human oppression. No more would we be threatened by these men who come to claim our homes."

"That's not a majority," the toughened woodsman noted coolly. "Aside from the fact that Faeron had oppressors of its own, we no longer possess the strength of magic it would take to build a new city."

"Of course not. We would simply inhabit the remains of our last home and repair the minor damages."

Here Umbrah stopped and looked at his cousin as if he were mad. He could see Litan favored the idea to leave Luminarron, regardless of the risks he undoubtedly was too young to recall, the reasons for the elves leaving Faeron in the first place.

"That place is a warren for monsters now! We would be facing an even deadlier foe, and we would have to rebuild the city again!"

Litan continued to walk, though at a slower pace, his flowing robes sweeping along the smooth, leaf-strewn floor. Umbrah stalked ahead to catch up, his anger boiling to a point of bursting. Speaking through clenched teeth, he fought to control his emotions while Jonathan looked on with interest.

"We won't survive the move. We'll have to fight our way through the barbarians to one of the rings and then through the creatures of Faeron. All to reclaim a city overrun with nightmarish things whose magic is more powerful than our own. Can't you see that we cannot win?"

"That is why we shall enlist the help of our distant kin, the drow."

"I cannot believe what I'm hearing! The dark elves would sooner spit on your corpse than lift a hand to help you! What idiocy is this? How could you possibly believe that they will aid us?"

"Didn't I tell you?" Litan asked with a chuckle.

Umbrah bore a hole through his cousin with a fiery glare of pent up fury. "I'm waiting..."

"The Guardian of the Wood has returned."

* * *

The Council chamber was a large room of polished limb, the winding branches smoothed and glossy. The leaves underfoot never bruised but gave off the odor of spring and renewal. Light shone through windows, as it did all throughout Pergolai, from a vantage that overlooked the whole of Luminarron. The misted canopy of treetop stretched out to the limits of the clouded horizon, a mass of silver-gray that stained the edges, and birds flew as groups of dotted ink spots in the distance.

A semicircular table of lustrous white cedar encompassed most of the chamber, with twenty high-backed seats lined in blue velvet cushion resting behind. The Council had yet to convene, so Litan and Umbrah sat and continued their heated argument while Jonathan remained quiet and listened. The guards stood outside the double doors, waiting to announce the arrival of the King and elders.

"The senquil," Litan was explaining, "will force the drow to help us. With Randor as mediator, they will agree to send warriors with us into Faeron. We have sent scouts into the old city, and their reports are not wholly unfavorable. Much of what you say is true, the place is infested with orcs, goblins and the like, but they possess no magic. There are no traces of dragons or demons to be seen, so it is wise to assume they have fled to some other realm."

"You're risking too much, cousin. You're asking many of us to give up our lives here in the hopes of returning to a way of life we abandoned countless years ago. There were reasons for our leaving Faeron. What makes the Mystic Kingdom so amenable now?"

"Time," he answered simply.

"Have things changed so much?" Umbrah asked the Prince. He put his hand on Litan's shoulder and saw the boy he watched grow up within the determined sapphire eyes. "You're too young to remember, Litan. I was there, and I fought against them. Having lived in this forest all your life, you have no idea what it was to exist in Faeron." He sighed. "We cannot go back to that life now. We must make our stand here in Luminarron. Stand or fall, we must not be driven away again."

"But the Guardian," Litan said and shook his head. "He can help us get back to the home of our ancestors, to where our magic thrived! If we stay here any longer, our magic will dwindle away to nothing."

"Randor can just as easily help us stay."

Jonathan cleared his throat, reluctantly interrupting the impassioned discussion. "Just who is this Randor?"

"The Guardian of the Wood," Umbrah replied and let out a deep breath. "He is protector of this forest and the last of his kind. He has not been seen in many years, but his return could not have come at a better time."

"That we agree on," Prince Litan laughed. "We have a few moments before the others will arrive. Perhaps you should tell our friend the story of our birth. The break from this debate might clear our minds and give us an objective point of view."

"That it might," the woodsman conceded. "Alright, Jonathan, the tale of the Guardian of the Wood it is. Know that it may contain a few things contrary to your beliefs, but try to bear with me. I don't want to insult you, but you must realize that it's for stories like these that man first drove elves away from them, seeing heresy where only minor differences existed."

"I'll do my best," the knight said seriously. "If anything, I'm an open-minded person."

"Then open your ears and your heart as well..."

* * *

Thousands of years ago, the woods of Luminarron were watched over by the senquil, the peaceful elves, and all of its inhabitants were kept free from harm so that they might grow in love and serenity. The senquil lived free from evil influence and resided within the song of life. Noreva, ruler of all, creator of elvenkind, was pleased with his people and remained so for quite some time.

It was only when a darker god found one realm to rule lacking in the ability to satisfy an insatiable lust that strife befell the gentle creatures of the forest. Xeranthiak, Lord of Death and Chaos, entered the kingdom of elves by stealth and forcibly took one in the dead of night. With this one, the Dark God performed unspeakable acts of pain and suffering, distorting and destroying his mind and soul. When Xeranthiak finished reshaping the elf to his liking, a new race had been created: the orugai.

Though springing from the blood of elf, the twisted creatures were no more elf than human. Standing significantly shorter than a senquil, its strength seemed compact and considerable, containing a physical might and endurance by far outstanding that of the woodsmen. Its green skin was leather-tough, its eyes a baleful red and its coarse hair black as pitch. The orugai possessed a piggish snout, one that rested above a cruel mouth littered with yellowed tusks. The one aspect of their nature that set them apart from their distant kin like a yawning chasm of inescapable black was the intolerable hatred they bore for the senquil, nature and life in general. Their brutal and vicious manner could only hold one possible future for all of elvenkind.

Hundreds of orugai entered the tranquil domain of Luminarron, seeking the ultimate destruction of the senquil. The new presence in the wood was easily felt by the Guardians, but the intent of these foreign minds were somehow masked. The creatures were able to resist the magic of the elfstones, the translucent gems that allowed the elves to see into the hearts of all who walked the forest floor. Unwitting scouts encountered the orugai and brought them back to the senquil home in the heart of the wood, offering food and shelter with song and love.

When morning came, only one senquil was left alive.

Adrianna, senquil Queen and Lady of the Wood, sustained what little life she had left with Noreva's aid, calling upon her powers of healing. After being abused as a spoil of war, she was struck by a mace and left for dead. She received a serious head wound, and it was many months in passing before her body was completely healed. Her soul, she knew, never would be, tormented as she was by nightmarish dreams and visions. Even with the helpful god's intervention, there was little the animals of the forest could do to assist. She fought desperately to sustain her life and that of her unborn son, for she knew that if she should die, her hybrid son not yet birthed, the senquil would forever be gone from the world.

When Randor, son of Adrianna, was finally brought to bear in the deep of the forest, the Queen recovered much of her strength. Though she would never be the same person she once was, harboring doubt and anger, she had yet to raise her son and ensure the fate of the elves. Her body and soul had been invaded, her visions of life as a peaceful and serene realm of invulnerability were no more. She felt no vengeance towards her attackers and would ever welcome those new to the trees, but her past would not be forgotten nor the orugai forgiven. The time for caution had arisen, so she took her son and fled, hiding within the depths of Luminarron. She was determined to teach Randor all she knew of the senquil lore and to prepare him for the life of isolation that awaited him, the last of a dying race.

After the senquil were almost utterly destroyed, Noreva unleashed his wrath upon Xeranthiak and imprisoned the Dark God far within the Abyss. A curse then fell upon the orugai – not one of mindless rage and bitter hostility but a self-deprecating scourge. All of the orugai females were rendered barren, making reproduction an impossible and futile prospect. Though Noreva would not purposely annihilate an entire race, he would let their malign and warring nature eventually destroy themselves by diminishing their numbers. The pure strain of the race would die out when none were born to take the place of a fallen warrior. It would not stop the interbreeding of races, which spawned the equally vile orcs, but it would lessen the immense hatred and bitter animosity felt towards the elves.

The orugai were still free to do as they wished, and Luminarron was left unprotected. Until the senquil could guard the wood as they once did, something had to be done to keep the malicious creatures out of the forest. It was then that Noreva created the other elves.

Thousands of elves roamed the wood, learning and living in song as their ancestors did, but these were unlike the senquil in many ways. The overall elven appearance remained the same, though these were slightly shorter at only nine span. The new elves would come to rely more on weaponry and physical skill for survival rather than their need for song and spell, but what made these fresh souls entirely separate from their senquil brethren was their ability to grow and become what they may. Being completely without fate or destiny, the elves were free to choose their own paths and carve a future for themselves out of the beautifully rich soil in Luminarron.

The senquil had been created for the specific purpose of guarding the wood and were given access to powers that enabled them to do so. Unfortunately, it was that very nature of the Guardians to protect all who entered the forest that was their downfall, for they had sought to safeguard their murderers. With an intentionally vague task set before them, the elves had only to live and exist. They would follow in the footsteps of their forebears in securing the wood but only to maintain their homes. The protection of their young and kin would take precedence over the denizens of Luminarron, as freedom to choose their fate would make them stronger and immune to the mistake of their predecessors.

Regrettably, their gift of liberty had an equal flaw.

The elves grew with individual views and personalities, rather than sharing the unity of mind, body and purpose shown in the senquil. Those who found themselves with similar opinions and mannerisms would join together, working and living in groups. While it was preferable to be among people who shared common feelings and persuasions, it caused the elves to grow apart. Six groups were formed with those of like minds, and the separated elves went about their own ways, becoming more independent of each other. The divided nation expanded to develop in isolation, forging new languages, customs and traditions based upon the lands they chose to live in. The breaks from the pure language of the senquil made communications between the elven nations difficult, and the decay of magic over centuries would make it near impossible.

The wild elves, the grugach, carried themselves westward to live in the feral woods of untamed lands. They called their tree village Karon-Rai and prospered in the wilds as excellent bowmen and hunters. With their magic all but forgotten, the grugach grew to become a savage nation of warriors not unlike the barbarian clans of mankind. A harsh environment and rigorous life-style toughened the hunters with painted faces and molded them as they adapted to the woods.

The wood elves, the sylvan, stayed within the senquil homeland, following in the ancient footsteps to protect the trees and inhabitants of Luminarron. Though a bitter history once drove the elves into the land of Faeron, to the city of trees called Geilon-Rai, they returned to the site of their birth, feeling ever drawn to the song of the wood. A people hardened by plight, the sylvan would become unparalleled woodsmen, skilled with the bow and sword. Though they never abandoned the magic, less and less of it was passed on until what remained was but a shadow of the past. Fewer young volunteered to pursue the Arts, while more and more chose the ways of the tracker and hunter.

The high elves, the noldor, made their way to the east. Though staying near the comfort of trees and nature, the conservative elves chose to live in spires of white stone and crystal, castles and towers that jutted up towards the heavens. Concentrating solely upon their magic, the noldor exceeded even the limits of their predecessors. Always a reclusive and reserved people, the high elves looked down their collective noses at the coming of man. Over the years that followed, the noldor city of Dergun-Rai simply vanished. Ivory castles, iridescent crystal strongholds, shining spires and all just up and disappeared from existence. The other nations lacked the magical aptitude to divine their whereabouts, and time soon smoothed the fear of possible destruction to resigned forgetfulness.

The dark elves, the drow, saw their future under the earth, within the dark and awful powers of rock and soil. The cavernous warren of obsidian structures was centered in an underworld of terrible monsters that seemed to spawn from the shadows themselves. Learning to survive in the hostile gloom, the elves of Tehkon-Rai became indomitable warriors and terrifying magicians. The art of healing was all but a distant memory to the strict and disciplined people, as they would not tolerate the crippled or severely wounded. Dying in battle was considered the only death befitting a drow, and anything less valorous was looked upon as dishonorable and reason enough for execution. Unfortunately, the grim environs that sought daily to destroy the dark-skinned elves had succeeded inasmuch as the drow were no longer the peaceful people of old. They were inexorably changed, a mirror image of the very beasts that endeavored to slay them.

The gray elves, the sindar, journeyed south to the farther reaches of the land. Within the towering trees of Sullenwood, the cheerless people found the means to build their sanctuary, the city of Gadrin-Rai. Devoting their lives to the serious pursuit of knowledge, the sindar became the foremost sages of the world, gleaning what information they could from their scrying stones and crystals. Heightening the powers of the senquil elfstones, the solemn people were able to see into the affairs of all living creatures, learning from their mistakes to the exclusion of having their own experiences. Focusing so much of their energies to the observance of others, the sindar had amassed unlimited wisdom into the lives of their subjects – and little if any into their own. Equally proficient in the arcane Arts as their brethren noldor, the gray elves disappeared as well, fading from their simple tree-homes to a place of deep seclusion.

The last group to leave the warmth of the wood were the valley elves, the sindor, who found refuge among the grassy hilltops to the south. Nestled between the semicircular chain of small mountains, the sturdy people discovered a satisfying life within the gentle hollows. Retaining the tranquil sense of peace inherent in the senquil, the valley elves were content to live as one with the land and gave of themselves what they could. When their human neighbors arrived, serenity and offers of love were misconstrued as subservience, and the violent men strove to enslave the foreign race. Regrettably falling back on their reserves of lore, the sindor struck back with magic. Once the invaders were driven away, the elves constructed powerful wards over the smaller land of Kergun-Rai, a precaution that would stave off more war. Living simple lives attuned with nature, abhorring the confines of fortified structures, the sindor roamed their lands and slept where they willed. Their lives were peaceful and would ever remain so while the wards stood firm.

With the new Guardians watching over Luminarron, the senquil Queen could concentrate on the upbringing of her child. Randor grew quickly during that time, a trait inherited from the orugai warrior. It had taken a great deal of time for him to tame the hot blood that coursed through his veins, the savage passions of a warlike race, but he was successful in channeling those intense emotions into running, hunting and climbing. Improving daily upon those skills, he became quite a strong individual, his muscles corded and bulky for an elf.

Though his skin was tinged a soft hue of green and his wild hair pitch as night, Adrianna often thought how truly beautiful her son was. Despite his odd parentage, Randor excelled at all he put his mind to. Drawing upon the best of both races, stubbornly overcoming the faults as well, he was becoming more than what his senquil heritage had to offer.

The Queen was duly proud of her son.

Mother and son found pleasure in foraging together, in stealthily skulking about the forest to watch their unaware kin, the animals. Randor found he still had much to learn from the Queen and listened with intent to each word she would impart. Countless lifetimes of experience spoke to him through her knowledge, and he was intelligent enough to heed her advice and wisdom.

Spending nearly all their time together, Randor was taken by surprise the day his mother asked him to remain behind while she moved ahead for some reason she would not explain. Adrianna had sensed something evil lurking in the trees ahead, an evil her son had sensed as well but could not recognize for what it was. The alien presence was nothing the likes of which he'd encountered before, being altogether new to him.

And yet it was not.

Unsheathing his long sword, Randor followed his mother's tracks. The task was not easy, by any means, as the senquil Queen was like a shadow flitting from dark to light, striking across the emerald grass with little trace of her passing.

Adrianna had sensed something dangerous, something she had felt once before and not again since the driving out of the orugai. One of the vile creatures had somehow entered the forest sanctuary and was feeding upon an animal. The monster was assuredly alone, for no group of orugai could hope to sneak past the new Guardians of Luminarron. With the loss of the senquil came the loss of the elfstones, so a lone intruder would have had a slim chance to slip through undetected.

When the Queen found the slavering beast huddled over a buck, she fell back to the trees in revulsion. Whether to protect the innocent animal's right to live or to satisfy an empty space in her heart, Adrianna moved forward with rigid determination. She closed her eyes against the ache in her heart but steeled her nerves with iron resolve, calling forth a spell to her lips. The senquil magic flowed through her body as she approached the pig-like visage immersed in gore. The orugai ceased its grisly feast and raised its snout with the warning of a warrior's sense, but its acuity came a moment too late.

The monster slumped forward in magical slumber, while Adrianna closed the distance between them. She knelt before the tortured animal and fought the wave of tears building up inside. Though dead, the deer could have been brought back to life, and such was her intention when she began to heal its wounds. Channeling the divine power of Noreva, she directed the glowing light to renew flesh and bone, closing the ragged hole in the deer's side. With tears clouding her vision, she worked tirelessly, her grief washing away the unseen wounds within.

Randor moved about the wood with the agility and litheness of a feline, the liquid grace born of disciplined practice. Living among the animals had influenced the fatherless elf, and he silently moved throughout the trees to where his mother knelt. Moving aside the encroaching brush, he saw the elf Queen unprotected beside an orugai, for no other creature could have so aptly fit such a horrid description. He watched in shock as the monster twitched, no longer prone under his mother's spell.

The nimble woodsman leaped clear of the brush and over a fallen log to land before her. With his long sword in hand in the midst of a full swing, he watched the orugai quickly draw a dagger and slip it into his mother's side. Randor's blade ended its life with undeserving swiftness, and he fought to keep from striking it again and again. With his anger held tightly under rein, he knelt and took Adrianna into his arms.

The unbearable pain in her side disrupted the casting of her spell. Halfway through recalling the deer's spirit, the shock of the interruption was more harmful than the knife could ever have been. Her strength fled before her like a broken dam, spilling over the edges of her being with the pent up magic.

Her son stoically removed the knife from her side and covered the wound with his hand. Blood flowed between his fingers as he softly called the words to a spell. Randor pleaded with Noreva to heal the terrible wound, but no power was forthcoming.

"It is time for me to join him," Adrianna said gently, a thin smile crossing her pale lips.

Randor understood her spirit was being called, but the pain burned in his throat nonetheless. He hugged his mother close for what would be her final moments on earth.

"Weep not, my son, for we do not grieve the loss of a full life." Their eyes locked together as they clasped hands. "Now it is upon you, dear Randor. In my chamber, there is a chest. Within it you will find what is rightfully yours, all that remains of our people." Adrianna wiped the tears from her child's face and added, "Be strong, dear one, for you are now Guardian of the Wood."

Randor leaned forward and touched his cheek to hers as she exhaled her last breath in his embrace.

He buried his mother that night, giving her body back to the soil as was the senquil way. When her body was properly at rest, Randor returned to their home in the bole of an imposing cedar. There he found the wooden chest Adrianna had spoken of, a slender piece of elven workmanship inlaid with tracings of gold and mithril. Touching his hand upon the lock awoke the dormant magic, and the lid opened of its own volition. A blinding light was then exposed, an incandescence that softened to a hazy glow.

The woodsman reached a tentative hand inside the box and stared in awe and wonder at the treasures he drew forth. *Turanqhai*, Keeper of Peace, was his to wield, the finest long sword ever crafted by the combined hands of elf and divinity. *Wendsorai*, Enforcer, as well was his to ply. An enchanted long bow attuned with its bearer, *Wendsorai* could strike a target at nearly any range like a bolt thrown by the gods themselves. As most senquil magic, the weapons would only be as strong as their wielder.

In the hands of the Guardian, they were immensely potent.

Even more precious than the two artifacts of the senquil legacy was the deep green elfstone, a magical crystal of emerald hue shaped simply like a small stone. Held fast by eight golden leaves and a chain of mithril, the beryl gave the ability to see all that occurred within the mystic wood. The ability to scry the breadth and width of Luminarron was the senquil heritage, and the power was passed on to the last of that peaceful race.

With the elfstone, Randor became the Guardian of the Wood, protecting those who lived within the boundaries of the elven homeland, and even some who did not.

Since that time, the senquil grew to be known among many races and each with its own name and story for the elf. The barbarian clans knew him as Chameleon;

those of elvenkind called him Lonely One and Guardian; the dwarves and gnomes referred to him as Springer, the legendary hero of the trees; humans and halflings knew the elf as Stalker, the skilled hunter without form; and among the darker, evil ilk, he was despised and labeled Unholy One.

Though each held dear a different tale and title for the lone senquil, the elf King was a legend and hero among many, a nightmarish scourge among others. Regardless of race or grandeur in story, all held a deep respect for the Guardian and the wood he protected. Where so many lives found a home in the forest, none were better suited to the task than a mixing of races.

And Luminarron could not have had a more appropriate protector.

* * *

A vision of Umbrah weeping over the green-skinned monster came unbidden to Jonathan's mind. Most likely, the orugai was one of the last to survive Noreva's curse of sterility. That something so horrible could be done to a person turned the knight's stomach, that magic should be used to torture and twist a soul beyond its control and drive it to such hatred. Then he thought of the pain the elves must endure, knowing the vile creatures are their kin. Fighting for their lives, the woodsmen would be forced to slay brothers and sisters.

For orugai were elves and of the same blood.

An understanding passed between Jonathan and Umbrah, a subtle look that spoke volumes in its silence. Without speaking a word, the knight nodded to Umbrah, and the incident was left in the past. The woodsman was very, very old in the way of years, and it would not be the first time he had dealt with orugai. Leaving the dead buried and focusing on the present, living for the day at hand, was the path of perseverance.

"Do you see why we must return to Faeron?" the Prince asked Jonathan.

"No, I don't. If your people were first here in Luminarron, then it would stand to reason that your magic can be restored here as well. I don't claim to know a great deal about magic, but I have had my experiences with it." Imperceptibly, Umbrah shook his head. Jonathan took his friend's advice and continued. "I know of a one in the Wizard's Guild, a man of many winters, and I can attest to the magic in this land. The answer you seek is in the telling of your past. The magic of the elves isn't fading away as a result of the forest or mankind or anything but your own negligence. Every generation of elves sees more hunters and less magi. Eventually your magic will completely fade out of existence."

"There are less magi because there are less with the aptitude for it," Litan explained. "When a child is born, we test for exceptional potency in the life lines. If a child shows no promise, steps are taken to ensure the proper training."

"You're forgetting," Umbrah interjected, "that some elves acquire the ability to work magic as they grow older. By that time, unfortunately, their task is set, and the magic becomes nothing more than a hobby. It is not uncommon for our hunters to know a few spells."

Jonathan scratched his hawk-like nose. "You really don't understand anymore, do you?"

Both elves looked at him perplexed and then in amusement, as if a human could possibly explain the intricacies of magic to them. Umbrah, however, stopped short his mirth and listened, if not politely paying attention. After all, the knight was Illuminate, and may have had insight into the workings of nature beyond even that of elves.

"There is magic in everyone," Jonathan went on. "It is not intended for a select few who show promise to be great magicians but is meant for all to use. Magic is a part of nature that cannot be denied or given to any one person. Just as any other ability or skill, it must be learned and perfected. As hunters, you know that anyone can be taught to track, to see the signs of deer in the mud and grass, smell its scent on the air, hear the snapping of brittle twigs. Magic is no different, and in my kingdom it is taught to any who seek to learn."

Prince Litan's smirk had weakened half way through the knight's exhortation, the playful set to his eyes losing its merry gleam to concern. He sat back against the heavy cushion, taking support from the hardened birchwood chair, and let out a soft harrumph in defeat.

"You have given me much to think on, Sir Knight."

"Glad I could help," Jonathan smiled, disarming the earnest Prince.

"Tell me, Jonathan. Do you practice magic?"

Jonathan's brows raised in surprise, and he looked to Umbrah for advice. Before the two could manage a response, two guards opened the heavy double-doors. In a clear and sonorous voice, the arrival of the King and Council was announced.

"The King approaches!"

Umbrah quickly grabbed Jonathan's arm and pulled him to the center of the chamber. Prince Litan went to his seat near the middle of the table and stood as the other Council members filed in. Nine elves to a side, the elders stood behind their chairs as well, awaiting the elf King's entrance. Preceded by two royal guardsmen, each dressed in mithril chain mail, King Arboran entered with little flourish. Dressed simply in flowing white robes lined with gold and silver trim, the King was presented to his seat, the centermost chair being only slightly taller than the rest. Prince Litan stood by his right side.

"All be seated," the King said once the guardsmen took their stance behind him. A circlet of mithril rested atop his silvery hair, and his unlined face was strikingly similar to Litan's. "This day we will hear the words of Umbrah, First Hunter and emissary." Arboran smiled as formality slipped from his voice. "It's good to see you again, nephew."

"As it is always a pleasure to see you, my King."

"Is your news so pressing that you could not remove your paint?"

Umbrah still wore the green and black coloring on his face and arms, the streaks of camouflage forgotten in his haste. "Yes, my King, I'm afraid it is. I would like to present to you Jonathan Esrald, Protectorate of Noria."

"Your Highness," Jonathan bowed. Without his shining plate armor, the knight looked almost roguish. "My liege, King Marik, sends his most heartfelt regards and hopes we find you in good health." Using the plural when speaking on behalf of a kingdom can be tedious, but such was the expected norm when amongst royalty.

"All is well," Arboran replied ceremoniously. "Your King is equally in good health?"

"He is, your Highness. I have been sent as a spectator to observe these barbarian disturbances and offer any help that I can. Once the situation has been assayed, I will send message to King Marik of my findings."

The elf King nodded his approval and turned his pale blue eyes to Umbrah. "And what news have you to report?"

Jonathan watched the Council members with interest. To the King's right sat Prince Litan and nine others approximately his age, each dressed in smooth blue robes. If hair color could be any indication of an elf's age, then the nine who sat to Arboran's left were advanced in their years. Though no lines of age crept onto their delicate features, silvery-white hair adorned the elves also in blue robes. Apparently, the term elder was a title of wisdom and not a badge of years.

Umbrah hesitated, forming his words before speaking. "I have come across an Illuminate, my King."

The intake of breath from the older Council members was palpable. The younger elves simply looked to each other in mild surprise, having heard the ancient name used in stories of their past. Only the venerable elders could have recalled the incredible magic of the Illuminati.

"Do you mean the Guardian?" Rutai asked. The younger elf's hair was so pale as to seem white. "We just heard of his return earlier this day by a hunting party."

Mention of the Lonely One brought whispers of debate, the heated discussion of whether or not Pergolai should remain in Luminarron or return to the mystical land of Faeron. King Arboran held up his hand for silence, staying the argument so that Umbrah could proceed.

"No," the painted woodsman answered. "I speak of another. As the sun was rising this morn, I watched a man change shape and fly in the form of an eagle." Cries of outrage was the older response, while the others were content to listen. "Yes a *man*! I know what I saw. The reason for my haste was not to tell you of this thing but to bring you the man in person. This knight is Illuminate!"

"Preposterous!" Garon bellowed. Though his many years were too numerous to count, his strength was far from lacking. "No *man* can touch upon the lines!"

Calls of "Well said!" and "Here, here!" echoed across that side of the table. Arboran again held up his hand, and quiet unwillingly reigned. The other elders were studying the knight as if seeing him for the first time, some in wonder and others expecting a sort of hazy glow to emanate from his person.

"Is this true, Sir Knight?" the King asked. "Are you Illuminate?"

"Ill-oom-in-ah-tay?" Jonathan asked tentatively. "I'm not sure, your Highness. I did change into an eagle this morning, but I swear that I don't know how." The venerable members were on the verge of exploding. "I fell from a rather large tree, and before I struck the ground, something strange happened. I didn't feel or sense the transformation, but I felt the grass beneath my wings as I flew to safety."

Jonathan Esrald was not a man to spin yarns, or stretch the truth in any sense of the words. His voice, his manner, his entire being spoke of an honorable man, and there were no doubts of his story from Prince Litan's young supporters. The testimony of Umbrah, First Hunter, was weighty enough for any elf with the sense to listen.

"I demand proof!" another aged member called and stood. Laerin's porcelain face was an unusual crimson as he leaned over the table for emphasis. "If this man claims to be Illuminate, then let him demonstrate to us his power!"

"No!" Serah stood in Jonathan's defense. The young elf had a steely edge to his voice, but his mind was ruled by reason. "You know well enough that if a man should touch upon the life lines he would be destroyed! You should not make such a demand of our guest."

"He should not have made such a claim!" Garon shot back. "If this *knight* –" he spit the word out as a curse –

"thinks he possesses such purity of spirit, then he should not be afraid to show us!"

"Please!" King Arboran commanded. "Let's keep our perspective here. Garon, you simply cannot ask a guest of this Council to lay his life down to prove a moot point. Whether Sir Jonathan is Illuminate or not is irrelevant at this time. He is here to help us, not entertain."

Though the elders opposed to the knight's proclamation may have seemed to be chided, the King had unconsciously shown his support of them. If Arboran believed the man before him was Illuminate, he would never have suggested that Jonathan's life would be in danger from tapping into the lines. He held, as well, to the belief that no man could harbor such purity of heart and mind.

The unspoken slight was not lost upon Jonathan.

"Excuse me, your Highness." The knight spoke in controlled tones. "I know it may seem difficult for you, or any here, to believe that a mere man could be so virtuous, but I tell you that he can. Your opinions are based on generalizations of man that have not been accurate for centuries. The clan of the Deer are your only persecutors now, and I am here to offer aid, to give what I can. There is more goodness in man than you can ever know, a greater probity than our ancestors could hope for." He paused and looked each of the protesting members in the eyes, and many faltered under that honorable gaze.

"All of you," he continued, "are guilty of the very crime you profess has been done to you. Crying out for justice against a racial prejudice that has driven you from one world to another, you only learned to mirror those failings you so despise. I did not come here to prove myself but came at your request for help. I have proven myself time and again to the only one that matters: me. What I said before was true. I took the form of an eagle, but to me, this means little. I made no such claims to the title you hold so dear, nor did I use your precious life lines to do it. In the bluster of all your self-importance, you never thought to ask yourselves if humans could have a magic of their own."

Letting his words sink in, Jonathan was pleased to see the silvery heads bowed in shame at the truths laid before them. Litan's supporters had found a new champion within the noble Protectorate, and nods of approval ran through their number. This one man who was so different from any other they had ever encountered was their salvation, their hope of survival.

For him, they would stay and fight the barbarians.

"I have said my peace," Jonathan said after the uncomfortable moment. "In the morning I will go and observe the barbarians and decide what is to be done next."

He gave a low bow to King Arboran, the word *guilty* still hanging in the air like an inky shroud. Without looking back, Jonathan turned on his heel and walked from the Council chamber. Excited murmurs broke out as he walked to the double-doors, some in fervent support, some in mollified chagrin. While the King was equally mortified at his own shameful behavior, he looked after the retreating knight with hesitant admiration.

Prince Litan was not so abashed by the Protectorate's revelation, and he chuckled inwardly at the much needed honesty.

"I think I'm going to like him."

* * *

Jonathan walked the winding corridors of Pergolai, not caring much for where he was going. His thoughts were churning in his mind, and many of them were not pleasant. The elves were more concerned about some ancient title granted magicians than they were the continued existence of their people. The prejudice so wrongfully inflicted on the woodsmen should have been an unforgettable lesson, but years of isolation and hiding had made the elves every bit as mistrustful and prejudging as their persecutors ever were. Rather than face their problems of fading magic, they would rather run away again. Jonathan held out a hand to aid, but the bitter sylvans only snarled and snapped like biting dogs.

Ideas of abandoning the elves to their own fate came to the knight's mind, but he quickly pushed them away. Turning his back on them would not solve the problems at hand but would only make them worse. The barbarians would not go away easily, and though he had a plan in mind already, Jonathan needed the elves to help him pull it off. The sylvans were just as important to the realm as any other people, and they would take his help whether they wanted it or not.

Finding one of the open spaces of tree and leaf, the knight leaned against a sturdy railing and watched the sun set over the forest. Like a smear of fiery ink, layer upon layer of crimson light melted into the dense collection of trees called Luminarron.

"Are you really so evil?" a little girl's voice asked from within the shadows of an elm.

Jonathan started at the musical sound and smiled despite his dark mood. "And why would I be evil, little one? I am no more wicked than you, though maybe a bit less furtive."

Her laugh was like the tinkling of silver bells. "I didn't think all men were evil, but you looked particularly bad just then."

She jumped down from her hiding spot and took a seat on a branch by his side. Her hair was like spun gold, a cascading length of shiny locks that rested upon her shoulders in a pool of spilled honey. With playful eyes the shade of sapphires, she looked the knight up and down with a professional gaze beyond her slight years. Her tapered ears were half hidden beneath her lustrous hair. Her pale complexion was touched with pink in the cheeks and a dash of blue at the eyes. Rosy lips parted in a smile, as if she found approval in the questionable man.

"You don't look like other knights," she accused.

"No, I suppose not. This is a bit more comfortable, though," he said and showed her the silver-tinged leather armor. "Plate mail makes it difficult for a man to run and climb, so it wasn't very well-suited to the trees. Tell me, are all elven women as beautiful as you?" Though he was teasing the young maiden, his voice held compliment enough to make her blush.

"Mother warned me about men, you know."

"Is it helping?"

She smiled sheepishly and batted her lashes at him. "My name is Serenia. What's yours?"

"Jonathan," he replied and took her tiny hand into his. "At your service, milady." He gave Serenia a flourished bow that set her eyes to dancing, and she clapped excitedly in return. Turning back to the rail, however, he set his thoughts back to the Council.

"You look unhappy again."

"Isn't it past your bed time, little one?"

"I don't have one," she proclaimed and stuck out her chin defiantly. "Besides," she added and smiled impishly,

"I can't leave until you're happy. I know, I'll sing you a song! My mother taught it to me when I was a little girl, but now that I'm older I can sing it to myself at night."

She began to hum the melody, light and sweet at first, and worked to build the momentum she needed to sing unaccompanied by instrument. Growing in scale and strength, the tune took on a life of its own, like the warbling of birds flying in unity. A long, resounding note escaped her lips to form the first word of the verse, and her descant went on unabated.

She sang of the Guardian, the Lonely One of the elves, and his life in the rich depths of Luminarron. Last of the mystical race of senquil, the ancient elf King lived with the knowledge that his people would never again enjoy the wild scents of spring, the lazy warmth of summer, the frenzied labors of autumn or the crisp chill of winter. Each of the seasons exploded into a world of shades and hues that fought their way into his eyes, a battle he gave way to willingly, for the scents that came to his nose were incredibly real and tangible. He saw leaves falling past in a shower of gold and bronze, the sun bathing his skin in a wash of light. Reaching a hand forward to take hold of a wild flower, he watched the bud expand and grow before his eyes. Time was a flood of visions that passed his eyes in cycles ending with the welcomed frost of fading day. The snow cupped in his hands was cold and fresh against his lips, cleansing a scarred soul with the revelation that the ending of life was also but the completion of a similar cycle. Life would continue to grow and mature as it passed from one season to the next, and the series of lives that seemed to end so abruptly would forever go on in the minds of those left behind.

Life would always go on.

When the visions faded to the moonlit landing in Pergolai, tears came into the gentle knight's soulful eyes. He turned and looked at the elf child again, a little girl who sang with all the magic in her heart. Her eyes were wistful when she saw the hidden pain inside Jonathan, the feelings he kept buried under years of discipline.

Jumping down from her branch to land on soft bare feet, she held her arms out to the knight. Scooping the little girl up for a hug, the Protectorate of Noria endured a kiss on the cheek and let Serenia go as he blushed a lighter shade of crimson.

"Well done," a man's voice said from the shadows of night. Jonathan pulled Serenia behind him protectively and drew his sword before the next words were spoken. "I see she has made you smile, though you lose your joy too quickly."

Stepping from the darkness was an elf, albeit the tallest elf Jonathan had ever seen. The wild black hair looked wind-swept, the dark eyes aged beyond the counting of years. Though the woodsman stood right before his eyes, Jonathan couldn't see him clearly enough. He looked as if he wore leather armor but favored a generous use of the green paint as opposed to the streaks of green and black most sylvans preferred.

"Your song is quite enchanting," the elf went on.

"Thank you." Serenia took the compliment in stride, as if nothing untoward were happening. "I do what I can for my friends."

"As you should, little sister."

"Is this your brother Serenia?" Jonathan asked. "Someone finally come to fetch you for sleep?"

"No," the elf said warmly. "All elves are brothers and sisters, and I have come only to hear the song of a loved one. And to deliver a gift."

The woodsman held out his hand, and moonlight struck off a piece of metal held between his fingers. He slowly brought the piece up to Jonathan, careful not to show that he meant any harm. A closer view showed the gift to be a leaf, an intricate working of elven mithril in the simple shape of a blade in full bloom. Touching the metal sparked a small globe of golden light, an ancient magic working its way through both bodies. Both souls were laid to bare and shared in a bond that merged their spirits into one being, an understanding of each other surpassing anything known to man.

"You are indeed worthy of the title, friend." The Guardian of the Wood then turned and disappeared into the trees, his voice a trailing whisper in the dark of night. "Seek Shimarra."

"Ahem." It was Umbrah. "Was that who I think it was?"

"Don't be silly," Serenia chided the First Hunter. "You know very well who it was, so why ask?"

"You should be in bed. Your mother would be furious if she knew you were out so late." He knelt and kissed her cheek, drawing a smile from her pouting lips. "Now off you go."

"She's adorable," Jonathan said and sheathed his sword. Serenia fled down the corridor, laughing mischievously. "She also has the most beautiful voice I've ever heard. She's quite captured my heart, you know."

"She does that often."

"What did the Council finally agree upon?" Jonathan asked and turned over the leaf in his hand. He was still unclear as to what transpired, but his insight into the Lonely One could very well have been greater than that of the elves. Randor had revealed all that he was to the knight, and Jonathan had done likewise.

Together the two would preserve Luminarron.

"You have not been given the title Illuminate, but your safety is now in my hands. The Council has also decided to stay in Luminarron. There wasn't much of a debate after you left. Litan's supporters were inspired by your words and feel more confident with you helping." He smiled then, a habit of Jonathan's that was quickly growing on the elf. "I'm glad you're here, too. With your help, reclaiming Luminarron may not be so difficult a task."

"I'll do what I can for you, Umbrah. I pledged no less to you when I first came into your home. Our chances of success are greatly increased now that the senquil has returned. Speaking of which, do you know what this is?" the knight asked and showed Umbrah the mithril leaf. "It's a gift from Randor... the Guardian, I mean."

Umbrah took it in his hands almost reverently, running his fingers over the stem and veins of the leaf. "He gave this to you?" There was something akin to awe in his voice. "Jonathan, this is a leaf from the Evertree."

Jonathan nodded wordlessly.

"The Evertree is said to be in-between Luminarron and Faeron, hidden there since before the senquil. It's the source of the life lines that run through the earth and lend magic to the elves. When Noreva created the senquil, he gave them the Evertree to teach them the song of life and love. When the wind blows through its leaves, they shimmer and ring like the striking of bells, but they don't actually become mithril until one is plucked from a branch. Only a senquil may do that. The Leaves of Elvenkind were used to bond the elves to each other in a physical manifestation of their spirits. With the leaves, they could feel each other's emotions, sense the other's thoughts. In essence, they would know each other as well as they knew themselves."

Umbrah took Jonathan by the shoulders. "They would only do this rarely in their immortal lives. The giving of the leaf is an oath of friendship, and receiving the leaf is an acceptance of that oath. The Guardian has chosen you to be his friend and brother, something not lightly done."

"But why me? Why would he not have chosen an elf?"

"Jonathan, you *are* Illuminate! I don't care what others may say or believe, but I know what I saw. You could not have done what you did, by any magical means, if your heart and spirit were not pure. This honor you hold so dear is what gives you that purity, and it's what must have brought the Guardian to you." He sighed deeply and added, "With the leaf, you can touch the life lines and draw upon their magic. The Lonely One would not have given you the leaf if he thought you incapable of doing so."

Jonathan thought over the oath he'd taken and found that he was glad for it. The connection he felt with Randor was very real, and he was honored to have been chosen. He took the leaf back and held it tightly in his hand. The whisper returned to him then, spoken softly in his mind.

Seek Shimarra.

"Where is Shimarra?" Jonathan asked. "Randor told me to seek it just before he left."

Umbrah chuckled. "Not it, her. She is the Queen of fairies and lives within the Mystic Kingdom, deep in its magical heart." He looked solemnly at the knight. "If we go there in the morning, we best get some rest."

"Wait, there's something I need to do first." Jonathan walked to the railing and stepped underneath. The forest floor loomed hundreds of feet below, with numerous jagged branches along the way. "I know I can make the change again, and I have to prove to myself that I can."

Umbrah's voice was stern, revealing his concern. "You have no need to prove anything to me, Jonathan. I saw you change, and it is enough."

"I need to do this, Umbrah. Besides, I have this." He grinned and held up the mithril leaf. "I'll be back in no time." He looked back and winked to the elf. "Unless I'm enjoying myself too much!"

Letting go of the wooden rail with arms spread wide, the knight fell quickly from sight. An inaudible gasp escaped from the corridor behind Umbrah, but the elf was too absorbed in his friend's sinking into the black of night. A soft nimbus of golden-yellow erupted from the dark below and vanished into the shriek of an eagle. A tear of heartfelt joy misted the woodsman's cheek as he watched Jonathan soar up and over the city of trees. A triumphant cry escaped his beak as powerful wings propelled him through the starry blanket of sky.

Away from the revealing light of the moon, Serenia clapped her tiny hands in a silent applause for Jonathan. With her little feet padding across the leaf-strewn corridor, she ran to tell her father of the news.

King Arboran was going to be very pleased.

* * *

Early the next morning, Jonathan went down to the forest floor in the hopes of finding a stream to clean away the soil of travel. Though the sun was beginning to edge its way over the horizon, its spilling light could not be seen from under Pergolai. It was still dark and cold when Jonathan entered the shallow water.

Gritting his teeth against the chill, the knight set about to shaving. From a leather pouch within his shoulder pack, Jonathan took out a hand-held mirror of polished silver, a straight-edged razor intended for shaving and a powdery substance the gray of lightless dawn. Wetting one hand and rubbing it into the powder resulted in a foam that he applied to his face. Careful not to shave off his mustache, Jonathan began taking away his two days growth of beard. Trimming his badge of knighthood with small scissors topped off that task, and he began to wonder if elves chose not to grow facial hair or if they simply couldn't. He'd yet to see one wear a beard or mustache, and Umbrah certainly hadn't grown any over the past two days. He shrugged it off and set back to cleaning himself.

Next came a smaller leather sack, from which Jonathan poured a handful of a gritty brown powder that looked more like sand than dust. Moistening his hands and rubbing vigorously produced a lesser foam that he smeared all over his body, looking as if he'd just brawled in the mud. When the brown cleanser had washed away, the Protectorate was again a shining example of purity, if not in spirit then most assuredly in body.

"Interesting," Umbrah called from one of the surrounding trees.

Jonathan hadn't even heard him approach. "What's that, my friend?" The knight was pulling on his tunic and breeches as he spoke. Leather armor is appreciably more comfortable with padding underneath. "You've never seen someone bathe before? Not to be offensive, but you could use a dip yourself." He grinned.

"We clean ourselves with scented water and fruja leaves." He took the pouch of cleanser and poured some in his hand. "This feels like something I'd find on the bottom of my boots. It smells too much of bergamot. Couldn't you use herbs from the forest? The barbarians will smell you coming for miles." He smiled and gave back the pouch.

Jonathan grumbled and pulled on his armor. "Who'd have thought your humor would be so bad?"

"So what is it called?"

"It's soap. I purchase it in the merchant's quarter, since most who live near the market have no use for cleanliness. I believe it's a mixture of salts, herbs, ground pumice, beeswax and spices for scent."

"Are you sure it's not intended for other purposes?" Seeing his friend had taken the bait, "Perhaps to drive away thieves and brigands?"

With eyes rolling heavenward, Jonathan slipped his feet into the deerskin boots and stood in readiness. "Umbrah, please. You are far too droll this morning."

"My apologies. I'll try to be less humorous."

The two were met on the trail by more elven hunters, three of the finest in Arboran's service. Umbrah handpicked them the night before, with permission of the Council, to ensure Jonathan's safety. Though they were no longer going to observe the barbarians, the knight's well-being was no less important to the nation he was visiting.

"This is Baran," the First Hunter said in way of introduction. They grasped forearms in greeting, and Umbrah went on to present Khotek and Breanna. The three were poorly masking their admiration for the knight, and Jonathan wondered if any watched him change from man to eagle the night before.

"There are barbarians to the North," Baran suggested, still unaware of their altered plans. He was a rough-looking elf, toughened by rigorous years in the forest. His hair was pale, but his skin was darkened, like Umbrah's, from hours spent in the sun. His eyes were fixed and stern, filled with intent, and his sword hung comfortably by his side. Jonathan felt he would be a good person to rely on if the need to fight should arise.

Khotek and Baran were much alike, confident and assured. Though the former chose not to wear a sword, the two long-knives at either side of his belt were equably deterring. Khotek was notably younger, but his manner was that of a skilled woodsman.

It was Breanna that took Jonathan for a turn.

The elf was beautiful beyond any woman he'd ever seen or heard tale of. Golden hair streaked with fine white lines, like froth upon a yellow sea, she looked more a goddess than mortal. Her delicate features made her seem frail, her milky skin like fragile porcelain, but the bold gaze that met his own dispersed all thought of her being weak. Losing himself in that fearless stare, in the swirling pool of jade and golden flecks, Jonathan could only return the look of wonder. The smile she gave him then could no more melt his heart than if she had cast a spell upon him, and in the obscure way of women, he mused that she had.

"We're not looking for barbarians this morn," Umbrah said to the hunters, breaking the silence between Jonathan and Breanna. "We'll be trying to avoid them instead. We will be going north, though. To find a ring and enter Faeron."

The three exchanged questioning looks, but none spoke out. Elven hunters were trained to obey the orders of those above them and would sooner break the prized hornbeam long bows each kept over a shoulder than question the commands of a superior.

"The Guardian has asked Jonathan to seek the Queen of fairies, so we will escort him through her land. If Shimarra refuses to see him, then we will demand audience as representatives of the sylvan nation." Umbrah held each gaze in turn, conveying the importance of this one journey. "The Lady Shimarra will see us."

Nods of understanding passed through the group, and all turned towards the trail. With only a days worth of rations in the leather sacks at their belts, the hunters were set to proceed at a fast pace. They could forage for more food once out of Pergolai, but the need to travel light demanded they live meal to meal.

Khotek looked in askance at Jonathan's backpack, but Umbrah was quick to reassure the young elf.

"Jonathan is more than able to take care of himself, and he won't slow us in the least." He gave Khotek a friendly slap on the back, and added, "You might even find it difficult to keep up with him."

The five hardy adventurers were then on the winding paths and keeping a steady pace. Their retreating forms melted into the shadows of Luminarron as one far above them watched their passing.

Serenia tried to keep them in her sight for as long as she could, but the group disappeared all too soon. Her honey-colored hair was mussed from a night of sleep, and tired eyes fought against her will to stay awake. Waving her farewell, the little girl laid her head against a comforting elm and fell asleep with the whisper of a wish on her lips.

"Good luck, my knight."

* * *

Another watched the group of five depart, perched high above the forest in the concealing arms of a cedar. His wild hair swept back from wind, his eyes forever sweeping the trees below, the Guardian of the Wood set after the elves and knight. No more than a shadow passing from limb to limb, the wraith of Luminarron kept an equal distance from the swift-moving group.

Barbarian scouts tracked nearby deer, some but a stone's throw away from the group, and the shimmering image of prey that appeared would send painted men in the other direction. Relentless in their hunt, the savage warriors would never know how close they had come to facing the elven hero and legend. His magic was strong, the senquil lore rivaled by none, and the illusory buck would fade into the trees as if having existed but in their imagination.

"Go with all speed," Randor called after his Chosen. "Bring back the sprites and fairies, the winged ones of Faeron, to their true home in the trees of Luminarron.

"And bring them its salvation."

Part Three:
Courageous Hearts

The blast of magic sent ripples all throughout the land of Faeron, its resounding whisper sending tingles through the ears of those with the power to hear. Across gloomy landscapes of barren wastelands, where biting winds could freeze a beast in its tracks and a lightless moon cast a hazy pall of listless fog, the magic traveled relentlessly. The shockwave was a palpable vibration felt in the twisted trees, the charred rocks and earth. Loose dirt the grimy shade of soot turned over in its wake, spreading like lifeless veins in a heartless body. Daggers of ice jingled from gnarled branches, sending animals below scurrying for cover in the gloom of a hollow trunk before dropping to pierce the ground in rows of jagged teeth. A webwork of cracks stretched across the frozen streams, the glassy surface marred to match its poisonous waters. Still the magic went on unabated, its invisible wall of force reaching for the edges of Faeron, where it struck the Keep of Shadows.

Deep within the heart of the ancient, darkened fortress beat the rhythmic cadence of a sleeping force. Steadily it echoed off the hollow ebony of twisting corridors, veins of red light running through the smoothed surface flaring with each pulsing thrum. As the magical shockwave approached the keep, passing through its glowing wards and hollow halls, the beat began to quicken. Keeping time with the increasing pace, red streams of light flashed and faded until a single glow of fire filled the corridors. Down winding stairs and stone-carved doors, the magic raced the deafening drums.

There, in the center of the keep, sat a single throne of silken stone. In its obsidian surface, black as pitch, were carved sigils and runes that erupted in a blaze of violet light. The wraith-like shade sitting upon the mystic throne began to stir, and its inky claws gouged long streaks into the arms of its chair. The pounding beat of its lifeless power reached a thundering crescendo that faded to a crackling roar as its eyes flew open.

Though having no human body, its shadowy substance formed that of a man. Where should have been eyes rested glowing orbs of a deep crimson, eyes that could be seen from behind and see behind as well. Its mouth was no more than a sliver of violet light and the only other distinguishable feature on its person. Its inky claws seemed insubstantial, but the pointed digits could rend stone apart or slice a hair.

Rising from its needed slumber, having slept for many centuries, the stretching stain of impenetrable black was the embodiment of power. Tendrils of magic strength ran along its appendages in bands of crackling electricity. Stepping to the center of the chamber, the shade waved its hand over the liquid surface of a standing mirror.

"Show me what disrupts my rest," it hissed.

The silver face of the mirror swirled and twisted in eddies of raging mist. Formless colors and crying voices fought within the tempest, struggling against the magic of the looking glass. Again the shadow passed its incorporeal hand over the surface, but this time its icy touch brushed against the magic face. The voices screamed as if from a distance, then suddenly near. Each shriek of pain brought the vision clearer, until the mirror finally submitted to the will of its master, and the colors sharpened to form a scene.

Within the mirror's glass, six children took on shape and clarity. Though varying in years, the group of brats could not even begin to conceive age as the shade understood it. By focusing the image, it could sense the powerful auras generated from these insignificants, how their life forces exuded much more than the normal person. Gathered as they were about a wooden table, the shadow focused its attention on the oldest present. In her hands was a leather tome, a weathered book that sparked a memory deep within its past. Fixing on the faded gold lettering sent the creature of darkness reeling backward, more taken aback by the implications than the rush of defensive energy that instantly blocked his scrying and slammed the images into swirling mist once more.

They were reading from the Chronicle, an enchanted book that recorded the history of the Guardians as it occurred. An intense sheet of loathing fell over the ebony form as it recalled the old and withered man that created and wielded the magic tome: Magarius. The wizard's name stung like a thorn in the creature's side, an unending pain that refused to go away. Knowing full well the Advisor would never leave, his presence forever ingrained into its own, the shade could only hate – and plot. Revenge was its central motivator, and nothing would stand in the way of its destroying the mage and all he loved.

"Why is the old fool not with the book?" the shade asked in its sibilant voice. "These pitiful children must be the Guardians of this time, but how can that be? They're insects barely able to walk!" Its booming laughter resounded off the keep walls, shaking the ebony blocks of its foundation. "I will crush these puny pests and revel in their demise as I drain their lives from under my thumb! No one can oppose me. Not feeble Magarius and certainly not the Guardians!"

Again his laughter filled the chamber, but it was a low rumbling of its chest, a snickering of secret knowledge. Throwing wide its arms, the creature called aloud a summons to its kin. Carried by the fetid winds of the Shadowlands, the invocation would be heard by all of evil ilk.

"Come to me, my children."

Vicious man-beasts reared their heads, pausing in their feasts of fallen prey. With blood-stained maws, they cocked their pointed ears. Shivers of excitement coursed through their orange hides, and they gave their answer with a screeching howl to the omnipotent night. The goblins roared again, and the tiny men took up their rusted swords to join together for their lord, the Shadow King.

Others answered the call as well. Monsters nine feet tall with thick leathery skin an oily jade and bristling black hair, the trolls were soon lumbering across the barren landscape with stone axes and clubs in hand.

Orcs, little pig-faced men, rallied in great numbers. Descendants of the elven race, the filthy creatures intermingled with other races and multiplied by the thousands. Though not as stout as their orugai ancestors, the orcs were long-lived and formidable when in large groups. A tribe of the cruel warriors would be nearly unstoppable.

Various foul creatures flew or ran, but each took heed their master's summons and scrambled with what speed they possessed to obey. Countless years had passed since last their lord had walked the land. Already they could feel the Faery King's powers dwindling, and with it his wards of imprisonment. Soon the shadow would lead them all through a rift in the planes, into the lands of men. Nothing would be able to stop the flow as armies marched through the gate, and once again the land of Faeron would encompass mankind as well.

Somewhere off in the lands of man rested the only hope of survival for that race. Though unaware of what true powers were in their hands, six children would be forced to defend their homeland, the only existence they've ever known, and pray their strength was enough. The Keepers of the Magic slept fitfully, already sensing the imminent danger, and all but one found solace in dream. One escaped through past, delving into the lives of her ancestors.

Stephany continued to read the Chronicle...

* * *

"I still don't understand all these references to the eyes and why they are so important," a man in priest's robes said in defeat. He pushed the libram across the large oaken table, where another priest turned the pages to read.

"You don't need to understand," said the older man. "You only need to translate." Pushing the book back to his brother cleric, weathered old Marcus went back to his own task. The skin on his aged bones looked much like the yellowed parchments he read, flaking in some areas and wrinkled all over.

"The text could be misinterpreted if I do not understand the implied meanings," Clarence reasoned. "Surely you must know, what with all the years you've spent in this library. What is the significance of the eyes as opposed to that of the other senses?"

"Do you read as you translate?" Marcus asked, acid dripping off his sharp tongue. Clarence winced at the reprimand but did not turn his eyes away. "Just do as your told!"

Such is the way of the clergy, Daren thought from above. He looked down from the rafters, in a small storage area reserved for older texts, and shook his head at the single-mindedness of the temples. Though most clerics lived in the holy quarter, where all the various places of worship could be found, a large number of priests donated their time to the library. In exchange for their services, rewriting scrolls into leather volumes or translating older texts into common, the priests were given control of the library's resources and availability to the public. They encouraged the commoners to read, but there were some works not meant for the average eye to peruse.

"The eyes, as a sense," Daren whispered from the beams overhead, "are venerated as being closest to the divine. Along with hearing, it is the farthest sense from the physicality of earthly things, that which binds man to this plane. Touch, reason and spirituality are the three steps to divine." Leaning farther downward, the little rogue whispered a bit louder.

"The eyes are windows to the soul."

Brother Clarence looked up from his text with a start. He craned his neck to see all about him, eyes wide with a fear that soon turned to fanatical fervor. Realization dawned on the priest, and he set his pen to a furious pace. Believing he just had a visitation, Clarence was busily scribbling his thoughts on the text before they slipped from his questionable grasp.

"What is the matter?" Marcus asked, raising a wary eye to watch the lesser clergyman. "You look as if possessed."

Clarence showed his yellow-stained teeth. "I've just been inspired by the gods! They told me what I needed to know."

Daren chuckled, trying to control his laughter and sorely losing the battle. He quickly made a retreat back to his lair of books, desperately fighting the urge to break into a fit of uncontrollable laughter. Scrambling out the darkened hole that led into his hiding place, the little thief barely made it out of the building before a guffaw escaped his lips.

The resounding *Ha!* that echoed all through the library sounded as if angels had come to mock poor brother Clarence.

Darting from rooftop to window, the agile thief raced towards his meeting with Cornelius. The ex-mercenary would be waiting for him, ready to teach more about how to handle a sword. The old soldier would want to meet at first light, never believing in wasting a precious moment of the day, and Daren could only smile as he thought of the grizzled warrior, the only man he thought of as family. No one had ever cared for the wily boy before. He'd never known his parents or even what parents were, so Cornelius easily filled the empty space in Daren's life, becoming the father he was denied since birth.

Knights of Virtue

Slipping through an open passage in the tops of a building, tracing his lithe form over the stout beams, the practiced thief moved more like an acrobat than a cutpurse. His unfortunate small size, however, had prompted Daren long ago to outmaneuver rather than overpower his opponents. Darting through occupied buildings without making a noise kept his senses alert and his skills honed. Normally, the boy would have been through the run-down structure in a matter of moments, but a trail of conversation caught his ear and rooted him to the spot.

"Half now and half later," a muffled voice intoned through the wood beneath his ear. There was a metallic chink as a sack of coins was thrown onto a table.

"I am quite aware of how this business is done," another more deadly voice replied. The sinister quality to the sound sent involuntary shivers down Daren's spine.

"Just be sure to complete your task at the appointed time. Too early and our men won't be inside. Too late and they'll have to deal with him, in which case you won't see the other half of the gold."

"You tread a dangerous line," the dark voice warned. "All shall meet with Morgon when their time has come. Be sure your conscience is always clear, for no man knows when that time may be. We will do our part in speeding the soul to its master." There was a drawing of steel and a frightened yelp. "Just be sure to do your part as shown to us here. The remaining gold is promised to Morgon."

Daren nearly fell through the ceiling at what he'd just heard. *Morgon!* Only one group of people dared speak that name, and only one group could worship the God of Death.

The Assassins Guild!

Somehow Daren had stumbled into a guild house of the Assassins and overheard a deal being struck. Though aligned with the Thieves Guild, the agreement was tentative at best and always tested by either side whenever the opportunity presented itself. Knowing where the guild house was located could prove valuable to the thief – provided he could make it back out alive.

"We'll do our part," the other promised weakly, his voice trembling with forced confidence. "I'm only concerned because a great deal of our plan rests in your hands."

Chairs scraped against the floor as two men stood. "You may go now," the dark one said. "Be assured that at the appointed time, the soul of King Marik shall lie at the feet of our god."

Daren didn't wait for the sound of a door closing but immediately pressed forward through the dusty shadows of the crawl space. Hoping he moved with the stealth of a master thief, he was all too aware that his fear spurred him on at an inadvisable pace. The cold hand that had a grip on his heart would not let him slow or calm himself. All he could think of was making it out of the building alive and running to tell Cornelius, or anyone, that the king was in danger of being killed.

The Thieves Guild may have been viewed as unlawful by all others, but there were none in the city of Noria more devoted to the king. Aside from the poor business during King Jaril II's reign, as most people are tight with their coin under rule of a tyrant, King Marik was a fair and just man who ascended the throne from the rank of a commoner. He understood people and respected their individual beliefs. As a result of his unique outlook on life in his city, the king had called the Guildmaster of Thieves to a meeting and struck a bargain with the man. Thieving would be kept to a minimum in certain quarters of the city, and he would pay a tithe to the crown. In exchange, the Guildmaster would be allowed to deal with his own, enforcing the unwritten laws agreed upon by king and guildmaster. With the treaty in place, both parties prospered greatly. Thieves could afford to live, cutting down on violent crimes, and the crown enjoyed an extra revenue to boost its treasury. In the end, the coin was returned to its rightful owners, the people of Noria, in ways that made it tenfold its original worth.

Now the Assassins Guild would destroy that relationship and all for the sake of some ill-gotten coin and the fanatical belief of their order. If the Brotherhood, which was more a clergy than a guild, could speed yet one more soul to the feet of their master, then so be it. Oftentimes the members of that group would walk among the commoners in the guise of priests. Where a true cleric would offer healing to a diseased or injured person, the Brotherhood offered only a swift death and departure to their lord. Self-justified in their missions of mercy, the assassins were the deadliest men to walk the streets. The treaty between the Thieves and the Brotherhood was merely to keep the two from destroying each other, but the assassination of King Marik would be seen as an intolerable breach in their agreement.

It only served to show how uncertain the treaty was.

Forcing himself to move even faster, pulling his cramped and shaking limbs through the small passageway, Daren made enough noise to catch the attention of one guard below. Grabbing a fellow assassin, the two men followed the scuffling noise above. Clad all in black, they looked more like shadows than men, and the way they kept pace with the soft scraping of shoe in the crawl space was more akin to the supernatural.

Daren found his way out of the guild house and quickly moved to the alley below. Keeping to the shadows, the little thief ran as fast as his trembling legs could carry him, fear spurring him on through crowds in the plaza and empty, dark alleys. Something nagged at the back of his mind, an uneasy feeling of being watched. As a cutpurse, Daren knew what it was to have the eyes of another upon him, and he cut a swerving course through the milling crowds before admitting someone was following him. Whoever trailed the boy was skilled in the art of stealth, for half an hour of misguiding trails left Daren with nothing more than the unshaken feeling of pursuit.

He was certain someone spotted him leaving the assassin hideout, but he had no choice but to find Cornelius. Surely the master swordsman could protect him if, indeed, he was being chased by trained killers. Breathing somewhat easier for the decision, finding comfort in the thought of the ex-mercenary's protection, Daren settled into a fluid run that more suited his craft.

"It's about time you showed up," Cornelius said and gave a half-smile. His tawny hair was tied back into a long braid, and he had a silvery long sword in one hand, a thick short sword in the other. "I brought your sword."

Daren had practically impaled himself on the extended blade, so tired and fast was he running. He broke into the alleyway with a smile of triumph, seeing the cheerful veteran waiting for him. He fought to catch his breath and grabbed a handful of homespun shirt in the process.

Taking the boy's hand from his tunic, Cornelius forced their eyes to meet. "What's wrong? Who's chasing you?"

Having finally filled his lungs with air, Daren opened his mouth to speak. Before he could utter a word, however, two slender men in night black cloth stepped from the shadows a few feet away. Neither Daren nor

Cornelius had heard or seen the two approach, but only the Guardian was dealt a blow. The hand that chopped to his throat was expertly aimed, and the old soldier could no longer breathe, let alone return the attack. He felt Daren torn from his grasp and a startled scream escape the boy's lips. All he saw was a flash of white as a lightning quick blow struck across his temple and another to his sternum in one simultaneous chop.

He felt the waters of the alleyway cooling his back and a figure kneel over his unmoving form. A tide of black threatened to wash over him, driving him into the deep of unconsciousness, but one thought kept him focused: Daren. The boy was in trouble and needed his help. Cornelius forced his eyes to open, to see past the glassy haze that swallowed his vision, but only a groan showed for his efforts. His world then exploded in a wall of red pain as the blade of a dagger drove through his chest and heart with the precision of a practiced killer.

Cornelius exhaled a breath, and his eyes no longer fought to open.

* * *

A black gloved hand clamped over Daren's mouth. The assassin was already dragging him through the alleyway when the other paid killer went for Cornelius. Fighting against the iron grip, Daren struggled to see behind him, but the man in black was too strong for him. They were in the shadows of the alley when Cornelius cried out in pain, Daren's captor reaching for a square slab of steel in the cobbled road. He could hear rushing water beneath the lid and tried to scream for help.

He was being taken into the sewers.

There was no doubt in Daren's mind. They were taking him to be questioned and killed. Hoping to buy his friend some time to catch up, the little thief bit down on the sinewy hand over his mouth. A gasp of pain escaped his lips as he nearly broke off all his teeth. Hidden beneath the palm and fingers of the glove were thin plates of metal, probably lead, and Daren succeeded only in drawing a chuckle from the slender man.

The assassin threw Daren unceremoniously down the open hole, landing him into a current of filthy water and ominous dark. Before the thief could catch his breath, he felt a body next to his and the familiar grasp. Taking hold of his neck between thumb and forefinger this time, the assassin put his masked lips up to Daren's ear.

"If you try to escape, I'll snap your neck like a twig." He tightened his grip to emphasize his point, sending spasms of pain all along the thief's arms and legs. "Whether you're at Morgon's feet now or later matters none to me."

Nearly gagging on the awful smell of floating waste, Daren was somewhat grateful he couldn't see the foul stuff. The only source of light in the waist-deep waters was the glowing moss on the rounded stone walls. An eerie green light emanated from the slick growth, casting a deathly pall over everything. Ignoring the lumpy objects bouncing off his legs, Daren strained to hear something other than rushing water and the echoes of his heavy breathing.

Sunlight disappeared as the second assassin returned the lid to its original position, climbing down the rusted ladder with only a nod to his brother. When they pushed Daren forward, he turned around and faced the deadly pair.

"What have you done with Cornelius?" he demanded.

The second one was almost indistinguishable from the first in the murky dark of the sewers. He shrugged and pushed the thief ahead. "I did nothing to him. He'll be along any minute now to rescue you."

The emotionless voice did little to hearten him. Daren knew that the assassin left Cornelius either dead or unconscious. Though he prayed for the latter, something told him the fanatical killers would not have left an enemy behind. There was no chance the ex-mercenary could follow them through the twisting passages and endless sections of the sewers. If Cornelius was alive, then he was better off not trying. Daren would never forgive himself if the grizzled soldier was killed because of him. Already his chest ached with the pangs of guilt, his breath coming in short gasps as he thought on his only friend lying dead in an alleyway.

The three stopped suddenly.

An unseen look was passed between the two in black. With a curt nod, one tore the sleeve off Daren's dirty tunic. As the assassin disappeared down a side passage, the thief could only guess at what was transpiring. When the three continued on ahead and began taking their turns at a faster pace, he began to get an idea of what was going on. Someone was pursuing them through the sewers, looking for Daren, and they used a piece of his clothing to throw the trail off.

A surge of hope sent warmth through Daren's chilled and numbing legs. There was a slight possibility that someone from the Thieves Guild saw him taken and was following, but the odds were better that it was Cornelius. Glad that the swordsman still lived, Daren hoped he could find them before they reached the assassin guild house or else not find them at all. His only chance of escaping was in Cornelius' freeing him before they entered the Brotherhood's den. Realizing he needed to help his friend in what little way he could, Daren began to slow his pace, blaming his lethargy on the cold waters of the sewer.

"Move faster, or I'll carry your unconscious body."

"If I move too fast, you'll think I'm trying to get away." Daren tried to look back at his captor, but the grip in the hollows under his ears would not allow it. "I need to rest," he protested.

"You'll get plenty of rest soon enough," the other remarked.

The three stopped again, waiting in the putrid muck. Daren watched the two men stand completely still, not even drawing breath into their slender forms. For the briefest of moments, he thought he saw a white flash in the eyes behind the mask but had no time to think on it. He was roughly pushed forward again.

But this time one stayed behind.

* * *

A small hand reached for the leather purse on his belt. Cornelius woke with a start, exacting a yelp from the little beggar boy leaning over him. With eyes wide in surprise and fear, the boy shook his short blonde hair and fought for the words in his throat.

"You're dead!" he whispered and looked around for help. The grip on his arm tightened, and he was sure the dead man was going to kill him as well.

"Where did they go?" Cornelius managed to croak. His throat was very dry, and a hollow pain in his chest ached with a fading throb. There was a bloodied hole in his torn shirt, where a dagger had entered his heart, but the skin beneath it was whole and unscathed.

"I saw him kill you!" the beggar gasped, struggling to free his arm. "I didn't mean to steal from you! I was just hungry!"

"Look!" Cornelius barked, his authoritative voice from years as a soldier showing through. "I only want to know where they've taken the boy. I'll let you go if you tell me." He loosened his hold on the boy and let him see that he was very much alive.

The beggar stood and led Cornelius to the square cover. He kept his face down towards the lid and gazed up at the swordsman in askance, as if Cornelius should know to just give up.

"They went into the sewers?" he asked the boy. "How long was I out?" He'd spent nearly every day of his childhood in the sewers, exploring and adventuring in imaginary kingdoms with illusory monsters. Some of his fondest memories of youth were of the days spent in the underground passageways in search of magic and treasure.

If Daren was in the sewers, Cornelius would find him.

"They left not two minutes ago," the boy sighed. In his eyes, whoever the assassins took was already dead, or at the very least would be by morning. "You're not thinking of following, are you?"

Cornelius was already pulling the lid up by its handles. He took a moment to flip a silver coin to the beggar before disappearing into the rushing waterways of the sewers, fighting the waves of nausea that erupted in his gut at the awful smells rising from the place. He pulled the steel cover back into place, and all fell into darkness.

Reflexively reaching for his sword, Cornelius gasped in astonishment at the glowing blade he drew from the scabbard. The entire passage ten feet ahead was bathed in a wash of silvery light. The globe of magic was strong enough that Cornelius could move at a quicker pace than his prey, or so he hoped, and might buy him the extra time it would take to catch them. A faint greenish light beamed ahead, emanating from the walls like a misty shower in the darkness. The two lights together cast the walls and water in shades of gray, the floating refuse rushing by his thighs in lumpy mounds of stinking garbage.

The ache in Cornelius' chest had all but gone, leaving no trace but the reddened hole in his shirt. He remembered the man in black coming at him like a shadow, a soundless and efficient attack. The knife entered his chest with ease, piercing his heart and ending his life. *Or did it?* When he woke, there was no dagger, but the bloodied tunic confirmed the melee had taken place. *Maybe the blade didn't go in as far as I thought,* he considered. *No, it did.*

The only other explanation he could come up with was that his newly acquired magic as a Guardian allowed him to heal his body. The wound he received should have been instantly fatal, and yet, he still lived. No scar remained, nor pain – nor memory. His body had healed itself without his being conscious. *Could I be immortal?* he wondered but soon shirked off the idea. Daren was depending on him, so he turned his full concentration to finding the boy.

There was absolutely no trace of anyone passing through the slick, foul-smelling sewer. Frothing gray water came half way up his thighs, numbing his legs with the biting cold. Autumn was no time to be playing in water in the cold reaches of Noria. He tried not to think about it and turned his thoughts to Daren, to the brief moments he saw the boy last.

Something tugged at his mind.

Cornelius stopped and looked all about, his silver broad sword the center of an unwavering globe of light. The lion's head pommel felt cool in his grasp, its flowing mane sending shivers of excitement up his arm. He'd sensed something just then, a presence or force. It was as if sitting with eyes closed and feeling when someone moved close. But it was more than that! He could perceive who that person was, and he had touched on Daren's presence.

Wading through the waters as fast as his legs could carry him, Cornelius headed in the direction he sensed the boy. He could almost see the trail in hazy shades of milky gray as the thoughts and emotions of his little friend pulled him forward. He gave up on all pretense of approaching quietly to surprise the two men in black but gave in to the hopes of now catching the three before it was too late. Whatever intentions Daren's captors had, Cornelius did not care. Sticking a knife in his chest was not something he could so easily forget or forgive, regardless of whether or not they were fellow guild members of Daren's.

The sewers opened up into countless different passageways, but the Guardian knew which way to go before even seeing the options arise. He turned down slender corridors and gaping tunnels without a second thought, his mind attuned with the boy's. Only when a flash of dirty blue cloth passed his peripheral vision did he stop, unsure of which way to go. He quickly took up the torn piece of clothing and knew it to be Daren's. All of his being told him Daren was just ahead, but the incessant pulling in his mind told him otherwise.

Abandoning reason, Cornelius dropped the false lead and continued on his previous course. He could feel the distance between the two lessening, and a wave of triumph flushed his face, spreading warmth through his frozen legs. The precious minutes that separated the two were slowly closing in.

There was a change in the trail then, a sense of urgency and warning. Without slowing his pace, Cornelius tried to focus on the change and determine its meaning. He couldn't be sure if Daren was in immediate danger or if danger was approaching. In either case, the insistent sense of a threat existed, some peril he could not put his finger on.

The assassin was out of the water in a heartbeat.

A garrote slipped over the Guardian's head, tightening around his neck and yanking him off his feet. His forward momentum nearly took his head off, but Cornelius managed to get to his knees. A man clad in black was mercilessly pulling two wooden handles, cutting off the swordsman's supply of oxygen. The rough wire of the garrote broke the skin, and Cornelius gasped for air. His face was red with strain and lack of breath. Struggling to get his fingers under the tightening wire, he realized he no longer held his sword.

Only the faint glow of moss-covered walls allowed him to see. The assassin, the only ones who employed garrotes, twisted around so he was behind Cornelius. Driving a knee into the swordsman's back, he pulled with all the strength in his skillful hands.

Cornelius gave up on trying to loosen the wire, and the numbing black of sleep was rising up to greet him again. Once more, the assassins will have killed him and taken Daren away, leaving the helpless man to die of his wounds. How many others must die before these professional killers are stopped? How long before they decide to take another boy? The questions burned in the Guardian's mind, and that burning led to a fire, sparked by a torrent of anger at the cowardice of cowled men who strike from the shadows at defenseless boys.

A claw reached back and raked the man's head, shredding the black mask that hid his face. A horrified cry of pain and shock broke from his lips, and the garrote fell into the coursing waters. The assassin regained his senses, long used to the idea of dying and meeting the God of Death. Many hours of meditation had prepared him for the time of his demise, but it all seemed somehow not enough. Having lost his eyes, he relied on his other senses: hearing the water plunge past him, tasting the salt of sudden tears that sprang from his unseeing eyes, smelling the nauseating stench of garbage and waste floating past.

And feeling the implacable bite of steel.

* * *

Daren felt as if they'd been backtracking for quite some time, turning in and twisting back on passages they'd already trudged through. Whenever the opportunity presented itself, he would lash out with a hand or foot, marking the green moss by scraping it from the slick stones of the walls. The two passed a triple opening, and Daren scratched the side wall with a nail as he was pushed by. Pain shot through his neck and jaw as the assassin pulled up short.

"Stop trying to help me," he hissed. "I can make false trails without you. And if you drag your feet one more time, I'll cut them off. You won't need them where you're going anyway."

With that said, he dragged the tired thief back the way they came and took another passage. They followed it through a hundred paces of dulling cold, then stopped in the largest opening they'd seen yet. It looked as if nearly all the passages, regardless of how many twists and turns they took, would have led to this one corridor.

It stretched as far as Daren could see, the glow leading far into the distance, and still no light beamed at its end. The network of sewer tunnels under Noria was a city unto itself.

Forcing Daren to his knees, the water pressing in against his chest as he labored for breath, the assassin knelt and felt along the wall under the water's surface. There was a click, though its sound was drowned away by the roar of coursing murk, and a section of wall swung open a bit as if on a rotating support.

"If you so much as move to mark this wall," the dark man warned, "I won't wait to have you questioned before finishing you. I'll let your body float into the Sea of Tears."

Pushing from under the water, the assassin swung the portal open for the two to pass through, keeping his eyes locked on Daren. The little thief kept his arms to his side and made no move to mark the door. The cold fingers that gripped his neck were anxious to end him quickly, so he gave no reason to do so. His only task now was to stay alive long enough for Cornelius to find him. If the master swordsman could track them as far as he had, he shouldn't have any trouble locating a secret passage.

The swiveled portal locked back into place with an audible click. The echoed sounds of rushing water abruptly faded to a muted thrum, and only the dripping of sodden hair and clothes could be heard. With each step they took, the resulting splash sounded all too loud, like the poisonous breath at Daren's back.

At the end of the silent passage was a single iron door. There were no markings, no locks, no handles or anything to distinguish it as a metal plate in the wall or a portal of some kind.

Daren searched the dead end for any trace of a mechanism, putting his thieving skills to use. As a trained member of the guild, though of no high standing, he had a well of knowledge to draw upon. Unfortunately, little of it was experience. There's only so much a book or spoken word can teach without the practical familiarity of actually doing a task. He could study the surface of the mossy walls, but without putting his fingers to their slimy stones, he would never find a latch or spring to trigger the door.

The assassin, however, did no such thing. He simply stood and stared at the door, or so Daren thought. It was difficult to see his eyes behind the mask, the gloomy dark just a series of jagged shadows. Without cause or warning, the tick of a lock could be heard on the opposite side as tumblers fell into place. The door opened slowly into absolute black, with no sign of light farther ahead or to either side. Daren could sense something waiting there for him, heard the soft scuffle of feet against the stone floor as he was shoved forward into the arms of two more assassin guards. He looked back to the dim green glow of the sewer passage, longing for that source of light.

But all became black as the door locked shut behind him.

* * *

Cornelius stared down at his paw, where used to be his left hand. He was so astonished by the rough wide pads and coarse brown hair, marveling at the sturdy retractable claws, that he barely noticed the tingling sensation of healing at his throat. The deep wounds left by the garrote were all but gone, the slender cut fully closed, before the Guardian could take his gaze away.

He quickly searched the fallen man, rifling through his possessions for anything that might help. Hoping to find a key of sorts, thinking Daren already closed away behind some door or barricade, the swordsman found only the deadly weapons of an assassin. A small glass vial filled with an emerald liquid caught his attention, and he stuffed it into the leather sack at his belt. Aside from the elaborate tattoo of a dragon on the killer's left breast, there was nothing worth wasting more time over.

The ex-mercenary was up and running through the icy waters again, his transformed hand a mystery he would ponder when time allowed. Focusing his mind on Daren's presence, Cornelius picked up the trail again and followed with as much speed as he could muster. The water pulled at his legs, weighing him down with each strenuous pump, but he would not relent.

There were moments when the trail went in more than one direction, but the presence pulled insistently stronger. Knowing the destination without worrying over the path to that point was the advantage Cornelius needed to catch his prey. The light shining off his broad sword reflected off the slick walls ahead, showing him the largest tunnel yet. Five men could have easily stood hand to hand across its breadth.

He burst into the open passageway just as something farther down caught his eye. Unsure if it was floating refuse or one of a million rodents that made their homes in the awful place, Cornelius rushed to the point where he thought he saw the wall move.

The movement was there again, but it was not. It was as if his memory was superimposing itself over his vision, except that the memory wasn't his. A flash from his sword sparked a picture in his mind of a man in black working his hand along the wall, which served to affirm his suspicions.

He was seeing the scene through Daren's eyes.

Kneeling before the wall, where he'd seen the assassin crouched, Cornelius ran his paw over the oily stones. Scraping his claws over the slick surface helped him find the depression, a stone that sat too far in from those surrounding it. He pushed on it with his other hand, holding the glowing sword under his arm, and gave a smile of victory as the portal swiveled open.

With sword in hand, he went through the opening. Not sure if he'd be able to get it back open from the other side, or if he and Daren would need to come back out that way, Cornelius left the portal open.

The single passage lead to a dead end. Somewhat quieter than the other corridors he'd passed through, the Guardian began to miss the deafening rush of water. It would have made his approaching the iron door a bit less noisome. Cornelius assumed there must have been drain pipes in the floor or bottom portions of the walls, because the water in the dead end remained at a lower level than the main passageway.

Once the swinging door is closed, the entire passage must empty of water all together. He approached the iron door, studying its plain surface for anything that could help him open it. *Not that it matters. Wet or dry, I'm not leaving without Daren.*

He couldn't find any way of opening the door, short of banging on it, but things had not gotten quite that bad yet. If he had to fight through every assassin in Noria to get to the boy, he would. He preferred stealth only to save time, or so he told himself as he ran his hand over the unremarkable door.

Hoping to find something useful in his leather sack, he emptied its contents into his paw. More disappointed than he was before, he tossed the food and other equipment back inside. Wet flint and soggy rations would hardly get past an iron plate that was who-knows-how thick. The small bottle of green liquid he picked off the assassin was probably nothing more than poison.

It certainly smelled bad enough.

If there were any cracks where the door should open, he could... do nothing. If he knocked and waited for the assassins to open the door, he could throw the poison... in the water, because they would sooner drink the sewer water than be hit in the mouth with poison.

He sighed in exasperation, feeling Daren's presence growing fainter. Removing the stopper from the vial, he pondered drinking the poison and then knocking. The assassins might bring him inside once he fell dead, and his new-found healing powers would keep him alive. He hoped.

Wrinkling his nose at the milky cloud of vapor that escaped the container, he took a closer sniff. Nearly burning the flesh on his nose, he threw the stuff at the door as if stung by its scent. As awful as the sewer water smelled, he took a handful of it and splashed his face, washing away whatever the stuff was in the vial. It was then that he realized it wasn't poison at all.

The smooth surface of the iron door began to bubble and smoke, hissing and popping with the fury of fire. Cornelius stood back, afraid some of the vile stuff might spray onto him. The concentrated acid was eating through the door with a voracious appetite, slicing through the iron like a knife through butter. Leaving only jagged burns and scorched metal behind, the acid completely disappeared into its surface. Where there should have been a handle to open the door was now only a crescent of tortured iron. Without any help from Cornelius, a chunk of eaten metal fell through to the other side, revealing nothing but inky black.

The Guardian kicked wide the door, casting a silvery light within.

* * *

Unceremoniously dragged all throughout the guild house, Daren was finally taken to a dark and tiny room. His captors didn't bother to blindfold him, nor did they make any attempt to keep him from mentally mapping his route. He had no chance of escape and no future to speak of. The Assassins Guild could not afford to let the little thief live.

And so he was thrust before the Headmaster Assassin, a feline-like man clad in a charcoal outfit of tight-fitting cloth and a violet mask. Not an inch of skin could be seen on his lean and muscular form. From the gloves on his hands to the black leather wraps on his feet, nothing could be seen but the piercing eyes beneath the visor of dark crimson. Consistent with his sinister character, his eyes were so black as to have no iris at all.

"Is this the thief?" the Headmaster asked in a sibilant voice.

Unspoken assent came from the two behind Daren. They stood by the doorway, ready to spring, but nothing was likely to come close to harming the Guildmaster of Assassins.

"I haven't done anything." Daren tried to stare into the man's black eyes, but he couldn't keep his gaze fixed there for long. Something about the man bore through his eyes and exposed his thoughts. Letting his gaze settle on the room's only light source, a single candle on the desk between them, Daren shifted from foot to foot.

"I never said you did," the slithering voice replied. "You were brought here before you did manage to do something. There is as much fault in intent as in deed."

With fingers steepled under his chin, the ominous man leaned back in his chair. "Tell me what you know, and your death shall be quick, maybe painless. Provided you know something else that might interest me."

Daren looked as if he were thinking, mulling over his options or organizing his thoughts before presenting them. In truth, he was buying time for Cornelius. The longer he could stay alive, the better the odds he would be saved. He nearly laughed while imagining Cornelius, let alone any one man, breaking into a guild house of the Assassins and living to tell the tale. Feeling less than mirthful, Daren was coming to the realization that he had no hope of escape. *Perhaps a quick death would be preferable...*

"I'm growing weary," the Headmaster warned. "Tell me now, or it will be extracted from you."

The threat struck something deep inside Daren, a spark of pride or stubborn optimism, he couldn't tell which. He tensed his stance and stood firm his ground. His eyes took on the steely edge of defiance, and he forced them to stare into the menacing black depths before him.

"I know nothing." Bile rose in his throat, but he fought the bitter taste back down. "Even if I did, I wouldn't tell you. Regardless of what you think, thieves do have honor."

"Honor is nothing but a word, little boy. A preconception that serves only the living and badly at that."

The guildmaster gave what passed for a sigh, a long slow breath exhaled with control, and nodded to the assassins at the door. Rough hands took hold of Daren, dragging him from the room. Over his shoulder, he could hear the snake-like voice calling to him, invading his thoughts like a poison.

"We'll just ask your corpse. I'm sure it will prove more cooperative."

* * *

The silvery globe of light extended into the darkness ahead, throwing the small antechamber into unexpected shades of gray. The two assassin guards once hidden in shadow were then revealed, one with a poniard and the other a garrote. Cornelius glared down at the choking weapon and moved forward with a menacing set to his features. The assassin jumped for a red satin rope hanging by the door, but the Guardian's reflexes were magically enhanced as he gave in more and more to his lion form. His sword cut the rope at a point four feet above the killer's head, showering the black-clad man in a blast of sparks. The shining metal of the sword made a grating noise as it was pulled from the stone, leaving a notch in the wall a finger deep.

Cornelius narrowed his cat-like eyes.

The other assassin crept up behind the strange swordsman, holding his needle-sharp dagger along the length of his forearm. A sticky black liquid was smeared across the blade, looking for all its color like the dried blood of a previous kill. Deadly enough to strike down ten men, the poison need only enter the bloodstream for a few seconds, so the assassin looked for an opening to slash and a quick end to the fray.

Unfortunately, the wavering man was in no mood to comply. The hazy aura that surrounded Cornelius made it difficult to define his shape. The edges of his body simply blurred into a cloak of gray mist, and his center looked uncertain of color. A slender beige tail hung down by his feet, its curled end covered with a bristly tip of chestnut hair. With his eyes transfixed on the changeling man, the assassin had no hope of seeing the claw until it hit.

Thrown against the far wall, his dagger falling from limp fingers, the brother slumped down to sleep. With head on chest, the poor man just couldn't find the strength to continue fighting.

The other thought twice about trying to slip his garrote over the shaggy mane of the man before him and grew more keenly aware of the sharp teeth that now stood out from the intruder's mouth. A cross between lion and man, the creature evoked only concern. The assassin had long ago put aside his fears, but he had no weapons to defeat a lycanthrope. What other creature could change from man to beast?

Cautiously backing away from the werelion, the brother kept his garrote loose to allow for the larger neck. When the beast sprung on him, sword flashing in air, he managed a kick and a hold round the neck, but he didn't have time to tighten the wire. A paw had been waiting to reach under the cord, and its sharp claws cut the garrote in half with less effort than swatting a fly. Another swipe of the paw, and the assassin was sprawled on his back as well.

Cornelius jumped atop the man and reached up for his throat, his dagger-sharp teeth just inches away. A wall of animal rage had come over his senses, an instinctive desire to destroy his prey. His body less resembled a man as his struggle brought him closer to the merciless spirit of a beast. The scent of fear had subsided, but the sweet aroma of fallen prey could not be so easily ignored. His teeth closed over the throat, jaws tensing to rend and tear, when a presence edged its way through.

Daren.

Something was wrong. The animal instinct was no longer so sure of itself, and the voice of reason interceded at the lapse. Where once laid fallen prey was now only a man. A cry of pain pierced his thoughts and further cleared his mind, drawing aside the curtain of rage and calming the savage beast within.

Daren was in pain, and Cornelius could feel him close by. Still retaining his feline eyes and left paw, the Guardian left the two assassins behind. Consciously dimming the light of his sword, he stalked through the shadows of a narrow corridor. The boy was so close that Cornelius' skin prickled with a surge of anxiety, a shiver of fear touching his spine, and the Guardian of Courage again knew the difference between one who is brave and one who is fearless. Neither the better in times such as these, it was all but a state of awareness. Facing incredible odds for a cause that's just, whether afraid or not, was the mark of a courageous heart.

The corridor opened into a circular room some hundred feet across. Four other passages went off into alternate directions, but a single door of stolid oak stood at the far end of the room. It was there that Cornelius sensed Daren was being held. From the constant note of pain, he knew they were torturing the boy. Cornelius offered himself to Daren, allowing the boy to share his pain, before storming towards the door. A fiery agony suddenly enveloped the swordsman, and he nearly fell to his knees. Though no mark stood upon his body, he could feel the agonizing touch of piercing steel and the sting of cuts across his body. Forcing himself to ignore the pain, for Daren's sake, the Guardian pushed on for the door. The light of his sword was faltering, its silver globe collapsing in on itself, but he would not give in to the torment.

He was in the center of the room when shadowy figures slipped in through the other corridors. The six men were waiting for the intruder, having heard the initial fray, and stood patiently in the dark. None carried a weapon nor felt the need to. They confidently circled around the swordsman, noiselessly moving with deadly intent. Looking every bit as much as any other assassin, covered head to toe in black cloth, these six had only two distinguishable features. A red sash was wrapped around their waists, and the imprint of a red dragon could be seen on their left breasts. The six master assassins were soon in place, and each gave a slight bow to the man before them.

Cornelius was surrounded.

* * *

The two assassin guards dragged Daren through a circular room, past a heavy wooden door. On the other side were the whirrings of metal machines and the pain-filled screams of tormented men. No sound escaped from beyond the simple door, nor did any who were brought through its massive stone arch. Daren could see the walls were easily ten feet thick as he was brought in, which meant no one would hear his cries for help – not even Cornelius. The light of a hundred candles burned all about the small confines of the chamber, casting light in a place where darkness was a welcome friend.

A small man was there to greet him, an old fellow with a pleasant smile and balding pate. A ring of white hair sat over his droopy ears, and thin spectacles sloped down his pudgy nose. He wore brown leggings and a white tunic, with a leather apron thrown on for good measure, and waddled over to greet his new guest.

Though terribly short and robust for a man, he was only average for a gnome.

"Hello! Come in, come in! I am Portlanimbinickerty, Portly for short, and I will be your host!"

The little man was shorter than Daren by a head, and the pudgy hand he held out was half the size of the thief's. They shook hands, and Portly led the boy towards a table in the middle of the small room. Another door stood against the far wall, the source of screams and grinding metal. The table was not the sort one would expect, as it had leather straps all along its edges. Daren imagined that once something was strapped in, there was little chance of it breaking free.

"You may go, of course," Portly said with a wave of his hand, dismissing the assassin escorts. "Now, you're a fine looking lad. What's your name, son?"

Daren was slightly stunned at the little old man's pleasantry, not expecting to even see the face of his tormentor. If Portly was the one who carried out such things. *What did he call himself? Host?*

"I'm Daren," the thief answered, eyeing the wooden door from whence he came.

"I assure you," Portly said in conspiratorial tones, noting the desire to flee, "that the guards remain outside the door. Much better to have this between you and me." The gnome patted him on the back companionably and slapped his stubby hand on the wooden table. "Good. Up you go now. We don't want this to take any longer than needs be."

"Wh-what's going to happen to me?" Daren sat up on the table and laid down as instructed. He squirmed only a little as Portly tightened the leather straps around his ankles, legs, waist, chest, arms and wrists. Another heavy belt went over his forehead, holding him completely still. "Are you going to ask me questions?"

Portly sighed heavily. "I'm sorry, son. Those who are brought to me already had their chance to answer questions. It's my job to do... something different."

The gnome opened a drawer beneath the desk, the candlelight reflecting off the polished steel instruments inside. Long, sharpened needles and razor-edged tools were arranged in order of group and size, neatly kept and spotlessly cleaned.

"I'm a chirurgeon, you know." Portly held up one of the thinner needles, inspecting the hair-like metal through the glass of his spectacles. "Or, at least, I used to be at one time. I've saved hundreds of lives in my own long life. Family, friends, sometimes complete strangers, would all come to seek out my services, to find the famous gnome from Fizicia." A single breath steadied his heavy heart. "It seems my fame stretched farther than I had thought it could."

Daren tried to see what Portly was doing, but his peripheral vision showed only the glint of reflective steel.

"What are you going to do?" he asked with a shaking voice.

For some reason, the boy couldn't stop the wild beating of his heart. He'd fought down fear before, but that was a fear of the unknown, with the possibility that things would be alright. He'd never before faced a fate that was a certain doom. The only hope he would escape alive lay in the hands of a man probably very far away. Too much distance and circumstance separated the two, and Daren's hopes were not enough to bring them closer. He began to shiver as the cold hand of fear took hold in his chest.

"There, there." Portly tried to comfort the boy as best he could, placing a withered hand over the boy's heart. "Have courage, son. You were brave enough to get this far."

Daren saw only compassion in the gray eyes looking over him, but he couldn't be comforted by the cause of his fear. The gnome understood and let the boy be, but he still had a job to do. He took a wet sponge and washed the thief's arm, paying particular attention to the biceps. Lining the point of the needle along the muscle sideways, Portly began to gently push.

"This may hurt just a bit."

* * *

The Headmaster Assassin sat at his desk, shrouded in shadow but for the single candle that shed a ghostly light across the oaken wood. Beneath the dark crimson mask, a sinister smile crept across his lips, engendering a throaty chuckle that escaped as a slithering hiss. Long, slender fingers, gloved in black silk, held up to the scarce light the source of his enjoyment.

A fist-sized crystal, smoothed to perfection, held his icy gaze. Not a single bubble or scratch marred the cylinder, and its absolute purity reflected clear beams of white light. The crystal itself would have been worth a small fortune, but the magical properties of this unusual quartz set its worth by far above priceless.

"And how are we this night?" the Guildmaster asked, his eyes penetrating the clear surface. "The first strike of night has come and gone, but I'm afraid your father is busy at the moment." Another cruel smile. "He's entertaining a guest of mine."

In the very center of the crystal was a tiny form, a small child by all appearances, with waist-length gold hair and a hard set to her delicate features. She stamped her small foot, sending eddies of pearly mist all about, and her flowing pink dress billowed outward. Eyeing the man with a "Humph!" of disdain, it was plain to see she had long lost her fears of him. Well aware she was needed to blackmail her father, she was simply an uncooperative little girl.

"I thought I would entertain in his absence," offered the sibilant voice. "I can imagine your boredom with the poor company you keep."

This brought a chilling stare from the crinkling brow, but still the gnome would not speak.

"Ah, it's just as well. The very sound of your voice might break my ears, so unused to the foul noise as they are. Sirella, why do you look at me that way? Are you ill? Tut, tut. Well, I'll be happy to convey your poor humors to your father." Her eyes opened wide as the hardness of defiance melted to pleading. "Perhaps you'll feel better tomorrow."

Sirella moved to protest, but the crystal was already away.

* * *

Daren looked more like a pincushion than a porcupine. With all the varied needles protruding from different areas of his body, long and short, narrow and wide, thin and thick, it was for his own good that he couldn't move. Foot long incisions had been made all along his chest, arms and legs, and then been sewn back up again with a hair-like black thread. Hours could have passed, but they seemed an eternity to the tortured young thief. Tears fell freely down his pale cheeks, and his body shook with the spasms of sobbing.

Having performed the task on many men since the capture of his daughter, Portly knew his heart would never harden to the sight. He could only marvel at the deeds men will do when the life of a loved one is endangered.

"Daren," the gnome called soothingly. "I have a potion that can ease your pain. You will drift into sleep and never again hurt."

"No!" he cried, pain wracking his body. "Cornelius will come! He's going to save me!" Daren coughed on his tears, his head throbbing with fire. "I... just have to... hold out."

"Daren." Portly tried to talk reason into the boy. "I know how badly you want to be rescued, but I've seen too many come through my door. There is only one way out, and it's through there." He motioned to where the screams came from. "My work here is done, and now it's time for you to move on. It either ends here or in there."

The gnome leaned close, pleading with Daren. "I can't help you once you pass through that door, and the pain that awaits is by far the worse." A heavy sigh passed through the diminutive man. "Do you understand that I've been chosen for this task for my skill at keeping men alive? I assure you, the men on the other side of that door are heartless and cruel.

"They will not have the same regard for your life."

Another sob tore through the thief. "Am I supposed to thank you? Are you proud of what you've done to me? 'Keep me alive!' Ha!" He then cried harder, his tears unable to wash away the pain.

"Just leave me alone," Daren said, his voice a whisper.

With a tear of his own, Portly gently began to remove the needles.

* * *

Cornelius was down on all fours before a strike was made. The six master assassins stood ready to pounce, watching the man as he thrashed his head about and cried out in pain. Whether it was some trick of the eerie silver light or not, something began to change about him.

Now backing away from the strange occurrence, the assassins watched as the silver long sword shimmered and shrank, folding in on itself with a liquid appearance. The intruder was surrounded in wavering light, the edges of his body losing their sharpness and flowing into something entirely different. Clothes melted and disappeared into his skin, while his hair grew darker and elongated to cover his naked body.

As the sword slipped away, becoming dagger-like claws, so faded the globe of light that encompassed Cornelius. When he turned to look at the men surrounding him, his eyes cast a glowing yellow light that pierced into their hearts and bred fear like a plague. Shaking a mane of coarse brown hair, the Guardian threw back his head and roared with all his animalistic rage, threatening to shake the very walls down.

The swordsman was no longer human.

Eyes went wide beneath their dark masks, but they soon narrowed again with determination and the fanatical promise of salvation. A low growl escaped the giant lion's throat, and its massive paw swung out. One of the men crashed into a stone wall, the resounding crack of his skull the only sound to be heard before he slumped to the ground. The other five moved to attack, but a sharp command from the eastern corridor halted their fluid steps.

"Let him go," the Headmaster hissed quietly.

The lion crashed through the wooden door, sending a shower of splinters to the other side. There was a scream and another crash, then the sound of claws on stone.

"When he leaves," the Guildmaster continued his orders, "you will follow him through the sewers. Weaken him from a distance, reduce this magical power he has and then kill them both."

The remaining five moved towards the far wall without hesitation, waiting for the immense creature to come running back out the door. Instead of the ferocious lion, however, two scrabbling forms appeared, a man and a boy. The man-lion was badly wounded, his body covered in a variety of new wounds, while the boy looked to have none. With this sudden change of events, the assassins looked to their master for new instructions. The slow shake of his head was all the answer they would get, so they made no move to attack.

Cornelius and Daren made a run for the sewers.

* * *

A wave of uncontrollable rage fell over the giant lion, running through its massive body with fingers of probing fire. Venting its frustration on an unassailable foe, it lashed out with its paw and sent a man sprawling. All was a rushing storm of indecipherable noise, pain drowning out all its senses until nothing remained but numbing dark. In the distance, far beyond reach but within mental sight, grew a single point of light. From that hazy star came an elongated sound, an urgent plea, that brought a chilling calm and focus.

A boy cried out for help.

With blinding speed and mystic strength, the lion was through the door. An explosion of shattered wood sounded on the other side, and a diminutive man scrambled away under a blanket of tinder. The giant lion was through the second door before its second stride. Thick blocks of stone came away this time, leaving jagged gray teeth where once stood a doorway.

A grotesquely large man stood in its path. He wore only black leggings and a matching mask, his hairy stomach hanging over the former like a giant ball of flesh. With the overall appearance of a bear, the man was menacing enough without the burning poker in his hand.

The tortured boy tied to the table behind the man was too tired and beaten to care anymore, but his head raised slightly off the sweat-slick surface at the sound of splintering wood. Terrible gashes ran all along his back, the result of a practiced hand and whip, and a myriad of swollen welts could be seen where the man had begun to use the hot iron.

The sight of Daren's battered form so shook and hurt the raging lion that it could not retain its anger. Wrestling with its emotions, feeling pity and pain for the boy, the lion was man once more. The grossly fat torturer had already retreated to a corner, his brand held ready to strike, but Cornelius paid him no attention. His yellow eyes saw only Daren, and tears burned down his cheeks.

"I'm sorry," he whispered and laid his hands on the boy.

Daren stirred at the pain in his wounds but slowly woke from his foggy sanctuary as his burns began to heal. The deep cuts in his skin all closed and faded, leaving no trace of their ever being there. Damaged muscle, aching joints and whatever wounds remained all vanished as if washed away in a stream of warmth.

The blanket of healing warmth he felt was, in fact, Cornelius' hands, drawing away each mote of pain with tendrils of flickering light. When the boy was completely restored to health, he sat up and rubbed his eyes as if waking from a dream. He was amazed that all of his wounds were gone and more so that Cornelius had found him, but the joyous embrace was cut short by a sharp intake of breath. Daren's soft green eyes widened, and he gasped in concern for his friend.

Cornelius now bore the boy's old wounds.

"How did you...?"

"Never mind," the swordsman said shakily. "We have to get out of here." He gave a shrewd glance at the cruel man in back but thought it a waste of time to deal with him at that very moment. "There's some people waiting for us outside, so we'll have to make a run for it."

Daren swallowed hard but declined to make a comment. He reached out to help his friend walk and supported him to the door. Cornelius knew if they were to make it out alive, he would have to run on his own. He could feel his injuries healing already, but they would not be fully gone for quite some time.

When they reached the second door, Cornelius watched the dark ahead. He drew his silver blade, shedding a globe of light before them. Daren saw the gnome watching from a distance in the room, his small hands kneading in worry. Portly opened his mouth to say something, but the thief shook his head, a stern look crossing his face. The gnome knew there was no forgiveness in those stony features, but neither did he seek any.

The Guardian saw no immediate threat and hoped his eyes saw the truth. Grabbing Daren by the arm, he motioned for them to go. The two were through the dark chamber and into the murky passageways of the sewers before the count of ten, a sprint that ached Cornelius' nervous stomach more than it did his wounds. They were free and alive, something they both promised to never take for granted again as they forced their way through green sludge.

The sewers no longer smelled quite so bad.

* * *

It wasn't long before the two realized they were being followed. No sooner had Cornelius reached an iron ladder in the passageway than a shadow fell over the finger holes and voices whispered above. Though the men waiting for them to jump out of the sewers were hired thugs, sell-swords from the plaza, the trailing shadows back down the stone corridor were most definitely assassins. Whether or not they were the masters Cornelius faced earlier mattered little. The swordsman was wounded, and any combat would be to his disadvantage.

"We can try another one," Daren offered. "They can't guard every sewer cover in the square!"

"No." Cornelius hurried them along as he spoke. "There's another way. I just don't know if I can find it. They'll have men looking for us all over the city, but they won't look for us outside of the city."

Daren nearly choked. "I hope you don't mean we're going to ride the river out of the sewers! We'll be killed!"

"Not quite." The Guardian chuckled then winced as another wound pulled taut and sealed. "When I was young, even younger than you, I used to come down into the sewers and play. Mind, they used to be much cleaner back then, and you could consider drinking the water... if you were thirsty enough."

They turned down another passage, the splashing sounds of pursuit not far off. The two made better time with Cornelius' sword lighting their way, but it seemed to the thief the assassins weren't trying as hard as their reputation proclaimed.

"While under the merchant quarter one day, I found an opening in the sewer walls and followed it deeper in. It was a stupid thing to do, granted, but I was too curious to care. What I discovered astounded me, and I haven't been able to explain it since. As a matter of fact," he added after some thought, "I hadn't thought about it 'til now either. Isn't that strange?"

"What did you find?" Daren asked, forgetting his fatigue in the depths of the tale. "Elves? They say if you meet elves that they make you forget, and you can only remember if someone or thing reminds you of it. Or sometimes, not even then. I'm not sure."

"You've been reading too many fairy tales," Cornelius said and shook his head with a smile. "Try picking up one of the classics now and then."

"I'd hardly consider The Strategies of War a classic."

"In any case," the swordsman went on without taking the bait, "I found some kind of city. The buildings were mostly falling or fallen, not more than a mass of rubble, but much of the place was still in tact. I only went in far enough to see roads leading out in all directions. One of those roads must lead out of the city, maybe into the forest."

"Why didn't you explore further or just go back again? Did you meet an elf?" Daren raised an eyebrow, a knowing look in his eye.

Cornelius would have sighed if he had the breath. "To tell the truth, I was scared out of my wits. I met up with a monster of sorts, or what I thought was a monster back then. Later I learned it was a hobgoblin, but that didn't make it look any smaller to this seven year old boy with his wooden sword."

The young thief laughed as he imagined Cornelius as a boy, dropping his play sword to run.

Such was the stuff of true heroes in the making.

The sounds of echoing chants rang out from behind, and Daren pulled up short to better hear the noise. Closing his eyes to focus his ears, a trick learned during training as a thief, the boy could hear the harmonious chanting of clerical summons.

"Did I mention that they can cast spells?"

"What?" Cornelius tightened the grip on his sword.

"Well, they're sort of priests –"

A gigantic rat the size of a wagon emerged from the rushing water ahead. A blanket of rubbish fell from its shaggy hide as it screeched a roar of challenge. Its red glaring eyes centered on the glowing sword, and its two front teeth gleamed like daggers of ivory in the sphere of dull gray light.

Cornelius hardly had time to curse.

* * *

With barely enough room to stand in the corridor, the rat could only snap with its sharp teeth. Its ruddy coat of soaking fur stood on end in bristles, scraping the green moss from the stones in the ceiling and upper walls. Again the giant teeth would snap, sounding as if two rocks had slammed together, and the swordsman scrambled away from being caught under the creature's bulk.

Cornelius had no time to appreciate its size or be grateful that it couldn't swing with its claws, which stood on the end of very stout legs. He contemplated chopping at its legs to bring it down, but the whiskered snout would come driving down on him like a battering ram before he could ever swing. For lack of a better means to attack, the Guardian slapped at its nose.

The flat of his blade struck against the beast's snout, and it let out a roar that shook the sewer walls. Daren fell from his feet and was nearly dragged away by the rushing water, right into the massive rat. Cornelius stood firm his ground and struck again while the creature reared its head to bellow. His enchanted spoon, then in its sword shape, scored a hit in the rat's upper chest. When he pulled the blade free, the Guardian was amazed to see that no blood ran free of the wound.

In its place shot a beam of reddish light.

"It's not real!" Daren cried, holding onto a niche in the wall.

"What do you mean?" Cornelius missed getting bit on the shoulder and struck another cut in its neck. The passageway was ablaze in red light. "It looks real enough to me! How do I kill it if it isn't real?"

"I think your sword is draining its magic! That's why it leaves behind those empty spaces of light!" The thief moved farther away as the fight pushed closer to him. "Leave your sword in next time!"

Cornelius frowned. *Leave it in? That's ridiculous! And what do I defend myself with, my charming wit?*

Letting the rat shoot right for his head, the swordsman ducked low at the last instant, feeling the whoosh of stinking fur and hearing the clack of empty jaws slamming shut. While the giant beast was completely on top of him, Cornelius drove his sword into its chest until the hilt closed flush against fur.

The rat went wild, slamming its head into the stones above.

Cornelius was no fool. He jumped back far out of its reach and watched it from a safe distance. Leaving the sword in had nothing to do with holding on to the blade. The terrible wailing of the rat was enough to deafen a man, and its thrashing fit was going to bring the entire city down on top of them. Stones began to slip out of their holds, the mortar breaking off in fist-sized chunks, but its screeching soon grew less energetic and its movement lumbered. Its massive form fell lifeless into the water, its head slipping under the green morass.

There was a faint buzzing that increased in volume and speed as crimson light erupted behind the fallen rat. Like a blazing fire, the light ate away the body's shell, for nothing could be seen inside but a foggy red mist. When the sizzling flames had completely eaten away the giant monster, there was no trace of its existence but the broken sewer passage.

Daren leaped from his place and snatched up the sword before it was carried away by the water. He grinned at his teacher and returned the blade, eager to let go of its handle.

"It's all hot and buzzing," the thief remarked. "Is it always like that?"

"No," Cornelius answered worriedly. "We better get going. I don't know why they're not attacking us, but I'm not going to wait and ask."

The assassins could have easily trapped the two while they faced off against the giant rat. Cornelius couldn't figure it out any more than Daren could, and the thief was a bit wiser when it came to the guilds.

"Is the entrance far?" Daren looked back over his shoulder as he plodded through the waist-high waters. "I don't know how much longer I can run."

"I'll carry you." It sounded more like a threat than an offer. "It's not far now. The street markings are worn and missing in some places, but I know where we are. Just a few more streets and we're there."

Street markings? Daren watched the walls carefully, but never noticed anything different in the moss-covered stones. He was about to ask when the globe of silver light fell over an iron mark, four thin letters in a spidery scrawl. MQ-CA. The iron was rusted and covered with moss, so that it blended into the wall as no more than a raised lump of green. They were turning another corridor when Daren pieced the words together: Merchants Quarter – Candle Avenue.

Cornelius slowed and stopped by an overgrown passage. The moss was much heavier here, swarming over the wall until it was obscured by a blanket of oily green muck. He pushed his sword into the sheet of growth and watched the blade disappear well beyond where the wall should have stopped it. In two quick swings, Cornelius had cut away a door in the moss. The two climbed over the stone wall and through the half-open door just as the sounds of pursuit came from behind. The moss was then pushed back into place, looking as if it had never been touched, and the muttered cursing of men could be heard rushing by.

Cornelius turned and led Daren out of the craggy tunnel, leaving the slippery sewer walls behind. The terrain was much rougher but easier to walk on then forcing their way through four feet of water. Not to mention that a band of murderous assassins no longer pursued them. When the two reached the end of the tunnel, they both stopped and looked on in amazement at the sight spread out below them.

An underground city stretched end to end in the faintly lit cavern.

All above was pitch black, dotted with green patches of mold in a semblance of night-time sky. Reflected off the webwork of waterways that ran along each street and building, what little light there existed was enough to see the enormity of the city. Cornelius could count twenty square blocks into the distance before the buildings and streets all blurred into an indefinite horizon of glowing emerald. Fires burned in some of the still standing constructions, peering back at the two as crimson eyes of the city's inhabitants.

"It looks like people already live here," Daren noted.

Cornelius led them at a slower pace and sheathed his glowing sword. If there were any guards posted along the city perimeter, he didn't want to alert them. Not until he knew what they were.

"Hobgoblins don't mind fire," Cornelius said in answer. "I doubt there's any people living here, but you never can tell. It'd be more likely that orcs, goblins or even something worse have taken refuge here. I don't know that any of those races prefer living in houses, or how they live at all for that matter, but this place seems as good as any to get out of the cold. The forest can be harsh this time of year."

They were carefully moving down a steep-sloped road of sorts, the loose rubble threatening to send them sprawling down to the rocks below. At some points, they were forced to climb, but their descent was not overly taxing. Most of Cornelius' wounds had disappeared, but it had been a long time since either of them had slept or eaten. Almost a full day had passed since Daren was taken in the alleyway. The thought sent Cornelius to wondering why they had taken the boy in the first place, and he would have asked if the sound of falling dirt and pebbles hadn't come from above.

The assassins were back.

"How did they know...?"

Cornelius snorted and moved them at a faster pace. "You're the one who said they could cast spells."

"I didn't say I knew what kind of spells." Daren's eyes were drawn to moving figures below. "Either we've been spotted or something's going on down there."

As unbecoming as cursing is, it aptly fit Cornelius' mood. "Those are hobgoblins," he said and looked over his shoulder to gauge how far off the assassins were, "and they're waiting to greet us."

"Well, look on the bright side." The thief gave a wry grin. "Things can't get any worse."

"Can't they?" Cornelius was slowly losing his temper, sure he was being punished for all his years as a single man. The Fates *were* women, after all. "When we get down there, don't say or do anything. I've dealt with hobgoblins before, so leave it to me."

The two score fierce warriors were waiting in a semicircle. Each of them had a burnt orange colored skin, tough as leather, that was hidden beneath bronze scale mail and battered helms. With small wooden shields and nicked short swords, they were well outfitted for their kind. At the front of the tribe must have stood their leader, one easily a head taller than the rest and bulging from his armor with corded muscle. An outrageous set of sharpened horns were mounted on his helm, proclaiming him as chieftain, and spittle ran from his yellowed fangs as he patiently awaited his meal.

Unfortunately, no one had explained the rules to Cornelius. The grizzled veteran simply walked up to the hulking monster and slammed his fist into its face. There was a resounding crack and the bending of poorly forged bronze as its helm caved in, but that didn't stop the chief from taking a nap. He was equally just as happy to loan the man his helm, and Cornelius put the monstrous thing on without a second thought. He turned and addressed the gathered tribe, who somehow managed to look shocked at the occurrence.

"Nahk mi cheid," he said in their tongue. *I'm in charge now.*

* * *

"What are you doing?" Daren asked, his eyes scanning the tribe of savage monsters.

"Don't look scared," Cornelius said out the corner of his mouth. "They respect strength but despise fear."

A nearby hobgoblin began to protest, an obvious supporter of their former chieftain. As a race, they hated all other races, including their own, and openly warred at every given opportunity. They also venerated strength and bravery and would follow whoever or whatever was strong enough to defeat their best. Usually.

"Nas te Cheuz," the hobgoblin sneered. *You not chief.*

Cornelius met the sword leveled at his chest with a fierce gaze and growl. He slapped up the blade and snatched it away before the monster could react. With his own sword pointed at his armored chest, the hobgoblin felt very vulnerable just then.

"Tagak mi," the Guardian said loud enough for all to hear. *I am now.* He handed the hobgoblin back his sword, gaining an avid supporter, and called for silence as he addressed the ferocious group.

"Gruek'i mitash u rhad fidzech. Khup ve'i yrulidz mi, u yruledz veank! Dask uil be! Dask uil oadh! Aeht vadkri ul velhom!" *Men in black come this way. They come to kill me, to destroy you all! Take up your swords! Take up your oaths! Vanquish all who cross [your path]!*

At hearing the famous hobgoblin call to arms, the tribe was driven to a frenzied banging of sword on armor. There was something more at work, however, something Cornelius was barely aware of himself. His very presence, his words and voice, were floating with undertones of magic, a source of confidence for the tribe to draw upon and cling to. Filling their dark hearts with the insurmountable spirit of courage, Cornelius was the living emblem of inspiration.

The hobgoblins rushed off to attack the assassins.

"C'mon, let's hurry." Cornelius left the chieftain's helmet behind. There was no telling what other monsters lived in the city, and proclaiming himself leader of a tribe would not be a good idea. "They should be able to hold them off long enough for us to escape. They may even solve our problem for us."

"I doubt it." A cold shiver ran down the thief's spine as he thought of the Brotherhood's ruthlessness and efficiency. "They'll buy us some time. Nothing more. Where did you learn to speak hobgoblin? I couldn't understand a word you were saying. And how did you get them to attack the assassins?"

The Guardian touched a finger to the side of his nose and gave a roguish wink. "Mercenaries aren't as ignorant as you might think. You'd be surprised how many languages I know, and all of them learned on the open road. Much easier to calm a raging orc or hobgoblin when you speak their tongue. You also get a kind of feel for the race just by knowing how they word their thoughts. Unfortunately," he shuddered, "it always leaves me with the need of a bath."

The swordsman led them through the winding streets, hopping over the irrigation system that ran all throughout the city, sending green waters beyond his vision. The clash of steel on steel could be heard and the rising battle cries of the hobgoblins as they faced their mortal foes. Cornelius and Daren were through a tumbled building of decaying stone as the distant sounds were fading away, replaced by the trickling run of water.

"Halt!" a voice cried from the shadows. "Skas ad si?" *Who goes there?* Five men of medium build and wiry form stepped from the shadows, but their faces remained hidden behind cowls. They each bore crossbows with nasty looking bolts, cocked and ready to fire.

"Thieves!" Daren whispered. "They're speaking the Cant, and they want to know who we are." He kept his hands in plain sight, trying not to provoke the men before given the chance to speak.

"Isn't there some kind of guild sanctuary you can ask for?"

The thief nodded. "Sa linh al'bes nedroon. Da sen, linhsi." *A friend who asks for peace. Well met, brothers.*

"Who is your master?" one of the men asked, an older man by his voice. "By what rights are you in this place?"

"I am apprenticed to master Jhedro, of the Third Tier, and we're here because we're being chased." Daren paused as the five moved into the light, their weapons then laid aside. "Members of the Brotherhood are trying to kill us."

The four younger men were much what Cornelius expected: young, lithe, agile and swarthy as a moving shadow. Dressed in black padded leather, with a variety of knife hilts protruding here and there, the young thieves were enough to frighten any merchant out of his wits. It was the older man that caught his attention and seemed so out of place. His graying black hair was tightly tied back, his aging features softened with time and his gentle green eyes seemed almost paternal.

"And what of this man?" the old thief motioned to Cornelius.

Daren couldn't help but smile and look up at his friend with admiration. "He saved me from them. Took me right out of the guild house."

This brought some uneasy glances from the four thieves standing behind, and the crossbows edged higher by a hair.

"Indeed?" The lead thief studied Cornelius, the jade of his eyes gleaming in the faint light. "So tell me, young apprentice, why is it this man should have to save you from our allies? The Assassins Guild must have had a good reason to take you." His tone was not as forgiving as his eyes.

"Yes," Daren agreed, holding Cornelius' attention as well. He never quite got around to asking what this whole thing was about. "They did have a good reason to abduct me, and they should have killed me when they had they chance. But now it's too late. They'll have to face the consequences of their actions."

He took a deep breath before continuing. "I accidentally stumbled into one of their guild houses while passing through crawl spaces in the garden quarter. I heard the Headmaster Assassin himself make a pact for a life in exchange for gold. Half was delivered then, and the other half is to be given once the deed is carried out. They must have heard me sneaking out of the building, because when I heard who they planned to kill, I did all I could to get out of there as fast as possible. I thought to go to our guild house in the garden quarter, but I spotted them following me by then. So I headed for Cornelius here instead." The big swordsman smiled down at the boy and nodded for him to go on. "They took me just moments after I found him and brought me back to their hideout. They wanted to make sure I hadn't talked to any other thieves before they killed me."

None of the five liked the sound of anything Daren was saying. The older thief was scowling half way through the telling, and his nostrils flared with barely controlled anger.

"Who is to be killed?"

Daren furrowed his brow in a show of concern, and a profound sadness settled over him. "They plan to kill King Marik," he said, drawing a gasp of shock from the thieves.

And Cornelius looked as if he'd just been struck.

Part Four:
Only the Strong

Stephany walked among the trees of a darkened forest, the slender trail beneath her feet obscured by ivory mist. The excitement of adventure coursed through her veins, and her heart beat to the tune of a frantic drummer. It was cold and wet in the dense woodland, but the spirited girl pushed on with vigor, ignoring her discomfort with eyes wide in wonder and full of elation. A heavy medallion hung from her neck with a glow like a soft blue nimbus. Warmth emanated from the enchanted necklace, a magic that sought to protect from the cold and bolster confidence, though Stephany needed little encouraging for her quest.

There was a sword in her hand, a silvery short sword with a leaf-shaped blade and claw crosspiece. The pommel resembled a roaring black bear's head, and it fit firmly into her left hand as she wielded the sword like a two-handed weapon. Though Stephany had a small frame and stood just under seven span, she moved purposefully through the murky shadows of the forest, unafraid and determined. Her love, Sir Beviar Lightsword, was in dire need of rescue, and Stephany wasted no time in coming to his aid.

Unsure of just what sort of trouble Beviar had fallen into, Stephany was cautious in her approach. If it were not for the special bond of love the two shared, she would not have known of his capture at all. A sense of urgency had come upon her in her dreams the previous night, and a vision of a terrible creature standing over the crumpled form of her knight woke her with a start. She grabbed up her sword and headed for Darkling Wood without a second thought, intent on freeing Beviar from whatever fate he had gotten himself into.

Her sword began to glow.

Trouble was near, a threatening and evil presence that would do harm to her if given the chance. A part of the medallion, the sword was enchanted as well. It sought to protect through forewarning. Stephany could feel Beviar was close, too, but the link was weak. Beviar was wounded and close to death.

The dark and twisted trees began to thin in the distance, but the area was still encased in a bone-chilling mist. A growing wind moved through the underbrush, drawing her attention from what she knew lay ahead. No birds cried out in the lightless warren, nor did anything make noise but the crunching of leaves and snapping of twigs underfoot. Moving as quietly as she could, each step still sounded like the clap of distant thunder, echoing off the hollow boles and blackened brush around. Sight diminished just ahead, where a standing wall of icy fog settled over the trees like a second nightfall. Boiling clouds overhead bespoke of a brewing storm, dark masses of silver-lined shadow that blotted out the sky and moon.

Passing through the standing mist, Stephany recoiled from its touch. Her medallion flared blue as it strengthened her body's protection, but still the unnatural cold pervaded her skin. Unconsciously holding her breath, she took in a deep lungful of air when reaching the other side.

Stephany walked into the clearing where Beviar was held captive. He was sitting against a man-sized tree, his hands bound behind his back in thick iron chains. His head was slumped forward onto his chest, and his weapons were cast aside. With his suit of platemail stripped away, gashes could be seen on his chest and body where claws had torn away flesh. The rise and fall of his breathing was imperceptible from where Stephany stood, and she hurriedly moved to his side.

Lifting his head, she gently woke Beviar with a kiss. His eyes slowly opened then winced from the cold and pain. She hugged her dark-haired knight close and wiped the grimy tears of joy from his cheek.

"I'll have you out of these chains in no time," she said, drawing back for a swing with her sword.

"I don't think so," another voice hissed.

Stephany's sword blazed to life with brilliant white light, warning of the potent danger ignored until now. Before her stood a filthy monster, appearing to be human but having long lost its natural life. The lich moved closer, and Stephany jumped up to protect her love. With glowing sword to fore, she calmly held the lich at bay.

Undead is a term often used to describe the animated corpses and cursed spirits that live on after death, but of all those foul creations, nothing was more terrible than a lich. Powerful and deadly sorcerers in life, a lich was one who endeavored to extend life and attain immortality by forcing the spirit to remain attached to the body after death. The sentient life force would not be able to move on once the sorcerer's body could no longer sustain life. Great magic would fuel the decaying corpse for many centuries, never quite achieving eternal life but coming close enough. Inevitably, these undead spell casters grow an unimaginable hatred for the living and a desire to cause pain and suffering. Unable to be reborn into another body or possess one already alive, a lich inflicts its miserable existence on others and feeds on the frailty of its prey.

"This one is mine," the skeletal face intoned, its lipless jaws moving to the chilling voice. Its eyes were crimson fires that flared when it spoke, and its tattered black robes gathered about its body like a death shroud.

"I don't think so," Stephany said, mirroring its previous words with deadly assurance. "Go dig yourself up something else to play with. This one is mine."

Fingers of yellowed bone, sharpened to needlepoints, probed the air with mystic sigils. The tarnished gold circlet that was the lich's source of power glowed from under the folds of its hood, a vaporous red light that rose from the single ruby gem in the crown.

"I sense your love." The lich's voice could barely be heard over the whistling of frigid air. "I also sense your uncertainty. It is true you love this man, but he does not love you." Stephany glanced back at Beviar for an instant. "How could he possibly love you? One so frail and unattractive?"

"Don't... listen," Beviar gasped. "She's trying... to break... your strength. She... feeds... on weakness."

The knight cried out as something clutched his heart. Blood pounded in his head as his body fought to live. His voice was choked off by the pain, and the chill that spread through his body like an infectious shadow dropped him deep in slumber.

"Beviar!" Stephany's eyes went wide with shock and concern, and she would have knelt to help her dying love if the lich had not moved closer. "Stay back! I warn you now," she said and leveled her sword at the undead sorcerer. "Release him from whatever spell you've worked, or I'll destroy you where you stand."

The rasping laughter that ensued was like the scraping of brittle bones.

"It is not my power that kills him," the lich replied with glowing eyes. "It is your own doubts and fears that threaten his life. His spirit wanes, as does your faith in his love. Deep within, you know he loves another."

The spell was very subtle, a slight twitch of its wrist and spark of light from the gem in its crown. Visions of an unfaithful Beviar flooded Stephany's mind, overwhelming her senses with exaggerated doubts. The fleeting moments when one wonders of the possibility that the other is untrue, when trust is not implicit, were the seeds of such visions sown. Taking hold of those seeds and nurturing them with magic, the lich was able to make them grow. The imaginary scenes blossomed into tales of recreant lust, a treacherous heart taking pleasure in abusing Stephany's love. Sir Bevier Lightsword was nothing more than a lascivious man driven by physical desire. One woman suited his needs as well as any, and Stephany was no more than a trifling toy to be played with when time permitted.

As the visions continued, Stephany's guard wavered. Her sword lowered, her stance no longer secure. She looked down at the beaten man at her feet with tears of betrayal clouding her vision. Wondering how she could have loved someone so cruel, she would have struck the knight with her sword had the medallion not burned so strong. Her left hand closed over the metal, cleaving the spell like the edge of a blade and clearing her mind of the lies and magnified doubts.

"No!" Stephany roared. The broken spell struck the lich a physical blow, sending it backward and fighting for balance. "It's not true! You're twisting the truth," she accused with a firm sword arm once more.

As she advanced on the magical being, a crackling aura of power began to grow around the tiny blonde-haired girl. The storm overhead spat forth great bolts of lightning, blue fingers of light that stretched down towards the earth to the crash of rumbling thunder. A wave of rain fell over the forest, drenching the trees with a silvery sheen of winter cold and driving the warmth from the ground in clouds of swirling mist. The preternatural eruption of nature's force could not penetrate the protective globe that formed around the girl.

But the lich's bony fingers could.

The razor sharp points of its skeletal digits punctured the enchanted sphere, a collision of magics that threw both Stephany and the lich some ten feet away from each other. The undead sorcerer landed in a smoking heap, its wind-blown bones now blackened and cracked in places. Stephany rolled to her feet, but the momentum was enough to slam her into the hollow bole of a nearby tree. Wood exploded into a shower of splinters, and her blade flew from her grasp. In pain but still conscious, she turned over and scrambled for the handle of her short sword.

A sizzling ball of fiery black struck her hand and arm, scorching her skin and clothes. Snatching her hand away from the circle of fire that burned wet leaves and ashen soil, Stephany rolled away and dodged two more flaming missiles. Hiding behind a heavy tree stump, she grasped her medallion in her left hand, and the warmth of healing spread through her right. Flexing the fingers of her sword arm, she saw no sign of the magical burns.

"Surrender, and I will kill you quickly," the lich offered in emotionless tones. "I hope you will choose otherwise, but the option still stands."

Balls of spellfire struck each side of the trunk.

"Imagine leaving your love unprotected like that." Fire struck dangerously close to Beviar. "As if you no longer cared for the man."

The top of the tree Beviar was chained to burst apart as a bolt of crimson lightning struck it from where the lich stood. Magical fire, tinged red and black, broke out in the remaining wood and slowly began to trail downward. The knight would be burned alive in a matter of moments, and the rain did nothing to stop the flames.

"What do I do?" Stephany whispered to herself, tears streaming down her delicate face. "I have nothing to fight with, and Beviar's going to die!"

Remain strong.

Stephany heard the voice in her mind, but it was not her own. A man's voice had spoken to her somehow, a voice she had never heard before but knew was a friend she could trust.

"How?" she asked the voice. "What do I do?"

Trust.

"Trust who? That monster plans to kill me whether or not I trust it! There has to be something I can do to stop it. Can you help me or not?"

Trust yourself. Strength comes from believing.

The ground to either side erupted in scattered earth and flame as more spellfire was hurled by the lich. *Trust myself to do what?* Stephany thought, and her left hand began to burn. She was clutching the medallion so tight that she hardly noticed the terrible pain from its blaring surface. It was then she realized that the voice had come from within her necklace. One of the previous Guardians was trying to help her – at least the memories of one of them – and she was beginning to understand how. Strength, the virtue she inherited, was derived from faith in one's ability. It was her confidence and certainty that provided her great strength of spirit, that was the source of her power. If she believed in herself, no obstacle could stand in her way.

Stephany stood and faced the undead Sorcerer.

"You are a brave one," the lich intoned. Stephany began walking forward, as if she intended to face the spell caster and throttle it with her bare hands. "Or have I misinterpreted courage for stupidity?"

The lich drew back its hand, and a ball of whirling red light appeared in its skeletal palm. The miniature sun cast eerie shadows across the glade as it coruscated in shimmering hues of fiery crimson.

"Courage is my sister's specialty," Stephany replied. "Mine's strength."

With a howl of inhuman rage, the lich threw the scalding ball of magic. Stephany closed her eyes and whispered a prayer in the brief moment before her destruction. An instant before the spell struck, her silvery short sword appeared in the air before her, suspended of its own accord. The spellfire missile was cut in twain as it smote the enchanted sword's edge. Fire was thrown in a wide circle around the girl, but not a spark came to harm her soaking frame. Stephany reached out and grasped the handle of the floating sword and took in a sharp breath as magic flooded her body. The fire reaching ever towards the unconscious Beviar was suddenly put out, disappearing into the wood as quickly as it had appeared.

"Impossible!" the lich said incredulously. "Nothing could have withstood such raw power!"

Rearing its head back with arms thrown wide, the undead monster let loose a howl of frustrated fury. Its eyes became intense embers of sweltering fire, and its gaze set the earth and trees aflame. Mounds of watery earth were upended as jagged bolts of electricity were thrown from the skies without relent. The rising wind tore trees from the slick soil, their roots like blackened fingers desperately seeking a hold in the ground.

"Now you will know the full extent of my wrath!"

Stephany narrowed her eyes in determination, holding her sword in both hands. The tumultuous destruction of the land around her was little more than a distraction, and she extended her protection to Beviar. Nothing could harm him now, but the raging lich would have to be dealt with.

"Talk about having a bad temper."

Driven beyond rationality, the sorcerer forewent its use of magic to destroy the girl. It chose, instead, to rend the recalcitrant human to bits of unrecognizable pieces with its claws. The deathly chill that surrounded the undead spell caster sent shivers down the girl's spine, but it was not sufficient to paralyze her like it did so many others. That this puny female human should be so resistant to the lich's magic was a source of unending indignation. If she could not be affected by its spells, then physically killing her was the only option. It might even offer some pleasure and satisfaction to the spirit of the coldhearted corpse.

The lich failed to realize, however, that the magic Stephany was resistant to was the source of its very existence. A touch from her magical blade quickly reminded the undead sorcerer, and it cried out in pain and horror as one of its arms fell free. The decaying limb simply broke apart and crumbled to ashes that scattered in the wind. It never reached the young girl, and the lich recoiled from the burning sword to avoid losing its other arm.

Stephany came forward after the thing.

She lunged and swung in tight arcs, taking her time attacking the lich without giving it the chance to hit her. It would occasionally lash out with its remaining claw or cast a hasty spell, but Stephany was the quicker. With a swordswoman's proficiency, she chipped away the undead monster until it could scarcely move to defend itself.

"Killing me will only free my spirit from this wretched existence," the lich said with its one arm raised in defense, its back to a burning tree. "If you let me be, I would be forced to continue life in this broken body, in constant pain and misery."

The lich was appealing to a darker part of humanity, something it truly understood and expected others to possess simply because it did. Revenge and vengeance were intertwined with the desires of power and eternal life found in darker souls, and the lich could think of no better way to convince the girl to let it live but to make her think she would be condemning it to perpetual agony.

Stephany knew better, though. She knew that to let the lich go on with its unnatural life was to give it the chance to hurt again. How would she feel if she let the undead sorcerer live, and it killed countless people as a result? She could not live with that guilt upon her shoulders. She would rather live with the decision of destroying an evil and malicious creature than leave knowing it could one day harm another. The only way to ensure the thing would never again inflict pain and suffering was to finish it, end its existence with one swing of her sword.

"Kill me, and my soul shall know peace," the lich continued its plea, working its one hand in the motions of a spell. "Leave me here to slowly waste away, and I will endure endless days of torture." The spell, like all the others, was not having any effect.

"Then consider this a favor," Stephany said and cut away the outstretched arm.

"No! Wait!"

Stephany swung again, cutting through robes and bone to slice the lich in two. The torso fell apart, the lower half disintegrating into a whirlwind of smoky gray ash. Imploring the girl to leave it alone, the lich stubbornly clung to its fragmented life.

"You'll thank me later," Stephany said and placed a foot on its skull while prying off the golden crown with her sword.

The steel edge bit into the bone and ground underneath the dulled circlet. Screaming its final protestation, the lich's eyes flared and faded to empty black as the crown was torn from its skull. Wind carried away the final remnants of ash and dying cries as the magical coronet rolled away to clatter against a muddy stone. Stephany decidedly strode towards the muddied band of gold and struck the point of her sword into its single gem. Red tendrils of light played up and down the blade but quickly died as the crystal shattered into shards of coal-stained glass.

The storm began to calm as winds and rain steadily lessened in intensity. A groan could be heard above the dying breeze, and Stephany broke from her reverie to see Beviar raise his head and smile.

"Beviar!" she cried and ran to his side, dropping her sword to hug him. "I'm so glad you're alive!"

He tried to chuckle but only managed a weak cough. "I'd return the favor, but I'm all tied up right now."

Stephany kissed him again and took up her sword to break the chains. With one swift cut, her sword went through the iron links like a knife through cheese. She helped Beviar to his feet, holding him close for warmth while he worked the blood back into his arms. The sun was already rising over the forest, sending its heated rays down into the trees and earth. The chill was growing into a distant memory, but it was a good enough excuse to never let go her hold on him.

The two lovers started their way back through the lighted woodland, taking their time as they walked arm in arm to the song of emboldened birds. The rising day could not have been more perfect, the passing tale no more romantic nor the fading dream undone.

Waking to the warmth of a comfortable bed, her arms wrapped tightly about her pillow, Stephany sat up and nearly wept for joy. *So romantic,* she thought and reached for the book on her nightstand. Her fingers ran along the aged pages of vellum, opened the hard leather cover and cast about for where last she had read.

Perhaps one day I will be the hero who rescues her fallen knight. She smiled at the thought. *One thing is certain: This fair maiden can take care of herself. I'll only be rescued if it suits me.*

With a winsome grin, she began to read.

* * *

What in the world could he want with a hundred swords and shields? Stephen had been asking himself that question for the better part of early morning. After taking the oath with his brothers, he came back to the forge to finish King Marik's order for armor and swords for his knights and squires. The blades were nearly done and the platemail ready to be fitted for straps, but the recent order from one Lord Hubreys made Stephen feel pressed for time. Though he hadn't slept for well over a day, he wasn't the least bit tired. His uneasiness, however, was giving him a headache and beginning to affect his work.

The three boys, his apprentices, would not be in until the sun broke over the city walls, at about the fifth toll of morning. Laying the hand-worn hammer aside, Stephen leaned a hand against the stone wall while rubbing his temples with the other. For some reason, the hammer rang more loudly than it usually did, and the simple sounds of city life – drunken sailors singing their way to a bed, the crying of moonstruck cats and dogs, cursing tavern keepers and breaking pottery – all resounded through the night to be caught by his sensitive ears. The cool, stone wall was comforting, though, and offered a sense of calm. The throbbing pain in his head slowly drained away, and noises grew more distant.

Had the burly smith bothered to inspect the wall, he would have seen five slight indents marring its surface, roughly the shape of fingertips.

"It's no use," Stephen said to himself and sighed. "If it bothers me this much, then I should do something about it. I believe he said Dirkemshire and Laudley. I think I'll just pay Lord Hubreys a visit this morning" – he took up a sword intended for one of the king's new knights – "and show him how things are progressing."

The master smith smiled to himself and blew out all of his tensions in one deep breath. This Hubreys fellow wouldn't know that a sword couldn't be forged in such a short time, and the excuse would be enough for Stephen to see the man's estate for himself. If the facilities to house one hundred men-at-arms existed, then all would be well. Otherwise, full payment in advance would be called for and the king made aware of the transaction before the monthly record of sales.

With all that settled in his mind, Stephen was able to get back to his work. The aim of his hammer again struck true, and his muscled arm was secure and strong as ever.

"Your neighbors must love you," a voice called from the wooden double doors, and Jonathan stepped into the heat of the forge.

"Of course they do," Stephen said and winked between ringing blows. "How else would they know it's time to get up and work? You're up awfully early." He picked the cooling length of metal off the anvil with tongs and slipped it into a bed of fiery coals. "And you certainly didn't come to see me work."

"No," the older brother admitted, "I came to say goodbye. I heard your hammer from the other end of the square and assumed no one but you would be up so early... or should I say late?"

"Where you off to?" the smith asked and took up the ladle by the end of a large table. He took a long drink from a water barrel and offered one to the knight. Wiping water from his bristly beard, Stephen took the silence as a hint of discretion.

"I'm not sure when I'll be back," Jonathan replied, as much answer as he would give, "but I'll send word if it will be overlong. Give the others my love and take care of yourselves."

"You too. Try not to dent that armor of yours." Stephen gave a toothy grin. "Took me forever to make."

An hour later, just as a caravan was making its way through the south gate, the three young apprentices came walking into the smithy. Wiping the grit of sleep from their eyes and donning the heavy leather aprons of a blacksmith, the two said their "good morning" and went to work. After four years of hard training, Stephen was needed for little more than supervision. His presence, though stern, was always welcome among the three young smiths, for how else could they learn all he had to teach? Though either one of his apprentices could have gone off on their own to try their hand at forging a brand, Stephen was a good man and almost like a second father – despite his only being thirteen years their senior. Two of the boys came from very large families, and the generous coin earned in the forge bought more meals and clothes than could be counted. So when Stephen said he would be gone for most of the day on business, the clanging and clatter of working smiths only increased to make up for his absence.

The tower rang half past the fifth hour, striking once in the cold autumn morn, just as Stephen was walking out of the shop. Though the sun had barely begun to warm the cobbles beneath his feet, the smith could see the plaza come to life. Wagons were delivering goods from the newly arrived caravan. Crates of salted meat from Littlemore, spices and herbs from Hawthorne and Newstead, wild livestock from Gransmere and Lincoln and countless casks of wine and ale from all over the kingdoms. Though a score of hired guards stood watch over the unloading, the last of their commissioned task, Stephen could see a number of broken arrows in the sides of some of the trail-worn wagons where brigands must have tried to take the train. The mercenaries were dirty from long nights on the road and must have been ordered to hand in their swords to the caravan driver, since they stood without weapons in the morning light. No hired blade did not have a knife or dagger to fight with, but few had swords to call their own. The less experienced or poorly skilled mercenaries could be gotten cheap, and the weapons lent to them for the hired task had to be given back when done.

Stephen passed through the crowd of workers with the bundled sword he intended to show Lord Hubreys. He wouldn't put it past anyone to try and take the package from him, regardless of his immense size, so he kept an eye on the hired men who stood guard over the unloading wagons. Since Stephen normally slept at the forge, he had no need for a horse. With plans to visit the stables to rent a horse for the day, the master smith couldn't help but notice the unusual amount of men hanging about. Most taverns stayed open all through the night, and groups of filthy rogues came stumbling out as if they'd been trying to prove that fact. Small bands of men just stood on the walkways, as if waiting for something to happen.

All that occurred from the smith's point of view was the increased presence of city guardsmen who patrolled the streets of the plaza. The market quarter had a larger number of guards than many of the other city districts, to ensure safety for those who wished to buy or sell goods and services there, but the swordsmen in black livery were seen more often than not this one sunny morning.

Stephen stepped lightly through a puddle of water left over from the storm and greeted a pair of the watch pushing on through the milling crowd. He wondered how long before the captain of the guard ordered the men from the streets. They were a bundle of trouble waiting to happen, and Stephen only hoped no one would get seriously hurt.

"Marnin' master smith!" a stout little man said as Stephen entered the stables. "Come to shoe me harses, have ye?"

Donald McNarlin stood with arms akimbo, his cheeks beaming brighter than the red of his beard. Just over seven span, the stocky fellow in homespun tunic and dark leather leggings looked as if he worked his horses sunrise to fall. His smile was friendly, his green eyes full of humor, but his meaty hands were hardened by labor and bespoke a man who stood his ground. If not for the mane of coppery locks, he would have been thought a dwarf – albeit a tall one.

"Actually," the smith began and extended his forearm, "I came to rent a horse for the day." The two shook arms, and Stephen let the stable master walk him down an aisle of stalls. "I need to ride out to Dirkemshire for a quick visit. Nothing too important, so I'm not worried about speed."

Donald gave his friend a wary eye, and laughter danced behind that glance. He knew horses made the blacksmith uneasy but didn't want to offend the man.

"How 'bout this gelding?" The sleek black horse snorted and shook its charcoal mane. "He may seem to be feisty, but he's the best o' the lot."

Stephen reached his hand out to pet the horse and barely pulled it back before losing a finger. "Maybe something a little less spirited?" he asked and rubbed his hand. "It really is a short ride."

"I've this lass here," Donald said and pointed to a cinnamon colored mare with a white star on her nose. "She's a good ol' garl, this one she is." The master smith reluctantly scratched her behind the ear, and the mare neighed softly in response. At Stephen's nod, Donald said, "I'll have har ready ta go in no time at all."

Once the mare was saddled and adjusted to fit the smith's size, Stephen dropped a silver into Donald's palm and led Sugar out the stable's double-doors. Short for

Brown Sugar, the mare was all Stephen could ask for in a mount: obedient, intelligent and... gentle.

More and more seedy looking men were walking the cobbled streets when Stephen turned down Taverner's Way that he thought to unwrap the blade tied to his saddle. Riding horses was prohibited inside the city, so the smith felt unprotected with one hand unavailable to him. The leather purse at his belt felt heavier and his back somehow naked as he passed the covetous eyes of brazen sellswords. A group of six men, each armed only with knives at their belts, began to follow him down the crowded way. It would have been difficult to spot them, but Stephen sensed them close behind. What they wanted didn't really concern the muscular smith. He could handle himself better than most, and they would find that out the hard way if any should try him.

Just up the street, Stephen could see the Mercenary Guild. He noticed more than a handful of armed men standing outside the whitewashed building, some sharpening their tools of trade while others simply watched. There was a feeling of uneasiness all throughout the quarter, and it wasn't only Stephen. The men who came in from the caravan didn't look like they were getting ready to leave with it, and a mercenary without a hire is no better than a cutthroat. With the sixth bell of morning past, Stephen decided to visit a friend of the family.

The guards outside the guild house were kind enough to keep an eye on Sugar while Stephen went inside. Lyam Steelheart, a companion of Cornelius' for many a year, was glad to see the smith. The swarthy swordsman was graying at the sides, but he still retained the sharpness of wit and strength that sustained a hired sword.

"I know you didn't come here for a social call," Lyam said and offered a cup of mead. "I noticed you've got a horse outside. You need a hire?"

"No, I'm not going all that far."

Stephen declined the drink but took a seat before the desk that Steelheart worked behind. Two men stood guard at the front entrance and another door leading farther back into the building. Other than the posted hires on a wall, the room was fairly empty. The heady smell of tobacco wafted into the room as a guard outside lit up his pipe.

"I was just wondering," the smith began, "if any of those men wandering the streets belonged to the Mercenary Guild. I seemed to have picked up a few stragglers and wouldn't want to hurt any of your men."

Lyam frowned. "Our men don't 'straggle,' Stephen. We're very strict about who we allow into the guild, and I can vouch for every one of them. Unfortunately," the mercenary captain said with a troubled brow, "I have no idea who all those men are. You're not the first to visit me this bright and early morning."

"Oh? And here I thought I was doing you a favor."

"Your brother was here." At Stephen's puzzled expression, Lyam stood and paced the room. "Valoran. He's an extraordinary general, don't misunderstand, but I expected someone from the watch. Your brother isn't very pleasant in the morning, though, I'm sure you already know that."

Stephen gave a lopsided grin and folded his arms. "He is a bit grouchy at times."

"So are wild boars. I don't claim to understand what's going on around here, but I know that not one of those men is on my roster. Most came with the caravan, and they don't look as if they're leaving." He sat back down and exhaled a heavy breath. "There can't be more than a hundred of them, but our gladiator-general must think they're going to cause some kind of trouble the city guard can't handle alone."

"Did you say a hundred?" Stephen sat forward and listened with interest. Something tugged at the back of his mind, and a very bad feeling settled over his chest.

"About that. I wouldn't worry, though." Lyam shrugged and picked up his paperwork. "They don't have any weapons."

"What if they were suddenly to have swords and shields?"

Steelheart looked up, as if the smith knew something he didn't, then laughed and shook his head. "That's a lot of coin, my friend. Unlikely to happen. If it did..." He shrugged again and let the thought go unfinished.

All the more reason to check this out, Stephen thought. *The sooner the better.*

"Thanks, Lyam," The master smith said and stood. "I should get going. I've got some business to take care of up in Dirkemshire."

"That's a good few hours ride. Want me to take care of the bunch that's following you?" Lyam walked him to the door and spotted the raucous bunch across the street. "I'm sure it wouldn't take much to dissuade them."

"I am in a bit of a hurry." Stephen untied Sugar from the wooden post and walked her down the path. "Maybe just keep an eye on my back?"

"Consider it done," Lyam replied. He nodded to two men, and they fell in step behind the big smith. "Keep a fair distance, boys."

Stephen was barely out into the street when the six men crossed over and approached him. The lead brigand wore padded armor, muddied from the storm, and had a knife at his hip about the length of his forearm. The others were similarly garbed and took the first one's lead as he called out to the giant blacksmith.

"You there!" The man waved a hand with what must have passed as a smile for him. Clean teeth and bathing were not very high on his list of priorities. "Were you lookin' fer a hire?"

"You speaking to me, neighbor?"

Stephen switched the reins to his left hand, ready to strike out with his right should the man make a move. The two men from the Mercenary Guild took to watching the exchange from the edge of the street, keeping a comfortable distance so as not to draw attention to themselves. Lyam and two others came to join them.

"We saw ya back at the plaza," the grimy man explained. "Someone as big as you sorta stands out in a crowd, ya know? So me and my friends think to follow and ask if yer lookin' for a hire. Be worth the coin, from what I hear."

The master smith studied the six with a critical eye then snorted. "Thought you were trying to rob me." The others gave an evil laugh, but Stephen's was short-lived. "What is this hire? I may be interested."

"You'd have ta talk with Gh'ruk 'bout that one." The others nodded to each other with silent mumbling. "He's a huge one. Half-giant from the Northern Isles. He's doin' the recruitin', but we get a few extra coppers for helpin' ta find some good arms."

"I have a few things to take care of, but I may want to know more about this hire later on." Sugar's nostrils flared wide, and she shook her head as the foul odor of unbathed men caught her nose. "Easy, girl. We're going now."

"Be sure ya tell em Derek sentcha!"

The six shared another laugh as thought of a free round of drinks crossed their minds, and they headed back down the street. Stephen waved to Lyam that nothing was amiss, but the two men followed nonetheless. The smith only shrugged, glad for the added security, but he felt all would be well until reaching Hubreys' estate.

That's when things would start going badly.

* * *

Aside from hearing strange splashing noises in the sewers under the city streets, the ride to Dirkemshire was uneventful. Stephen was becoming more and more concerned about his ears. Hearing sounds from far off as if they were magnified a hundred times, his head was beginning to ache again. When he thought he heard the sound of voices in the waterways below the market quarter, the smith used the newly forged medallion at his neck to ease the pain. A wave of soothing coolness swept out from the metal disc, spreading all throughout his body like the feeling of comforting stone he experienced that morning.

The countless noises that barraged the smith faded back to a steady hum of normal activity, and Stephen was soon riding Sugar through the heavy doors of the south gate. The guards posted at the busy city entrance barely paid attention to this burly man as he left, but others coming in were not so fortunate. The watch was strict when it came to knowing what goes on in Noria. Those who seemed suspicious to the guardsmen could have their weapons confiscated, refused entry or, even worse, held for later questioning. All who passed through the mighty stone gate had their names and purposes recorded in a daily ledger, with no exceptions to the rule.

It was always easier to leave than it was to come back.

A variety of roads branched out from the city of Noria. The main highway led directly south, towards the kingdom of Nuorn Haet, but other lesser roads wound towards nearby hamlets and villages. Farther off were larger towns and communities, some run by appointed administrators and others by elected officials. The individual holdings of the various nobility stretched far and wide throughout the kingdom, some with estates by far larger than an entire quarter in the city. Minor lords held lands as well, some with barely enough staff to maintain a small keep, but each did his part contributing to the welfare of Noria.

The distant tolling of the tower was marking the eighth hour of morn when Stephen hailed a bondman. He kept Sugar away from the tempting stalks of wheat and led her to the edge of the road.

"Can I 'elp you, sirrah?" the serf asked with a thick accent. He wore a short brown cap but still had to squint to avoid the bright sun.

"I'm looking for Lord Hubreys," Stephen answered. "I was told I could find him in Dirkemshire."

"This is Dirkemshire, milord."

The serf seemed confused for a moment but only shrugged at the city man. He wiped calloused hands on the front of his tunic and pointed down the road Stephen had just come from.

"You'll want to go back the way you came, and 'ead west at the crossroad. 'Ubreys is at the center of Laudley, 'bout another two bells in." The serf held the horse's reins while Stephen got back in the saddle, then headed back to his master's field with little more than a wave.

"Two bells," the smith said as he clucked Sugar forward. "Most of the morning will be gone by the time I get there."

When Stephen finally did reach the lord's country home, he'd passed countless fields of tireless serfs, each working the soil to feed and clothe their family the only way an indentured servant could. Hubreys' holdings were very large, from what the smith could see, and the main estate was no exception.

A white stone arch stood over the road at the entrance, where two men stood vigilant guard. A wooden barn could be seen in the distance, closer to the fields, but near the main building were a considerable stables, a barracks large enough to house much more than a hundred men and another stone structure just half the size of the immense stronghold. Aside from its blocky appearance and archer's crenellations, the keep looked every bit the beautiful home of a noble. Ivy hung from heavy walls in a blanket of emerald leaves, highlighting the wild red and white roses blooming at its base. Ornately carved wooden shutters were open to let in the cool autumn winds, and a scene of frolicking sylphs done in marble was placed over the iron-barred door in front. Though out in the open hills, with only a small forest to the south for protection, thought of attack from any direction would have been unlikely. Guards could see for miles all around the estate, and the large hill the keep was built upon gave greater advantage to defend.

"Good morning, sir," one of the guards said to Stephen as he approached. Though very polite, the two men quickly stepped to block the smith's path. "Are you expected?"

"Not quite." Stephen smiled, but he felt alone in his jollity. "I was commissioned to forge some swords for your lord, and I've brought one to show how work is progressing." He hiked his thumb back at the bundle wrapped in his saddle.

"May I?" the guard asked.

By the polished helm and oiled chain the man wore, Stephen gathered the guard would know a quality sword if he saw one. The smith dismounted and handed the reins to the other guard before removing the sword from its cloth wrapping. The gasp of recognition was what Stephen was hoping for.

"I know this mark," the guard said. "Are you the master smith?" He showed the blade to his companion.

"I am," Stephen said proudly, his smile this time shared. "I hope it won't be any bother to see –"

"Oh, no! No bother at all!" The sword was handed back to the smith. "Bring his horse to the stables, Mik. I'll escort the master smith to the keep."

The two started walking up the path towards the stronghold.

"What's your name?" Stephen asked as they passed another pair of guards. The place seemed as busy as the city, though less noisome, as servants hurried to do their tasks and guards moved from post to post. The ring of sword on sword could be heard as soldiers practiced in the distance.

"Name's Jake, milord."

"Well, Jake, call me Stephen." The two grasped forearms in informal greeting, and the smith ran his gaze over the entire estate. "This all belongs to Lord Hubreys? It really is a magnificent place."

"Milord? This place is Hubreys, but it belongs to Lord Duncan. It's named after my lord's great-grandfather."

Stephen stopped. "Lord Duncan?" He softly swore and grumbled, "I knew something was amiss."

When the two arrived at the keep's entrance, two guards let them pass with a curt nod to Jake. Inside, a servant was told to fetch Lady Diane and inform her of a guest. Stephen was led through the fire-warmed hall to a large chamber where he could wait. Taking a seat on a silken couch, he laid the bundled sword on the bear rug at his feet and began to worry his lip. Jake was standing by, watching the master smith closely.

"Lord Duncan will be back from his ride shortly," the guard explained. "Can I have a drink brought to you? You suddenly don't look so well."

"I'm alright," the smith assured him. "I just have a bad feeling about something is all."

The Lady Diane came into the room, her waist-length blonde hair tied into a long braid with white ribbons matching her elegant dress. She gave a charming smile as Jake introduced Stephen.

"This is master smith Stephen," the guard said to his lady. "And this is Lady Diane Buchann. Master Stephen needs to speak with Lord Duncan."

"Thank you, Jake," Diane said and offered Stephen a seat again. Jake stood behind his Mistress as she sat opposite the smith. "Are you from the city, master smith?"

"Please, call me Stephen. There's not much formality in the life of a blacksmith, and I rather like it that way." The lady giggled at that but seemed happy to oblige the smith. "I am from the city, and I've come to clear up something of a dilemma. I don't suppose your daughter is to be wed in two months?"

"My daughter?" Diane looked somewhat surprised, a hint of laughter in her eyes. "I've heard my son called many things, but I don't think anyone has ever accused him of being a woman." Seeing Stephen's distress, she laid a hand over the big smith's and let out a girlish laugh. "I am sorry, Stephen. I was only jesting. You've just been misinformed is all. I'm sure my husband can clear up whatever it is you've been told."

"That's what I'm afraid of," he said with his head in his hands. The pain in his head was coming back.

"Unless Lord Duncan is planning to purchase a very large order of arms and armor, there may be a great deal of trouble in the city."

"I have no such plans," Duncan said from the doorway.

He still wore his riding pants and gloves, but the fair-haired lord with the heavy build of a soldier was not the oily man who visited Stephen the day before. Duncan Buchann, with his slate-gray eyes and confident air, seemed more a seasoned commander than the soft nobility the smith was used to seeing in Noria.

"Please excuse the way I'm dressed, but I wasn't expecting any guests." He sat in the chair beside his wife, regardless of her silent plea not to soil the fine cushion. "As far as my purchasing weapons, you can see that all of my men are already well-equipped."

"Can we speak in private?" Stephen asked.

Jake was sent back to his post, and Lady Diane left the two men to their discussion, closing the sliding doors behind her. Lord Duncan sat forward, his eyes intent upon the smith.

"I came here to verify that order of arms. You're obviously not the man who placed it, so that only leaves me one avenue left to explore."

"Why did you come here to verify it?" Duncan had a quick wit, and already he didn't like where this was leading.

"Someone claiming to be Lord Hubreys asked me to make him a hundred swords and shields, as well as ten rapiers. He claimed they were to better equip his men for his daughter's wedding. I wasn't quite sure at first, but I soon realized something was amiss. He didn't quite hold himself as a nobleman would. His arrogance was forced, as if he was playing the role of a nobleman. No offense."

"None taken," Duncan said with a dismissive wave of his hand. "Someone is abusing my family name. Do you know what this fellow looks like, where I could find him?"

If Duncan was angered, he hid it well. He stood and paced the cold stone floor, his mind running through a list of those who might want to harm him. Placing a false order, without intending to pay the honest – and well known – master smith, would have easily dishonored the Buchann name. *But why would they call themselves Lord Hubreys? None of my enemies are that ignorant, nor is this idiotic caper their style.*

Stephen picked up the sword and stood to leave. "I really don't think this was meant as a personal slander, Lord Duncan. There's an unusually large number of hireless mercenaries, armed and unarmed, in the city right now. I have a feeling these weapons were going to be used to equip those men."

"And then what? There are hundreds of soldiers and city guard inside those walls."

"I don't know," Stephen answered honestly. "But that's what I'm going to find out. Once I know what they're up to, I'll inform the king. I've already been offered a place in their ranks. Maybe I'll take them up on that offer."

The smith headed for the door when Duncan laid a hand on his arm.

"Let me come with you." The nobleman called a servant to fetch his sword. "Give me a moment to change into my armor, and I'll help you get to the bottom of this."

"I'm not sure you'd fit in with that crowd." Stephen was trying to be polite, but Duncan was being insistent. "They're sellswords without a hire. They'd just as soon kill you for some coins than answer your questions. You'd just be in the way."

"Nonsense. I inherited my title when my father died seven years ago, but before that I was a mercenary." The spirited lord gave the smith a slap on the shoulder. "They won't know what him 'em!"

Stephen rolled his eyes but waited for Duncan to change. With a sigh, he massaged his throbbing temples. He could hear the calls of men outside, directing servants and soldiers alike. Before clearing the pain with help from his medallion, the smith heard lord and lady exchange their loving goodbyes.

"Where are you off to now?" Diane called out, exasperation creeping into her voice. Her husband's reply was both apologetic and assuring.

"To settle a score, my dear."

* * *

It was Duncan's idea that the two of them put on the travel-worn clothes of a mercenary, rummaged from a chest buried under countless boxes in a storage room under the keep, and muck it up a bit in the dust. A borrowed helm, a pair of leather gauntlets and a black neckerchief topped off the makeshift disguise. Stephen smelt like he hadn't bathed in weeks, of oiled leather and something else he was glad he couldn't distinguish. He felt foul and dirty, but even his brothers would not have recognized him. Tying a band of black leather around their foreheads told anyone interested they were mercenaries looking for work.

The two were now swords for hire.

It was another hour before Stephen and Duncan were riding back towards the city, the roguish lord astride his charcoal stallion, Onyx. Although Sugar was not pleased with Stephen's new odor, the smith approved of the overall change. While it was true he didn't get out of the forge very often, his face was still known to many. That someone might find it odd Noria's finest blacksmith wanted to join a rugged group of merciless sellswords never crossed his mind. Not until Duncan pointed it out.

"You tend to stand out, friend," was all he said before making Stephen change his clothes. "This way you'll be someone who's supposed to look big and menacing!"

"I hope that was a compliment." Stephen looked dubious.

Duncan slammed his hands down on the smith's shoulders, sending up a thick cloud of choking dust. Fanning away the stuff with a smirk, he replied, "Of course it was."

The sixth bell of afternoon found the two at the stables. It took Donald a few moments to recognize the smith, but he eventually brightened a smile and let the two in. Stephen thanked the dwarfish man for the use of Sugar for the day, and Duncan paid five coppers to have his own horse stabled. They weren't sure where they were going or for how long, but very few mercenaries could afford their own horses – let alone the excellent swords each of the two wore at his waist. It would be better for them to appear as ordinary as possible and be able to go wherever the hire led them.

The majority of jobless mercenaries seemed to be gathered around Taverner's Road, a length in the market quarter where a man could bounce from one alehouse to another at least ten different times. The avenue ended in a heavy brick wall that separated the market quarter from the crown quarter, so city guards only patrolled its open end. Men were known to brawl when they drank, but they all had to come out sooner or later. As most taverns hire their own protection, the place was perfect for a mob of sellswords.

Duncan had the most experience with the rowdy lot who lived day to day, by the edge of their swords and strength in their arms, so he did most of the talking. Stephen told him about Derek and his recommendation, so all that was left for them to do was find this half-giant, Gh'ruk. In the crowd of men that choked the street, that should not have been so difficult. Unfortunately, they couldn't see him right away and needed to ask around, which brought attention to the smith.

"'E's a big one, in't 'e?" a drunken man laughed with an elbow to his three friends behind. "I reckon I can take 'im!"

Catching the swing in one hand, Stephen leaned into the filthy man's face and spoke with a chilling voice. "Care to rethink that move, neighbor?"

Struggling to remove his hand, the mercenary began to wish he'd stayed inside with his drink. Stephen drove him to his knees, putting enough pressure in his grip to draw a crowd around him. One of the others tried to take a swing at the smith, but Duncan was the quicker and didn't waste time in a show of his strength. He blocked and punched to the sternum, knuckles extended, before the drunk knew what hit him. The poor man crumpled to the dirt road.

"Awright, I give! I give!" The giant swordsman let go his hold and took a step back for measure. "Gods yaw strong! I thought you was goin' to break me bloody 'and!"

"He should have!" one said from the gathered crowd with a laugh.

"I would've!", "You couldn't if ya tried!" and "Bugger off, ya sot!" came rumbling back through the milling voices, but one man stepped forward to stand before Stephen. He was about the smith's size in height, with muscles hardened from years on the open road, but he was more sporting than sinister.

"Name's Ren," he said and took Stephen's arm in a friendly manner. "Care to go inside and 'ave a go?" He made a motion with his arm, but the meaning was lost to Stephen.

"He wants to arm wrestle," Duncan said in Stephen's ear and spoke aloud for his friend. "Make it for three silver, and you got yerself a bet!"

The crowd was quickly filtered through the door of a tavern where room was made and a table cleared. Mud-stained mercenaries filled the place from wall to wall, drinking to the bawdy songs of a minstrel and his lute. A barmaid here and there unwillingly danced with a patron, until hired muscle intervened, and an all-round festive atmosphere hung about the room. Coins of silver, bronze and copper changed hands as bets were made on the wrestlers. The odds were against Stephen some three to one.

"Ready?" Duncan asked the two when they were squared off from each other across the table. The two gave a nod, grim determination set into their eyes and jaws, and the nobleman slammed his hand down on the ale-soaked wood. "Go!"

Stephen held Ren's arm in place, watching as the sellsword strained against the sheer mass of the smith with all of his might. There was some technique in his pull, where he would have twisted his wrist to put his body weight behind a quick thrust to the table, but the huge mercenary in beaten leather armor was just too strong. He was immovable as a rock and nearly as stubborn. When he sensed Ren was close to giving up, his body pushed to its limit, Stephen brought his arm down with the force of a battering ram. The table broke into four separate pieces of distinguishable wood, while the rest flew apart in splinters great and small.

Most of the men groaned as they counted their losses, but Duncan was one of the few happy ones. His leather purse bulged forty-five new silver when another wanted to try his luck.

"He's strong," the next man challenged, "but can he balance all that muscle?" He then stood with his right leg and arm extended while crouching low. "Let's see, why don't we?"

The sturdy man stood and wiped away pieces of wood from his leggings. He helped Ren up and dusted the merc off with a roguish wink.

"Shire wrestling?" Stephen asked. "Alright, but I have to warn you –" the two took a firm grasp of the other's hand, laying their right feet flush against the other – "I'm rather good at this."

Patiently waiting for all bets to be made, and for Duncan's signal, the two men assessed each other. The purpose of shire wrestling was to pull or push your opponent off balance, forcing him to move the stationary foot without moving your own. Stephen was capable of pulling a horse off balance, but keeping his own might not have been as easy – that is, if he hadn't spent so much time playing the game with five brothers. His competitor was lean and stout as any man who lived by his arm, but something about the wiry rogue said he had better balance than most. The odds against Stephen were five to one, what little support the smith had no longer so sure.

When the signal was given, the match began, the two pulling and pushing in a test of the other's strength and balance. Stephen pulled to his front and back, never exerting too much force but enough to know his opponent's limits. The other kept his body loose and moved with the liquid grace of an acrobat, only resorting to brute strength to keep from being pulled on top of the massive swordsman.

Blood pumping with adrenalin, Stephen was enjoying the competition too much to realize his hearing was growing acute. The fast-paced thump he thought in his chest was the increased rate of his opponent's heart. His controlled breath and stretching muscle drowned out all other sound. Stephen's attention was so fixed on the match and his adversary that his keen hearing became focused as well. The crowd of cheering and cursing mercenaries was just a muted hum in the distance, and a strength grew up from the cool stone floor as the smith's leg became more firmly rooted.

Stephen wasn't quite sure what happened next, but the well of strength that flowed to him through the stone could only fill so much. The power needed a release, and the man opposite the smith was unfortunate enough to feel the result. He went flying over Stephen's head in a swift but graceful arc. Two or three others broke his fall, but all tumbled to the ground with a grunt and a thud. Stephen was able to channel the rest into his medallion, the rough leather armor hiding the faint blue glow, but a buzzing sensation remained, tingling up and down his arms.

The crowd wasn't even fazed by the show of strength but groaned aloud a wave of discontent. Money changed hands again, and Duncan, smiling wide, was forced to exchange his silver for gold to fit all the coin in his purse. It wasn't everyday a lord got to play a rogue and win ten shining gold. The barkeep would have to be paid at least one gold for the damage to his costly furniture, or so the three doormen warned, but Duncan was more than happy to make amends. After all, it wasn't really his coin.

Concerned for the slender man's health, Stephen rushed over to help the men up. He expected all four to turn on him with savage glares and brandished blades, but they accepted his apology and offer of a drink with a somewhat consoled resignation. The smith wasn't fooled into thinking this lot a goodhearted bunch who take life's misfortune in stride. He knew the only thing holding them back from his throat was a fear of his beefy arm and the sword at his waist, or perhaps they just hadn't had enough to drink as yet. In either case, Stephen was glad the whole thing was done, and he turned to find his now wealthy friend. Instead, he looked into the widest chest he'd ever seen. He wasn't truly stunned by the pure size of the man until he realized what he thought was a broad chest was actually a hefty waist.

The enormous man stood over thirteen span.

Stephen didn't even want to try and guess how much the mass before him weighed, but Duncan judged him some fifty stone. There was no doubt they had found Gh'ruk, or more troubling, the half-giant had found them. The question at that point in Stephen's mind was, *Now what?* Fortunately, he didn't have to wait long for an answer.

"You strong?" the giantling asked in a voice like rumbling stones, its incredulity masked by a profound lack of wit. Before Stephen could answer, the voice went on as the smith slowly craned his neck to see its full height. "We wrestle outside!"

"That didn't sound like a question," Stephen said in response, but the giant-man was already ducking low to move out the door.

Duncan came over and gave the smith a friendly slap. "Does this mean I have to bet on you again?" He ignored the icy stare and led Stephen out onto the dusty road. "I'd understand if you didn't want me to."

"Your confidence overwhelms me." Stephen eyed the ten foot tall giantling, his tree trunk legs, bulging mass of muscles and long wiry hair. A sloping forehead rested over deep-set eyes of black, and his skin was a leathery beige. "Then again," the master smith mumbled to himself, "maybe this isn't such a good idea."

Standing with legs wide and hands flexing in front, Gh'ruk was crouched and ready to fight. With mismatched strips of fur and cured hide, he looked a craggy mass of iron-corded sinew. The bets were made, as usual, and needless to say, the half-giant was favored ten to one. Stephen couldn't see if Duncan put up some coin in favor of the smith, but he could see the deep concern in his eyes.

This wasn't the sort of wrestling one normally walks away from unhurt, and taking on a giant, half-breed or no, was never an advisable task. Stephen could draw some comfort in that he didn't have a choice in the matter, but it was a small comfort to have. The best he could hope to do was survive. There really was no chance of him putting the giantkin over his head and slamming the monstrous body to the ground at his feet. He was pondering whether or not he should feign unconsciousness at the first given chance, but the half-giant grew restless and moved to attack.

A cloud of filmy dust went up as the two met with growling determination. Stephen had Gh'ruk around the waist and squeezed for all he was worth, trying to throw him off balance but only succeeding in turning him about and kicking up more dust. The giant-man raised his massive arms above his head like twin clubs and brought them down with enough force to drive Stephen to his knees. Another blow sent the wind from his stomach, and Stephen fought to get air in his lungs. All he got was a mouthful of dust.

Gh'ruk lifted Stephen from off the floor, chuckling as he wheezed and coughed, and brought him up overhead. With a deafening roar of inhuman delight, he threw Stephen down at his feet. The sickening thud and rising cloud of loose dirt brought pain even to those watching the fray, and Duncan was sorely pressed not to draw his sword. He hoped the smith was smart enough to stay down, provided he had the ability to stand, and wouldn't continue the match.

The giantling had other ideas, however, and knelt over the choking man. Gh'ruk pulled a chalky powder from under his belt and, hidden in the shroud of dust, threw it in Stephen's eyes. Stephen screamed as the grounded salt hit his face, making him blind as well as breathless. A punch to the ribs and more scuffling about only brought more dust in the air, but still the smith struggled to gain his feet.

Don't give up, he kept telling himself, or was it some other voice within him? *Strength is more than the physical; it's the inner spirit of a body that gives one strength, and that knowledge makes one stronger. Only the strong of heart and mind can defeat the strength of body... Only the strong.*

Forced back to one knee, Stephen no longer fought to stand. Laying a hand flat on the ground, he called for help instead. The earth was quick to respond and gave of itself what it could. Stephen's breathing cleared, though he was still surrounded by dust, and the cool touch of power that flowed into his body glowed a soft and tingling shade of blue. Gh'ruk continued to punch and kick the smith, but the stone-like fists never quite struck. They came within a fraction of an inch of touching but met some kind of resistance that felt very much the same as flesh. The giantling couldn't tell the difference and continued his savage beating with increasing voracity.

With a direct tap into the earth's reserve of power, Stephen intensified his already unnatural strength. Gripping both of the giantling's wrists and holding his arms wide, the smith slammed his head into the leathery wall of flesh that was Gh'ruk's stomach. The monstrous body doubled over, and Stephen raised it high above his head. The half-giant broke over the top of the encircling dust then disappeared swiftly into its confines. The crackling of joints as his back struck against Stephen's outstretched knee left all who watched in a wide-eyed amazement. Gh'ruk managed a pained groan, sat up and shook his head to clear the steady buzz that grew there. Tears streamed down Stephen's face, washing away the powdery mixture and clearing his vision as he spun around behind the sitting giant-man. Massive arms struggled against the smith's hold, fighting to get the human's own flimsy arms from off his neck, but the man had too good a hold. His arms were locked, and the small space in which Gh'ruk's neck strained for breath was too small to allow air to pass through.

The dust cleared to show Stephen standing over the still form of an unconscious giantling, his arms bunched tightly around his neck. Duncan rushed over to stand by his friend as the smith let Gh'ruk slump carefully to the ground. Others watched on in astonishment, but a handful yelped as they hurried to collect their winnings. By that time, however, six guardsmen thought it time to break up the boisterous crowd. Ten more were on their way when the horsemen arrived.

"You two," a city guard yelled to Stephen and Duncan, "pick up that thing and drag it inside! The rest of you, find a place to go!" He looked around menacingly, his gaze stern and level as he warned, "Or one will be found for you!"

A total of thirty watchmen made sure the street was clear, relaying the king's order that any suspicious men outside after dark would be brought in for questioning. If the mercenaries wanted to stay and drink, they would have to do it inside the tavern. The crowd grudgingly dispersed, none doubting the fine skill of King Marik's own, and grumbled low complaints as they all disappeared into various alehouses or away from Taverner's Road altogether. The watch had taken it upon themselves to leave a tenmen behind to patrol the dusty road, something that did little for business and less for those who preyed on drunkards.

Duncan took a hold of Gh'ruk's legs, while Stephen hefted the brunt of the load at the shoulders. Together they carried the motionless body into the Dragon's Maw, the tavern where all this had began. Four doormen cleared a space in the corner for the giantling soldier, and a barmaid brought the two a drink for their help. Gh'ruk and his men were a great source of income to Talmon, the barkeep, and staying on the good side of one who can best a half-giant was one of Talmon's mottos.

"How in the hell did you do that?" the tired lord asked from his chair across the smith.

The two sat at a table in front of Gh'ruk, and even though the giantling sat on the floor, he still met the two eye to eye. His massive body leaned against the wall, and his snoring was enough to drown out the rasping minstrel.

Stephen shrugged. "I've always been kind of strong." He saw the expression of disbelief but didn't think it safe to tell anyone of he and his brothers' new-found powers. "Ask me again, some time later. It's quite a story, and I'll be more than happy to explain it to you once this is all taken care of."

"Here ya go, Stark!" the barmaid said and slapped down a mug of foaming ale in front of the smith, slopping only a quarter of its contents onto the stained table. She nodded her head towards a group of men who tipped their mugs with respect.

The two had taken to calling themselves by different names, and Stark was what Duncan dubbed the master smith when pressed for some kind of title. Calling himself Garoth, the seasoned lord gained himself a reputation as Stark's swordmate – a term identifying a close bond between two soldiers that goes far beyond partnership – and a sharp gambler as well. His winnings totaled over seventy gold, and four of his coins were platinum.

"Well, we found Gh'ruk," Duncan remarked mildly and eyed the giantkin. "Supposedly he has his own outfit, and he's waiting for confirmation of a hire. He's looking for more men, because it's the biggest hire anyone's ever heard of. At least three hundred men are waiting for work, but –" he lowered his voice when he thought someone was listening – "only a hundred of those without their own swords will be given hire."

"Then we're on the right track. Now all we need is for this one to wake up. I hope he isn't as sore a loser as he is a cheater."

Stephen resisted the urge to kick the half-giant. His eyes and throat burned less, but the pain in his neck and back still throbbed. He was lucky to be alive, he knew, but that didn't make the pain go away. There was never much satisfaction in winning a fight, but that's why Stephen had won. He was defending himself, attacking out of necessity and not for the pleasure of victory. Gh'ruk may thrive on the pain of others, but the smith was a man who believed his strength was a gift meant to be cherished. He was special and proud of the fact, but it didn't give him the right to abuse that gift and use it to hurt those of a weaker frame.

Gh'ruk didn't see things that way.

Life to the half-giant, who was feared by man and scorned by giant, was nothing but a series of events that were the results of exploits or missed opportunities. Using everything at one's command is arguably just, and failure to employ every advantage one has over others is an insult to the gods. As a half-giant, he did not question why he had great strength. All that concerned the immense brute was how it would affect his life and how it could be used to further his needs and wants. His views might have seemed boorish and savage to a civilized human, but giants were a pragmatic and simple people who lived by the creeds: *What's best is best* and *The best shall lead*. Raised among giants for a time and then with humans, Gh'ruk chose an adapted lifestyle of his larger kin and surrounded himself with less than civilized men. It all made for a pleasant arrangement, and being bested by a human would do nothing to change that.

"Oh," Gh'ruk moaned and laid a hand on his head. "My head is killing me. Is that drink for me?"

Both Stephen and Duncan sat dumbstruck, mouths hanging agape as the smith nodded mutely. The giantling chuckled to himself and picked up the miniature mug with two beefy fingers the size of a normal man's forearm. He downed it in one gulp, then roared for a normal sized mug.

"Bring Gh'ruk drink!"

He gave a wicked grin to the two seated with him, his penetrating black eyes resting upon Stephen. In the fashion of giants, Gh'ruk's teeth were filed down to deadly points, and his smile sent chills down the backs of both men.

"It's a ruse?" Stephen asked with eyebrows raised.

Duncan laughed and paid for the massive drink brought over by a muscled doorman. A full silver for the foot-high wooden cup inlaid with the faces of dueling dragons and enough foaming ale to choke a man. The mug usually hung from a peg behind the bar, and only those who didn't know the half-giant saw it as a jest – or a dare.

"It's worth it," the lord said lightheartedly, "just to see him drink it."

Gh'ruk downed the ale in one tip of his head and wiped the foam from his lips on a furry forearm with deep satisfaction. He slammed the mug, which looked more like a bucket to Stephen, and called for another. Duncan told the giantling he was on his own from then on but enjoyed the display in any case.

"Comes in handy," Gh'ruk said with a nod to the smith, "to have people think you're stupid. Only my captains –" he indicated two men watching the three from across the room – "are truly aware that I'm literate. You're different," he said to Stephen over his second large mug.

"Is that good?" Stephen asked. Gh'ruk laughed and held out his arm to shake in the human fashion. "I almost thought you'd want to kill me."

"Not for losing a fair competition." Stephen didn't rise to the bait, and the giantkin nodded as if approving of something. "I like you. You're strong and disciplined, important traits in this business."

The half-giant surveyed the room, his irisless eyes watching each detail and marking them in his mind as he drank. Stephen was fairly shaken that someone so large should have such a shrewd demeanor. The half-giant was frightening for his mere size, but coupled with his obvious intelligence, he was an extremely dangerous person. The smith's appraisal was reflected in Duncan's eyes, and the two made a silent agreement to keep a wary eye on the giantling – always.

"We were told to look for ya," Duncan said and called for a drink of his own. "Derek an' his boys said you were lookin' for men for a pretty big hire. Said we'd be welcome 'cause we got our own blades."

"He said that, did he? Too bad he's rotting in a watch cell, along with his drunken friends. Well, if you're good enough, you'll be provided with the weapons and armor needed to finish the hire. You've already proven yourself," he said to Stephen then turned back to Duncan, "but you'll need to be tested just like all the rest. We're waiting for a Lord Saxmont to call on us. Once he does, we'll move into the poor quarter and set up a base where whoever is hired will be trained to work together. This isn't a hire for individuals to run amok. It will be a concerted effort."

Stephen nodded, absorbing all Gh'ruk offered. "My name's Stark," he said as late introduction, "and this is Garoth. He's my swordmate, so I hope you think him good enough."

"I won't be judging," Gh'ruk said and shrugged, "but if he's anything like you, he won't have a problem."

The three sat and spun tales of old hires, Duncan doing most of the talking, until the tower rang the first bell of night. They drank only a little bit more after the third round, nursing their last mugs as they listened or added to the conversation, and kept their wits about them. The call everyone had been waiting for came just after the toll, and Gh'ruk led the way out of the market. Dispersed into groups of threes and fours to avoid suspicion and notice of the watch, hundreds of mercenaries filtered through the streets from one section of the city to another.

They met outside a disheveled wooden building that should have been condemned. It stood some fifty feet high, had a few windows, of which all were broke, and looked no more than a fire hazard. The collection of heavy wood was stained and scarred an oily black, but for the poor quarter, it was a castle. Few in that section asked for better protection from the weather and a warm place to sleep. This building, at least, provided the former.

The mercenaries seeking hire were herded into the building, and all was done quickly and quietly. No one who saw them would speak about it, regardless of coin or threat – unless one or the other was to an extreme – and Lord Saxmont was counting on it. Stephen and Gh'ruk stood on the first floor as men were brought into blackened rooms to wait for approval. The smith caught only a glimpse of the man handing out the single silver piece to each man he found sufficient, but there was no doubt in Stephen's mind as to who the employer was.

Lord Saxmont and Lord Hubreys were one in the same.

* * *

Most of the mercenaries given a silver piece as retainer removed the strip of black leather – either from heads, arms or swords – that said they still looked for hire. Others, swordless men, were not so optimistic and left for the next meeting place knowing that only a hundred of them would be kept on for the continued silver a day. The lengthy interview given by Lord Saxmont was to ensure no unwanted guests were hired on to learn what the man had planned. A handful of city guard were caught and asked to leave, and even three others were suspected of belonging to an elite group of soldiers called The Unicorn, though no one knew how Saxmont could know it. Those who were approved were moved to what would be the mercenary base, a stone building deep in the heart of the bards quarter.

A den for assassins, thieves and any other murderous cutthroat in Noria could find comfort in the unpatrolled section of the city. No city guard would dare walk those streets unless in great force and then only when absolutely necessary. As far as the king was concerned, the vermin that grew there could do as it wished, provided it didn't leave. Patrols along the outskirt of the quarter were the largest in all of the city, greater even than those surrounding the castle.

It was to this lair of demons that Lord Saxmont would make his base, where those brave enough to follow him would fight for their hire. Only the best would stay on, living in the two-level structure while they continued to train together. The others would be forced to leave, defenseless stragglers no longer in a large number of men. Few would make it back to the poor quarter alive.

"You won't be needing that anymore," Gh'ruk told Stephen as quietly as a half-giant could and pointed a massive finger at the leather headband. "You'll still have to train with the others, of course, but that will be to both our advantage."

"Something I don't understand," Stephen said in a low voice and unrolled his sleeping pallet. Rows of bedrolls were lined up in the commons, numbering a hundred in this one room alone. There were six other large rooms where men made their beds, a hundred to a room, and Stephen made his with Gh'ruk on one side and Duncan the other. Because of the giantling's immense size, the three were in their own corner a short way from the others. "Why did you let us know that you're not what you appear to be? I thought only your captains knew."

Gh'ruk chuckled, drawing the attention of some who were trying to fall asleep. He glared at them for only a moment, and they found it wasn't so difficult to sleep after all. They turned over without a word.

"It was a mistake," the half-giant commander admitted and shrugged his massive shoulders. "There was no sense in continuing to pretend when you knew it to be otherwise. Besides," he added as he laid down over two sleeping mats, "I think you have good potential. I plan to make you one of my captains, and your wealthy friend here one of your lieutenants."

The lord from Laudley put a hand to the bulging purse of coins at his belt and eyed the men to his right.

"It's not all that much coin."

"If you say so," Gh'ruk replied with a smile, his eyes already closed. "But even I would be wary to keep gold around the likes of these men." He chuckled again, a rumbling that came from deep in his chest. "After all, isn't that what we all fight for?"

Duncan didn't answer but slept with one eye open.

* * *

Early the next morning, each common room was cleared as every man rolled up his pallet and laid it along one of the walls. Lord Saxmont left to take care of whatever business needed to be done to prepare for the elaborate hire. Gh'ruk and four other commanders were left in charge, one for each of the hundred men that would stay.

Some two hundred were to be weeded out that day.

Gh'ruk ordered those in his area in a simplistic, pragmatic system. The men would pair off randomly, fight and the losers would be marked with a red strip of cloth. There were no arguments as to who struck first blood. When a dispute did arise, the half-giant ordered the men to continue their fight until only one stood. Not only did it prevent further disputes, it proved which one was truly the better.

Divided into two groups of victors and defeated, those men would face off in another random pair. Again, the losers would be marked. The two groups of bested men would then pair off, the same for those who prevailed, and the results would leave eighteen men removed from competition. Of the remaining eighty-two men, half that many were marked with one strip and another sixteen with two.

What mercenaries were left then paired once more, with no particular order as to who faced who. Many of those marked twice rushed to face those of their own skill. Gh'ruk said nothing, watching impassively at all who fought. Some of the bouts lasted longer than others, and the anxious men waited either in anticipation or dread. Another eight were counted out, leaving thirty-four marked twice, twenty-six once and ten unscathed. Most of the men were tired and sweating from the exertion but stood firm and ready when the giantling called for yet one more match.

Without complaint, those with two strips engaged in melee. Others fought to satisfy their curiosity, to determine who among them was the better swordsmen. When all was done and told, seventeen more men were asked to leave, and three stood without marks.

Lord Duncan Buchann was one of them.

Six of the mercenaries, all of them swordless, were killed during the matches, but that small number couldn't possibly compare to the carnage some of the other commander's were responsible for. Hanrold Bladestain, a merciless fighter said to once have been an assassin, stood before his gathered men and let them make a choice.

"Forty of you must go," he informed them in a passionless voice, "and I don't give a damn how it gets done. Either leave or fight, but only sixty may stay." The coldhearted man gave a careless wave to a corner in the room. "Leave the dead over there."

Fifty-seven men were killed in the chaotic battle that ensued, a far cry from the original quota. The other three commanders were no better than Bladestain, and they exceeded their limit as well. Only Gh'ruk, with an extra loss of three men, seemed truly able to lead well and follow his orders – the orders given by Lord Saxmont. Unconcerned, another commander, Claeryn of DuMont, sent back for some of those who were turned away. In the end, there were five hundred skilled mercenaries worthy of hire.

And exactly one hundred were without swords.

* * *

The rest of the day was spent determining the abilities of those who remained, testing their sword arms for strengths and weaknesses. The hundred men under Gh'ruk were drilled by each of his four captains, who were also responsible for a quarter of the mercenaries. Stephen was made one of those in command and Duncan named his lieutenant. That left twenty-three swordsmen, not including Duncan, the smith had to control and lead to wherever Lord Saxmont was taking them.

The noble imposter had caught three more infiltrators, men from the city guard who had learned of the building's whereabouts and attempted to join their ranks by stealth. How Saxmont had ferreted out the soldiers was beyond any to explain – or question. Rumors quickly spread that the sinister lord was touched by magic, that he could see into a man's mind by looking into his eyes. It all made for an army that feared its employer, for no one in his right mind would embrace something as foul and unpredictable as magic.

Stephen had met the man, so he paid no mind to the whispered warnings that passed between men as they paired off to spar. He'd met the man and never sensed anything other than arrogance and an underlying sense of duplicity. Saxmont could have used magic to hide the fact he used it, but such hypothetical reasoning was a useless endeavor. Stephen thought it best to concentrate on the task ahead: learning what it was his swords would be used for and keeping distance between himself and Lord Saxmont. If any should find out who the smith really was, he had no doubt his life would be forfeit.

So he and Duncan had their men in twelve pairs, each fighting with a sword of his own. The weaponless mercenaries must have been kept in one of the other common rooms, since all of Gh'ruk's men bore arms. The Lord of Laudley was one of the greatest swordsmen the half-giant had ever seen, and he would've made captain had Stephen not been his better. One didn't become a master smith without knowing how to wield a sword.

"Disarm him," Stephen told one man in a pair. "Be careful not to hurt him, because he will disarm you next."

It was important that no one sustain an injury during these periods of practice and exercise, or so the half-giant said. The practical-minded giantling had no desire to lead wounded men, nor would he lead any who could not control his sword. Fighting with real blades would keep the men on their toes, and anything worse than minor cuts would result in one less man to lead.

"Yessir," the merc answered with a grin and moved in.

The two exchanged blows for a number of minutes, but neither looked as if he gained any advantage. Holding back to avoid being hit had long since been abandoned. These men were fighting with all they had, drawing upon years of swinging a sword on the road. The clanging of steel on steel as each took full swings was only a small fraction of the deafening noise that filled the room.

"Hold," the smith said and stepped between them. "I want you to do it like this. You just try to hold onto your sword," he told the other. "I'm going to come at you pretty fast, and the slap will be less than gentle."

The mercenary sneered, thinking his captain a condescending braggart who needed a lesson in manners. What he mistook for conceit was actually confidence, an attitude of assurance that held no secrets. Stephen said what he would do and did what he said. He swung his sword up into the other man's blade with such force that it was driven far above his body's guard zone. With sword still raised in the air, the burly smith twisted the edge and drove the flat of the blade across at his opponent's wrist. The sellsword yelped and dropped his sword, standing with wide eyes as he watched a thin line of blood well up at the base of his hand. If the captain had used the keen edge of his sword instead of the flat, there would be nothing but a stump where his smarting hand remained.

"How in the blazes...?"

"You're too confident," Stephen explained. The smith no longer seemed a patronizing imbecile but now spoke as a man with the skill and knowledge of an accomplished swordsman. "You're also too tense. Your muscles are all stiff, as if you intend to strike at any time. Loosen them up a bit, and only tense before you strike. It makes for more fluid movements and an easier switch from attack to defense. Keep your body turned to one side or the other but not full forward. It makes too big of a target if you show the breadth of your chest..."

The lessons went on until the third toll of night, when Lord Saxmont returned from his business in other sections of the city. He gathered all of the commanders, captains and lieutenants. It would be up to them to explain to the rest of the men what was said as preliminary plans were presented. Saxmont laid out a map of Noria and began a strategic recounting of a reconnaissance and attack, designs for movement in and out of the city to avoid being seen by the watch and the intention of leaving early on the morrow. The others accepted their orders with confident nods and steady hands, but Stephen was no longer so sure of himself and his plan to find out the truth.

For the army was marching on the village of Parsons.

* * *

"You're damn good with that sword of yours," Duncan told the smith as they marched through the eastern edge of Lightwood. "Maybe a little too good."

Stephen was careful where he put his feet, the supposed trail overgrown with brush and littered with protruding stones. The men under his command moved ten paces behind, keeping a good distance while their captain and lieutenant discussed plans for their attack.

With the sun just barely lighting the tops of the trees, the whole of Saxmont's army had been marching for three hours. One quarter-command at a time, the five hundred men were led out of the city through secret passageways in the sewers. The smell of refuse lingered in their clothes, but no city guard had seen them leave.

"What do you mean, too good?" Stephen shifted the heavy leather strap on his shoulder that kept his long sword within easy reach over his back. "I'm not much better than you are."

Duncan gave a mirthless laugh. "If I were that good, I would still be a mercenary. Not to swell your head, but you're damn near the best swordsman I've seen, next to the gladiators in the arena." Stephen smiled at that but didn't say anything. "No, what I meant was your instruction. This small army will be hard enough to defeat without you teaching them how to fight. Hell, you even showed me a few things I never knew about!"

"I'm hardly teaching the entire army. I've gained Gh'ruk's trust, and showing these mercenaries a few tricks won't hurt us." He took a drink from his waterskin and offered some of the tasteless stuff to his friend. "I've thought this over now, and I admit I would rather have been just an ordinary soldier in this army. It would be easier to see what's going on and leave if necessary, but things didn't turn out that way. The half-giant trusts us, and I think we can use that to our advantage to save some lives and put an end to Saxmont's plans."

Duncan handed him back the skin, shrugging noncommittally. "If you say so. I think we should find a way out of this right now and warn someone at the castle. Let Marik in on this before it gets out of hand."

"If either one of us tries to leave, we'll be cut down before we make it past the city walls. Saxmont has more men working for him than those in this army. We can't do anything that will make Gh'ruk suspicious of us, or else we'll never know what their true intentions are."

"Isn't that obvious? They plan to oust Marik from the throne and replace him with this Saxmont fellow." Duncan looked over his shoulder, seeing the men trudge silently along, and lowered his voice even more. "Not that it matters. Regardless of what they plan, raising an army for it can't be good. If we put an end to the army now –"

"Saxmont will raise another one," Stephen said, completing the thought for him. He sighed and shook his head. "Don't you see? We really have no choice. In order to stop this from happening again, we have to see it through to the end and find out who's behind it all. We'll do what we can to help the people of Parsons, but we must not give ourselves away."

"I won't kill anyone," Duncan said with a fierce cast to his brow. "I'll kill every man in this quarter-command before taking an innocent life."

"I'm not asking you to," Stephen replied evenly, "but we might have to look the other way. I may have a plan to keep us from fighting altogether, but we cannot stop the other commands from what they're told to do. We'll be cut to shreds with Noria no safer for it."

Duncan nodded, his eyes fixed ahead. "I hope your plan works."

Stephen slowed as he caught sight of the rolling grasslands beyond the forest edge, where Gh'ruk and the other three quarters were to meet. The five commands were gathering at different areas surrounding the large village, some coming through the very fields in which the commoners worked while others would bear down from the tall grass to the north. Gh'ruk's command came from the trees, just south of another. Gathering together to converge on Parsons, the five hundred men would act as a vice that crushed from all angles, and the village had no hope but mercy.

Stephen prayed for a miracle.

*   *   *

"Lord Saxmont has given me special orders," Gh'ruk was telling his four captains as they gathered in a tight circle away from the men. "The smith who was to be making weapons for us has disappeared, so we're to gather what stray swords we can from this small raid. There's fifteen of the king's soldiers here, as well as a small militia of thirty or so farmers, so hold on to any weapons you find. I'm putting you in charge of taking and holding their supply building, Stark. Don't let anyone caught without a weapon find one, if you catch my meaning."

Stephen nodded once and turned away as the giantling bellowed over the milling crowd of soldiers. Gh'ruk roared at them to move and only grunted in satisfaction when he saw the four quarters break off into the tall grass south of the village.

Why me? Stephen asked himself. *If Gh'ruk is so impressed with my fighting skills, then why put me in charge of guarding something? Either he sees the supplies as having precedent, or Saxmont knows who I am.* He knew the smith wasn't making swords for him. *This could all be an elaborate trap.*

No, he said to himself as he saw the giantling's approving nod of luck. The nod seemed to say, "Let the others take care of the fighting. You handle what's important." *If I was found out, Saxmont wouldn't waste his time with an elaborate scheme. He'd either kill me or have me making swords for him somewhere.*

Stephen was wondering what sort of signal the others would give when they moved into position, but all he heard were the war cries of a hundred men. Gh'ruk's command was then off and running, trampling through the golden blades of tall grass and into the cold clearings of fields. Stephen led his quarter towards the far building to the east of the village, away from the thatch-roofed cottages and makeshift structures where woman and children already screamed. Everywhere he looked, bloodthirsty mercenaries ran like madmen in search of prey, heedless of the shouted orders from lieutenant and captain alike. They met little resistance and quickly cut down those that appeared.

The twenty-three men who trailed after Stephen and Duncan looked on with lustful eyes, their hands itching as each drew forth his sword. The bear-like smith was first to reach the sturdy building where food and weapons were stored. Gh'ruk's report of the village was thorough, so much so that Stephen wondered if one of the villagers hadn't betrayed his own for a few tarnished coppers and a blanket.

"Surround this building!" he ordered his men, anxious to keep them from the fray. "Hold, you! If I see one of you break from this position, I'll personally cut your throat! Garoth, go keep watch on the other side."

And then Stephen was inside the building, barring the door and kicking over a crate. The sounds of battle had ended, all of Parson's guard and men cut down in the wash of steel. Passing over the village like a monstrous tide, their swords flashing out like froth, Saxmont's army had completely devastated all traces of resistance, but still his men fought on. The helpless cries of women and children, the tearing of clothes and breaking of pottery were all magnified twenty fold. Fire began as a slight crackling in the distance and grew to an immense wave of noise that deafened the smith.

"No!" Stephen cried and fell to his knees, the amplified sounds overwhelming his senses and threatening to burst his ears apart. He tugged at the medallion beneath his shirt, but he had no magic to store or take. With a desperate sob of pain, Stephen drove his hands towards the earthen floor.

And his fingers sunk in to the palm.

Without knowing why or questioning how, he pushed further into the cool surface of earth, drawing into himself the essence of nature and strength of the element. He was into the packed soil clear up to his elbows when the clamor faded away. Quiet again reigned in his mind and with it a sense of reason. He could still hear the cries of mistreated women and frightened children, but he was now the one in control of its volume.

The door was then kicked in, the heavy bar snapped as if no more than a thin branch, and its metal frame twisted in protest. Stephen was showered in finger-length splinters as sunlight flooded the musty room through the valley between Gh'ruk's powerful legs.

"I heard screaming," the giantling said with suspicion clear in his brow. "What the devil's goin' on in here?"

Stephen was leaning back on his knees, his arms covered in dirt and the floor before him torn asunder. The smith had a startled look to his face that soon turned to nervous confusion. His mind was buzzing with explanations, but his mouth found no reason to work. Just as he was settled on fighting his way out, pitting himself against the half-giant again, Gh'ruk knelt on one broad knee to overshadow the smith and give him a hearty slap on the shoulder.

"Good work, man!" Gh'ruk reached down into the ground where the glint of dark metal was hid. He reached two meaty hands into the hole and pulled a wooden box out with little effort and a spray of soil. "How did you know the weapons would be buried? You've a sharp eye, that's for sure."

Rising to his feet with a dull ache in his stomach, Stephen felt bile rise in his throat as three more crates of weapons were raised. Gh'ruk gave orders to carry away the blades, and Stephen was cheered by all. Hoping to somehow thwart an army in the midst of Noria, the smith had managed to arm them in a fraction of the original time...

A traitor ironically made hero.

* * *

Lord Saxmont stood before his men on one of the crates brought back from Parsons. He was smiling wickedly, his dark eyes intent as they touched each and every one of his men and pierced them to the soul. With all five hundred standing in the common room, they were tightly pressed together, and Stephen found it easy to avoid the sinister noble's gaze. Saxmont looked taller somehow, stronger than he remembered the dark lord, and his gloating made Stephen feel terrible.

Sneaking back into the city was no trouble at all. There was no one left in the village to ride for help, and no one saw the army come out of the sewers in the bards quarter – at least, no one who would tell of it. All had gone according to plan, though it worked out better than Saxmont had anticipated. The extra swords, obviously a weapons cache for Marik's soldiers, was a valuable find. Attributing the success to the army as a whole, Saxmont never asked to see the man who had found the crates. He simply praised his commanders and called the men together.

"It is time we begin our plans," the lord said softly. All fell instantly quiet, straining harder to hear the light-spoken voice that did more than reach their ears. "You have proven yourselves in the field this day, and I congratulate you on your success."

The men took their cue to applaud, a single cheer that died away to unnatural silence. Stephen could feel something working beneath the voice, a magic that soothed and subverted. Taking Duncan by the arm, the smith shielded them both from the sound without really knowing how.

Something's not right, Stephen said with his eyes, afraid to even whisper. Duncan gave a nod, narrowed his eyes and looked about him, alert.

"Our battle today has made us stronger, brought us closer," Saxmont went on as his eyes trailed from man to man, "forged an army made of iron. No longer are you hired swords but a brotherhood of men that rely on each other. No more are you individual blades but a single sword to be reckoned with. From one man to the next, you are as strong as your brother, a part of a whole, a sign of perfection, a ring of unbreakable spirit – an Iron Ring."

A nod from Saxmont sent each commander to his captains, a large leather bag in hand. Gh'ruk gave Stephen a sack from within and orders to distribute one to each man in his quarter, with one for himself as well. On the half-giant's massive finger was a simple band of iron, where before there was none, and Stephen then saw the connection. An iron ring, one for each man, was what would bind these rogues together. The feel of belonging and sense of kinship, coupled with Saxmont's subtle magic, would bind the group of heartless sellswords into a formidable army with spirit and purpose. Stephen forced himself to put on the ring, though the feel of it turned his stomach.

"By this ring," Saxmont continued and raised his hand, where a gray iron ring like all the others was set upon his third finger, "we shall know each other and stand for each other. Never will one of us stand alone, for if one faces a fight, we all face a fight. The simple rule we will live by is one of respect, respect for the Ring and respect for each other. Do nothing to harm another Ring or suffer the wrath of us all."

Lord Saxmont went on with his speech, molding the minds of each man before him as a sculptor works a stone: chip away the unwanted and free the desire. The plain iron ring each swordsman wore soon became more than its metal or shape. Imbued with the magic in Saxmont's voice, the rings were a constant reminder of purpose and brotherhood, an unspoken code of discipline and loyalty – to each other and to their lord. Not one mercenary wore his black leather strip once given the ring, for their hire now was permanent. They belonged.

Only Stephen and Duncan were free from the charm, and the Lord of Laudley thought he'd had more than an earful. Saxmont and his Iron Ring were a threat to Marik's reign, an army within the city that did not have Noria's best interest at heart. Not a word had passed between the two, but both knew the other was resolved. They would get free of the building and warn the king. Better to take the teeth of this growing beast before it finds use for its bite. The people of Parsons would be avenged and their bodies put to final rest.

Just when the smith thought he'd heard enough, Saxmont went on to tell of his plan, confident his spell had a firm grip on each man. He talked of times past when Jaril was king, of a time when mercenaries could make a good hire without paying a tithe to a useless guild. He spoke of what could be, a band of men pledged to a cause, backed by the gold and power of a king. He promised the Iron Ring a future of fortune as the king's private guard in Noria. In exchange for their loyalty, they would be given protection, amnesty from the rightful king...

A pardon from Jaril II.

* * *

It didn't take long for Stephen and Duncan to realize they were prisoners, that no one was being allowed to leave. Lord Saxmont trusted in his magic but would take no chances now that the men knew of the plan to dethrone King Marik. Stephen noticed a change in the men as well, in Gh'ruk specifically. The big half-giant was still personable with the smith, but he was nearly fanatical with things concerning the Iron Ring.

"Why do you need to leave?" the giantling asked heatedly when Stephen asked permission to go into the plaza. "What do you need that can't be brought to you?"

"Freedom," Stephen muttered, but Gh'ruk didn't hear.

Rather than push the point, Stephen just shrugged and went back to the shadows at the rear of the commons. He and Duncan would have to find some other way to get out of the building. Food and ale, even women, were brought in to keep the men happy, and Saxmont would have it no other way. It was in their best interest, he would say, that they all remain out of sight until word from their ally arrived. Stephen had no idea who that ally might be, but he knew someone had to be funding this small army. With nothing to do but eat, drink, train or sleep, the burly smith felt helpless and trapped.

"A lot of people died today, and there's nothing I can do about it." Stephen fumed, his fingers unconsciously sinking into the earthen floor, drawing from its coolness to calm his rage. "Everything I love in life is threatened by this maniac Saxmont, and there's nothing we can do but wait for him to attack our king!"

"Keep your head," Duncan warned. "You do us no good by angering yourself. There must be another way out of here. I mean, after all, we're on the first floor of the – what the...?"

Stephen looked at the lord, his new friend covered in dust from marching most of the day, stinking from the sewers, and his anger subsided at the sight of astonishment. He followed the gaze down towards his right hand, where it was buried in solid earth up to the wrist and glowing faintly blue.

"How are you doing that?" Duncan asked and turned about, blocking the light with his back. They were practically invisible in the heavy shadows, but any source of light would draw attention to them. "Are you a magician?"

"Hardly," the smith replied, surprised at himself as well. He pulled out his hand and saw it was covered in rich soil. "I wonder," he began as he turned towards the wall. "If I can put my hands through packed dirt, why not through stone?"

He pressed his palms against the wall, the cool night seeping through and filling his body with a sense of serenity. The magic came to him then, without any thought or hesitation, and he became one with the stone. There was some resistance, hardly noticeable, but more than the ease with which he drove through the soil. With a gentle push, his arms were through the wall, and a biting breeze washed over his hands.

Freedom never felt so good... or cold.

Duncan looked nervously over his shoulder, afraid that others would see the thin wisp of blue light that surrounded the smith's arms. "Can you take me with you?" His look was grave. "If you can, good. If not, I'll stay and try to cover for you as long as possible."

There was no doubt in Stephen's mind that he could do it, but that was not what he had planned. They would need to come back, to keep watch over this army and its ambitious leader. He needed only to send warning to Valoran or directly to the king, but Duncan would have to stay behind. If it was discovered that Stephen was gone, the Lord of Laudley would have to find some excuse for the smith.

Stephen shook his head, his brows furrowed in thought. "If they come looking for me, say you're not sure where I am. Say I was asleep beside you one minute and gone the next. I'll figure something out if I need to." He forced a grin before passing his leg through the thickset stone. "This way, at least one of us can keep an eye on that madman."

"If it becomes necessary, I know what to do." Duncan gripped his sword for emphasis, but Stephen didn't question him. "Saxmont will fall long before Marik does."

"Just be careful, Duncan. Don't give yourself away unless you have no other choice."

"Don't worry about me," the roguish lord said. "I know when and when not to act. I lived by my sword once before, remember? Some things you never forget."

"Be strong," the smith said and disappeared through the wall.

It was dark in the bards quarter, the crumbling buildings kept in shadow without the street lamps common to other quarters. The Lampers Guild refused to enter this part of the city and with good reason. If the thieves and cutthroats wanted light in the streets, they were more than welcome to carry a lantern – or so went the argument of that organization. Only the moon was brave enough to shine its light over Darkling Street or Webwork Way, avenues notorious for the darker dealings in Noria, and that silvery light was pale and wan as the tower struck third bell.

Stephen was a confident swordsman, a master with the blade compared to those in the streets who lived by club and crossbow. There was rarely a standoff of swords in bards quarter, as those who made a home in the unpaved streets preferred silence as well as dark. It was more common to find a body riddled with slender bolts, coated with foul-smelling poison, than it was to see – or hear – a sword fight. All Stephen could do was stay to the shadows and make his way to a safer section of the city. No one would stop him so long as he carried his sword out in the open, but an arrow might find its way to his back if he didn't watch his step.

Bards quarter was as duplicitous as its name, its residents a facade of beggars and urchins alike. Its inhabitants preyed on each other in a battle of cunning, strength and alertness. Nothing more than a series of traps and plots, the place was avoided like the plague by all who could. Those who could not fell in step with the game or died as a result.

Though the smith had never lived in bards, he knew better than to trust his eyes. A drunkard sleeping off his cheap wine in a doorway was just as likely a seasoned thug baiting his prey. Child beggars gauged the worth of their targets, allowing thieves to carry out the job. Hired killers sought their mark, moving swiftly and deadly like the shadow of death, for no thing or one could not be bought in bards. The beggars were the eyes and ears, the information gatherers, and the thieves were the arms and fingers, reaching the purses of all in Noria. The Bards Guild was the heart of the quarter, the black market merchants and dealers of all from arms to zinc, people and poison included. Cross any one of them and deal with retribution, the Brotherhood of Assassins.

So Stephen was more than wary of any he saw and went out of his way to avoid coming close to the roving groups of swaying drunks that pulled themselves from tavern to tavern. It took some convincing to get the guards at the gate to let him through, since the great wooden doors were barred at the fourth toll of night when the city wall was closed off to all outside. There were other ways through the gates, established long ago by the differing guilds, but Stephen had no idea where those would be.

He explained who he was and that he had urgent news for his brother, General Valoran. The guards let him through and were told to expect him back within two hours. Once he passed his message on, he would need to get back into bards. The watchman would have offered use of his horse, if he had one, but Stephen was forced to run the whole way, his lungs burning as he reached the cobbled streets of the merchant quarter. It was minutes later when he entered the plaza and smiled at the sight of a fire burning at his forge.

"Hide those out in the back," he told the boys and pointed to the blades they'd been working on. "You've been busy. Good. I know I look a mess, smell even worse, but I need two of you to take a message to the castle and one to my brother Valoran.

"This is extremely important," he was saying as he searched a desk drawer in the back for ink and paper. He found a black feathered quill and sheet of old parchment, and he began penning a letter with hands more accustomed to hammer and anvil. There were splotches of ink on his hands and the paper, his writing smeared but legible.

"Take this." He gave the first letter to Jarod. "Bring this to the castle and give it to no one but King Marik himself or his Advisor, Magarius. Show them my seal. Good lad," he said and slapped him the shoulder, sending the boy off through the doors and into the quiet streets.

"I'll take this one to the general," Warren offered. "He's at the arena, right?"

Stephen nodded and sealed the letter with red wax and a stamp. "He usually sleeps there, but check the barracks first. He stays there if he's up late with the watch." Warren took the missive and ran with the tireless energy of youth. "Lock up, Kaern. We've done for the night, and I need to get back someplace in a hurry."

Kaern closed and barred the windows and was putting away a handful of tools when Stephen had a second thought. He pulled out another sheet of parchment and scribbled a third note, not bothering to seal this one in wax but folding it in haste.

"Slip this under master baker Tristan's door at the bakery." Kaern was hanging up his leather smock as Stephen stuffed the paper in the apprentice's hand. "I don't have any time to explain, but keep these doors closed until you hear from me again. No more swords are to go out, and no one is to be let in here unless on orders from the king. Understand? Good lad. Now off you go. I'll be back as soon as I can."

Stephen bolted the double doors to the forge after his apprentice was gone and slipped out a back way that he locked with a key. The boys would be able to keep working the forge, but he didn't want any of Saxmont's men getting their hands on his finer blades. It was bad enough they were armed with excess iron from Marik's stores. High-grade steel from Stephen's forge would only make them stronger, and that's something the smith would not allow.

Stephen was off and running again, taking only enough time for a quick drink of tepid water before striking out into the night. The cobbles were harsh through his thin leather boots, but he ignored the throbbing pain and focused on making good time. He was through the gate and into the bards quarter with little more than an hour gone by, and he hoped Duncan was not forced to make some excuse for him. He hadn't thought much about it before, but if he stumbled back through the wall – provided he could find the building again – and others were looking for him, he would have a difficult time explaining himself. What would he say? He decided to worry about that later and instead sought out the dull gray stone and featureless walls of the Iron Ring stronghold.

It took him nearly half an hour and three trips down the same avenue before finding the darkened alleyway. He ran his hands over the gritty stone, his fingertips melting into the cool surface and dragging along as he scanned for the area of warmth. Just a few feet away, he found the spot, the section of wall he had passed through. He knew it to be dark, with Duncan nearby, and it was the most logical place to go back through. With little effort, he pushed through the wall and heard the heated exchange just a short distance away.

"And you didn't see him leave?" Gh'ruk was asking as Stephen stepped through, his right leg still outside. "How can you sleep next to a man and not wake up when he moves?" The giantling was furious, but the mercenary turned lord was not daunted.

"I didn't think it was important," Duncan replied, and Stephen could see him shrug. "Sometimes he goes off to meditate, so I'm just used to him leaving when he wants."

"Meditate!" Gh'ruk waved his arms in the air, his voice a booming growl that forsook all pretense of hiding his intelligence. It was more evidence that something was amiss, and the monstrous giantling seemed on the verge of crushing poor Duncan. "I suggest you find him before –"

"Here I am," Stephen said and walked out of the shadows. He waved off the half-giant's questions and accusations with brows raised high and hands spread wide. "I just slipped off into the shadows to collect my thoughts. The trance is sometimes so deep that I don't hear anything around me."

Gh'ruk snorted and glared. "Must be useful when enemies are about."

"I didn't realize there were any," the smith countered and managed an innocent look. "If I knew it would be this much trouble, I would have just went to sleep."

"Good idea," the giantling agreed, his sloping forehead shaking in earnest. "Try to stay in sight. I trust you," he added as an afterthought, "but others might not. Don't give them reason not to."

Stephen nodded and turned away, Duncan at his heel. The two were on their mats and under a thin blanket as the lanterns were dimmed to dark. Duncan leaned over and whispered to Stephen, his voice a harsh rasp that reflected his fading fear.

"I bet he trusts you. Something's wrong, Stephen. Gh'ruk used to trust you more than this. He's changed – or changing, just like the others. It's those damn rings," he said and showed his unadorned hand. "I've taken to wearing gloves, and so far no one's minded."

"I don't think that's a chance we should take," Stephen said softly. "I'm pretty sure I can protect us from whatever it does, but I can't keep them from killing us if they think we're traitors. Keep your ring on, and I'll do the rest."

"But what do we do now?" the Lord of Laudley asked as he slipped the iron band back onto his finger. "I thought all we wanted to do was find out what they planned and take it from there."

"Exactly. Now we know what they in have mind, and staying here will give us the chance to thwart them somehow. If we can stop Saxmont by acting at just the right moment, then staying becomes a priority." Stephen propped himself up on one elbow and looked at the ring on his hand. "The Iron Ring. It sounds ridiculous that someone should be able to build an army within the city's walls, but this Saxmont could very well succeed."

"You mean Jarill II." Duncan spat the name. "That spineless whelp will drive us all to ruin, and it won't take him very long. I guess there's nothing we can do now but wait, so we might as well get some sleep. At least we'll be on our toes in the morning."

"Yeah, at least," Stephen said and turned over to sleep.

Part Five:
True Magic

Magus watched from the confines of his lair, its enchanted walls drawing life from the land to strengthen him further. The earth outside the Shadow Keep was a blackness that spread out from the ebony structure, seeping through rock and tree alike. What unfortunate animals could not or did not flee that impending murk were frozen in their tracks, left helpless as their life force was drained away. All that would remain was a colorless, gray husk. As all of the energy was drained for miles around, it coursed through the veins of black marble walls, pulsing a fiery crimson and flaring with life. The constant thrum, like the beat of a heart, raced along the halls and corridors, reaching the shade in undulating waves of power that danced across his shadowy frame. A violet flame emanated from the lord, a flickering nimbus of magic and power.

"We have arrived at the gate, master Magus." The crackling voice came from the mirror, drawing the shade's attention from the pulse that filled his being. "We await your pleasure."

Magus stepped closer to the silver surface, seeing the crowd of his children gathered round a ring of mushroom. There were goblins, orcs, stalkers and worse, but what delighted the shade were his darker minions. Hundreds of trolls had answered his call, nearly all there were in Faeron. The lumbering giants were rare and their strength unmatched among the dark folk, but it was their regenerative powers that would serve Magus best. With the aid of his magic, he would help the race grow, swelling their ranks beyond that of the countless – and equally dispensable – goblins.

"You know my desire," Magus told the troll.

A heavy mist surrounded the scene, but he could see the troll's eyes narrow and a wicked smile cross its swampy-green face. The long, pointed nose dipped as it nodded off to the side, and a dance of sorts began to take place. Five orcs cried out at the sky, their shrill voices like a call to war. The blackened earth was torn and twisted where their boots stomped down in successive strides, and a wind blew through the leafless trees that ringed the small group. A wailing shriek rose up from the ranks of thousands that were gathered, keening to the drums that answered the dance and set the winding pace.

Three full circles were made by the orc shamans when they threw their arms wide and danced with heads low. They looked possessed as they lost themselves to the drums, spinning and kicking up black soil in a wild frenzy of tireless steps. Fully enveloped in the spell of summoning, controlled by the orcs' erratic pounding, the snorting pig-men circled another six times before falling dead upon the enchanted ring. The ashen mushrooms blazed to life, searing the eyes of those who didn't know to look away. A hush fell over the assembled mass as the black flaked away from the ring and was replaced by a shimmering azure light.

It was then that gate appeared, a solid door of nighttime black and winking stars that appeared to lead to oblivion. A curt order from Khajoz, the troll who had spoken to Magus, and others of his giant-like brethren were taking up the fallen orcs and casting them into the gate. The bodies disappeared in a flash of blue, with no sign of their passing left behind. When all five were cast to the void, Khajoz turned as if looking to his master.

"The gate is still protected, my lord." A thin stream of spittle ran down the troll's chin as he showed two rows of rotted teeth. "The Fairy King still has some strength left."

Magus regarded his general through the mirror, the crimson orbs of his eyes flashing for an instant. "Then we must tear away what little remains. You will march your army through the gate until the protection fails."

"Yes, master."

Khajoz turned quickly away and ordered the goblins be marched through first. There were thousands of the orange-skinned savages, and the gate could only kill so many before its wards were stripped away. Magus watched impassively as goblin after goblin stepped unwittingly through the enchanted portal to an almost certain doom. There was a slight chance of one slipping past the protective shell, but that was a slim chance indeed. Magus expected a few thousand of the goblins to silently meet their deaths, but that mattered little. With each dispersing life force, the Fairy King would be weakened trying to maintain the gate. When that happened, the horde of waiting monsters would cross the void into the lands of men, and Magus would lead the throng.

The lands of men. There was a time when Magus belonged to those lands, when his was the darker side of a man, the shadow of his thoughts. A bitter anger rose up in the shade, and he slashed out at the mirror, drawing anguished cries of pain from the voices within as his shadowy fingers trailed across its surface. Again and again he struck at the mirror, never enough to destroy it but just enough to cause it pain and misery unknown to mortals. Wishing each swipe of his chilling hand could grasp the throat of the withered sage, the Shadow King sat back in his ebony throne and remembered the day of his tormented birth.

The day when Magarius had cast him out...

* * *

After the six brothers had taken the Oath of Virtue, they filed out of the Advisor's chambers and went about their respective tasks. Magarius continued to go over his notes and set aside the various components he would need to present his findings to the Wizards Guild. He had a fresh tome pulled from the shelves, its soft leather binding gilded in a spidery framework of precious gold, and was seating himself before a table when the pains came stabbing through his stomach. Magarius fought for air and struggled to gain control of himself, but something was very wrong.

Flicker was nowhere to be found, probably off in the woods with Humphrey. There was no mirth at the thought when pain tightened every muscle in the sage's body, his stomach burning with the intensity of magical fire. Magarius cried out in a hoarse whisper, his throat seized by the spasms of tingling flame, and he gasped when he saw himself in the mirror against the wall.

His salmon robes were thrown open, as if blown wide by a brisk wind, and its ends were burned to tattered shreds of ashen sun. The snowy mane of hair and beard were bristling with energy, and a halo of golden fire spread out from and down his body. The flames spread like wildfire, glowing and dancing with the sparkle of magic and the heat of true fire. He could see his features contorted in pain, the withered flesh and mapwork of wrinkles creased deeper in agonizing spasms. Magarius dropped to his knees, pulling the empty libram with him, and fell forward with his twisted hands wrapped tightly around the black leather book.

There was a flash and a flaring of white light as the fire swarmed around the tome, leaping from the mage's hands in a flickering dance that engulfed the book but did not burn the pages. Like fairy fire, a heatless and magical glow, the flames were drawn from his body and into the spine of the tome. The gold melted and ran like quicksilver but left no trace of its passing. Where there was once an intricate work of spiraling gold there was left behind a bare surface of hardened black leather, a single word adorning its center: Wisdom.

It was then the words began to form on the pages.

Magarius was utterly drained and fell into a deep sleep without any prompting from a fluttering fairy dragon. When he woke to the unforgiving light of the morning sun, all was as it had been, but a full page had been written in the now enchanted book, chronicling the history of the Guardians. The magician watched on in fascination as the words were scribed without ink or quill – or a hand to scrawl them! There was only one explanation for what had happened just hours ago.

Essence had transformed the mage, and now he too bore the magic of a Guardian. The single word on the libram's front left little doubt as to his virtue, but still Magarius couldn't figure out at what time he had been effected. He was sure he'd been careful not to ingest the powder, and there was barely enough of the mixture in Tristan's cookies to spark that taste of essence. He felt no different, but there was an absolute certainty that he had gone through the transformation he had witnessed the Esralds endure at the tavern.

"Perhaps there is enough in the cookies..." he began to muse but then waved his hand in dismissal. He picked himself off the floor and took a seat at his table. With the Chronicle set aside for later inspection, Magarius gathered his notes and read through them again with a careful eye. "It must be touch. I touched the powder, and it entered my body through the skin. That's it! Ingestion only makes the process work faster, and touching the concentrated powder is enough to bring about the transformation."

The revelation was an exciting one. Magarius was working furiously on his notes, comparing his new findings to old theories and vice versa, when he felt that a change had truly come over him. There was no longer the weariness that accompanies old age, and Magarius was one who had lived far longer than the normal span of a human life. A sense of clarity had settled over him, as if a thin layer of mist that was blocking his view had been removed, and life seemed suddenly bright and clear. It wasn't so much a learning of new and different things but an understanding of what was already known, the switch from knowledge to wisdom. He understood, both what essence was and what effects it could have, and with his comprehension came a terrible fear.

All of his being had been enhanced.

Not only was his magic improved, his power heightened by essence, but so were his desires, his fear and hate. All of his human emotions would be expanded to their very limits, pushed beyond the balanced norm of human behavior. While the same would hold true for the Esrald brothers, the extent to which it would affect them could not come close to that of the mage who had lived for over three centuries. As one who delved in the Art, Magarius had more opportunity to acquire different desires, touch upon powers that few had ever seen in their lifetimes, than the other Guardians, and his great many years had made him the most prominent of that few. Decades of learned discipline and control had kept such lust for power and wealth in check, making them nearly nonexistent. His hatred of evil, of wasteful things or prejudice against magic, had been previously stayed by rational thought, as opposed to the usual fear of consequence that played a large role in such things. But perhaps it was the growing fears, the intense concern of losing control, that caused Magarius to act. He was afraid there was little time left before he was consumed by that which he had struggled so long to control, and driven by his anxiety, he sundered his spirit to allay those fears.

Drawing upon the potent magic at his disposal, Magarius summoned up all the excess emotions he felt would be harmful to his clear thinking. All the sexual desires, lusts for power and wealth, the fears and hatred were pulled from his life force like the tearing off of a limb. The darkness that swirled out of his frame, embodying that which he no longer wanted as a part of him, formed an eddy of murk upon the stone floor, too weak to even stand on its own. Taking up the foul-smelling shadow, struggling to keep a hold of its oily surface, Magarius imprisoned the remnants in a shard of obsidian.

Its wailing cries echoed through his mind, even as he cast the obsidian into the sea and watched it fall beneath the dark waters. Magarius sighed in relief when the task was done, certain that his sanity was secured, but there would forever be an emptiness inside of him. There was no telling that the discarded shadow would have taken over his thoughts or changed who he was, but the fear of what could have happened was so strong that doubt could not be considered an excuse for inaction. Like many men who have held great power, Magarius did what he had to do – or at least what he thought was right.

Magus, the shadow remnant, did not agree.

Its magic began to grow, trapped within the confines of the cursed obsidian. If the old sage hadn't been such a bleeding heart, with an intolerable sense of romance, he would have chosen a more practical prison. A diamond would have held the shadow forever, with no chance of its magic reaching beyond its bonds. The volcanic glass, however, proved no such deterrent. Magus reached out his slithering thoughts and guided his fall through the inky depths to a source of magic and power.

The shard was only so much black in a sea of darkness, but its smooth surface reflected light when it drifted in through the cave that housed the magical column. Giving off warmth and a soft yellow glow, the Pillar of Life was exposed in this cavern, a trace of its girth sprouting up from the floor and disappearing into the rocks some fifty feet above. Magus lay the obsidian down beside the massive column and began to draw power from its carved surface of elven kings and heroes at battle. The thin stream of light encircled the prison and seeped through the glassy exterior to feed the shadow within.

"Yes!" Magus cried, his sibilant voice echoing through the waters in ecstasy. "I feel strength again!"

Somewhere deep beneath the tons of rock, where the pillar was fully exposed, its life-giving force wavered for a moment, and its magical light burned less brightly. This little concerned Magus, who absorbed his fill and glowed a black luminescence within his shell. All that mattered to him was freedom... and revenge.

With the power taken from the enchanted stone, Magus called out to one of his own, summoning his distant kin to break the bonds that held him. There was movement in the water an instant later, and a wave of absolute chill settled over the cavern, spreading out like the settling of a dark winter night. The shadows cast by the glow of the column seemed to grow, stretching further out than they had before, but then Magus felt the fiery eyes upon him.

With one swipe of its mutable claw, the shadow dragon destroyed the shard, shattering the obsidian into a thousand fragments of powerless glass. The manlike form that stepped from the pieces was in more ways than one the shadow of a man. With a wicked smile of his violet mouth, Magus bowed and disappeared through the darkness in the cavern. He was a part of the foolish Advisor, possessing the skill and intellect of a master magician, and he planned to use all of his power to exact revenge upon his other half.

The shadow dragon turned its narrowed eyes back towards the murk it sprang from, but the yellow orbs were drawn back to the strange column of glowing stone. Moving closer, it could feel the pulse of magic flow through the thing, as if the column rested upon one of the ley lines that stretched out from that wretched elven

Tree of Life. Without a second thought of hesitation, the monstrous shadow settled its bulk around the pillar and slowly began to feed.

And deep beneath the Sea of Tears, chaos reigned again.

* * *

Tristan and Cornelius hadn't bothered to go to sleep. Neither one of them was tired, and there was a great deal of work to be done. As agreed earlier by Magarius and the six brothers, some cookies would be distributed among the people at no cost. Only a few batches, mind, else the master baker would no longer be able to afford such generosity. A small amount of the Recipe, the mixture that was the key to unlocking essence magic, would be added to the cookie dough. There wouldn't be enough to initiate a transformation, a drawing out and intensifying of the inner being, but the pinch of enchantment would suffice in causing some reaction.

Those who ate the cookies saw a glimpse into their own hearts, touching upon what few in life could ever know about themselves. Many would not have liked that fading glimmer of absolute truth. A soul laid bare, for even an instant, could be an unsettling experience for anyone. One of the fundamental teachings of all ages, without exception, was that mankind is not perfect. Another was the hope of one day attaining perfection.

It was this lasting promise that was left behind once the magic faded. Some saw the bright light of smiles and the fire of love, while others saw the shadow of guilt or the blinding shroud of greed – but all remembered the hope. It was in their power to better themselves, to take away the empty darkness and replace it with happiness. The moment of pleasure or bitterness on the tongue was soon forgotten, leaving only a flash of memory, but the aftertaste of certitude was not so easily washed away.

The hope was what kept them coming back for more.

Early morning came and went, Cornelius leaving as the sun stretched over the castle walls and cast the plaza in long shadows. With the intention of keeping his promise to Daren, the ex-mercenary had two swords thrown over his shoulder, one much shorter than the other, and a basketful of fresh cookies. Steam escaped through the thin, blue cloth covering the basket, further proof beyond Cornelius' aching muscles that it truly was cold that morn.

"Just be sure those are given out," Tristan told his brother as he was stepping out the door. "I've noticed your tunic is fitting a bit snug these days. Maybe you should concentrate more on baking and less on eating."

"Bah!" Cornelius ran a calloused hand over his stomach, perhaps rounder than his earlier days but still hard as a shield. "How else am I supposed to know if what I'm making is any good?"

"The customers come back for more." Tristan smiled but turned to put a tray in the oven before his younger brother could see. "You can have just one," Tristan called over his shoulder.

Cornelius laughed aloud, already walking away from the shop and shaking his head. There was no doubt that if the veteran sellsword wanted to eat every last cookie, he would. Of course he wouldn't, but that didn't mean he would give Tristan the satisfaction of saying so.

"Hullo? Master Tristan?" A lean man with a bald pate and a ring of thin brown wisps poked his head through the open window. "Open for business?" the man asked, a smile slipping across his face as the smell of baked chocolate blew past his nose.

"Master Ferran," Tristan said with a bow of his head. "Yes, please come in. What better way to thank you for your considerate help last evening than to give you a batch of cookies?"

"Oh, it was nothing!"

Ferran waved his hand in polite dismissal. Wearing the soft white shirt of a courtesan, the rich silken vest of a merchant and the long brown leggings of a commoner, the man had enough coin to care for his comfort and little for appearance. Not paying for merchandise was beyond his business-like mind, though he'd received some things seemingly for free before. Ferran simply preferred to exchange coin for goods, and favors for favors.

"Consider it a favor then," Tristan said, not knowing he had seen the truth of Ferran's response without having heard it. "You could take some for yourself and give the rest to your family or customers as a bonus for doing business with you. Your patrons can only eat so much bread, master Ferran."

"So I've been noticing," Ferran replied with an appreciative nod of approval. "It won't be too long before someone else comes along to take away some of your business. Of course, they'd never be able to match your quality –" Ferran shut his eyes tight to savor the taste of a cookie – "and I will remain forever faithful to your service."

"You're very kind," Tristan said and chuckled inwardly. He began putting new trays into the oven, the long silver spoon slapping against his leg as it swung from his leather belt. "I hope you won't think me rude, but I really do have a lot to get done before the day's end."

"Not at all." Ferran wiped the corners of his mouth and licked the chocolate off his fingers. "If you don't mind some friendly advice, contact a stonemason. I think you're going to need another oven." Tristan nodded, his expression thoughtful. "Any chance you might show me how to make these things?"

Master baker Tristan, the Guardian of Truth and Keeper of the Magic, thought for the briefest of moments, then plainly said, "No."

"I didn't think so."

Ferran took his cookies and left with a sigh.

* * *

Magarius was tired from his ordeal. He could only pray that what he had done had been the right thing. But with such power at his disposal, he reasoned, how could he take the chance of just waiting? There was plenty of time to think on the matter when time allowed. It was more important that the Wizards Guild be warned of the coming renegades, the guildless magi who will seek out the explosion of magic caused by the brothers' transformations.

And the smaller one this morning, Magarius added silently.

The white marble towers and far-reaching spires of the guild's keep was surrounded by spiraling gates of gold and silver, woven into the intricate sigils of strength and protection. No less splendorous than Marik's castle, the home of all wizards in Noria rested in the center of the garden quarter, in the midst of tall trees and wild flowers. Ordered paths of colored stone led through the maze of rainbow gardens, leading a winding route both to and from the gate entrance.

With the melodic cry of playful jays, the swooping pass of bold sparrows and the wordless lay of songbirds, the gardens were a beautiful and peaceful place to walk.

Magarius was too caught up in his thoughts to appreciate the magnificence and didn't even notice the manlike darkness that stepped from the shadows of an elm and hurriedly disappeared behind a nearby birch.

No matter that Magarius had not stood before the gathered members of the guild's council in over eighty-seven years or that he hadn't worn the official robes of a guildmaster in just as long. He was more concerned about how to address the problem at hand. If he could not convince the guild to prepare for the renegades, it might be too late when they finally did arrive. Countless lives would have been needlessly lost before the council could intervene.

"Master... Magarius?" a young man in robes asked at the closed gates. The Advisor would have kept walking, no doubt through the gate and all its wards, if the stammering youth hadn't said something. "It is you, isn't it? I recognize you from your picture in the main hall."

Magarius nodded, once. Whether or not he was agreeing that, yes, he was Magarius or yes, please get on with it, the young man couldn't say. Without waiting to find out which it was, he opened the gate to let the old mage in. The first thing all apprentices learned was that wizards were a testy lot, always self-absorbed and rarely did they have patience for anything but the Art.

He was certain the guildmaster, Magarius, would be no exception.

The Advisor continued up the gravel walk, the rose-colored stones blending with the myriad flora and perfectly-shaped rows of hedges. The gardens outside of the gates were beautiful, serene; inside the courtyard, where meticulous wizards dwelled, the flowers were no longer wild, the trees and few small animals were painstakingly proportioned and all was – for lack of a better word – organized. No less pretty to look at, the handiwork of the spell weaving guild seemed an attempt to shape nature, presuming to guide her to a more perfect state.

Magarius shook his head at the vanity, walking under a series of hand-carved stone and wooden arches. Set some ten feet apart from each other, the arcs were inscribed with ancient symbols and pictures that depicted the birth of magic to the world and its passage through the four Ages of time – Darkness, Stone, Fire and Iron.

The winding patch led into the main keep, a solid structure of ivory stone, marble buttresses, crystal parapets and mottled crenellations the hue of open sky. All of which made for a breathtaking sight to behold but not one of very much use where the practicalities of war were concerned. If not for the runes etched into every inch of the place, enhancing its strength tenfold, it might have toppled over years ago. The towers built into its four corners gave some support, with their stout girth and heavy stone, but the far-reaching spires of icy white – capped with azure tiles resembling a deep blue sky – would not have been enough without the spidery scrawl of magic stretching across their surface in a webwork of complicated design.

The portcullis was open, and the two swordsmen standing guard snapped to attention when Magarius passed, offering a stiff salute of fist to bowed forehead. Magarius shook his head, that the once mighty hunters, who bore enchanted weapons and armor to seek out renegade magi and bring them to guild justice, were reduced to standing guard over a place no one could invade – or even had the desire to. It was visible proof that the council's power had become but a shadow of its former self, that magic was no longer respected as it should have been.

"Too long have you been hidden away behind enchanted walls," he whispered to himself as he passed from the darkened corridor to a brightly lit room.

Magarius stepped into the main hall, a large room with exits leading in many directions. The source of light came from an unnatural sun hanging from the ceiling on golden chains – a comic attempt to harness nature that only Magarius seemed to find amusing. Tapestries taller than three men, head to foot, cascaded down in flowing cloth to flash against the bright white of the walls. A thin red carpet wove a trail throughout the place, following along the walls so that one could walk the path and admire the paintings of each of master mage or the carved busts of ancient wizards. A memorial to awe apprentices, teach them to appreciate the magnificence of their mentors and give them something to strive for, all in one gesture of ordered creation.

Salmon robes sweeping across the warmed stone floor, Magarius marched through and past the hall, heading for the opposite end with a single-minded determination. There were no doors in the corridor he walked, and the rows of lighted torches led to a pair of wooden double doors. No guards stood outside those doors. None were needed. The black metal bands that both reinforced the wood and secured the doors would not open for any but members of the council.

"Open!" Magarius commanded, before reaching the doors and walked past them without a second thought as they slid soundlessly closed behind him.

There was a meeting in progress, as he knew there would be. The room was built in a semicircle, with a hundred cushion-backed chairs facing towards a marble podium. An oak table rested behind the stand, called the High Table because the seven who sat behind it resided over the conferences. From doors to table, the room sloped downward in a manner that placed those who spoke at the center of attention.

Saunin, acting guildmaster, sat at the table's center, the silver circlet of authority resting securely on his shaved pate. Three others, old in body and spirit but powerful nonetheless, sat to either side of the blue-robed Saunin, their own green cowls signifying them as council elders. A dark-haired woman in long yellow robes was addressing the council, the hundred men and women who filled the seats before the podium.

"– saddened to report the loss of two apprentices. The trials, however, were a complete success..."

All heads turned to see the old guildmaster, now Advisor to King Marik, burst into the room with the calm of a patient storm. Magarius simply stood at the top of the room, the doors sweeping closed behind him as he waited to be acknowledged.

"Thank you," Saunin said smoothly, "for your diligence, mistress Lisona." Dismissed, she took her seat among the council. "The Table recognizes master Magarius." Former guildmaster, his tone seemed to say.

Magarius said nothing at the slight but stepped purposefully down the aisle between seats. He had no intention of trying to reclaim his position as head of the guild. What he did want was to make them listen, and he wondered for a brief moment which of the two would have been more difficult. Those gathered in the assembly and at the Table murmured amongst themselves, some in disbelief and others in poorly hidden concern. Saunin watched on with cool impassivity, a sure sign of his discontent. Magarius bowed to the seven elders and then to the council, his sun-burnt salmon robes so colorfully out of place. An elder leaned over to whisper in Saunin's ear, but the acting guildmaster silenced the man without taking his eyes from the frosty gray mane of his political nemesis.

"I see there are more new faces than old," Magarius began, seeking out the handful of familiar ones who had supported him at one time, "but many of you should know the reason for my... absence." A significant look at Saunin. "My experiments in what I call essence magic have been successful. Though not fully explored, I have proof of its existence."

"Yes," a voice muttered in the assembly, "so we've heard."

"Have you come to gloat?" Saunin asked from behind. The shadows under the Table grew longer, thicker. "We had very little interest in your experiments when you described its full potential. What makes you think we would be interested in something less?"

Saunin was old, much older than he looked. Privy to the secrets of the elders, both Saunin and Magarius had extended lives. What was originally intended to prolong the rule of wise and noble men, in the case of Saunin, had become a double-edged sword that left the guild ruled by closed-minded ignorance and vanity.

Magarius waved away the question impatiently. "I did not come to interest you in my endeavors. I came to warn you." His eyes swept across the sea of raised eyebrows and incredulous looks. "You've all heard the noise last night, and no doubt this morning as well. Such noise will travel far, calling out to any with the desire for power. The flood of renegade magi and reckless spell weavers will cause untold chaos in the streets of our city. You must prepare to meet them."

He lies, a soft voice whispered in Saunin's head, sounding like his very own. *He wants the seat back. This is a ploy.*

"How many will come and how do we prepare?" one in the yellow robes of a young master asked.

They were all so very young.

"How indeed?" Saunin asked before Magarius could answer. *He wants your power.* "Would we not be better prepared to face such an obvious onslaught –" sarcasm here – "if you shared with us your findings?"

Magarius shook his head, his bushy eyebrows forming a V of stern disapproval. "That cannot be. The magic is too strong."

"Too strong. For the council of wizards?" Saunin stood in outrage. *Take it from him.* "Have you been gone so long you forget who holds true power?"

"No. I remember all to well."

Banish him. He threatens your power!

Saunin's eyes narrowed as a thought came to him, one he mistook for his own. "You will share this essence with the council, or you will be forever banished from these walls, on pain of death, and labeled renegade." He paused as a ripple of shock and mute approval raced through the assembly. "And make no mistake, we will come for you."

Only once before had Magarius looked so sad, his soft blue eyes filled with shadows of years gone by – almost eighty years.

"For the same reason I left before," Magarius replied calmly, "I will not share essence with you. It is for your own good."

He would make decisions for you.

"Who are you to decide what is good for the council?" Saunin sputtered, nearly losing his fragile hold of reality. The shadow moved away before driving the man insane. "That is for the High Table and the council itself to decide!"

"It is only my absence that makes you head of the Table," Magarius noted, as if pointing out to Saunin his robes and shoes didn't match. "Keep what power you have now. I gladly leave you to it.

"I have done what I came to do," he went on, facing the assembly. "You have been warned that renegades are coming to Noria, and where do you think the first place they will look will be? The center of magic for this realm, perhaps? That's of no matter to me."

He faced Saunin now, as much as the High Table. "If you do not ready yourselves for this, the countless lives that will have been needlessly lost as a result of your inaction will rest on your conscience for all eternity."

"Have no fear, O Wise Magarius," Saunin nearly snarled. "We will act. And for you, it will be all too soon."

With a little shake of his head, the King's Advisor turned and walked from the council, heading up and out the double-doors with no more than a sigh of old disappointments.

And no one noticed how dark his shadow had become.

* * *

The next day passed much the same for Tristan. Packs of children came in search of Cornelius, who had not been around the shop lately for some odd reason, and were each given a free cookie anyway. Passersby were drawn by the delicious odor, and other shopkeepers left their trade in the able hands of apprentices while they came to sample the cookies that so many were speaking of. It's not that none of them had ever tasted the Esrald cookies before, which of course they had, but there was something magnificently different about them now. No one could put a finger on it, and the common curiosity made for polite, if somewhat bold, inquiries.

Tristan turned them all away with a small shake of his head that in others would have prompted more questions. The master baker, however, was a serious man with little time for pleasantries. He was courteous to all but stopped his work for none. It was soon evident that only an expert tongue would decipher the mysterious recipe – but even these were hard-pressed for an answer.

Even the gathering mercenaries from the caravan managed to put in an appearance, wandering into the shop as if they hadn't eaten in weeks. One free sample offered, and the sellswords bought all he could make. It was the first time Tristan could recall ever turning away business, having to sadly inform other customers they would have to wait until morning for more.

So when morning did come, a crowd of hungry people arrived with it. "Not that I really need them, mind," one explained to the others. "It just seemed a good thing to go with my breakfast."

The crowd heartily agreed. What better to go with a cup of that dark drink from the south – what was it called, coffee? Oh, and just think of having one with your eggs and bacon... or with a thick slice of honeybread and berry tart! I have no time for such a large breakfast – I'll have to settle for a hardcake... oh, cookie, what's the difference?

There was a steady flow of people through the shop that morning, and Tristan began to seriously consider master Ferran's advice. A new oven, and possibly an apprentice, seemed to be in the master baker's near future. He had no idea the touch of essence would have such an effect on the cookie's taste that it would move so many to absolutely loving it. The plaza was most definitely a happier place.

He almost felt bad, that people should suddenly love his father's work because of the magic and not the cookie. The cookie was only a means to an end. Or was it? Could it be that the magic affected the cookie just like it changed him and his brothers and their spoons? It wasn't inconceivable that the magic could transform the cookies.

The essence of cookie.

What could be the true nature of a cookie? Tristan wondered if it was the taste, since few people ate pastries or cakes for their nutritional value. But then he remembered, long ago, when his mother had helped bake with his father. Being the oldest brother, he still could see her noble features, the straight nose over full lips and the caring, blue eyes that glittered as bright as her golden hair. He remembered how he had felt the first time she gave him a cookie, how it tasted all the better because she had made it for him. There was love in the exchange, a tangible something he could grasp in his child's hand, but it was something more than that.

It was hope. A momentary feeling that all was well or that it one day would be. It was fleeting as time, passing in the breath of an image, the taste of a cookie. But the memory remained.

He truly cared for the people who came to his shop, no matter if he knew the face or they knew him. He cared. Like so many things, the cookie became more than the sum of its parts, more than the ingredients that made up its whole. Hope, love, caring... the essence of cookie.

"Hello, master baker."

Tristan looked up from rolling dough. Not that he complained about a break in the bustle of people in and out, but he could have sworn the shop was full just a moment ago. Now, there was only one man standing before him, a foreigner by his accent and dress. The knee-high breaches, dark hose and billowy tunic were out of place, and if it weren't for the brown cape and cowl, Tristan would have mistaken the man for a buccaneer. He had long, chestnut hair tied back with a black leather thong, eyebrows as dark and bushy as his mustache and eyes that seemed forever searching.

"Can I help you?" Tristan asked, looking over the man's shoulders. A group of people were waiting outside, as if Tristan had left and they patiently awaited him. "A free sample perhaps?"

"Of course." The man took the cookie and studied it before wrapping it in a handkerchief and placing it in his pocket. "I can see something very odd about your... cookies."

That was when Tristan saw something of his own. Magic emanated from this man, an aura of strength and power but somehow masked with illusion and darkness. Only by looking into those searching, brown eyes could Tristan see the truth. This was one of the renegades Magarius had warned of.

And he was standing right in front of Tristan.

"Oh?" Tristan asked, fingering the long handle of the spoon at his belt. "And what might that be?"

The man leaned forward on the counter, his eyes boring into Tristan's. "I won't insult you by playing this game. There is magic in your cookies, and I want to know how it's done."

Tristan found he couldn't look away from those eyes, their amber depths drawing him in and probing his mind. When they met with the stone fortress of Tristan's will, the man backed up a step as if he'd been slapped.

His eyes went wide with surprise, then narrowed in determination.

"Really," Tristan was saying, "You must be mistaking me –"

Then all went black.

* * *

Johnny Filch slowly pulled himself through the castle window, quiet and lithe as an alley cat. The room was dark, but the sliver of moonlight cast from behind was enough to light his way. No one was there, but then again, he didn't expect anyone to be. The Thieves Guild had been climbing in and out of the castle for as long as kings have claimed rule of Noria.

There was urgency in the thief's movements this day, however. This was no ordinary note he was leaving on the chest at the foot of the bed. It was a warning, stamped with the seal of the guild. It explained the danger King Marik was in, how the Assassins Guild planned to have him killed for mere coin.

The betrayal was shared, and the Thieves Guild would place themselves at the disposal of the king. The guildmaster of thieves himself gave his word to aid Marik, having learned of the treachery from a young thief named Daren and a courageous ex-mercenary known as Cornelius.

Filch lay the letter down and turned on his heel, heading out the window again. It was a long climb down, and he was needed elsewhere.

A shadow disengaged itself from the closet just then, a separate and secret room where the king could be spied upon. No one in Noria was safe from the Assassins Guild. There were no secrets.

The brother took up the note and smelled its surface, as if the very odor of the letter could tell him who had penned it. He slipped it into a pocket on his vest and stepped into the light. Dressed as a simple porter, no one would question his presence in the castle. After all, he'd worked there for years.

He went back into the closet and down a set of stairs that would lead close to the gates outside. Thieves were born climbers, like rats bred in the streets that could scramble up buildings or walls with feline speed. Assassins were more pragmatic.

Why climb when you can walk right in?

* * *

Tristan opened his eyes, his hand still clutching the spoon at his belt. He was no longer in the bakeshop, and the bustle of activity in the plaza was no more than a fading echo of abrupt silence. Lush fields of blue-green grass stretched out for as far as he could see, thick blades that brushed against his leg and brought the heady smell of earth. A handful of trees dotted the landscape further off on the horizon, and though the sky was free of clouds and sapphire-blue, Tristan could find no sun.

"Tell me of essence," a voice called from nowhere, the voice of the renegade wizard. "Tell me, and I will return you to your world."

Tristan pulled the spoon from his belt, and it elongated into the silver long sword he had made the Oath with. The unicorn pommel fit snugly in his hand, crafted to be an extension of his arm.

As Guardian of Truth, Tristan would never lie, but a little misdirection never hurt anyone. "I sincerely think you're wasting your time with me. I am a simple baker, a man who makes treats for those with a sweet tooth. How could I possibly be of any help to you?"

"You could tell me the secret of essence," the voice answered smoothly. "Do not play games with me, Tristan Esrald. I know, from your own mind, that you do know the truth of essence magic."

"I know many truths... Norin Falgwyn. Or should I call you Norin Far-Sight, renegade wizard from the kingdom of Garand?"

The same magic Norin used to probe into Tristan's mind could be used to read the renegade's mind as well. Tristan was rather pleased at the thought, but he was suddenly thrust out of Norin's mind by a red wall of rage. Dark clouds began to form on the horizon, ominous and foreboding.

"I will not play this game with you, baker!" The renegade did not sound happy. "Tell me what I want to know, or I will give you use for that sword you hold."

Tristan shook his head. "I will tell you nothing."

"So be it!"

Thunder rocked the earth, shaking Tristan off his feet just as jagged bolts of blue-white lightning raked across the skies. Dark soil was thrown in the air in an explosion of grass and rock as the bolts drew closer. Rain began to fall in a sheet of heavy drops, skipping the gradual drizzle that came with natural showers. The bright and sourceless light dimmed to a dull gray that cast all in long, cold shadows that clutched at the heart. Another flash of lightning, a few feet away, and something stood in its aftermath. It was a troll, one of the most foul creatures of darkness to walk the blessed earth. Standing over nine feet tall, with leathery green skin and bristling black hair, the gangly monster was reminiscent of a nightmarish scarecrow. So tall and thin was its frame that it forever stood in a crouch. A long, pointed nose protruded from under deep-set eyes, charcoal orbs with a cast of crimson. Warts covered its entire body, as well as the ochre slime that protected it from the diseases of the swamps it normally inhabited.

Its teeth, small and widespread but sharp as needles, gnashed together in anticipation of food. It moved closer to Tristan, testing his speed and litheness by taking halfhearted swipes with its talons.

Tristan watched those hands closely. The black nails were long and sharp, like tiny daggers, and he knew they could tear him apart as swift as any blade. He was no swordsman, like his younger brothers, but he could hold his own. One doesn't grow up the oldest of six brothers and not learn how to defend himself.

The Troll struck, swinging its wiry arm with the speed and ferocity of a bestial hunter. Tristan blocked with his sword, sending up sparks of silvery lights as the blade cut away a talon.

"Ahhh!" the troll screamed and clutched its wounded hand. "You pays for that, little mans!"

It snarled and spit but didn't move to attack again. Instead, it waited and glared at its prey while healing its hand. Trolls had an unusual ability to regenerate wounds. If given the time, they could grow another limb and continue to fight... while the severed limb grew into another troll.

Too late to act, Tristan could only watch as the fingertips quivered and grew. Now facing two of the noxious things, Tristan could only think one thing. *Something's not right. The troll should not have regenerated so quickly.* No expert on the foul race, Tristan knew that it took at least a day to form a new body.

So what was amiss?

There was no time to think, only to defend, as the two rushed in with swinging arms and snarling maws. Again Tristan wounded his opponents by defending himself, cutting away a hand and a nose. Two more trolls grew from the fallen pieces.

Norin's laughter could be heard over the roar of rain, echoing like the distant thunder. "Do you yield, my Guardian? You cannot win here. If you fight, they grow stronger. If you stand, they'll cut you to shreds. What's it to be?"

"This isn't real," Tristan gave as answer, staving off another assault. The trolls were surrounding him, and he tried to avoid cutting away pieces of them. "I will see the truth!"

"But what is truth in a dream?" Norin laughed again as the trolls moved in closer, threatening to engulf the baker. "Give in now, while I can still save you."

"That won't be necessary," Valoran warned, stepping from the substance of dream. His eyes were yellow, with cat-like slits for pupils, and when he cut down a troll with his two-handed sword, it screamed and writhed as fire consumed it, leaving nothing but a wet pile of ash behind. "To me, brother!"

Tristan moved to his younger brother's side, so they stood back to back against their foes. "I'm glad to see you! I wasn't sure if I'd think of something before it was too late."

"You did," was all Valoran said before striking out, cutting down another troll. "Think of fire as you hit them. The sword will set them aflame and interfere with their regenerative powers."

He did as he was told, sending out white-hot flames along the edge of his sword, but still Tristan could not kill the trolls. The rain fell harder, drenching the magical fires and putting them out. There were twelve of the lanky monsters around them now.

"You look like you could use some help!" Stephen called, waving his beefy arm at the two encircled brothers.

Then Cornelius and Jonathan were standing beside him, rushing towards the fray. When Humphrey arrived, he was astride a pearl-white horse, an ivory spiral jutting out from its head to a sharpened and deadly point. He held tight to the unicorn's mane as it reared and smashed two trolls with its hooves.

It was all too much for Norin. He couldn't maintain the troll images against such magical strength.

"Enough!" he commanded, and everything disappeared. Only Tristan and darkness remained. "Enough. You cling so strongly to the truth, then tell me the truth! Tell me the secret of essence. Show me the truth."

Tristan narrowed his eyes, anger boiling within him. "You want the truth, Norin? Then have it, have it all. Look into the eyes of *true* magic!"

The renegade wizard, Norin Falgwyn, screamed and clawed at his eyes. His life, every misdeed and foul act, came back to bare the bald truth of his soul. The death of his parents, the knife in his small hands and the bloodied coins he got from the deed; Ygaerna, his mentor in the Art, her broken neck laying lifeless in his hands and the tear-stained books he'd gained from her; tens of peasants and lords alike, each face distinct and hateful, returning to point accusatory fingers devoid of flesh; all these things flashed in a heartbeat, destroying his mind with guilt and self-loathing. With eyes wide, rocking back and forth on his heels, Norin stared off into the distance at nothing, the blank and tortured future looming over his brow.

But for Tristan, the darkness bled away.

* * *

When Tristan opened his eyes, the renegade called Norin was standing before him with eyes glazed and mouth hung open. The wizard was swaying from side to side, as if he'd been struck a blow and was about to topple. Tristan moved quickly around the table and bound the man with the hemp rope used to tie off large bags of flour. With arms and legs tightly bound, Norin would prove little trouble, but Tristan stuffed a rag in his mouth as an added precaution. There was no chance of him casting a spell if he couldn't speak, or so Tristan rationalized.

Calling to one of the city guard passing through the streets of the plaza, Tristan handed over Norin to the authorities. A handful of sellswords came rushing over as well, having grown fond of the master baker and his wares, to see what was amiss. The guardsman took one look at the fallen man and looked in askance at Tristan.

"He's a renegade wizard," Tristan explained. "He tried to attack me with some kind of spell, but I hit him with my spoon."

The others chuckled at that, imagining the mild baker crack a man on the head with the large cooking spoon. The guard bent over to pick up the trussed man with a grunt of exertion, and the others lent him a hand.

"Good thing you didn't use a rolling pin," he said while carrying Norin out the door. "I'll have him dropped off at the Wizards Guild. We'll let them deal with their own. We've been having all too many reports of wild spells going off in the city."

"I hadn't heard anything about that."

"Not a problem," one mercenary said, watching the guard disappear down the streets with the slumped body over his shoulder. "Seems most of the buggers are off in the eastern end, near bards and the poor quarter."

"We'll keep an eye out for ya," another beamed and took in a deep breath. The odor was visibly pleasing to him. "I just can't get enough of those cookies."

"Would you gentlemen care for some?" Tristan went back inside to check on the oven. He'd been out for a bit and didn't want anything to burn. "It looks as if I've got a tray ready to come out."

The next morning was much like the one before, with lots of hard work and happy customers. Tristan was tired but still had no real need of sleep. He went to bed at night, out of habit, but found himself daydreaming and feeling refreshed without ever having actually slept. He was always told that sleep was extremely important for the body and the mind, that strength was renewed through it and healing sped along its way. For whatever reason, sleep no longer came to him.

Which left him time to think.

A renegade wizard had walked right into his shop and attacked him, in the middle of the day no less! Magarius warned that they would come, that the noise of their transformation would attract power-hungry men for miles. They had arrived all too quickly, and Tristan wasn't sure what to do. With a promise to visit the old Advisor at the end of day, Tristan went about working his trade. There were always more cookies to be made.

"Master Tristan?" a guard called from the door.

"Yes, please come in." The man turned down the offer of a seat or a cookie, and Tristan could tell that something terrible had happened. "Does it have to do with the renegade who was in here yesterday?"

The guard shook his head. "No, it's... have you seen your brother Stephen? It's important that we talk to him, and his forge is locked up tight. No one's seen him in the past couple of days."

"Actually, I haven't seen him. But that's not unusual. We only see each other a few times a week and then at week's end." Tristan decided to take the seat himself. "What's happened?"

"Last night, young Kaern, Stephen's apprentice, was found dead in the streets. His throat was cut and all of his coin taken." He cleared his throat before going on. "The boy must've just finished a hard day's work when some thief just attacked him from the dark."

"I'm sorry," Tristan offered, his voice sincere. "Kaern was a good lad. Have you told his family? No? Well, I don't envy you the task. Are you worried that something may have happened to Stephen as well?"

"That's hard to say. We would just like to ask him a few questions about that night, maybe pick up some clues as to who might've done it. If we don't hear from him soon, we'll be forced to open his forge and look around ourselves."

"I'll stop by there tonight," Tristan promised. "If he's there, we'll both stop by the guardhouse. Has Valoran been told?"

"The general is out inspecting the militias. He won't be back for some time, but we did send out a message to him." The guardsman saluted smartly and headed for the door. "Thank you for your time, master baker."

With such troubling news, the day then on went by much slower. Worrying over what to do or what might have happened, Tristan found it harder to concentrate. When the sun was passing just beyond the high walls, Tristan was glad to see the day end. He cleaned up as best he could, hurrying to finish without doing a bad job of it, and locked up before heading out for Stephen's forge.

That's when he saw the flashing lights.

There were explosions of bright color and streamers of foxfire surrounding one of the castle's towers. Others rang through the night and cast their glow just streets away. He could smell smoke in the air and hear screams in the distance, men shouting out orders and the whinnies of frightened horses.

Renegade wizards, he thought. *Stephen will have to wait, and Magarius will have seen for himself what's happening.*

Unfortunately, Magarius was getting a firsthand view.

* * *

Magarius was in his tower when they decided to attack. The old sage was amazed that the council could come to any kind of a decision in so short a time.

Only three days had passed.

Taking up the Chronicle, Magarius began the arduous climb up the winding staircase that would lead him to the top of the tower. With the Book of Wisdom in one hand and the other held fast to the battlement, the Advisor fought to stand as winds buffeted against him. Through the dark of night, Magarius could see the attack coming towards him.

It streaked past the stars in a roaring arc, four tendrils of fiery crimson lashing out from the towers of the guild castle. The brilliance of starlight faded in comparison, and the night seemed to draw in on itself to pull away from the unnatural light.

Saunin and his high council were invoking the mightiest of powers at their disposal, calling upon the depths of the void to fasten its hold of nothingness. The elders who held knowledge and power so highly would seek to strip it away from the outcast Magician, leaving behind a helpless husk of a man to wither into oblivion. It mattered not that Magarius once held the position of guildmaster, that he had held the fate of every wizard in the palm of his hand. That fact merely fuelled their rage, pushed the guild to greater heights of outrage at his betrayal... and jealousy of his power.

Magarius did hold power, and if he wasn't for the guild, he was against it. Nothing could be simpler, in the eyes of the council. True, there were tens of renegade spell weavers combing the city streets for the taste of magic they'd heard resound through all the realm, but the old wizard was not one to be left alone. All else could wait until Magarius had been dealt with.

So they made their decision and came to take what would not be freely given. Not only would they seek to strip the Advisor of all he knew, but they would take that knowledge and use it toward their own ends. With the added strength of essence magic to the repertoire of power they already possessed, wiping renegades from the streets would take no more effort then sweeping an arm across a cluttered table.

It was for this very reason that Magarius refused to share the secret of essence with the guild. He could barely trust himself with such immense power, and the shadow that had grown within him showed all too plainly his weaknesses. Magarius was convinced that he couldn't possibly trust essence in the hands of the guild. They would use its might to clear the streets, of that he had no doubt. It was the innocent people who would be swept away in that fearsome wake of magic that concerned the venerable sage.

"Then come for me," Magarius called to the fires, standing firm against the threat. "I still hold the guild secrets in my mind. Take them, if you can!"

The fires struck, enveloping the stone crenellations in a dome of wild luminescence. Waves of heat battered the stone, shaking the tower and the very foundation of the king's castle. And in the midst of the onslaught, Magarius stood tall, the Chronicle held high. The burning flames of ignorance were kept at bay and thrown back as the book began to change, growing upwards and out.

Magarius threw down the book and backed away, watching it transform with a stern defiance. He knew the only defense against ignorance was knowledge, and where once lay the Chronicle now stood a semblance of the One Tree, the essence of wisdom. All of the earth's precious knowledge is housed in nature, in the blowing winds, the flowing rivers, the glowing fires of molten rock and the ever-growing trees. The hungry flames of ignorance could blaze to the end of time, but wisdom would forever be its counter, an equal balance of dark and light.

The ley lines emanating from the Tree were stretching out and down the tower, glowing the blue of wind-swept ocean and wild flowers. Magarius stepped forward and placed his aged hands upon its surface, lending his strength to the sprouting limbs and bristling leaves. The Tree had grown to fill the open top of the tower, the Advisor safe beneath its boughs.

"Now," Magarius said and touched his hand to one of the ley lines, "the fighting will end."

His voice reached out and took hold of the fires, gathering up the fiery lashes and molding them to his desire. Into a swirling ball of light, the crimson and gold of flickering rage were quenched and reborn to the shape of a bird. With the shriek of life and promise of death, the phoenix turned its baleful eyes west and plummeted towards the wizards castle like a fiery bolt of heaven.

And from its mouth came Magarius' voice.

"No more will you seek this power," he said as the phoenix spread its wings over all four towers, engulfing the council and its spent magic. "You will continue in your efforts to protect this realm, to keep your pledge against renegades and their wild magic. This endless quest for yet more power must end, or you will bring the deaths of us all with your greed.

"Keep your promise," the voice echoed, and the fires began to fade, "or you will be stripped so that others may take your place."

Magarius was not one to make threats lightly, and Saunin knew it. The others could feel the strength of his words like a hand upon their minds, fingering the knowledge they held so dear. With a seeming flick of his wrist, the old sage could render any one of them helpless, bereft of wit and without magic. Magarius was wisdom, and they knew the truth of his warning.

Saunin sent out hunters the instant he could draw breath.

* * *

Tristan raced down the cobbled streets, guided by the sounds of chaos. He could already see the ashen clouds of smoke, and he was struck by a wave of heat as he turned down center street. His vision seemed liquid, distorted as it was by the fires licking their way up the plastered buildings of white and gray. Shopkeepers and merchants were busily working to put out the fires, forming a water line from the nearest well while guards kept black-robed men at bay.

Black robes, the badge of a renegade. Tens of outcast wizards were gathered in the large avenue, spread apart to do more damage but still banded together to attain a common goal. A full squadron of city guard were fighting off the magical attacks, but sword and shield were rarely a match for spells.

From where Tristan stood, he could see that the heavy wooden buckets wouldn't be enough. Without putting an end to what caused the fires, Noria would burn to the ground. More help had to be on its way, for such a fire would be seen at all ends of the wall. Tristan had to lend a hand until that help could arrive.

With so much destruction, he didn't know where to start.

Dragons clawed their way through stone and wood to claw at those who chose to hide. Swords were battered away by claws the length of an arm, like curved black knives sharp enough to rend steel and earth. The fires reflected off their glistening scales, bouncing off the invulnerable hide as surely as the useless weapons the guards employed. When the red and green dragons reared their saurian heads, the membranes behind their pointed ears flared and fire erupted from their throats, fire so fierce and strong, it burned white as it struck and splashed a silvery blue.

None of the common folk there had ever seen such a monstrous sight, and the fear was enough to paralyze. They fell like wheat to the scythe. And though each one of the reptilian giants was an illusion, formed of light and will, the mere believing in them was enough to kill. The illusory stab of a claw was enough to burst a heart from the overwhelming fear of death and pain that took hold in the mind.

On another street, two renegades walked side by side, hurling balls of energy at all in their path. Wagons were overturned and shattered into thousands of splintered remnants, neatly stacked bales of hay thrown wide while catching fire from the explosions of golden light. Horses bolted in fright, one still holding its thrown rider in the stirrups by a foot. Cobbles were torn from the streets in mounds of dark soil, and those remaining soon cracked from the intense waves of heat.

And yet on other streets, billowy clouds of noxious green gas engulfed all, leaving behind a straggle of helpless men, coughing and choking the stuff out as they gasped for more air. Thick bolts of blue-white lightning erupted from outstretched hands, shattering stone into hundreds of deadly missiles. When one of the dark-robed wizards clapped her hands together, the surrounding guards found it impossible to continue holding their swords and shields, and they watched in horror as they took on a crimson hue and melted into slag. Then they screamed and fell writhing to the floor as buckles and greaves melted as well.

Tristan faced the dragons first, scared out of his wits but forcing himself to stand nonetheless. He had the compelling urge to fall to the ground and ball up like a child. The mere size of the scaled monsters, the thundering of their massive feet striking and cracking the cobble, shaking all to the ground, was almost more than he could bare. With the reassurance of his silver long sword, Tristan stood before the dragons to see the truth of their nature.

But only translucent light reflected back.

They were illusions, colorful lights shaped and molded to the forms of dragons, given life by the fear of those who beheld them. As soon as Tristan saw what they truly were, he strode up to one and struck with his sword. A flash erupted from the jagged cut he'd made. Without a sound or inch of continued movement, the illusion ceased to be. It simply fell in on itself, disappearing from sight with a whoosh of air.

Its creator gasped, his face paling visibly. Tristan turned to face the man, holding his sword menacingly before him. He was no master swordsman or even very adept with a blade, but he knew how to swing and stab. He moved quickly to strike down the renegade before he could cast another spell, but a portly woman was even quicker. With a cry of revenge, she lifted a clay pot with both hands and brought it down on the robed man's head, making a satisfying thump as it broke into countless shards. She gave a gap-toothed smile, and Tristan was then moving off to face the remaining illusions.

Both guards and citizens cheered his coming, not knowing how he defeated the dragons but not really caring much at the time. Fight fire with fire, they always said. Plenty of time for questions when the fighting was done and the children were safe.

The enormous fires atop the castle tower were enough to blind those down in the streets, but still Tristan fought on. He dispelled all of the illusions, but the other attacks were all too real. Lightning snaked out and struck with its jagged clutch, like ice-blue fingers tearing and rending all in its path. Without knowing quite how, Tristan drew the bolts to his sword, absorbing them in a burst of sparks. His sword was growing warm and buzzing with power, so he pushed forward to engage the renegades.

Well-armed guardsmen followed his attack, moving like the head of a spear to cut away at the black robes. Spells rang out with the clash of steel, but they bounced harmlessly off the invisible sphere generated by Tristan's sword. Each time a blast of energy or some fiery missile would strike at the men, the protective globe was outlined in blues and reds, but nothing penetrated its surface.

As well as their advance was progressing, Tristan knew they were outnumbered. There were far more of the renegades then he first had thought, and they were charming the guards to turn against their own. Those men who possessed blank looks on their faces but fought like tireless demons were no longer men. They were the extensions of another's will, attacking their brethren and slaughtering with emotionless efficiency.

What was a warm sting against his palm soon became a wild heat, the unicorn pommel glowing with a yellowish incandescence. Recalling how Humphrey had rode in with his brothers to save him from the trolls gave Tristan an idea. He formed the thought in his mind, giving it life through will and the stored energy in his sword. When next he opened his eyes, the unicorn stood before him, a neighing symbol of beauty and truth. Its coat was a pearly white, and a thick snowy mane flowed down its back from the ivory spiral in its forehead.

Intelligent black eyes turned back towards Tristan, and the unicorn bowed its horn to him. With another cry, it reared up high and faced the snarling renegades. There was hatred in their eyes and a lust for power that fueled the fiery deaths of all who had fallen – and would yet fall. Staring back at them were the eyes of truth, an unyielding mirror that bore into their souls and reflected back the nature of who they had become.

A cheer rang out as more soldiers arrived. For some odd reason, the black robes had stopped fighting, but the tumult still raged around them. With eyes filled with horror, most stood unblinking at something only they could see. Others had fallen to the ground and cried aloud as they clawed at their eyes, while others took the fetal position and wept like month-old babes. Members of the Wizards Guild had arrived as well, hopefully to clean up the mess that should have been theirs in the first place. When Tristan looked back to see the new help arrive, a flush of relief passed through his body with a single sigh, the rigors of his endeavor enough to make him fall with exhaustion.

King Marik had arrived to set things aright.

* * *

> *My Liege,*
> *The army that destroyed Parsons today is within the city walls, holed up in one of the larger buildings in the Bards Quarter. I have infiltrated their ranks, with one Lord Duncan Buchann, in the hopes of discovering the secrets of their plans. A man calling himself Lord Saxmont leads the rabble, but he is merely hired help for the true problem: Jaril II. There are at least five hundred fully armed men in this newly-named Iron Ring, and it is possible they are all under some sort of spell cast by this Saxmont fellow. The mercenaries work for coin, of course, but also for a pardon from Jaril... once he is returned to the throne. I fear you are in grave danger, my King. I will try to send more detailed information at a later time. For now, I am returning to Bards.*
> *Your Loyal Subject,*
> *Master Smith Stephen Esrald*

For the first time in a long while, there were heavy patrols in the dark alleyways of the bards quarter. Drawing men from his own castle guard, Marik made sure there were three times the normal number of men protecting his city streets. If there was an army, or any kind of large movement within the walls, he would know about it. It was possible for five hundred men to travel from one quarter to another, if they went in pairs, but that would take a great deal of time. He had a dark feeling that this Iron Ring would strike hard and fast, much like Jaril had so long ago.

The sewers provided yet another avenue of traversing the city, but a skillfully penned missive to the guildmaster of thieves would make the rotting passageways unobtainable. Marik decided to call in a few favors as well, hoping the spy network set up by the thieves could help him put down this attack before it happened.

Valoran was already riding out in the countryside, inspecting the soldiers and militias of neighboring towns, villages and hamlets. If Parsons was attacked, Valoran would know of it by now. There was nothing for Marik to do about it, though he did send a squad with healers and provisions to aid those who still lived. What concerned him most was the weapons cache hidden away in that remote place.

It could not have been a coincidence that they chose to strike there, Marik thought to himself. *This Saxmont must have magic indeed.*

Having done all he could, for the time being, Marik had settled himself to rest. The next day he ordered more guardsmen to reinforce the poor quarter and each of the gates. With only two score men to protect the castle, Marik took to wearing his sword loosely in its scabbard. There was a sense of foreboding that hung over him, like a heavy shroud of impending dark and stormy nights. Magarius was locked away in his tower, inaccessible even to the king when such moods took him, and something was on the verge of occurring. He wasn't sure what it was, but his knuckles turned white as he gripped the stone battlements in anticipation. Marik could see the whole of the city stretched out before him, and the tingling at the nape of his neck grew stronger. Then he saw the oily smoke laid bare against the setting glow of the sun.

There was fire in the streets.

"Jaunce!" he called, and the general was at his side in moments. "Sound the bell in the south tower! There's a fire in the market and another in the merchants quarter by the looks of it. Then gather what men we have left and prepare to ride."

"Yes, sir!"

Jaunce was off at a run, his frame as solid and strong as any man in his prime, though he'd lived long enough to serve in the original mercenary company with Marik. The gray-haired soldier was already on in years when Marik had first met him, but he couldn't imagine anyone else more suited to protecting Noria. Valoran had youth, strength and skill with weapons, but Jaunce had experience and the cunning to strip a fox of its catch – and the canine glad to be rid of it!

Even though there was trouble within his city, with plots and counterplots brewing in the shadows, Marik felt the rush of old excitement. Memories of his youth came flooding back, to days when he rode the wilds of distant lands for no more than a meal and the chance to prove himself. Magarius was there, offering advice but never interfering, and Jaunce stood like a monolith. With the old soldier riding at his side, there was nothing Marik could not accomplish, no enemy he could not vanquish.

Twenty horses gathered in the cobbled streets outside the castle gates, with ten more guardsmen standing close behind. What few men were left to hold the castle were given orders to bar the gates and let no one in until the King returned.

"Forward!" Marik called and led his men out of the crown quarter.

It was all like it had been. The thundering muscles of a horse beneath him, the rushing wind in his eyes, steel in his hand and men at his side. The scene may have changed, and Herne knows the circumstances *always* changed. There was a familiarity to it, though. There was a battle to be fought, there was honor to be won and there was... an ambush.

From the shadows of a building top, a lone archer took silent aim. Dressed all in black, no one had seen any trace of him. No one but Jaunce. The steel head of the poisoned arrow glinted off the orange haze of sunset, and the old campaigner didn't think twice. He knew who the arrow was intended for, being only one of four who knew of the treacherous plot. Jaunce threw himself from his horse, taking Marik with him.

They both landed hard against the cobbles and were nearly killed by the horses coming fast on their heels. Marik was bruised and battered, but he was still alive. He attempted to roll his friend onto his back but pulled him forward at the sudden cry.

"Jaunce?" Marik turned him over and saw the black-feathered shaft protruding from the small of his back. "Oh, Jaunce. What have you done?"

Men were dismounted now and surrounding their king. Having seen the arrow, they had swords drawn and were searching the surrounding area. Heavy shields were ready to block any more attacks, but it was doubtful any would come. Whoever had taken down the general was long gone by then, or they would have fired again already.

"It's poisoned," Jaunce said, his voice a mere whisper. "I'm... warm. Tingling... in my legs."

Marik broke the shaft off and cradled the old gray head in his arms. "You!" he called to one of his men as the shock wore off. "Go fetch a healer, right away! Tell him to bring something to fight off poison! Don't worry, Jaunce. We'll stay here with you until the healer comes."

A weak laugh shook the dying soldier. "You know, Mar... I always knew... that I would go first, but... this –" Jaunce closed his eyes, his body weary and his mind gone numb. He meant to keep talking, to tell his friend and king how much he cared – how much he loved him. *The son I never had*, he thought, the words on his lips like the whisper of a ghost. Marik heard him, held him all the closer, but it was too late.

Jaunce was gone, and the city still burned.

* * *

While Marik and his men were pulling into the street where Tristan fought, a band of hunters from the Wizards Guild accompanying them, Magus was a hundred miles away. In the forests on the outskirts of Noria's borders, the shadow had found an open gate. The Fairy King was either weak or foolish to leave such an opening unguarded, but Magus neither cared nor worried about the mistakes of others.

He only wanted revenge.

Calling out to his foul brethren, gathering them like lost children from the land of Faeron, Magus held open the shimmering gate as countless monsters filed through. Like a silken blanket, dotted with stars, the portal held firm under the shadow's will. Ogres, trolls, orcs and goblins were amassing in the trees, all of them eager and pleased to be free of their tyrannical king.

Magus had plans to march his growing army through the collection of wattle and daub huts the humans called Hempford. The small hamlet would be no significant victory, but the taste of blood and battle would evoke rage in the fell races. Once they were driven by unfailing bloodlust, nothing would stand in their way. Magarius would fall, and all the old mage loved would be razed to the ground.

With violet eyes burning, the shadow urged them on in anticipation of his revenge. So concentrated on keeping the gate open was Magus that he didn't notice the three wraith-like forms off in the distance. Much like the vengeful shadow, these three were spawned from the darkness and wore their long cloaks as the sky wears night. Great beings in their own right, the three were lords of Faeron, and nothing would please them more than to see their king destroyed. The puny human, Marik, and his utterly disgusting city of stone and mud were nothing more than a means to an end.

Fe'anellan, Father of Dreams and Fairy King, was directly linked to the gates that led into his realm. Expending his own power to keep others from entering and the lesser races from leaving, Fe'an could be weakened by attacking the mystic portals. Magus, being the darker half of the most powerful man to ever live, needed only exert his will to force open the doorway to Faeron. Every monster that passed through was a slap in the face to King Fe'anellan.

Yes, the Lords of Faeron looked on with satisfaction, knowing that soon they could return and destroy their soft-hearted liege. Why should they care if the 'lesser races' made a new home in the lands of man? That left all the more room in Faeron for those with the strength to take it. For long hours did the lords watch this Magus free the nightmares of human dreamers, and they were very pleased. Soon Noria would be no more than a memory...

And Faeron, essence, all would be theirs to take.

About the Author

J.A. Giunta has been writing poetry and short stories for over ten years and had his first fantasy novel – *The Last Incarnation* – published in February of 2005. With a BA in English from Arizona State, he is both an avid reader and gamer. Though his current career is in software development, he hopes to someday write novels full-time.

He lives with his wife, Lori, and daughter, Ada Rose, in the perpetual summer that is central Arizona.

Visit him online at www.jagiunta.com.

Made in the USA
Columbia, SC
05 December 2024